The Changeling

The Changeling

a novel

kate horsley

SHAMBHALA
Boston & London
2005

SHAMBHALA PUBLICATIONS, INC.
Horticultural Hall
300 Massachusetts Avenue
Boston, Massachusetts 02115
www.shambhala.com

9 8 7 6 5 4 3 2 1

FIRST PAPERBACK EDITION
Printed in the United States of America

⊗ This edition is printed on acid-free paper that meets the
American National Standards Institute z39.48 Standard.
Distributed in the United States by Random House, Inc.,
and in Canada by Random House of Canada Ltd

LIBRARY OF CONGRESS CATALOGING-IN-PUBLICATION DATA

Horsley, Kate, 1952–
[Changeling of Finnistuath]
The changeling: a novel / Kate Horsley.—1st ed.
p. cm
Originally published under title: The changeling of Finnistuath.
ISBN 1-59030-194-3 (pbk.: alk. paper)
1. Women—Ireland—Fiction. 2. Identity (Psychology)—Fiction.
3. Passing (Identity)—Fiction. 4. Gender identity—Fiction.
5. Sex role—Fiction. 6. Ireland—Fiction. I. Title.
PS3558.06976C48 2004
813'.54–dc22
2004017076

for

AARON

ACKNOWLEDGMENTS

Thanks most of all to Joel Segel for his editorial acumen and passion. I am also grateful to Stephen Andrews, who generously gave of his knowledge of history, horses, and literature. Thanks to Margaret Murphy, scholar and teacher of tourists at Jerpoint Abbey in County Kilkenny, Ireland. I greatly appreciate poet and storyteller Maura Stanton, who was the first creative writing mentor to make me face my calling. I also want to acknowledge the expert and humbling editing work of Larry Hamberlin, the intelligence and warmth of editor Beth Frankl, and the continuing help and support of Victoria Shoemaker. Finally, I thank Morgan Davie for his love of this manuscript and this writer.

The Changeling

prologue

BEFORE THE TIME OF THIS STORY, in fact before human tribes inhabited Ireland, a loud-mouthed and mutilated species called the Fomorians dominated the island. Led by Cichol the Footless, they were giants with varying deformities, which made them mean and lazy. They created a race of bag men to carry sacks of soil from the valleys to the stony mountains where the loud-mouthed giants preferred to farm and oversee their holdings.

At this time, only a few other beings who chanced upon Ireland tried to claim it, since much of the water was impure. Some was brown and gritty from the Fomorians' slopping around in it. Some was corrupted by the salt of the sea. Other water was soiled by the urine and feces of cattle or tainted by their blood in scores of cattle-stealing battles. These battles often involved the Partholonians, the followers of the hero Partholon, a hardworking race fond of farming and herding. But they were all killed by a plague, which some say came from the spilled contents of a snoring Formorian's dream.

Into this world, the Tuatha De Danaan—the tribe of the sparkling-eyed goddess Dana—came from the north, wanting to purify and enjoy everything, including the water. The Tuatha De Danaan saw the sacredness of time and space inherent in all the land's aspects: trees, hills, pools, flowers. In the light of such affection, the waters, which were the earth's fluids—blood and semen and tears and saliva and sweat and the lubrication for lovemaking—became revered.

But in those times of shifting fortunes, the Tuatha De Danaan were forced underground by human tribes in a series of battles too tedious to describe. Still, their love of the land was so passionate that they did not want to leave it. They chose instead to reduce themselves in size and influence in order to stay.

In one forested and boggy corner of Ireland was a crystalline spring that flowed from the ground beneath a Fomorian skull-sized stone under a rowan tree. The sensuous fairies, who dug passages between the spring and their underground world, made the grasses around the spring intoxicatingly lush and sweet and engineered the bushes and trees so that the wind played them in harmonious, sometimes melancholy, tones. It was this seductive spring of jeweled water that caused the first human settlers to stay and give the place a name: Finnistuath—the tribe of Finnis. At festival times they decorated the spring with yellow gorse and rosy foxglove, rowan berries, holly, and mistletoe, and they were grateful.

But the priests who came to Finnistuath told the people not to be attached to the earth, for it was foul compared to Heaven, where they would go if they obeyed the Church. And the fairies asked each other how anything could be more beautiful than this land. To the people of Finnistuath, such fairy riddles sounded like a tinkling aspect of the spring's melody, and most paid little attention. It was a time when ignorance began to be confused with wisdom, when humans began to see their lives as bleak and were quite willing to believe that Heaven was more real and permanent an environment than Earth.

It was a time when fleas began to outnumber fairies.

the BOY

 1

ALL OF MARY OF FINNISTUATH's flea-bitten body was in darkness except for her cunt and the thick, sweating thighs branching
out at wide angles from it. It would have been more convenient to have gone
into labor during the day. At night, in such a household, one could not afford
the luxury of light, of candles or slow-burning, smoking torches. The poor
simply went to bed with the sun and slept heavily. They were always weary,
and considered weariness the physical nature of being human. At night it
was good just to lie down and listen to the sounds of wind or of restless creatures, both seen and unseen, to hear the breathing of one's children, even
the snoring of one's spouse. It was also good to use the darkness as a black
sea in which to sink into one's lust or piety or sorrow.

Despite the trouble darkness could cause, Mary had prayed to go into
labor with her eighth child after sundown in case God would not answer
her fiercer prayer that the child be a boy. In the dark, it would be easier to
hide the child's gender from its father, easier to conceal the truth if the
truth was as horrible as Mary suspected. Like the vast majority of poor and
conquered people, Mary did not expect God to give her what she wanted or
even what she needed, only some meager solace, just enough solace so one
had to continue to believe in God's power and show the proper gratitude.
She thanked God for his wise mercy in starting the labor after sundown.
She did not scold God for the fact that she would have to pay the Midwife
for the beeswax candle she brought with her in addition to paying six hen's
eggs for her services. And what was the need of such services after seven
children had slid from her womb without assistance? None of them breech,
none of them sickly, although three had died within the first two years of
their skinny lives. But the Midwife showed such kindness to Mary and
seemed to be the only one in the village who could keep secrets. During
negotiations for a lump of goat cheese, Mary had thrown into the bargain
the story of her woes with her husband and the new creature inside her
belly. The Midwife, who spoke little and listened with all her features, gave
everyone in Finnistuath, even people on opposing sides of a scuffle, the

impression that she was an ally. So Mary had poured out her soul with her tears. Whether as a matter of business or compassion, the Midwife offered her services, which would include an unimpeachable discretion and aid in keeping Mary's husband well away from the infant's naked arrival.

In the candlelight, the Midwife saw the head of the child squeeze between the thighs. The eyes were shut tight, and the hair, dark and thick, was slick with its mother's fluids.

Gregory, the man of the house, had been sent out by the Midwife to stand by the door and keep unwelcome invisible entities from slipping in to enter the newborn's soul with its first breath. Gregory the Goatherd, though a half-wit, had learned to be enormously vigilant—to wait and watch for wolves and other dangers for hours. He stood outside, his back straight, hearing only the groans of his wife and the coaxing whispering of the Midwife behind him in the cottage. A strong wind was beating the pines and rowan and oak trees about, and Gregory was staring up at the stars, wondering how they remained so still in all that wind. So still and so clear. His mouth hurt where a tooth had recently come out, all black and as crumbly as coal. He had only six teeth left, four in the front, which he thanked God for. He was a grateful, humble man, aware that he knew very little about the world in general, and a lot about goats in particular. He also knew that in the world a man who died without a son was pathetic. Gregory of Finnistuath was happy to be humble, even half-witted, but not pathetic. He would rather be a criminal, hanged in the public green, than be considered pathetic. And that is exactly what he told his wife when her big belly became taut with another baby. He said, "I'll tell you this—and may Jesus, Mary, and Joseph haul me away to Hell in a cart if I'm false— I'd rather be hanged in the public green for a criminal than be pitied for an unblessed lout. I'll not have another daughter born to me house after seven. I'll kill the thing with me own hands rather than waste the food we have on a weakling thing that can't carry me name or ease me work. It'll be a son or it'll be dead, and I'll hang for the sin." That's what he had told Mary, who had had enough of babies dying. She had lain three down in the ground, and touched their cheeks gone cold. She heard them some nights, crying from beneath the ground. Muffled, distant crying, weak but persistent.

Inside the one-room cottage where a new life was compelled to emerge, the Midwife and Mary—and perhaps the baby now—could hear the sounds of the wind. The four sisters were sleeping fitfully in their place in the corner, side by side like logs at rest at the bottom of a hill.

The child fell out like a calf from its mother onto the twisted blanket. Mary fell back and moaned. The Midwife hummed one low note and shook her head. She lifted the child, which began to wail in breathless, quivering cries, and wrapped it in a stained blue cloth.

"I will pay you what I said," the mother whispered. She could see the Midwife's dry yellow hair and wrinkled face in the light given off by the candle that the woman now held in her right hand, cradling the newborn in her left arm.

"Her cheeks are red," the Midwife said. "Her hands are grabbing the air. In old times she would become a warrior, I would say."

"'He.' You must say 'he,' Midwife." Mary propped herself up on her elbows. "He is to be called Gregory, for his father."

The Midwife handed the child, who now looked silently and wide-eyed at the candle's flame, to its mother. Mary lay down to receive the infant and said, "You'd better tell him to come in now."

Outside, Gregory muttered, "I'm no bad man." He was speaking out loud to the stars, which he didn't understand, though once the Baker had explained that they did indeed move, only not by wind, and that they could determine the fate of a man, even of a whole village or country. The Baker had told him and the Plowman one night that there were seven planets, stars that wandered the night sky and were like urges that passed over men and countries. In fact, it was Mars that caused the King of England to steal other peoples' lands. Gregory had no idea, among all the sparks in the deep blue sea of sky, which ones wandered, much less which one was Mars. "I work hard," he said. "I'm no bad man."

The Midwife was suddenly beside him with her candle blown out, standing still as though she had been there for a long time, forever, or was formed of wind and darkness.

"You've got a son, Gregory," she said.

"Is he sound?" he asked. The hole in his gums throbbed. He didn't want to show this Midwife, a woman he did not like, the joy that was pounding in him.

"Oh, sure he's sound. He's as sound as can be." She looked merry, and even laughed to herself and looked down at the ground. She was wrinkled but spry, even pretty in some way when she smiled, her teeth being good.

"I'll go in then," Gregory said.

"Well, but there is, after all, something you ought to study on, Gregory. The child had a suspicious encounter coming out. A moth fluttered by its genitals, a yellow moth."

"What does that mean? What harm's been done?" Gregory's mouth hung open, moisture collecting on the lower lip. His eyes, though, seemed dry and ready to blame the Midwife for any trouble.

"No harm that I can see. But it's best to take precautions. It's best to keep the boy's manhood covered well. There's been an interest shown by spirits. The boy should never go naked in front of anyone but his mother until he is wed or put in the ground. That's how I divine the thing." She looked casually up at the stars as Gregory nodded and rubbed the wiry curls on his chin. He was befuddled.

"I'll walk on home, then," she said, "while the moon is still up."

Gregory was muttering something about the hardship of maintaining such a rule when the Midwife left him. She walked down the road laughing a little to herself, past several other hovels. She wondered how she had so quickly thought up the good excuse for Gregory's not checking on his son's parts. She felt sorry for Mary and hoped the Goatherd's wife had the wit to remember their ruse when Gregory said something about the moth or the protection of his son's penis.

The Midwife felt no sin in lying, because she didn't believe in sin. She believed in grace, in God's understanding of human dilemmas and suffering and in his sense of humor about it all. God knew a fine joke, she thought. Look at the creatures he created—the waddling hedgehog and the twitching mouse—and look at the situations he arranged people in—men scurrying from a neighbor's shed with their trousers around their ankles followed by the neighbor's wife pulling straw from her hair as she answered her husband's call for supper.

And to prove the point that God, or at least his minor cousins, made mischief, the wind took her shawl from around her shoulders and kicked it down the road a bit before she could step on it and snatch it up.

"Be mischievous, then," she said aloud. On a night like that there was no telling what unseen characters were out and about to have a little fun. But the Midwife had a streak of merriment in her that diluted her fear. And she loved God like a brother. She talked to him often, though the priests taught that a layperson could not speak directly to God. That windy night, she re-

minded him that she had finished his work many a time, making sure that
a new being breathed its first breath, just as Brigid of Ireland had been midwife to Mary when she gave birth to the baby Jesus. The Midwife had let
this one's strong little hand grab her finger. She wanted it to be one of the
children who grew to walk and to speak.

"I want to hear what this one has to say," she told God.

2

*t*HE MIDWIFE had been born in another village—to the east, near a port town whose name she couldn't remember. She had been born to an Anglo-Norman father who, when pushed to decide between allegiance to the King of England or to the people of his wife, whose hands he shared work with, chose the people. They could identify the lavender blossom that cured a festering sore or the tea that could restore a man's ability to be reasonable. What did the King of England know but how to dress in brocade and fly a hawk for sport while sending his loyal subjects to murder thousands of people in some foreign place?

The Midwife remembered only images of the troubles caused by the King's men in her father's town. Dust. Sweating, grinning horses kicking up dust. Her mother's orange hair falling in spirals from her comb. Her father striking her, his youngest child. She didn't know why. Perhaps because she was wailing as her older brother and two older sisters were putting things in baskets. They went into the woods with others from the village. And she kept hearing the phrase "swept out." And this put a picture in her head of huge straw brooms pushing flailing people and dust and dogs and chickens and baskets and cups out of the town and into the woods.

"Who is living in our home now?" she had asked her mother.

The father had answered, "Some English bastards and their lazy children."

And there were constant stories of men going to avenge their displacement and humiliation, going to join various chieftains whose names ended with "the Great" or "the Industrious" or "the Undefeatable." "The Normans and the Irish are on the same side," some Norman or Irish inevitably said when in the company of both. Every man was under suspicion, his allegiance unreliable until a sword's blade was run through his chest or his son or brother was hanged. Then one knew the man's loyalty, because one knew his enemies. One could speak at his wake about his sacrifice for the cause, or count on the surviving members of his family to hold a grudge like a flag and be first to fight. Most Normans in Ireland called the English their enemies, were said to have become more Irish than the Irish, speaking Gaelic and letting their hair grow long, going barefoot into skirmishes, later sung as battles.

On the way to Finnistuath, the mother's village, everyone in the family but the Midwife perished. A traveler, who knew the fate of the little girl's family, took her on his back to Finnistuath and handed her to her grandfather. She had no recollection of what had happened to her parents and sisters and brother. She had no recollection, in fact, of their journey after leaving the woods near their home other than dreams of a small girl crying out to trees and bushes and hearing no human answer.

No one asked the Midwife to recall those days or explain her heritage. All they needed to know in Finnistuath was that she grew up to be the Midwife and she was poor. A midwife had a status that transcended lineage or nationality, like the druids who used to be able to go from one chieftain's table to his enemy's and be well fed and welcome at both. A woman screaming in labor, her husband sweating and powerless beside her, cared only for the skill of the midwife, not her heritage. If anyone asked her about it, the Midwife of Finnistuath said that she belonged to the same hungry tribe as most of the people of Finnistuath, except those associated with the English Manor that sat like an arrogant cow at the south end of the village.

"But we all live on the same land and drink from the same spring," the Bailiff had grumbled one afternoon when a few of the villagers had gathered to watch the felling of a dead birch.

"Ahh," the Midwife said, "the greatest trick of kings is to fool the poor into thinking we have common cause with the rich simply because we live on the same bog. Then the poor get their heads split open in the battles they fight so the rich can keep their wine cellars well stocked."

The Midwife talked to herself now, rather than God, as she walked the road past the Big Bog, wondering if a child born female could truly live her whole life as a male. And if this were possible and offended no god, then perhaps the world had no order other than what was arbitrarily imposed by humans. In that case, perhaps a poor man could decide he should be rich and take himself and his friends and sweep the English from their manors. Perhaps the English and all rich men understood this well enough—the flimsy nature of one's identity. Hence they protected their status with guards and stone towers, and with priests who explained the allegedly fixed and god-approved nature of their privilege.

"That's why the world needs fairies," she said and supposed that scores of little heads, hidden behind ferns and rocks, nodded with her.

Every now and then a fairy proved how silly humans were to think themselves born into some fixed identity. The mischievous spirit switched babies, a rich for a poor, or human for fairy. Then the Midwife had to pour scalding foxglove tea down the malingering and strange infant's throat; soon enough, the fairies took the changeling back and returned the child.

The Midwife laughed and shook the ends of her shawls at the invisible entities around her. She had pulled many humans into the world, most of the humans in Finnistuath, English and Irish, and they all looked equally as naked and miserable and confounded when they came double-fisted from the womb. Of the twenty some households, twelve had called upon her to bring new lives to the community. There, behind her at the start of the Big Bog, was the Weaver's house. She had attended the birth of his three sons, seen the deformed ears of the third. And there, where the village took up again on the south side of the Big Bog, were the three cottages all belonging to the Plowman's family, his own house and that of his two sons. The Midwife had one day brought the old man's youngest daughter into the world and the next attended his son's son's birth. The old mother had died in childbirth amidst a lot of blood and a bad smell, like the smell of warm, spoiled mutton. The Plowman lived with his two daughters now. His two sons argued over who would take the father's place at the plow when he died. The oldest believed it to be his right to inherit the Plowman's title, but the younger was more able to guide the plow and make straight furrows. The older one could do the lesser job of driving the horses but was insulted by this role. Their wives participated in the feud, sometimes dumping sewage onto each other's poultry yards. A day's work was wearying enough, thought the Midwife, without having another man's shit among the chickens.

The Midwife walked on, aware that a man was coming up the road toward her. She stopped near a row of cottages across the road from the Plowman's home and in front of the Small Bog. Of these houses, the Baker's, the Smith's, and the Flax Grower's, she had been in the Smith's and the Flax Grower's. She knew that the Flax Grower's wife's third son was in fact the son of the Baker. She knew how the Smith's first child had died.

She stopped by the Baker's house in case the man walking down the road were not truly a man. At night, or even during the day in remote places, spirits took many forms, sometimes no form at all, but came upon a person as a voice or wind or pain. It was a grave mistake to assume that what looked like a familiar face was indeed that face, especially on the road at night. Only two years ago, an Englishman accused of raping and bludgeoning to death a young girl in the village across the river was set free when it was determined, with complete certainty, that it was not he who had done the sickening deed but a demon who had taken his shape.

The man coming down the road toward the Midwife looked like the Bailiff, a thin-faced man with a long nose and swirling, thin hair. He always wore a wide-brimmed hat and shuffled awkwardly in tethered cloth shoes with lead soles—an eccentric but friendly man. He believed that lead shoes would protect him from demons who lived under the ground and grabbed men by the feet and pulled them down to Hell. It was his shape that was on the road that night. What business did the Bailiff have on such a night when his home was in the other direction, between the large stone box of the Manor and the copse of oak on the southeast side of the Small Bog?

When he passed the Midwife, he nodded and said, "It is I, the Bailiff."

"I know well enough the shape," she answered, looking uninterested. To show concern or fear to a mischievous spirit taking the shape of people or animals or trees was to entertain it and risk its continuing and relentless harassment.

"God bless you, Midwife," he said, walking on.

He was a kindly man, the Midwife admitted. He had neither wife nor children, poor soul, and would die alone. She was alone, of course, but her loneliness was fated and comfortable. She had no longings, as the Bailiff clearly had, for he had told her once, when they were at the spring alone, that he had meant to go back to England to find a wife but had been too busy to make the journey. He had hoped that among the English settlers there would be a young, perhaps comely enough girl to be his bride. He had confessed all this with his eyes shifting to the Midwife's bosom. And he had finished by saying that he did not want to die alone. This was none of the Midwife's concern. Seeing to the Bailiff's lonely death would be the Smith's job. She could see a dim light in the Smith's cottage and the dark movements of someone inside. The Smith, a disjointed man with hands too large for his body, acted as undertaker to augment his living repairing hand tools and the three brittle iron plows in the village. The Smith had buried his own son in a fine oak coffin with iron clasps, claiming that he had been trampled by the Plowman's horse one morning, early, before the Plowman was even awake to know that the animal was loose. But the Midwife knew the truth of it, because the wife had said during labor, "He'll not beat this one to death." She had heard many truths from the mouths of women in labor.

There were those in the village who were afraid of the Midwife, who spoke only a little and said too much.

The Midwife walked on, past the Small Bog, thinking that perhaps the Bailiff would return to England when his death was near. Perhaps he had some kin there. He was neither of the people of the village or of the people of the Manor: too English for the first, too common for the second. His main company was with the two free tenants whose homes were just west of the Manor and south of the Small Bog. The Midwife had been treated well by the free tenants, who were English but who deeply admired her for her skill in turning a breech around and delivering it alive, which she did for the Barley Grower's wife.

The Midwife lived in the last cluster of small cottages, hidden in some trees west of the Manor, where the bretaghs, the Irish laborers who had inherited from their fathers a debt of allegiance to the English Lord's family, lived. They each had their one acre of wheat and of oats each, which they and the few unfree Englishmen could use for themselves, as long as they gave a portion of their goods and labor to the Manor. The Midwife lived among these unfree Irish alone, loathe to marry and determined never to give birth, still a virgin and almost beyond the age of childbearing. And everyone in the village felt blessed to have a virgin as Midwife. They even came to her support when the Old Priest, a man who died of tumors in his neck, wanted to examine her to substantiate officially that she was undefiled.

"I'd not trust a priest with a virgin's naked arse in his face," the Flax Grower's old father had said. Everyone laughed at the old man and pretended to scold him.

The Old Priest never got his chance to substantiate the Midwife's virginity before he died and the New Priest came: a pale, apricot-haired man who turned a raging red after a moment in the sun. He had no interest in insulting or toying with the Midwife. He was obsessed with promoting the village Church as a stopping place for pilgrims on the way to holy wells, pilgrims who would buy meals, relics, prayers, blessings, stockings, bread, leather bags, and wine.

A fox scurried across the road in front of the Midwife, who wondered if this is what the thing that had presented itself as the Bailiff had turned into, still teasing her, playing with her. Perhaps not. Perhaps, after all, it was just a fox. Doomed to be hunted by the Lord of the Manor, a yellow-skinned man with an uncommonly large brow. He hunted sloppily with his sullen sons. Perhaps tomorrow she would see them flying across hedges on their shiny brown horses, laughing stupidly. Perhaps the fox was running from the premonition of this hunt. Perhaps tomorrow the fox would be dead, and the Lord's heavily powdered wife would have a new, orange fur collar for her cape.

The Midwife walked past her own cottage to a cluster of rowan trees and squatted down to rinse her hands in the slow-flowing spring that came up from under a rock that was the size of a giant's skull. She stayed still, quiet, respecting the beauty of the water, laced with ferns under a yellow moon.

The spring was always holy and necessary, a place a person came to refresh herself, away from the crowds at the river, a place to weep, or to meet another woman's husband, or to bathe a weak infant, or to get drinking water. The people needed no rules or signs to understand that they must not abuse the spring for washing or for watering their herds, that only the Priest could fetch water from there for his daily needs. Whispering fairies, drunk and urinating soldiers, masturbating priests (who blamed the fairies for their lust) came to the spring for more than water. The Midwife's grandfather once told her, as he let a sheet of sparkling water flow through his crooked fingers, that the misery or happiness of the world depended on the purity of that spring. It didn't matter that he had little knowledge of the size of the world and didn't know that there were many springs and rivers and oceans.

The Midwife drank water from her palms and thought again of the woman from whose body she had coaxed a new human being that night. She whispered into the water in her hands a request that the child would live a long life, a long and free life as a male, and that she, the Midwife, would remain a virgin until she died. Then she flung the water upward, throwing her hands out high above her head, pretending that she had the power to add stars to the sky.

# 3

tHE WATER the Midwife flung into the air the night before became rain that fell down in a thin sprinkle the next day.

The Lord of the Manor knew the cold rain would be a reasonable excuse to postpone the hunt, but he roused the two sons who still lived with him, glad to test their stamina, their ability to endure cruelty. This was his purpose as a father—to prepare his sons for cruelty. He kicked them awake and laughed when they moaned; one was twelve, the other thirteen. They were lying with three dogs on a pile of goatskins in front of the big hearth. Just out of their dreams, they could smell the dampness and see from the light in the hall that the day was an uncomfortable one.

"Get up! We're hunting today. Did you forget?" their father said, grinning yellow teeth. The dogs, three large wolfhounds who scratched at fleas most of their waking hours, creating unruly tufts of wiry gray hair, raised their heads and thumped their tails.

The boys, one red-headed and the other with his father's dark brown, greasy hair, glanced at each other and got themselves solemnly to bent-over sitting positions. They said nothing.

"Paddy has the crossbow. I'll be having the use of that today," the Lord said. "Go get your own bows. You had better have repaired some arrows or you'll not have enough."

"Why does he take the crossbow for hunting fur collars?" Joseph the dark-haired boy mumbled.

"I'll take my daggers, too," said Richard, who was called Red. He said it to himself and perhaps to his brother, whom he loved but didn't understand. For his brother Joseph was never playful, always obedient.

Red was confused by his brother's obedience, by his constant amnesia concerning their father. Red never forgot that his father took every opportunity to test, to harass his sons because he suspected they were as weak as his own shallow soul. And weakness revolted him.

"You'll take your daggers will you?" the Lord said, showing the same snaggled, yellow eye tooth that his two sons had. "I'd not put my back to him if I were you, Joseph, or he'll place himself closer to my fortune with one of those daggers." An old joke—constantly repeated in one form or another—a reminder that one was surrounded by enemies, lying, immoral enemies, that one could not even trust one's brother. And the Lord constantly referred to the Irish with obscene slurs. "These molting carrion, the Irish," he would spit. "They're stupid, dirty, constantly fornicating, and stink of poverty." No matter that the poverty had much to do with the Lord's wealth, their poverty was their worst sin. Such are the lessons a rich father must teach his sons.

Still sitting, Red put his arms around the dog who was standing beside him, the dog they called Hercules, the youngest and sharpest of the three wolfhounds. Hercules wagged his tail, creating a wind. Joseph got up, holding one of the goatskins around his shoulders and shivering. He was a thin boy, as his father mentioned often. "You walk about like a starving dog," he would say, or, "You're lying there like an old Irishman's corpse."

Hercules trotted after Red as he went to the table against the wall to search among the breads and cheeses for something unstale to eat. He got himself a hunk of goat's cheese and black bread, giving the grateful dog the dark crust, which was too hard for Red's taste.

His mother was sleeping, and Red was sorry to leave without telling her good-bye, without showing her affection, for he had heard her weeping again the night before. He wanted to take her hand and see her eyes sparkle a little for him and forget about her longing for England and her family there.

Not an hour later, in the wildish woods to the south of the Manor, the Lord's hunting party made a forlorn tapestry, soaked and running colors into the surrounding trees and ferns. In such a texture Red could feel the nearness of the Other World; he could sense the ability of the yew tree or the blackbird to shift subtly between its mundane shape into its true form as a displaced god with mournful eyes and reaching fingers. The father and his sons all rode dark brown horses. On foot beside them was one of the unfree laborers, Paddy, with the dog, Hercules, who felt no misery from dampness and wagged his tail whenever either of the two boys spoke, which was rare. Joseph rode in front of Red. They both could see their father many yards before them, drinking ale from a large skin he always took on the hunts. They were walking the horses slowly, not in deference to Paddy, who had to trot as it was to keep up, but because they were waiting for Hercules to sniff a fox and chase it out.

"It'll be hard for him to smell anything in this rain," Red said to Joseph, who turned around and said, "Father knows how and when to hunt." When the father also turned, Joseph made a gesture to his brother with his hands, turning them both up and letting the reins drop, a gesture which said, "Why do you make trouble?"

And the Lord said to his red-haired son, "Shut up, you fool! Every animal in the woods will hear us coming."

Red grew hot and reached into his tunic and grabbed one of his daggers hard in his fist.

The Lord's party rode on, Paddy staying back once to urinate behind an oak and then running to catch up. Hercules thought this was a game and tried to gambol with the peon.

"That dog is always merry," the Lord said after a few long swallows of ale. He had dismissed the rule of silence for himself and adopted a melancholic admiration for the dog that made the sons nervous, for it seemed that whenever the father revealed any tenderness, he had to bring himself back into balance with some senseless cruelty. "Come here then, Hercules," he called, and the boys wondered if he would somehow try to make a fool of the dog, perhaps by saying something insulting in a kind voice and then laughing at the dog's good-natured pleasure. But the Lord leaned down to pat Hercules, who was only a few feet shorter than the horse.

"He treats the dog better than he treats us," Red said to Joseph, for he was close enough to whisper to his brother.

"Take your horse away; you're unnerving mine," Joseph said. "Look at his eyes gone wild."

And so they went on, and Red began to imagine the twinkling and friendly eyes of small, mystical beings watching from behind sodden piles of winter leaves. He became lost in a story he was telling himself about the enchantment in this wood, the woman who would love him into a spell from which he would never emerge, and the fairies who would show him worlds where a man need not be so heavy on the earth, but could rise up and visit the stars. In this way, the boy had learned to take himself away from his loneliness. He learned this talent from his mother, whose longing for another world manifested in lavish stories told in whispers to Red, about ceremonies where dresses and swords glittered, and afternoons of reading and the singing of ballads. She held her son close and told him, "You are my soul, Richard the Red; you are a dreamer like me."

"You're dreaming again," Red heard Joseph say. "Hercules has found a fox. You'd better get your bow ready."

In front of them, the Lord had stopped his horse. He was yelling at Paddy in Gaelic to get him the crossbow. The Lord had learned all the Gaelic phrases he needed—all orders, none of the niceties he had learned in French and Italian. The peon, who understood English but never spoke it, loaded the bow with masterful grace and handed it up to the Lord.

"That damned, filthy dog!" the Lord yelled. "Look at him! He's chasing the fox away!" He yelled to the dog, "Chase him this way, you idiot cur!"

The boys and Paddy were still, silent.

"Look at him, look at him, merrily trotting back as though he'd done a great thing, chasing that fox into oblivion. I am surrounded by idiots!"

Hercules did indeed seem pleased with himself, wagging his tail at the sound of the Lord's voice. And then he yelped, horribly, an echoing yelp that brought birds up from the trees. The crossbow arrow was stuck through his chest right behind his front legs. He fell over, his legs moving as though running. He was yelping now, speaking to the pain.

"What have you done!" Red howled. He clutched his horse's neck and leaned forward. "Hercules! Hercules!"

Joseph slipped off his horse and walked to the dog. The Lord was sitting very still, his mouth fallen open. He let the crossbow slip from his hands to the ground. "I didn't intend . . ."

Paddy walked around and around in a small circle, shaking his head. The rain fell a little harder, tapping on the leaves and beading on the flanks of the horses.

The dog's tail thumped weakly as Red shoved Joseph aside and came to him. The boy said with tears streaming down his face, "There's a boy. It's all right. There's a good boy." Then he looked up at his father and said, "You've got to finish him. He's suffering." The dog tried to move and yelped, then wagged his tail as if to apologize for his situation. Joseph called out, "No. We'll take him back. We'll carry him back and tend to him."

Red squatted beside the dog and looked at the wound; he had a love of science, faith in the physician's art of examination and prescription. But he could see nothing but pain and slow death in the wound and in the dark blood that streamed out of it. He patted the dog's head and then stood up and said firmly to his father, "You've got to finish him."

"No. We can take him back and tend to him with medicine and surgery." Joseph's lips trembled convulsively.

The father started weeping, the liquid coming from his nose and dripping off his chin mixed with rain. "I can't," he whispered. "I can't. I didn't intend . . ." He shivered and looked away, knowing finally that the air was too chilling and gray for hunting that day.

Red shook his brother's hand off his arm and spoke to his father in a cold, flat tone.

"You shot him. You've got to finish it now. You can't leave him to suffer." Red's hands had become fists.

"I can't," the Lord growled. "I can't do it."

Red took out a dagger.

"Paddy, kill the dog, finish the poor animal," the Lord called back, no longer weeping, but mastering the situation as though he hadn't caused it. Paddy stopped on his circular path.

"No," Red hissed. "I'll do it."

He took the dagger and squatted beside Hercules, whose eyes were wild and confused, but whose tail still thumped when he saw Red's face so close. With his left hand Red stroked the wiry hair on either side of the snout.

He thought of praying to God for something and finally pleaded in his head for a swift end to the dog's pain. He said, "You're a good dog," as he thrust the blade into the spot behind the dog's ear and pulled it down with all his strength, through the jugular. The dog's eyes closed and everything was still.

Then Red said, "God have mercy." He looked up at his father, who had turned around, trotting back toward the Manor. Red threw the dagger on the ground and said, "You're all fools." Joseph stared blankly at the dagger on the ground lying on the mulch of winter leaves.

The party went back in silence, even when a fox scrambled out of a rotting log and ran right in front of them.

When Paddy and the two boys had stabled the horses and come into the hall, Lady Margaret, the boys' mother, looked up from her sewing and asked how the hunt had gone. Her weary eyes could not easily focus after so much time following the needle.

"We got nothing," the Lord grumbled from where he was giving his boot to a young maidservant to pull off. "And Hercules was killed."

"Oh, no," she said. The white powdered creases around her mouth stayed when her smile fell away.

"Another hunter shot him, mistaking him for a deer."

"Do you know the man? You should have hanged him on the spot!"

"He was too fast getting away when he discovered what he had done."

"Oh, no," she repeated. "Poor Hercules."

She didn't like to think of death, since she had let God take four children from her, all of them now so far away under a chapel floor in England.

She looked around to speak to her sons, but Joseph had gone to the back of the hall to read his Latin lesson by candlelight. Red looked at her with a secret standing in his eyes as tears. Then he went to sit up in the wide, square tower that made the west edge of the Manor. He looked out over the village and the forest, aware of the myriad kinds of suffering in all its detail: a broken hawk's wing, a twitching insect in the mouth of a rook, a feeble grandfather's trembling head, a dying infant's putrid diarrhea.

He was weeping openly, looking down at the ground below, when the Goatherd's wife came to the little Church with her new baby, a squirming bundle whose black hair he could see, even from that distance.

Mary had explained for the fourteenth time to her husband that the child must be baptized as soon as possible so as to be protected from fairy mischief. She then took the infant from her eldest daughter's arms and scurried, giving no mind to the soreness between her legs, out into the twilight. She found a few loose oats in her pocket and chewed on them as she walked.

It was almost evening and the rain had stopped. Marigold light lined the western horizon. Red leaned out of the window and thought of spitting on the woman and her baby. He thought of being mean, as mean as he could be. But instead, he prayed that the child be strong and able to endure the cruelty of the world. He prayed this as the woman trotted into the Church, having noticed a drop of water fall on her infant's forehead.

Red sat until it was dark in the tower, and his back stiffened against the rough stones as he resisted thoughts about the corpse of the dog lying still and cold in the dripping woods.

 4

"THE END OF THE WORLD is coming, woman. It's coming soon. And all the souls who have not confessed their servitude to God and Jesus Christ, their servitude to the Church will be forever tormented in Hell. Do you know what Hell is, woman?"

Mary squinted to understand the Priest's garbled Gaelic, full of mispronunciations, yet with such an arrogant tone she almost believed that she and the rest of the village spoke their own language incorrectly.

"I know well enough, Father. I'm married to Gregory the Goatherd."

"And I suppose you want me to baptize the thing," he said nodding toward the infant.

"Yes."

"Well, I'll not do it."

"If you'd just drop a little water on the poor thing's head, I'll pay you with meat and cheese. We'll be killing one of the goats. Gregory is so pleased to have a son, Father."

Her breath smelled of goat cheese, in fact.

"Woman, you haven't paid me for the other seven."

"Six, Father. It was only six you baptized."

"Why are you wanting the child baptized so soon and without attendants?"

"It would please his da, and I have a need to please Gregory as often as possible. The ache in his teeth has been making his hands heavy on me and the children. And I wanted to tell you, I'm going to raise the child to be a cleric, for service in the Mother Church. I want to know, Father, what I should do."

"You should show your own *timor et amor* to the Church. Do you come to Mass on all the holy days, daughter?"

"I can't be living the life of a saint, Father, with children to feed and clothe."

"You're not listening to heresies are you? The Devil is speaking through many who say they're Christian."

"I've stopped listening altogether, Father, when the words do naught but confound me."

"Now, Mary, you don't believe in fairies, do you?"

"Oh, no, Father. I know they exist, but I don't believe in them."

The Priest closed his eyes for a moment and sighed.

"Have you ever seen a thorn from the crown of thorns Christ wore on the cross? Come here, woman, and I will show you something truly miraculous."

The Priest, his face now as red as though he had been plowing a field, led her like a dog to a niche in a darker corner of an already dark little chapel. There a small silver box and a few bottles nested in a red velvet cloth that was dusty and showed some bare spots where moths had feasted. He brushed off the silver box and opened its lid. Mary peered in, leaning over the baby in her arms. The Priest leaned away from her breath and held the box out more as protection from her stench and ignorance than as an offering to her.

"I'm afraid to touch such a thing, Father, so precious."

"All right. All right. Come away then. No, no—don't touch that bottle. It's very fragile—of great value. Come on then. Does it have lice?"

They went to the doorway of the Church, where the Priest could examine the baby for any infectious condition.

"No lice, Father. He's as pure as dew."

"Then let me have it."

"He's a good child. Hardly cries and sucks all he can from both breasts."

The Priest dismissed the picture of this quickly as he took the wriggling bundle of rags in his arms.

"Here, then, lad. Let me look at you."

"He's a strong child."

"You'll be ready for the end of the world, will you then?"

"Look at him smile at you, Father."

"He has wild eyes."

"They'll stay that bluish gray color, like his father's, I know they will."

"If he lives."

"He'll live. Even Midwife said he's strong."

"To the Devil with the Midwife. Here, hold him and uncover his head."

"He'll live, Father."

"*In nomine Patris, et Filii, et Spiritus Sancti.*"

The baby struggled, as though to free itself as the Priest reached toward the stone font just inside the entranceway. He dipped his pink fingers into the cool water and spattered it on the infant who twitched, seemed to hold its breath, and then gasped and wailed.

"You startled him, Father," Mary said, digging the bundle out of the Priest's arms. The wailing came in waves and filled the small stone room.

"Go on home now, woman."

Mary jiggled the baby and held it close to her.

"Aren't there other words to be said?"

"I can hardly hear my own thoughts with that wailing. Go home."

Mary stepped outside and scurried around the west wall of the Church. She ducked under the branches of an alder tree, which were low and gave her protection from human eyes. She lay the infant on the ground and unwrapped it so that it lay naked against a warm, wet layer of rags. Mary sighed. There was no change. She had hoped that the Priest's touch, that the holy water—that the child would have been transformed, that a miracle would have taken place. But the tender twin puffs of flesh between the squirming thighs hid no penis. Mary put the soiled rags on the outside, putting the cool, dry ones against the baby's skin. She looked right into the blue-gray eyes and said out loud, "Then it would be best you're an idiot just like your poor, addled da."

The baby grinned.

*e*VERYTHING DEPENDED on the rusting plow. And that is why four men were standing around it in the middle of the Plowman's stubbled, brown-and-yellow field. The brittle blade was bent and stuck in the low, gray stump of a long dead oak. The four men—the Goatherd, the Baker, the Plowman, and his youngest son—all tilted their heads at the same angle, looking at the configuration of stump and plow. A large white horse with a tan mane and tail stomped its hoof and shook flies off its back with a rippling shudder. It was still hitched to the plow by the hairs of its tail.

"Let the horse loose, son, for God's holy sake," the Plowman chided.

The son raised his eyebrows in innocent compliance and went to speak to and untether the horse.

"The thing is," the Baker said, "if you pull it loose, it's likely to break clean off, the tip at least."

"I have some good knowledge of the problem," the Plowman said, and his son, who had returned to the little group, exchanged a sympathetic look with the Baker.

Gregory cleared his throat, which he did whenever he was about to speak, and said, "We could burn the stump around it."

"You might have an idea there." The Baker wanted everyone to be in a good humor. But the Plowman rubbed his thin hair until it stuck up frantically around his shining scalp. He was not inclined to believe that anything was going to save the plow blade. And since they all knew that Gregory the Goatherd was dimwitted, there was surely no point in considering his idea.

"I warned you, didn't I?" The Plowman addressed his son and raised his arm to swat the young man, who ducked in time from many years of practice.

"Oh, and there goes the Bailiff," the Baker said, having twisted around to see the world beyond a stump and plow and a man hitting his son.

"He's off to Smith's, no doubt," the Plowman said, "who'll be in no humor to repair a plow when the Bailiff's done with him."

"The cow is it?" Gregory asked.

"And what else?" The Plowman coughed and then spat. All four were now turned to look at the Bailiff, a hundred yards away, striding swiftly toward the Smith's home.

"He's owed a cow for two months now," the Plowman's son said. "Or so the Bailiff claims."

The Baker shook his head, "When an Irishman has a debt, he has one forever, but when a Lord has a debt, it never existed."

"And when an Irishman collects what's owed him, he's called a thief," the Plowman added.

"They'll hang him," Gregory mumbled. He was afraid.

"Oh, they won't hang him," the Plowman's son assured him. And the others agreed, matter-of-factly, in order to comfort Gregory, who everyone knew had been given too much fear and not enough wit by the Good Lord. He had thick arms, though, and an uncanny communication with his goats. He was a good man to weight a plow or hold onto a horse.

"We'd best be solving our own riddle." The Plowman drew their attention back to the stump.

But the Baker couldn't hold back his thoughts.

"If they go to hang him, I say we go to MacFaelin and to the chieftain there."

"What are you saying, man?" the Plowman yelped. "What will we get from a chieftain who fills his pillows with English coins?"

"A man's soul can't be bought, I'll tell you. There's many a chieftain has taken coins and waited for the time to fight the bastards."

"And how many have won?"

"The Bruce!" the Baker said as though the name could silence the world.

But the Plowman spit, "Killed at Fochart. And a Scotsman along with it!"

"Some say he wasn't killed," the Baker retorted, stepping closer as though to beat the Plowman into the earth with his fists if his words didn't do the job. "And he fought under O'Neill, who was, in case you've forgotten, the King of Ireland."

But the Plowman didn't let himself be intimidated, especially with his son present, and said, "Also killed, his head put on a pole and danced like a puppet before the King of England. You're all mixed up with your stories, man, and now saying there are hero ghosts among us, come to save us all from famine and injustice."

"And you were there to see it all, were you, in the King of England's court, were you, all those years ago in London?" were the Baker's final words on the matter, and hadn't they had just that conversation ten or eleven times before.

Gregory stood and watched the two argue, holding his mouth open as though to catch whatever he could of the discussion with the largest opening on his face. The Plowman's son looked at the ground, not yet ready to speak up, at least not in front of his father.

"We're treated like rodents in the granary," the Baker growled. "Only it's our grain and our land."

"You go and fight, then, Baker. Take your wooden spoon and attack! There you go, up to the Manor with your spoon and a big loaf of stale bread. They'll see you coming and run for the Other World!"

"The Smith has weapons hidden," the Plowman's son finally said, but he didn't look up. So he didn't see his father's hand coming before it slammed against his head and put him on the ground.

Gregory shut his mouth and looked wildly at the three faces.

"You don't know such a thing," the father said, standing over his son. "You don't know and you won't say it, will you? You'll say a prayer instead, that your mouth be sewn shut before you talk about hidden weapons?" His face was red.

"Look, you're frightening Gregory close to death," the Plowman's son said, standing up.

The Baker put his hand on Gregory's back.

"It's all just talk, man. Just talk . . ."

The Plowman shook his head and sighed.

Then all four of them looked up toward the line of trees and brambles and bushes that hid the river, about a hundred yards away as the horse took nervous steps and switched his tale vigorously. From that place came a cacophony of wooden utensils and metal, a chaotic beat and tinkle of items that turned out to be hanging off of a pack worn by a man, a stranger whom no one could recognize. The stranger, bent over to get through the tangle of growth, emerged at the end of the field and stopped. He saw the four men, saw the plow, saw the situation, and nodded.

"Who is that?" the Plowman's son asked.

"I've never seen him," the Plowman said.

The stranger straightened up, jangling his pack into a steadier balance and letting a breeze play with the ends of his long hair, which was tied back with some twine. He then stood still, locking eyes with the Plowman as though he had assessed who had authority on this piece of land. Curious, the Plowman nodded, putting the stranger into motion. He strode toward the group, and they could see soon enough that he was barefoot and his clothes worn, but a calm in his mouth and eyes made him seem as though he were not desperate for anything.

When he was near enough, he patted the horse's haunches and spoke. "I see the horse turned too sharply and stuck the plow."

And so it was. And the other men looked again at their dilemma.

"Are you passing through?" the Baker asked.

"I might be," was the answer.

The Plowman's son was unhappy with the answer, not liking to be confused or toyed with, and in a suspicious mood after their talk of rebellion and hanging.

"What's your business?" he asked.

The stranger lifted his pack off and leaned it carefully against the stump.

"Tinkering and bartering. I barter with good candles and have tools with me for building, if building is needed."

"We've got to get the blade out of the stump," Gregory said, leaving his mouth open after the words were out of it.

The three companions chuckled to themselves to show that they didn't take the half-wit seriously. But the stranger began to converse solely with Gregory.

"Have you thought of burning the stump around the blade?" he asked.

"That we have!" Gregory answered, grinning. "But now we're talking about the Smith's weapons and fighting the English."

"For God's sake, man," the Baker yelled. "Keep yer gaping mouth shut for once, will ya!" He hit the back of Gregory's head.

Still addressing the Goatherd, the stranger said, "You know, don't you then, what they did to a man up north, a Norman knight, he was. That stone mason from up there in Naas told me. To be sure, you've heard?"

Only the Baker nodded. "That's Niall, the Stone Mason. Tell the story, man."

"Well, I'll tell you." He looked each of them in the eye, smiling at the Goatherd. "The knight, a Norman man who'd found common cause with the Irish in that area, gave himself up after a night in the woods, huddled under a yew tree, I was told, exposed to mischief from this world and the other. They say a number of disembodied spirits came to him, telling him to surrender to the English whom he'd been fighting for three weeks. And sure he was starving and his sleeves torn." The stranger looked down at the stump. "And his sword was broken, snapped by the leather of an English soldier's breastplate. And he took this as a sign and sent word, by a servant, that he would surrender and pledge loyalty to Edward."

The four who listened didn't even notice that the Bailiff was on the road again, having left the Smith's cottage, pulling hard on a rope that was tied to a solidly reluctant brown cow. The Bailiff was leaning forward, almost to the ground, with the rope over his shoulder, making his way south by inches as the beast behind him took one reluctant step at a time. But the four men in the Plowman's field were in another time and place, oblivious to the Bailiff's struggle behind them.

"The wind was howling and blowing in a black way," the stranger continued. "The servant returned with a message, written on a scroll with a red seal, and it promised pardon and safety to the knight if he came to meet them and pledged his loyalty as he had said he would. And so he did. He rode into the English camp on his horse, his hands held out with his palms up, empty of weapon. His head was bowed."

Gregory involuntarily bowed his head.

"He rode alone, no soldier to threaten or cause doubt of his intentions."

The stranger paused and let the four see in their minds the scene. Then he continued. "The English Lord was seated on a blue velvet chair, like a throne, in a clearing, underneath a large sycamore with servants and ladies and soldiers around him. There were three black crows on a branch that hung over his head. And the knight got down and kneeled in front of the man and swore peace even though he knew well the lands of his family and of other families had been taken and the people cast out from their own homes. And he said, 'I am here to receive your pardon and promise to be faithful to the King of England and his laws.' And the Lord nodded and said, 'I accept your promise and will send you to God to keep it.' And he ordered his soldiers to hang him."

Gregory rubbed his jaws and the Baker looked up to the sky, where the sun was coming out from behind a billow of clouds. The Plowman's son asked, "Who could hang a man who comes to surrender and is promised pardon?"

"They hanged him, they did, from that very sycamore tree, and laughed afterwards, leaving him to swing in the wind for all his men to find."

"I hate them," the son said. "I will always hate them."

The Plowman looked satisfied and nodded with affection at his son.

The four waited, shaking their heads.

"Let me help, then . . . with the plow," the stranger said, "in exchange for supper at one of your houses this eve, and then I'll be on."

"Sure you can come to my table," the Baker said.

And so the stranger took out an adz, and all but the Goatherd took turns chopping at the stump around the blade.

"He'll be cutting his own fingers off and one of ours, too," the Baker said when Gregory held his big hand out to take his turn.

When the stranger worked, the others eyed him and puzzled him out, making notes to discuss among themselves later. He was barely a man, it turned out, hardly whiskered, though his smooth jaw was firm. They noted, too, that his hands were coarse and grimed beyond his years. He liked to talk when he worked, as though the use of his body set his words free from his mind. When the Plowman's son asked him what he was called he said, "I'm called many different names, including a horse's ass, but I prefer to be called Colin, since it's what my mother named me, and so far she has loved me most."

He went on to explain his plans, to unload as much of his pack as he could and then go to the Monastery at Tarmath, for he was weary just now of wandering and was thinking to turn into a cleric, since he had a knack for reading and writing.

Talk of the monastery quieted the others, who let the Priest and their wives determine their religious fervor.

Just before sunset, the Goatherd wandered home, wandering on the road and worrying about his goats. He wished that the Stranger Colin were coming to his house; he felt that he would bless it somehow and excuse all that it lacked. He would understand the wisdom of goats. Gregory had left the oldest girl with them. Sometimes she did well, other times she wandered off and left them. Gregory kept his mind focused on worrying about the goats so as not to think about the man hanging in the sycamore tree with the three crows laughing at him.

The air was heavy around him, until he could hardly breathe, and then he saw the Priest coming from his home.

"You owe me Goatherd," the Priest said, passing and turning around to walk backwards so as to deliver his message. He held up a cloth bundle. "I've got this, but I'm owed six more. And the end of the world is coming soon, man, soon. And all debtors will be thrown into the pit of fire."

Gregory stood still and watched as the wind turned the Priest around and headed him toward the Manor. He hadn't understood a word the man said.

"The plow's broken," he called after him.

But the Priest had no interest in this.

When Gregory went through the door he saw little Gregory, three years old now, standing on a stool, staring into the hearth where a small flame flickered. There was no one else home.

Grey, which is what the child was called as a shortening of his father's name, was most certainly not like his sisters. Perhaps the difference was a result of the larger portions of food he was given as well as the longer time on his mother's warm lap. Free of fear and raging hunger, Grey became a bolder child than the others in the Goatherd's hovel, a child who loved to feel, to smell, to taste the world. Perhaps, his mother considered, the Midwife had done some magic, had arranged for a changeling to take the place of the girl infant—a boy without a cock. The Weaver's wife had once said that a changeling child will always wander and dream, indulging too joyfully in the senses.

"Grey," the father called out cautiously, as though to waken a sleepwalker.

The child turned to him with a sober, furrowed expression and then let his mouth hang open, imitating his father's commonest expression.

"What the Devil are you doing all alone standing up there, Grey? You want to fall into the fire and burn yourself to ashes?" There was so much disaster in the world. What could a man do to oversee it all?

"No, no," Grey said as the father came and lifted him off the stool.

He held his son tight, rocking him in his big arms. The child repeated, "No, no," and reached his arms toward the stool.

"No, no," the father echoed. And the child finally laid its head on the wide shoulder.

Mary was outside, up on the hill behind the cottage. She was listening, putting her finger over her mouth to shush the wind so she could hear what she was listening for—the elder Fiona, whom she knew was in the woods with one of the bretagh's sons. She heard, instead, Grey saying defi-antly, "No!"

Some of the Weaver's cheapest cloth, thin and rough brown wool, the material from which her family's clothes were made, hung from her hand. The wind caught the end of it on a thistle. For a moment Mary thought a fairy was tugging on the cloth. She looked down at it, thinking now of the trousers she would make for Grey. It no longer occurred to her that Grey was not a boy, for a boy was defined by his trousers, his boldness, his strength and good prospects for the future. He would grow old and respected. This was a certainty in Mary's mind. Grey would not end up in the woods inviting a man's branch of flesh between her spread legs—never! Mary raveled the cloth around her arms and cursed her eldest daughter.

*t*HE FACE of Grey's mother was always close, always implying that the child was about to be the victim of some disaster. It was a round of doubt and worry that Grey loved and hated. His father's face had more bone in it, as though it were something whose edges one could hold onto and lift oneself up by. Whereas his mother fondled and held him like a fragile precious thing, giving him more broth, more oat cakes, more cheese than his sisters got, his father treated him as something solid and capable. But he was closest to his second oldest sister, the Second Fiona, named this because the oldest and First Fiona seemed ready to die of a fever when the second one was born. Mary hadn't wanted to waste a good name and so gave it a second time, figuring that soon the First Fiona would answer to no name. But the First Fiona lived and thrived, and the Second Fiona did, too, though her legs were thin and crooked.

The Second Fiona confided to Grey that she spoke to beings of the non-human type, some of them not even visible.

"They whisper," she said, imitating their tone herself, "so you must listen with all your bones and every piece of hair on your head. You don't believe me, then, do you?"

Grey said, "I believe you."

Fiona pointed out the faces in the trunks of trees, explained the thoughts of a beetle crossing the road: "He's thinking of his little home in the woods beneath a rock where he stays with his wife. They have five children, whom he teaches to stay away from the crows. If you're kind to him, he'll repay the kindness someday. So mind where you step."

To Fiona the world shimmered with something—fairies, laughter, sobs, dead heroes—something beyond the name of the particular item: tree, fern, stick, shoe, cloud. If one looked long enough at anything, it looked back.

"I want to see spirits," Grey said to his sister. "I want them to speak to me, too."

And Fiona explained, right into her brother's oily ear so that the words tickled. "You must look and look, quieting every thought in your head. You must stare and stare at tree or cloud, or even acorn, and be so still, sooo still you are, that the spirit of that thing forgets you're there and starts to show itself. Maybe at first just a little movement, hardly there at all, or a sigh you can hear if the wind dies down. And sometimes, if you've freed yourself of everything but the will to know the truth, the spirit will show itself and open its eyes. And when your eyes look into the spirit's eyes and you listen well, it will speak to you and know your sorrows and your wishes."

Grey tried, while pinching blackberries from laden bushes in the northern woods, to stare fiercely at things: a pool, a tall stone, a rowan berry. But his eyes often drooped closed before conjuring the spirit, or he felt in the flesh nearest his bones that the spirit was about to open its eyes and he looked away, afraid.

Until the time that Grey was seven years old he slept close to his sister, fitting like bark on a curved log. He had no resentment toward her for being the one his mother sent along with him with the same instructions: "Don't be lettin' him show his pisser to a soul. I know how the boys play."

So often hobbling behind Grey, Fiona went to join the boys who gathered by the old stump in the Plowman's field. They threw rocks at a hole in the stump; all of them had come to know that Grey was the surest marksman. He had strong arms and could fix his eyes on his target, never losing his mark, even when another boy shoved him or the whole lot of them challenged him to step farther back. He was almost to the road throwing at the stump when he was seven. The Baker's youngest son tried to distract him by singing a ditty about a man who ate shit and drank urine, but Grey was able to laugh and throw well at the same time.

"I will be a warrior," he announced one day, and no one laughed. All the boys nodded. It was the surest sign of a warrior to be able to laugh and still hone his skills as though both lightheartedness and perfection were equally sacred. He could feel the skill of a rock or a stick when he held it, its connection to its target, what it would take from him to allow the stick to do its best. He tried to explain once to the boys, and one of them said, "It's God's angels give us help." Another argued, "God's angels is up in Heaven." And another, "But God can see everything we do—everything." Grey shared a look with Fiona, who understood that God watched from every grain of dirt, every dark pool, every sprig of oak.

The only place Grey went to without Fiona was the Midwife's house. The Midwife, who had never received payment from Mary the Goatherd's wife, asked Grey often to go gathering with her, for some mischief was causing her vision to throw clouds of light around all the things she looked at.

He told the Midwife that he wanted to be a warrior, and she had not laughed at him but had asked, "And for whom will you fight, Grey? You must have a cause, something to fight for."

At Grey's silence, the Midwife laughed and said, "Well, you have time to think on it, then."

"It will be easy to be a warrior," Grey said aloud to his mates in the field. "I'll fight the English." For with his chums, he remembered clearly whom warriors fought.

Fiona watched Grey and wound a long blade of pale green grass around her dirty finger.

The Weaver's son with the deformed ears said, "Your mother says you're going to be a cleric and learn all the Latin prayers and live in a monastery."

Fiona hobbled up to the road. No one ever asked her what she would be. And Grey felt guilty for not having to suffer being a girl and being deemed worthless because of a deformity. There was often talk between the Goatherd and his wife about not being able to marry their second daughter off because of her legs.

As soon as Fiona was unable to hear him, the Plowman's grandson, who ached for adventure every waking moment, said, "Now then, Grey, show us your aim with your pisser and we'll show ours. Seamus here can make an arc with his water bigger than the arc of the Manor door."

Grey looked over at the Weaver's boy, focusing on the ears and suddenly wondering if there were anything at all perfect in the world of humans. He looked at each of the boys, and each in some way seemed misshapen: the Plowman's grandson with his big teeth, one of the bretagh's sons with a scar on his neck, the Flax Grower's youngest son who had the Baker's skeletal arms. They suddenly seemed like a pack of ill-fated demons.

"I'm not allowed," was all Grey said.

Of course, he knew that he was deformed with a pisser badly shrunken. His mother had reassured him, and Fiona had said that they were both marked by fairies. But he knew, like birds know which berries were poisonous, not to let any of the boys of Finnistuath see that he had a penis so small that it was buried between two folds of skin.

In the evening light, a little yellow like a healing bruise, the other boys pissed toward the hole in the stump as Grey walked alone on the road back to his cottage. He wanted then to sit in his mother's lap and to fall asleep with his fingers tangled in his sister's hair. He hoped his father would not call him to help with the goats. He hoped he could just stay warm inside the cottage.

The Midwife was on the road, coming from the Weaver's cottage, where the Weaver's wife had just given birth to a dead child. Grey wanted then to stop and go with her and wander in the woods looking for treasures, dry wood and berries to take home to make Fiona and his mother smile, but the Midwife looked so sad that Grey only nodded and muttered a greeting.

The Midwife stopped and looked at Grey and sighed.

"How are you then, Grey?"

"I'm doing well, Midwife."

The Midwife stood there, her arms crossed over her chest to keep the fluttering shawl tight against her. She laughed softly and said, "Well, that's good, then."

Grey smiled at her, jerking his head up to look into her eyes, which seemed to search the air for what they wanted to see.

"I'll fight with O'Neill," Grey announced, suddenly hostile toward the Midwife, who didn't understand the simplicity of enemies as the boys did. "And I'll fight whoever causes wounds and deformity."

Grey ran hard away with the Midwife looking after him, marveling at his speed and not wanting to tell the child that one cannot easily fight with dead kings.

"Fiona," Grey whispered that night, his mouth touching the edge of her ear.

"What?" she answered.

"I'll carry the water for you tomorrow."

"No, you won't, because Da wants you to help him with the goats because the one's ready to have her kid."

It wasn't bad working with the herd when his father was happy. When his father was happy, he touched Grey often, lifting him, or patting him, or grabbing his arm and pumping it a little. But when his father was sullen or confused, he looked at Grey and said things such as, "You're the only hope I have," or "You'll have to be Goatherd soon," things that felt like black rocks tied to one's insides.

The next day, Gregory the Goatherd was not happy. He had been unable that morning to separate dream from reality and had accused his wife of slaughtering the pregnant goat. She smacked him hard on the arm with a bowl and called him an idiot, and so his day began. Sure enough, the pregnant goat was still in the pen, alive and round-bellied.

He sat next to his son on the lichened boulder in the middle of the clearing where the goats started their day. Grey asked him what he wanted him to do, but his father said nothing except for, "I don't think it'll be today."

When the sun was above the trees, the Goatherd fell asleep on the ground beside the rock and Grey sat atop it, holding his knees to his chest and watching the goats. He watched and thought about being the Goatherd of Finnistuath and a familiar cool nausea came over him, some kind of horror, that he was stuck somehow in a life that would render up nothing good. He had begun to think about death, about how he would have to die someday, and he put together being the Goatherd of Finnistuath with living just one long day, one long day of everything being the same, of always being afraid and miserable, of being a warrior who never fought a battle.

He was glad to see his cross sisters, the taller one, named Deirdre, and the smallest, a feeble soul named Caerla, coming into the clearing with a round of black bread. He was sorry the Second Fiona wasn't with them and glad the First Fiona wasn't. His oldest sister had run off with some boy, or so his mother said in arguments with his father. She had gone off to Tarmath—a mythical village across the river where there were a hundred houses and a hundred goats and a hundred cows and sheep and loaves of bread and where his mother had gone twice in her life.

Deirdre and Caerla, like two different-sized versions of the same straw dolls, made no conversation with their brother, whom they resented for being always given the biggest portions at meals. They placed the bread on their father's sleeping head and then left giggling at his sleepy confusion. He told Grey that he had dreamed that God had made him an angel by putting a crown on his head. He was happy because he knew that this had been a dream and that the crown was really the loaf of bread.

After eating the bread, the Goatherd and his son had to move to the northernmost point of the clearing, where the goats were strung out in a curving line at the edge of the woods. Grey got to sit between his father's legs and doze against his chest, and so his terror left.

And then an hour or so before sunset, like a flame dressed in ragged pants, the Plowman's grandson ran across the meadow toward the two human mushrooms sprouted on the moist ground. Panting, the boy said,

"Grey, you must come with me. You must come on and see something, then. You must, before it goes away." His eyes darted surreptitiously to Grey's father.

"A bird?" the Goatherd asked.

With impatience, the Plowman's grandson answered, "No. Not a bird. Now come on, Grey you must, you must! You'll never see a thing like it, never again!"

Grey looked to his father, whose eyes were excited.

"I'll be back soon, Da."

The Goatherd nodded quickly.

"Don't hurt yourself," his father called out after him, still sitting with his legs spread out, making a space where his son had been.

Grey had to slow down not to run ahead of the Plowman's grandson, whose legs were not as long as his. Trotting along the road he asked, "Where are we going?"

"Down by the spring," was the answer.

The two boys went down off the road and behind the Midwife's home. Then they slowed down and crept to a thicket of holly and young oak. The holly leaves pricked their arms; Grey felt their teasing stings but stood in silence and parted the branches slowly so that the flesh color they saw between the leaves became a naked man.

"He's still here," the Plowman's grandson whispered.

It was Red, the Lord's youngest son. He was kneeling, and just as the two boys began to watch him, he leaned back on his knees. He held a long stick in his hand and laid this across his knees.

"What are those marks on his skin?" Grey whispered.

"He's been beating himself with the stick," the Plowman's son said, staring at Grey's face to see the same disbelief he had experienced an hour ago when he first came upon the Lord's son as naked as a fish.

Grey watched the breath heave in and out of the man's chest, saw the swirls of red hair, which glistened a little. Besides the self-inflicted welts, Red's body seemed to Grey undeformed, perhaps perfect. But he was some distance away.

"Beating *himself,* you say?"

"Yes!" The Plowman's grandson knocked on the trunk of a sapling to show his truthfulness, for if one wakes spirit to hear something, it had better be the truth.

Red's movement drew them back to look as the Lord's son straightened. He said something in Latin and after lifting the stick struck himself hard on the back, bringing on a silence in the woods around him. The Plowman's grandson covered his mouth to keep from laughing. Grey stepped backward, meaning to leave both the self-inflicted pain and the careless laughter of his playmate. He meant to run up to the road and run all the way back to the goats and sit with his father. But some spell had him and made him stay still and look. The man hit himself again and again. Grey watched the face, watched the pain on Red's face, and knew that it was not caused by the blows of the stick but was the pain the man meant to abolish with the stick. What was the sin or the suffering that a beating assuaged?

Red hit himself three more times, the last time gasping loudly, almost sobbing. This is when Grey turned away. But the Plowman's grandson said, almost too loudly, "Jesus, Mary, and Joseph, you must look at that!"

Grey did look, and he and the Plowman's grandson saw the Lord's son standing with a long erection leaning out from his loins. A flowing heat, an intense embarrassment and dizzying wave of wanting to touch the man's cock, went through Grey. He knew that his cock would never be so large. It was enough to wish that it were the size of the boys who pissed on the stump, but he could never make it grow like that, to the size of the Lord's son's erection.

"He's ready for the mount," the Plowman's grandson whispered in awe.

Then Red began to hold his erection and swaying back and forth he stroked it and moaned a little.

"Who is he fucking? He must be fucking a fairy! We can't see her! She must be beautiful! She must have gotten him to beat himself! Jesus, Mary, and Joseph!"

Grey didn't respond but started up to the road with his companion following. They were silent as they walked, picking up stones and throwing them, kicking at the rocks wedged into the mud. Finally the Plowman's grandson said, "He was fucking a fairy woman!"

Grey breathed heavily as though he needed a new supply of air for the new world of mystery that had just opened up beneath his feet. "Why would a fairy woman want him to beat himself?"

The Plowman's grandson seemed to have figured it out: "Because God wants men to suffer, and since the rich don't suffer like we do, they have to beat on themselves so when they die they won't have to suffer in Hell for all their sins."

Grey shrugged, seeming uninterested, not wanting to say what he was really dwelling on, which was Red's erection. He recalled that his father had once said that fairies made men's pissers grow at times, made them grow and got men into mischief. There were fairies around that spring—everyone knew it. And no one could say if they were in the service of God or the Devil.

These thoughts were in Grey's head as the Plowman's grandson peeled away from the road to find his own home in the dusk. Grey picked up a hawthorn switch at the edge of the Big Bog and it became a sword with which Grey fought the oncoming night. But night won. The sword became a stick again, and Grey threw it away, watching it spin and fall.

That night, lying close to his sister, Grey asked her, "Do you want to die and go to Heaven?"

She said, right away, "Yes."

"What is there in Heaven that is so wonderful?"

The Second Fiona turned to him and said, nose almost touching nose, "There is all the food you want or need—milk and meat and bread and butter. And there are no fleas or sores or bad teeth or anything bad at all."

"The fairies can go back and forth from this world to Heaven any time they want," Grey said.

"I don't think they're allowed in God's Heaven," Fiona said.

"Why not?"

"They laugh too much."

"Why doesn't God like them to laugh?"

"Oh, I don't think it's God that minds. It's all the solemn priests and saints that go to Heaven that don't like the noise. If God made everything, He surely made the fairies."

"Who made the demons, then?" Grey asked.

Fiona and Grey could hear their mother snoring now, a soft windy inhalation and a whistling exhalation. Father was staring at the embers in a pot kept by the hearth. There was no fire, not enough wood or peat for a fire that night.

"God made the demons, too," Fiona said.

Then God must have made her crooked legs and the pain in them, Grey thought. And he wondered if the only worthy thing to fight when he became a warrior was God Himself.

Tears filled up his eyes and slithered down, making warm trails on his dirty skin.

"Don't cry," his sister told him. "You're going to be a man. You mustn't weep."

And Grey was soothed by the notion that the secret rituals of men could very well mean that life was much more interesting than herding goats and making cheese, involving pleasures so profound as to make a man do battle with himself.

 7

*t*HE BAILIFF had been standing quite still in the Midwife's wattle hut for several minutes, watching a line of diffused sunlight lengthen along a crude pine table. It was covered with dried herbs, which the Bailiff did not dare touch. He held his hands folded against a red girdle that hung low on his hips, a quilted velvet fashion he had recently been given by the Lady of the Manor as a kindness.

The Midwife found him in this pose. She was breathless from her return journey from Tarmath. She had gone there in the morning to buy cloth and a glass bottle, which she carried in a bundle under her arm. She had hurried to get over the old footbridge before sundown, for soldiers there were building a new bridge over the river, one that could accommodate horses. The new bridge would be a miracle, but the English soldiers gave the women who crossed the bridge alone, or with poor and powerless men, devilish glances. They said things in English that had the ring of abuse.

After the bridge she trotted the three miles beside the river, glad to see familiar men and women and children doing various chores at the water— repairing boats, fishing, washing. Two women ran up to her with their children, toddlers, whose births the Midwife had attended. Her mood had been calmed and cheered by these encounters, and so she was not prepared to be presented with any danger, not after the bridge had been crossed without incident. But there was a man standing in her home.

She recognized the Bailiff quickly, after the first confusion passed. He was wearing his wide-brimmed hat, which he did not remove when she entered, but he touched the brim to acknowledge both hat and woman.

"Midwife," he greeted.

"Bailiff."

"I have business here."

The Midwife set the goods she had bought on the table. These English with their colorless bluntness, she thought. The varied thickness of the glass bottle gave the impression of green sea waves enchanted into solid form.

Beside the bottle were the folded dark green cloth, made of rough linen and a light piece of undyed wool large enough for skirt or small blanket.

"I've been to the town," she said unnecessarily.

The Bailiff looked around the one-room hut, at wooden bowls, cups made of dark metal, a bent brass platter, and a pockmarked caldron. The hearth was cold. If the Bailiff were not there, the Midwife would have gone to one of the nearby huts and borrowed a faggot to get a flame going for the night.

He brought out of his long sleeveless coat made of fox skins a scroll, so short and tightly rolled that it was hard to hold open. He read, "This is notice from the Lord Robert of Finnistuath Manor that you must leave your present residence by the new moon of this month, May of the year 1335."

He rolled the scroll back up and said, "It is sealed and signed."

The Midwife sat down on the one stool by the table and slumped over. She looked up at the Bailiff, whose gray eyes and thin, straight mouth showed no malice, nor any hope. She could see neither his eyes nor his mouth with sharp clarity, but she could see and feel his stillness, a patience that was stoic but not particularly kind.

"But I've lived here for more than fourteen years. I've lived on this very ground. What is the reason to turn me out of my home?"

"There is no record of your ownership, Midwife."

"And well you know this village was settled without your versions of ownership. It is the earth below us which gives us a home when we have made use of it, not a piece of paper with a cracked seal upon it."

These Normans, more Irish than the Irish, the Bailiff thought, with their baskets of words. Her father's people were Norman, everyone knew that, but ignorant Normans who had been slaughtered in the woods. Poor woman, he thought, turned out of her home again. He felt a tickle of shame at the back of his throat as he said, "There are new settlers coming who will live near the Manor. From England. The King of England has sent them to improve the land. He has granted land here to five good households."

"Improve the land?" The Midwife was dazed.

"You've already seen the new bridge."

"Yes."

"They'll bring wealth, more cattle, and farm the land."

"But the land is already being farmed. What of the others?" She looked around as though she could see through the walls to her neighbors' huts.

"They must move also." Now the Bailiff sighed and looked away. He pulled a ledger book from out of a wide pocket inside his coat. He opened it on the table and then bent down to pick a piece of charcoal out of the cold hearth. He wrote in the book as the Midwife leaned in to pretend to see the marks he made, which she could not decipher even if she could have seen them. The Bailiff shut the book and put it back in his coat.

"Where will I go, to the bogs and forests?"

"You may go to the north end of the village."

She stared at the table for a moment and then looked back at the Bailiff.

"But that's where the Goatherd herds his goats."

"There's room enough there."

The Midwife put her hands on the table and felt them tremble. So easy it seemed to turn someone out of his home, so thoroughly one moment could alter years of contentment and certainty.

The Bailiff stated, "Become my wife. Then you will have a good home."

"I'll not do that," she said, shaking her head.

"All right, then." He folded his hands in front of him again and nodded. Then he left the Midwife sitting in the darkening hut.

She felt sick in her chest, a little girl's sick terror at being swept aside by forces that had no concern for the individuals whose hearts it squeezed, whose eyes it pounded shut, and whose arms it tore from what they embraced. But this time, she told herself, placing her hand over her chest and breathing deeply, this time the move was not so brutal. "But what next? What next?" her child's voice whimpered. She stood up and touched the things she had bought in Tarmath: the bottle, the cloth. She put her mind on the Bailiff, his pathetic loneliness and his arrogance when the people of the Manor called him a milksop and the boys of the village played with him as though he were a crippled tomcat.

As he walked up the road to carry his news, just as he carried news of debts owed and services required, he waved his hand in front of his face to swat away visions of himself as the village fool as he passed the Plowman's field with the stump in it. That was where the village boys insulted him, he the Bailiff whose ledger had all their names and birth dates, all the debts their fathers accrued for them to take on. The Bailiff liked to sit on the stump where the boys came to play their hurling games.

That day, the clump of boys hung back, standing at the edge of the road and whispering. The Weaver's son was doing most of the talking, a boy who was full of words, both English and Gaelic, and whom the Bailiff had made a note of in his ledger as a future scribe, someone to keep the records for him when his own eyes went bad. The Bailiff ignored the boys but saw out of the corner of his eye as the Weaver pushed the Goatherd's son toward the field.

So Grey walked up to the Bailiff, who was eating a piece of bread dipped in a small honey pot he got from one of his pockets. Grey was distracted by the delicious appearance and aroma of the honey—a precious luxury for any of his kind. For it was actually a law that any honey found by anyone in Finnistuath was the property of the Manor. Sometimes the poor would find a hive and sit deep in the woods to have the sweetness in secret. But no household outside the Manor kept the stuff openly.

The Bailiff nodded and said in Gaelic, "What is it, boy?" And Grey spoke the words the Weaver's son taught him, promising they would flatter the man in his native language.

"Ya are tha son o pig ahnd dog."

The Bailiff's face grew orange, and he carefully placed the honey pot on the ground with the bread on top of it before he knocked Grey to the ground with a blow to the side of his head. The other boys laughed and ran up to the road and down into the marshy ditch on the other side.

The Bailiff took up his meal and left.

Grey understood the trick that had been played on him and the Bailiff, and the laughing Weaver's son darted around corners whenever Grey came upon him for the rest of the day.

"I'll put my fist in yer nose," Grey called out to him.

But soon their feud was diffused by the hatred and misery of all their elders who were, by the end of the day, aware that the Lord of the Manor had decided to rearrange Finnistuath according to a whim that the Bailiff bothered to explain only to the Midwife.

And so went the changes in the village, after the Bailiff had trotted from home to home as though the people were huge pieces in some game played by the King of England. And though there would be inconvenience, the Bailiff had announced, never looking into anyone's eyes, "In years to come, you will prosper, you see, for there will be more English to labor for."

Then the stranger returned, the one named Colin. And the villagers wondered if there was any providential meaning in his arrival at this time when they felt their impotence so keenly.

His strong legs and arms and his long brown hair looked the same as years before. But his skin was darker. His pack of goods, mainly candles and scrolls, did not bend his back and had less rattle to it. He smiled and sang often, indicating that he had none of the troubles of husbands. His autonomy was disturbing to some, for everyone had to be known by his or her family, even if just cousins, or at least by the lake or valley or hill one was born near. But Colin gave out no such information, and so rumor supplied it.

The Smith said to the Plowman's son, "He's well in with some men from the north, plotters, good men who want their rights and their lands back, Chieftains' men." The Plowman's son said to the Baker, "He doesn't say who his father is because it's too dangerous, that's what I say. I say he's one of the O'Neills, a descendant of the King of Ireland himself." And the Priest said to the Lord, "He's an educated man who knows Latin; he's a criminal, I'd say, who's lowered himself to tinker in order to escape his due punishment." And then Paddy told the Midwife that Colin had "murdered an Englishman up north." The Midwife said nothing.

Colin had his own legends of himself, but they all took place in the future. He had not yet lived up to his own standards of manhood, which required more than petty bartering and repairs. But he was putting off any other effort because he didn't want to risk seeing himself as a failure when he could still imagine himself as a legend. There was all manner of fame to choose from: swordsman, poet, chieftain, saint. He hadn't yet landed on any one, so furtive was he in running away from certain doubts—in himself and the world.

In Finnistuath, he made himself a crude hut with boughs of trees covered in mud, much like the huts built by the unfree laborers who had been moved to the north to make room for the new settlers. But he built his dwelling among the first trees of the northwestern woods, apart from the others.

Still, he knew that curious souls passed by or lingered around pretending to look at the sky. He saw the boys pushing each other toward his hut and then running off when he stood and stretched. He felt young women stand and let their skirts be blown by the wind as they watched him pass on the road. He tried to give them all something that they wanted of him, some image or entertainment. Every morning he sang:

I arise today
Through the strength of heaven:
Light of sun,
Radiance of moon,
Splendor of fire,
Speed of lightning,
Swiftness of wind,
Depth of sea,
Stability of earth,
Firmness of rock.

This argued against any of the rancorous rumors about Colin's being a clever spy, a warrior for their enemies. A poet was the most noble thing a man could be, and no English knight or peasant or king or angel could be such a poet—only an Irishman. In fact, Colin had learned most of his poems from the Stone Mason in Naas, whom he drank ale with from time to time. But he was beginning to make his own verses, about the particular lay of the land in Finnistuath, its grove of holly trees and its brambled woods by the river.

Only the Midwife, among the new cluster of huts at the north end of the village, kept away from Colin, because she heard in his tender voice as he greeted her on the road a recognition of a tragedy that paired them, an orphan's long-ago horror and loss. She knew, without knowing the details, that Colin was sad and had spent years making himself free and strong in response to an old and heavy sadness. And like her, he knew herbs as though he were the Earth's lover. For these reasons, the Midwife kept her heart and her virginity well away from Colin, lying still one day in a tall carpet of flowering bugles, so that the light blue blossoms and thick green leaves hid her as she heard him coming near and singing.

The bushy leafy oak tree
is highest in the wood.
The forking shoots of hazel
hide sweet hazelnuts.
The alder is my darling,
all thornless in the gap,
some milk of human kindness
coursing in its sap.

Colin knew the Midwife's coldness toward him was a response to a passion she did not want to let loose. He respected a person's need of distance. He was skilled at rummaging through other people's lives and picking out the best in them, just as he rummaged through various landscapes picking out the edible bits and the healing herbs, or a good place for nesting out of the rain. He liked to travel as lightly as possible and left even the most enticing things alone after letting their essence penetrate him a little. There were parts of Finnistuath that became his favorites. He liked the Bailiff's shoes and thought to mimic them and pass them off as fashion in other places; he loved the spring in the southern part of the village woods; and he was oddly fond of Grey, the Goatherd's son, who was the most skilled among the boys and the least annoying.

He understood Gregory's love of the goats and spoke with him about the crooked paths the animals made and their magical eyes. He stopped one day with a load of logs on his shoulders and said to the Plowman's youngest son, "Listen . . . there . . . hear it? the cuckoo deep in the woods, its call echoing in the dusk like a true love's secrets." The Plowman's son heard it and nodded.

In the Flax Grower's house the stranger sang songs while sharpening scissors and knives.

> *I hear the stag's bellowing*
> *Over the valley's steepness*
> *No music on earth*
> *Can move me like its sweetness.*

And the Flax Grower's wife asked to meet him by the spring. But Colin laughed and said, "I'm saving my martyrdom for a nobler cause. I don't want to be killed for taking a man's place between his wife's legs, as fair and sweet as those legs might be."

It was the Smith who was seen often going into Colin's hut, coming from the woods instead of the road. He stayed late into the night, even when Colin did not use his own store of candles to light their conversations. Those who came to have the ear of the outsider for themselves often stood and heard mumbling voices coming from the dark hut in tones so serious that the visitors turned back for their own homes.

Colin received more confessions than the Priest, who had come to despise the man and his handsome face. The Baker admitted that he was the father of the Flax Grower's youngest son; the Plowman's youngest son spoke about his hatred for his brother. Two boys, sons of the peasants, admitted that they had gone into the Church and urinated on the altar. Colin nodded and stirred his fire with a yew stick.

He didn't speak of his own troubles, and he made no speeches against the rich who fed well from other people's labors, but he sang a song whenever he passed by the Manor, sang it loud, as though hurling it:

> *In the fierce glen where water roared*
> *I found a place where game was stored*
> *The fatted pheasant and elk so lean*
> *But alas this poor young thief was seen*
>
> *For many a night I spent in tethers*
> *And had naught to eat but dry old feathers*
> *When I returned to my mother's side*
> *I found that she and my sisters had died.*

Sometimes he wanted no company, but became a shadow in his hut so that people did not enter, thinking it empty. He went into the northern woods often, to sit and listen and wait for whatever happened.

Grey was there one afternoon, staring fixedly into a pool. Colin watched the boy, intrigued with his fixated gaze and utter stillness. Then after carefully crouching and picking his weapon Colin threw a fat stone into the pool. It fell hard with a deep and sudden thunder. Grey scrambled backward until he heard the laughter and saw Colin pointing at him. "Your face—your face!"

Grey stood up and strode over and put his fist under the man's nose, as his own nostrils flared with the effort to recover his breath. "My fist," he yelled. "My fist, right up yer nose."

Colin held Grey's wrist and, still laughing, pulled it down.

"See here. I was just trying to break the spell you were under, about to be pulled to the depths of that pool."

Grey shrugged and Colin asked, "What were you doing then, staring like that, like a ghost that sees its own grave?"

Grey shrugged again.

"You're surly like all lads, like I myself was. So let's be chums, then. Let's agree to be chums and I'll ask your forgiveness."

"Where do you wander to?" Grey asked, and Colin sat down on a fallen oak and tossed smaller stones into the water.

"I go anywhere I want to. Everywhere."

"Where have you just come from?"

"Well, I was in Tarmath for a while, and before that in Naas, and before that in the Monastery at Tarmath."

Colin stood up again. He didn't want to go back further, back to what he had left behind years ago, in a graveyard to the west where corpses light as sticks were given rest from the hunger that killed them. And he wanted no questions about the Monastery. Once he had been a good companion of the Old Abbot, who had been removed right before Colin left, taken God knows where by order of the Pope. It was too bad, for the two had fallen into the habit of sharing a bottle of wine from time to time, Colin and the Old Abbot, and talking long into nights when Colin became the old man's confessor. And one night, when the drinking made the Old Abbot sullen, he told of something else, of a box he guarded for the Pope. Cursing and whimpering oddly, he showed Colin the place where the box was kept, and he wept and clawed at his companion. "It is a curse," he moaned. And ever after that, the two drank in silence until Colin demanded to know what was in the box. The Old Abbot shook his head vigorously, purple wine drooling from the corner of his trembling mouth.

Monks whispered and became scornful of the noise that Colin and the Abbot made. The Librarian scolded Colin one day outside of the chapel about his inappropriate merriment and inability to keep to the schedule of Offices.

Colin had stared at the moist lips moving, glistening a little above the flame from a candle the Librarian held. "You are no monk," the Librarian had said, looking him over. And Colin laughed in agreement and was grateful toward the Librarian for telling a truth he had been reluctant to say to himself. He knew that he was not going to take the final steps to be a monk, that he would keep his hair and other things that this place would take from him.

"But there's knowledge here I'll have before I leave."

The Librarian laughed this time and said, "Beware what you seek to know. Be sure that you don't carry knowledge so heavy that it pulls you down to Hell."

In a few weeks, three men arrived, one the New Abbot, an athletic and energetic man; the other two, agents for the Pope. The Old Abbot was gone with the two emissaries that evening. Colin sat up on the ridge west of the Monastery that night, letting the bells for the Offices ring and ring. He didn't move. With some humor and some self-pity, he was himself metamorphosing back into the outsider—a man who does not belong. A few days later, he had been abruptly tossed out by the New Abbot, a robust man his own age who was purifying the place of particular dangers, which included himself.

Grey threw a large stone, calculated to land heavily between Colin's bare feet, which it did. He did not flinch but looked up as though waking, his eyes puzzled.

"Did I break the spell?"

"Is that all you meant to break," Colin asked, nudging the stone with his big toe.

Grey laughed and ran away, racing between holly and oak as Colin sang to him

> It's the wild horse that runs so hard
> But the saddled horse feeds in the yard.

He watched the boy appearing and disappearing between the trees, until finally there was nothing moving but his own eyes and the softly smiling ripples of the pool.

# 8

IT WAS COLIN who first noted that the Goatherd's eldest daughter, Fiona, who was fifteen and recently returned from Tarmath, was with child. He told the Goatherd about it one day as they sat together watching the goats. Colin didn't want the man to be tormented more than he was already for his lack of wit, so he said, "It's well that you're keeping your eldest girl in your home and not sending her out on errands." In fact, Fiona herself had been sullen and unwilling to go out on the road much. But the Goatherd let himself be given credit for something he didn't yet understand. "In her state, being with child and without husband, well, you know, man, the words and abuses a village can hurl at such a one." The Goatherd nodded and later told his wife in a loud voice that she had a whore for a daughter who was breeding in Tarmath.

"And how do you know such a thing?" Mary asked, though she had suspected it herself.

"The stranger told me it," the Goatherd said, nodding not toward Colin's hut but toward the clearing where he and Colin had watched the goats and had their conversation.

Mary looked over at Fiona, who was sitting against the wall, rolling lumps of cheese in her hands.

"Ahh, you're a whore and I always knew it!" Mary said, and Fiona looked up without moving her head, her eyes as narrow and dark as buttonholes.

Apart from rage over her daughter's lustful ways, the news gave Mary respect for Colin's wisdom and observations. So she went to his hut and told Colin the plans she had for her son, whom she hovered over constantly, even though Grey was almost eleven years old. She would not let him play any longer with the nearby sons of the unfree, nor with the grandsons of the Plowman.

"He's to be a servant of the Church," she said, holding Grey's hand as they both squatted before Colin, who had only skins to sleep on in his hut. He used the doorway as his hearth, and visitors had to step through wavering heat or wait until recently fed flames had quieted enough to let them pass. The Smith had often returned home with his cloak hem burned.

Mary and Grey had their backs to the doorway, for Colin liked to face the opening to see who was approaching at all times. He stared at Grey, who smiled and shrugged, rolling in his hand a rock that he intended to hurl at something outside as soon as this discussion was over.

"He's a strong boy with fine features," Colin said. "But why drown your husband's good heirs in the Church before they're born? The new orders require celibacy. The English already pervert their priests and do not let them marry. They consider Irish priests wild and immoral. And who makes the laws more and more, Goatherd's wife—is it the Irish or the English?"

"I do not want my son to marry," Mary said. "I made a promise to God."

"Ah, yes, a promise to God. That's the whole loaf, isn't it? Once it's out of the oven, it must be eaten or spoil."

"I promised that if the boy lived I would raise him to be a priest or a monk."

"And what do you say, Grey?"

The boy shrugged.

"Come here, then." The man held out his hand, and Grey walked to him as the mother watched with a cat's vigilance.

"What desires do you have concerning the knowledge of words and scripture? It's a high calling to read and transcribe God's words."

"I know more about rocks and goats than about words," Grey said.

"Do you keep the commandments?" Colin asked.

Grey nodded, still looking fixedly, almost defiantly, into the man's face, as the big hands pulled bits of leaf from the waves of the child's rich black hair. Colin thought the face stunning, worthy of a song that he himself would compose.

"Do you pray?"

"Yes," Grey answered.

"And what do you say in your prayers? Do you ask forgiveness for threatening to put yer fist in a person's nose?"

Looking firmly at each other, the two pressed a smile off their lips as Mary nodded at Grey to make an answer.

"I ask for the health of mother and father and sisters. And the goats."

"Good boy. Do you ask to be kept free of sin?"

Grey hesitated.

"He doesn't know sin," the mother answered sharply.

Colin asked her, "Where will he be cloistered?"

This was an easy question to answer, for Mary knew of only her own village and the town of Tarmath. Finnistuath had no monastery.

"In the Monastery at Tarmath."

The man tightened his mouth and raised his eyebrows.

"That's a dark place," he said.

"I've spoken to the Priest. He says that he will speak with the Abbot there."

"I stayed there awhile once."

He poked his yew stick into the warm ashes.

Mary stood up and pulled Grey to his feet.

"I've heard naught but it's a religious place, where the monks keep pure and pray to God all day. That is what this boy will do."

The heat from the hearth was burning Mary's back. She hurried out with her child. Grey looked back at Colin, who winked.

Grey went to Colin's hut alone the next evening, lying about with his hands under his head in imitation of a man, letting a silence grow ripe enough for a question to be planted in it. And then he asked, "The Smith says that you are a warrior, like the Bruce. He says you'll give us back our rightful homes and pastures."

Colin wouldn't look at the boy's face as he said, "It's a pretty thought, sure it is indeed, a pretty thought."

"I am going to be a warrior," Grey said.

Colin laughed. But then he looked steadily at Grey's eyes and suddenly felt the lure of comradery, for Grey looked back without wavering like a person who wanted to know and not be told. But there was something else that lured him. There was the neck, the shape of Grey's neck. It wasn't thick; it was delicate like the boy's chin and wrists. It was then that Colin guessed that Grey was not a boy.

A man walked briskly by, came back, then leaned down to say into the opening, "There's a meeting tomorrow evening, Colin." It was the Plowman's youngest son.

Colin asked, "In what household is there the least threat to the Manor?"

The man answered, "The Goatherd's. He is a half-wit," the Plowman's son explained, and Grey drew his knees up and looked down between them. Colin put his hand on top of one of the knees and said to the Plow-man, "I'll be there."

Then he said to Grey, "I see a fine life for you." He laughed. "A fine and interesting life. What manner of game are you playing to turn a man's notions upside down?" He laughed again, falling backward and shaking his head. "I'll not tell," he said.

"Not tell what?"

"I'll not tell for I love the notion of it, a person not being at all what others believe he is!"

Grey stood up, his face hot, and looked down at the man who was chuck-ling softly and still shaking his head.

"The people here think you're going to save them, so you'd best be doing something besides wallowing around on the ground laughing like a lunatic."

"If you want to be a man," Colin said, looking up fiercely, "you'd best learn to listen to more than what people want you to be. You'd best be lis-tening and watching for what needs to be done, rather than what people want to be done."

He stood up and put his fingers on Grey's cheek, "You'll be a gentle man, I'd wager, gentle and fierce. And that's the way to play the game, isn't it?"

"I'll be fierce," Grey said.

"So you will, but don't be so fierce that you end up like me, a man with-out a home, without a soul to tell his dreams to in the morning."

Grey looked away and Colin passed by him to the outside world, think-ing to himself of what he should take and what he should leave behind when he left Finnistuath.

Seven men met in Gregory's hut, including the Smith; the Plowman's youngest son, who had brought with him his ten-year-old boy; Gregory him-self; two of the unfree laborers; and one of the Irish free laborers who farmed his acreage near the Manor and bartered more with the English than with the indebted bretaghs. Some eyes cast suspicious glances toward him, but he had suffered, like them all, the unfair reduction of his rights and lands, while the English laborers of Finnistuath were all free and all treated fairly. Mary sat outside happily churning with a newly repaired churn in the dim light that came from the two candles Colin brought into the hut. Chickens wandered among the men and were kicked fluttering and clucking outside.

Grey and his sisters were asleep at the Midwife's new hovel nearby, scattered about the floor like unfinished statues. The Midwife could hear the men talking, and when the voices rose twice in the same moment, Grey opened his eyes. He looked to the Midwife, who made no movement of her head or lips. And so Grey rose up and walked to his own home. He stood in the doorway next to his mother, who had fallen asleep leaning against the wattled wall. Shadow and light floated over the faces of the men inside. Gregory saw his son and came to get him.

"Here is my boy, who will be a man soon. I'll let him in so he knows the business of men." It was the only thing that the Goatherd had said or would say that night. No one paid much attention to Grey's presence except for the Plowman's grandson, who scowled vehemently whenever he caught Grey's eye. Grey stood by his father's thick legs and stared mostly at Colin. He heard the phrase "King's devils" often.

The Smith spoke the loudest, mentioning several times the cow that was stolen from him by the Bailiff to give to the Lord of the Manor. The Plowman's youngest son said, "We are all scattered about, with no common leader or common knowledge. And that is how they overcome us so easily. We have no common army. We have no weapons."

"I have weapons," the Smith said. "For every pitchfork I make, I make a blade." The men fell silent, mouths sealed for a moment by the Smith's dangerous secret. Grey felt his heart pound hard. He wanted, more than anything, to have one of the Smith's blades as his own. He would fight like a hero.

But there were tears in Colin's eyes. In a dizzying moment, he had seen the future, centuries worth of the future. He looked at Grey with an expression of pity and stern warning mixed together. He said, "I'll take no glory as your leader today without telling you that tomorrow you want to fight against men who make weapons by the thousands that will kill your sons and your daughters."

The free laborer said, "The word about, even in Tarmath, is that the world will end soon."

"What better way to make sure that we stay quiet," the Smith said loudly, "than to tell us that all our earthly matters are without importance in the face of Judgment Day? I believe nothing the priests from England say. Nothing."

A few other heads nodded.

The Plowman's son said to Colin, "So you go from place to place freely; you can make allies in many towns and villages, gather numbers of men to stand against the Lords."

"I have listened in many places to the injustices, to the need to . . ."

"Then tell us now the plan, the day."

Colin looked around the room. No face turned away.

"There is no plan yet."

Many cursed and shook their heads.

A scraggily bearded unfree laborer who grew a goodly share of the Manor's oats said, "You've no commitment to anything, man. You're naught but a wanderer, full of legends."

"This is useless," the free laborer said, and he left. No one spoke for a few minutes.

Then Colin said, "It will take time."

The Plowman's son asked, "What do we do then? There are more who are with us, and the Smith's weapons . . ."

"Keep yourself quiet," Colin answered. "Say nothing to anyone who gains from the English, no matter how they speak. Look hard at all things, and see not what you want to see but what is there."

"And what hope can you give us?"

At this question, Colin could barely keep his rage from turning his words red. He spoke through a tight jaw, saying, "You must give yourselves hope, man. Why are you always looking for some hero to humble you and lead you? Why do you keep yourselves ignorant, letting others tell you what to think and do, what to believe, what to eat and when to eat it? Where are your own convictions?"

He was scolding himself, in fact, for now he saw that, like these men, he had wasted much time in not admitting certain unsavory truths to himself, that there are some things that no hero can overcome but still must fight against. He, too, kept waiting for something outside himself to determine his cause and ensure his success.

"Are you calling us ignorant, then?" one man cried out, stepping forward and being held back by two men in front of him.

The Plowman's son spoke up: "He's just flea-bitten with frustration, like the rest of us."

And Colin said, "Yes, and I see that there's a whole way of thinking that needs to change, not just which hand is on the sword or which ass is on the throne."

There was some laughter at this, and when Colin left shoulders were clapped and shoved in comradery. But he was feeling the urge to move on.

Grey defied his mother and walked with Colin back to his hut in the woods. She said it was too dark to walk back alone, dark enough for wickedness to occur at the quick hands of some bored spirit. But Grey went on, making himself free as a boy does by defying his mother. He clung to the hand of the outsider, a hand fleshier than his father's but not as strong.

"I'll sing you a song my father sings when the goats and I are napping," he said, because he felt that Colin in his silence was already partially gone somewhere else, and Grey wanted to get him back.

After the singing, Colin said to Grey, "Are there fairies in your throat, then? You're a rough lad for such singing."

"I'm wanting one of your stories," Grey said.

"They're not my stories. They're the land's stories."

"Call them whatever you like, but I want a story about heroes and warriors."

"Like Cuchulain, who guarded a chieftain's house like a dog so as to pay for killing the man's hound? He was an honorable man. He even sent leeches and herbs to his enemy to help him heal and fight another day."

"And what did he fight for? What did he look like? Was he tall, with his hair free and long?"

Colin stopped and put his chest out and said, "Why he looked like me, didn't he, just like your own Colin here."

Grey shook his head as the two walked on, and Colin's voice got a little louder for story telling.

"It was Cuchulain protected the Bull of Ulster from thieves when Queen Mebd wanted the bull. Many were killed; fierce battles occurred for days and days."

"And what was the end of it?" Grey asked.

Colin rubbed his face hard and sighed, "So many killed . . . and you know, the bull itself died in the end, died of its own foolish and brutal aggression. After slaughtering a rival bull, its own heart burst. And in the end, the brave fight had no cause other than the pure duty of it."

Colin was thinking about the meeting, about the men's ambitions and their motley weapons hidden in the Smith's hovel.

"The thing of it is, to be a hero like Cuchulain is to fight for noble causes, but he must not mind that the fight is doomed. I'll say that a true warrior must not care what the odds are, or what fate dictates. He must not be cautious, committing only when he is sure to win."

Colin was thinking out loud now, and Grey let him go on and listened hard to the words without making a noise or a gesture that might stop them.

"But he must not be stupid either." Colin stopped and raised a finger. "He must not be a fool. He has to hone his skills, choose the best weapons and horses, fuck the strongest women. If he is to protect a bull or steal a cow, he must do it well and do it so that it makes others brave for other noble battles, no matter what the outcome."

"No matter if he himself dies?" Grey finally asked after some silence.

"No matter if he himself dies, if the cause is noble."

"And how does he know if the cause is noble or not?"

Colin took Grey by the shoulders and found the eyes in the half moonlight, eyes gone dreamy with visions of heroes.

"Give me more time to answer that, if you would," he said. "But you should know that Cuchulain learned his skill and got his weapon, the finest sword in all the world, from a woman. You should know that."

Grey's mouth hung open a little and he closed it quickly and looked away.

And then Colin said, "I'll sing one last song for you."

"Do you mean one last song this night?" Grey asked, for he felt that the tensions in the cottage, when the men were speaking so seriously, had been like the first spot of mold on a loaf of bread, and that Finnistuath would soon be inedible for Colin.

"Here's the song," he said. "Remember it when you are in the Monastery at Tarmath and there is too much solemn worship inside stone walls when all the glory is in the day outside:

Ah! When Finn and the Fian lived
They loved the mountain better than the monastery.
Sweet to them the blackbird's call
They would have despised the tonguing of the bells.

He winked, but a chill grew up his spine like a grasping vine.

Grey grabbed Colin's arm and asked, "You're not a traitor, are you?"

"No," he said wearily. "I am no one."

Grey squinted his eyes and stood in the road as the man walked on to his hut in the woods. Grey himself walked along the road, a little sick in his stomach with wanting the stranger to stay and to keep making the village more entertaining.

The next day the rebellious hope of the village was greatly tested. The Smith's home was entered by four armored soldiers who tore and smashed everything in the dwelling and in the foundry. They uncovered a hole beside the hearth, but there were no weapons, so they took the Smith.

The Smith was hanged by the new bridge. His wife begged that their two cows be unmolested and left to her for some solace. For she wanted nothing more than to be obedient on this Earth so that she might spend eternity in Heaven. She kept saying, "I am a good woman. I ask for little." And she twisted her hands around in her hair until the Baker's wife had to help untangle her fingers and walk her home.

"Who'll bury him?" Mary asked her husband, forgetting for a moment that he was a half-wit.

The Goatherd covered his ears and rocked back and forth.

"I'll not go to the river until I know he's down, may the Lord protect us," his wife said to his deaf hands.

Colin's hut was empty when the soldiers came for him. Some suggested that the outsider himself was the traitor. But a few refused to think this and spoke of him as a hero who would come to them again, on a huge black horse, followed by thousands of Irishmen. Now he was Bruce's son or an incarnation of the hero Cuchulain; the women said he was a fairy playing with the human form; or he was an angel sent to judge the village of Finnistuath. The Priest still contended that he was a lost man, ridden by sin or tragedy; or he was of the old clan of druids, an un-Christian bard able to compose satires and transform himself into a black raven and do other Devil's work.

Grey wrapped sticks and rocks in cloth and tied the cloth to his back and walked north until he came to a place that seemed most wicked. A tree had fallen across the road, and its scraggly branches were reaching out to beg for help and entrap travelers as eternal company in its despair. Grey saw himself transformed into a rag, forever caught and blowing in the tree's claws.

Drooping back to his home, he met the Second Fiona's black shape limping to fetch him. She did not scold and kept a hand on her brother's shoulder; she said nothing, and only nodded when Grey said with a teary voice, "I hate them all."

9

GREY'S BODY felt to him like a satchel of lumpy secrets in different shapes and colors. In the satchel there were figures made of the polished red wood of the yew tree, there were blackbird feathers, striped pebbles, the green speckled shells of birds. And there were essences of other people in the satchel: Colin's wink, the Midwife's calm smile, the naked erection of the Lord's son, his mother's hands, smelling of bread and cheese, the Second Fiona's hobble, and his father's strong embrace.

Carrying these things inside him, Grey heard words at every turn about who he was to become, what he was to do: his mother's most frantic and profound assumption was that her only son would be a monk. The First Fiona, malicious with the embarrassment of her pregnancy, knew—for she had lived for some months in the town of Tarmath—that a cleric must be able to read. She said to Grey, "You're an idiot like Da. And you can't read or write!" His friends taunted him with when his mouth drifted open as he concentrated and threw a stone. "Oh, look, he's like his da, with his mouth hanging open and all." The Goatherd himself stayed silent until the women in his house shut their mouths over some bread or porridge, and then he said, "He's my son and he'll be a goatherd like me and have sons named for me." Any further discussion invited blows from the parties involved, except Grey, who tried to become as invisible as he was being treated. He considered any blow not struck against the English or other devilish enemies a waste of might. As far as he could tell, he wanted to live the warrior's life, unrooted, free, wise in the use of the woods, not dependent on any but his own knowledge and hand for food. He wanted to return to Finnistuath as a hero someday, unfettered and unharmed, someone to whom people spoke and listened.

Grey realized the limits to his freedom. He could never be rich like the Lord's son Red because he was born a poor boy—a goatherd's son. But he also began to realize that being human, rich or poor, involved large limitations. Pain and disease made equals of everyone; for example, it was said that the Lady of the Manor fell mysteriously into bouts of searing pain that could not be alleviated by any herbs her son Red tried with her or any prayers said over her by the Priest. And in Grey's home, there was often a terrible ache in the stomach that passed through all who lived there. In this way, Grey began to note the raw material of the human condition, which included, if rumors of the Lady's illness were true, inevitable suffering.

One autumn night Grey lay in the rag bed in the corner, complaining of stomach pain.

"You'd best get over it to help with the harvest—there's no boy not needed to haul the baskets and pull the carts. You'll cause evil gossip if you don't do the work." His mother was easily hysterical when it came to what others thought of Grey. So he said, "I'll be right. I just need to rest."

The youngest girl stopped churning and narrowed her eyes; she said, "He always has a rest when he wants, when we all need one. And which of us girls can lie down?"

"He's not even like real boys," Fiona the Elder said while wrapping a wet lump of cheese in cloth, for she was bold now, thinking that becoming a mother herself would exempt her from her own mother's discipline. But Mary was swift in cursing her with words and slaps. When Fiona was sitting against the wall next to the hearth, covering her head from the blows and screeching, Mary said over her, "Grey will be our salvation for his differences, and you'd best keep your foul thoughts to yourself. You couldn't keep your legs shut, but you'd best keep your mouth shut."

When Mary was a few feet away, Fiona muttered, "The whole village knows Grey's been marked by the Devil."

Grey's stomachache surged. He had not heard the thought put so straight before, and it was made louder by a powerful silence that followed until the Second Fiona dragged in the water. Then there was a new discussion about who would have what portion of it for which task.

Grey lay with his face buried in the pile of cloth, thinking, testing his mind, wondering if he had wit or if he had signs of becoming like his father. Perhaps Grey was the same, not knowing who he really was when everyone else did. But he did know the stars and their influence. He understood which were wanderers and which were fixed. He knew how to add things together, how to count the goats, which his father had a hard time doing. The Goatherd didn't know when to stop counting when the goats were spread around the meadow, and so he counted many more goats than were really in the herd.

Grey rolled over and saw the Second Fiona standing over him. She asked, "What is ailing you, brother?"

And Grey said, "I'm going to find Colin and go with him."

She leaned down, swaying uneasily on her bad legs; she whispered right into her brother's face.

"And our mother will chase you down the road with a stick and herd you to the Monastery. She'll take whatever beating she gets from Da to win you for her plans, that I know."

And so Grey accepted that there would always be two lives: one his body led and one his heart led in secret—and that there were moments when body and heart were woven together, a rare ecstasy. He had seen ecstasy on his mother's face once when she stirred a pot and tasted a spoonful of broth that had some meat in it. And his father also seemed to feel it in a simple form, such as when he freed a goat tangled in briars.

The Goatherd had taught Grey useful things about simple comforts and goats: how to be gentle with a doe so she would let herself be milked, how to understand and respect the hierarchy the goats established and always milk the dominant doe first, how not to pull above the teat and pinch the milk glands. Grey had gotten a sharp kick in the shin for that carelessness and lost the trust of the doe. His father matched the doe's kick with a smack to the back of his son's head. But his smacks were never harsh, and the Goatherd often roughly wiped tears from his own eyes after hitting his son.

When the Goatherd's hillside was usurped for the huts of the displaced villagers, he had to take the herd farther into the woods. Several goats were lost in their new territory, and the eldest daughter refused to search the deep forest for the strays. She had become surly; she disdained the life of a herder and ridiculed her father's slow mind. She had, she reminded her family often, been to Tarmath. She even told Grey that in Tarmath his friend Colin was known as a common thief, not a hero at all. She said she saw him steal bread and give it to a dirty group of thieving children.

Grey knew about his sister Fiona, that she met with one of the Lord of the Manor's servants and they rubbed their bodies together and breathed loudly. He recognized this particular ecstasy and wanted to understand it more. It intrigued him to see the enchanted expression on his sister's face, an expression he saw in no other context, even when there was meat for supper. There were other secrets like this one that were not themselves answers but riddles to be solved. For example, Grey could only forget for a

while that he had a most shriveled prick. He recalled images over and over
in his mind—all having to do with penises: years ago his mother took him to
the river to bathe and he saw the boys, whose penises bounced around as
they jumped and leapt in the water. He was never allowed to go naked and
play as those boys had played. Never. He guessed even then that his body
was something for which his mother had shame. There was something terribly, horribly, shamefully wrong with his body. He envied the enjoyment his
sister and her lover in the woods seemed to have with their bodies. And he
wondered if Red, the Lord's son, shared this shame—this shame about his
body, because perhaps he, too, was deformed. Perhaps his deformity also
involved his penis because it was too large and extended.

According to Grey's mother, God had blessed him by not giving him a
prick. She said he must keep this fact a secret from everyone, though, for it
would humiliate others who were not so blessed and fill them with mean
resentment. They had pricks that made them sin and forget all reason and
dignity. Certainly, Grey thought, being forced by a fairy to beat your own
flesh and then fuck an invisible partner was a loss of reason and dignity.
Mary told Grey that the villagers might stone him to death out of envy for
being chosen by God if he didn't keep his blessings to himself. Another riddle: why would people choose to stone to death a person chosen by God?
Wouldn't they rather stone him to death because he was marked by the
Devil? Mother promised that all of these riddles could be solved in only
one place—the Monastery, where God, His relics, His words, His promises
were all kept and explained to the initiated.

Fiona the Eldest soon became a lesson for the mother to use in encour-
aging Grey to seek God's mercy and succor in the religious life, for her
lover from the Manor saw that she was pregnant. He guessed by her belly's
size and more by Fiona's defensive demeanor that his was not the seed
planted in her. He got drunk one night outside the Manor and began
yelling loudly to the Bailiff to record that there was a whore in Finnistuath,
a woman with many husbands. He named Fiona, and the news of her condition and her whoring was a point of discussion for several days.

"You must do for us, Grey," Mary said, her face always wide with anxiety
and weariness. "You must go then to the Monastery like a good lad and learn
to speak to God and say prayers on our behalf." Her hands brushed at her
face, trying to grab the desperation that caught on her skin like spiderwebs.
She told Grey, "You've got to do this for us, your Da and your sisters and me,

your old mother whose lot it is to be married to a half-wit and have whores for daughters."

At first, Fiona could go about her chores, walking the road, with only sneers thrown at her, but after a week of the village's mulling over her disregard of propriety and social order, a stone hit her cheek as she passed by the houses south of the Small Bog. She ran home and hid in the corner, letting her mother scold her and her father shame her. It was her fault, they said, for being wicked.

Grey finally felt pity for Fiona the Eldest, but he did not like to look at her or be near her. He was afraid to offer any words of kindness, for he didn't understand the circumstances being discussed. And he had a sense of how dangerous his sister's mood was. He had been kicked by her before when he had said something well meaning. But his mother kept bringing the two to each other's attention, thrusting Grey forward and saying, "See, this is why you should be glad you're a boy going to the Monastery, sure you won't end up like this whore, your sister." Fiona would look up at him through strings of sweated hair and spit.

"See why you must stay pure and speak to God on our behalf, Grey," the mother said, "so that we'll all go to Heaven and be there without our cares."

In her seventh month of pregnancy, Fiona lived for weeks cowered in the corner, getting up only to relieve herself outside. Her mother yelled at her to help with sewing or culling or churning, but Fiona glared out from the corner like a badger. No one, not even the Goatherd, was willing to go after her for fear of getting an arm torn off or an eye scratched.

But the Goatherd did speak to her. He said, "A girl who has more than one husband at the same time is like a dog in the yard with its tail up in the air, letting anything come into her."

After a fortnight of staying in the corner, Fiona had a stillbirth. Grey saw its tiny hands, limp and translucent. The elder mother, angry and officious, cleaned up the mess. The Second Fiona cried, for she had wanted a little baby to be born into the family and had told Grey many times that she was going to look after it herself. But Mary screamed that it had been a withered changeling with a tail, and everyone was silent. The elder Fiona slept for a day and a half and then left the cottage, which had grown eerily silent.

She went on the road, heading for the spring, where she had in mind to display herself to the Manor, hoping the servant would see that she had lost the offending child and was available. She had forgiven him for his part in her persecution, or at least she considered it less important than her desire to have a husband. But she was again across from the houses south of the Small Bog when a rock fell at her feet. It was hurled by one of a group of people, the sons and daughters of those houses. Another stone hit her thigh. She ran back to the cottage and tied up a small bundle containing one candle stub, a lump of cheese, and a cup.

That night Grey stared at the empty spot in the corner where Fiona had crouched for almost a month. He knew that she was gone and would not be back, for he had seen her crying bitterly and walking across the Big Bog toward the river. He had never really understood his sister, but he wanted to ask her if the pleasure of breeding made the cruelty of the world disappear for a few moments. He guessed as much and admired her a little for grabbing at least that much of Heaven. It seemed better than Red's encounter with the invisible fairy woman.

"It is a miserable thing," Mary muttered into a pot of broth so clear as to be mistaken for water.

What exactly was that miserable thing was not clear to Grey, since there was so much that his mother could be referring to.

 10

ONE YEAR after Colin left, when Grey was twelve years old, his mother took him to the Priest, a man who had become obsessed with the niches and boxes that housed several relics that he had accumulated over the years: a thorn from the crown of thorns worn by Jesus on the cross, a piece of Saint Augustine's thigh bone, a piece of the cloth of Mary's veil, and a lock of the hair of the mother of Ireland—Saint Brigid, she who had been a goddess until Saint Patrick had reformed her into a saint. Now it was said that she had been midwife to the Virgin Mary when Jesus spilled out into the carnal world.

When Mary the Goatherd's wife came in with her only son, Grey, the Priest was sitting on a high stool at his small writing table, writing a letter to Avignon, the little French town where the Pope now resided. It was the sixth letter requesting that the Pope acknowledge Finnistuath as a site for pilgrimage. The Priest was sure that the official sanction had been granted but had not yet reached him. And he determined that it would do no harm to send off one more reminder that he was waiting patiently and reverently for the Pope's most cherished and generous acknowledgment. He was not sure which order was in favor with the Pontiff, and so in one letter he praised the devout Benedictines and in another the formidable Dominicans.

Mary had hurried to the Church because for the first time in all her life she had been summoned there. The Priest had asked her to come and bring Grey with her. When he saw them in the door to his chambers, he actually smiled, showing his small teeth, like baby's teeth, thought Mary.

"He has such fine features," the Priest said, holding Grey's face in his hands. "Cheekbones like arches, and gray eyes like stained glass." He took the leather cord off Grey's hair and plumped out the dark brown waves. "He looks like an angel, but he smells like goats."

The Priest's hands were cold. Grey stepped back.

"You have never paid me, woman," the Priest chided. "There are many people in this village to whom you owe payment."

Grey took his mother's hand, feeling the calluses below each finger on the plump palm.

"The Bailiff has threatened to cast you out and disperse all your property among those to whom you are in debt. Hard times have come. There is not so much patience with debtors."

"I pray for forgiveness, Father. I pray night and day."

"And you, do you pray?" He looked down at Grey.

"Yes." Grey answered this question confidently, as he had determined that talking to blackbirds and bilberry bushes was the same as praying.

"Well, you mustn't pray to God directly, only to the Saints. If you pray to God directly you risk your soul being burned like a straw in a great fire."

Grey had no reply to this.

The Priest smiled, for he liked to render children speechless with fear.

"Well, I will help you, Mary, for the boy who was my helper has died. He did not recover from the worms, though the Bailiff leeched him. So now I am in need of another boy. I will take him in exchange for what you owe me in tithes and payment, and I will train him in the care of holy items. This is what you wanted after all, is it not?"

"Oh, yes, yes. It is. I . . . but, I . . . was hoping, that he . . . I was going to take him to the Monastery."

The Priest's already red face grew as red as a pool of blood.

"You ignorant people. You always want more than you have. Always! That you should owe me payment and not be on your knees with gratitude for my offer! To think that you believe that from your manure-covered hut you will produce a scholar, a boy fit for the Monastery. Listen, Mary the Goatherd's wife, you give me the boy as a helper or you face public stoning for sins against God."

And so Grey became the Priest's helper. Gregory pushed his wife down on the ground and wept when he was told. He babbled about Fiona's careless whoring and about the three girls left to him as helpers, one with crooked legs, one already showing the boys her thighs, and the other who had lost all hope of being a herder, having spent most of her youth throwing stones at the goats.

Mary calmed him with reminders that indeed the Second Fiona was slightly lame but was good with the animals and because of her lameness would probably never marry and therefore could help him until he passed on. This quieted Gregory, not because it comforted him, but because it diverted his mind to thoughts of his own death, which always made him hot and silent with terror. He had never been able to understand the stiff stillness of an animal whom he had named and whose tricks and character he had known.

It was in such a terror of death, or at least of a loneliness like death, that Grey passed his first few nights in the Church. The Priest slept in his chambers near the hearth. Grey was to sleep across the threshold that separated the Priest's small room from the chapel. In this way, any man or beast coming to do harm would step first on the boy, whose howls would alert the Priest.

This theory did not comfort Grey but added to his certainty that this new life was cold and full of danger. His homesickness permeated every part of his thin body, making him ache. He thought he was going to die. When the Priest's breathing became loud and then acquired a strange whistle, Grey prayed to the saints, any saints, to be in his home again, where his father's snore was warm and solid, and his mother's eyes seemed always to be open when he was afraid, where the Second and most wonderful Fiona slept close to him for warmth.

The first night away from home, Grey was exhausted enough to drift into a half sleep for a few moments at a time. At one point in this state, he believed that goats were standing around him. He could see their shapes in the dark. They were looking at him, waiting to be milked or taken somewhere. What were they doing in the Church, Grey wondered. What would the Priest say about the goats' getting in among the relics?

Then Grey came to full consciousness, and the terror of his loneliness and vulnerability came back in a hot wave. He heard scuffling noises and imagined rodents scurrying along the wall, or the spirits of the dead buried in the nearby cemetery whispering to each other, making plans to suck the life out of the Priest's new helper as they had done to the old one. He thought that if Colin ever came back to Finnistuath he would be his helper and disappear with him.

Grey told himself that he was fit, almost a man—he had legs, he had some wit—why didn't he just get up and leave? Why didn't he just get up and go home to his mother? Ahh, that was just it—he still wanted to go home to his mother. He was afraid to be by himself, so he was not a man, and may never become one, so shriveled was his penis and his courage.

The Priest was not harsh and gave him warm cow's milk and a hunk of cheese for breakfast. This luxury resulted in a dizzying shift in emotion, for Grey was first overjoyed and then trembling with sorrow because he wanted to share his good luck with his family and could not. Finally, thinking of the lumps of oatmeal his sisters would be eating—his sisters, who had always complained of the favors he got, being the only son—Grey could only swallow a few bites of the cheese.

"You will get used to it here," the Priest, whose moods were whimsical, said kindly. Then he put Grey to work, cleaning the stone floors with a rag. The Priest left him alone to do this work and went about some business at the Manor, which caused him to be in a rancid frame of mind when he returned and stood over Grey. He could find no fault in the boy's work and so attacked the boy himself to relieve himself of a strong inclination to bellow about something.

"You are too quiet. Are you witless like your father, or has the Devil got your tongue?"

These two choices did not suit Grey. He answered, "I am unused to being here."

"You also stink like goats. You must bathe. Leave off that work and go and get water to clean yourself with. And wash those clothes."

"Take them off?" Grey was barely used to the strange way the Priest spoke Gaelic, mixing up words and leaving out sounds.

"Take them off and wash them. Yes. That's what I said."

Grey stood up slowly. What if the Priest found out that he had no pisser? Then he would surely say the boy was some kind of demon.

"What modesty is this, and in a child?" The Priest laughed meanly and then said, "Go on to the stables and ask for leggings and a tunic to replace yours. Ask Patrick or Paddy or whatever he calls himself. He'll have some for you. And then go to the spring and rinse your body and roll in the grass there to sweeten the stench. Go on, now."

At that end of the village there were many cows, more so since the new settlers had come. Grey made his way through them and their droppings and found the stables where the Lord's laborer Paddy was applying a poultice to a gash on one of the horses' flanks. With few words, the servant got Grey the woolen leggings, full of holes, and a tunic made of brown linen, clearly too large for Grey. The servant's weariness and foul-smelling breath infected Grey with sadness about the world in which he must make his way through piles of dung.

At the spring that came out from a big rock under a rowan tree were long shiny grasses free of cow dung, for it was forbidden to let the cows mill around that water. This was where Grey had seen the Lord's son assaulted by a lustful and wicked fairy. When Grey lay down in those grasses, he was hidden even from the nearby cottage where one of the English families lived. He rolled around in the grass as the Priest had instructed, stopping often on his back to look up through the branches of the rowan and oak, which seemed very grand. The sky behind the green leaves was a large blue face veiled by thin cloud. For a few moments he looked around for a stick or switch; he considered kneeling and whipping himself just to see what it would feel like, and perhaps see if it enticed a prick to grow. But a thrush kept calling out in three slow notes as the soft trickling of the spring re-placed these ideas in Grey's mind. He rolled onto his stomach, and naked among the grasses, he fell asleep looking through the curving green blades at the gracefully arced roots of a tree.

When he awoke, he thought only to hurry. He pulled on the leggings and the tunic, grabbed the ball of old clothes, and ran to the Church. No one was there. The Priest was gone. Was he looking for him? To scold? To beat? For a moment, Grey thought to run away. He would go to his mother and she would hide him. The idea of warm milk and cheese for breakfast con-fused his plans. He wandered about the empty chapel, touching the pine box in which the precious thorn lay on a little velvet pillow, picking up and shaking the piece of thigh bone inside a blue glass bottle. He knocked a candle off the niche when he put the bottle back. Replacing it, he looked around and saw the rag left on the stones where he had been working that morning. He walked over to it and stared down. Then he sank to his knees, took up the rag and began to rub the stones. Perhaps he would work for the God that lived in the sky and watched people from a great distance, living a life rich with mysteries and bizarre miracles. He scrubbed carefully, seeing a face in each stone. Perhaps he would become intimate with the saints and spirits whose names had the power to pull everyone he loved into Heaven. He would then be a warrior whose weapons were prayers as well as blades, like the fellow slaying the dragon, a warrior saint. He bent lower and scrubbed with fierce determination to please God, or at least the Priest.

This is how the Priest found Grey. He had brought a piece of mutton and some carrots and made a stew for their dinner while Grey finished his work with a growing sense of joy at the prospect of eating stew with meat in it for dinner, as though it were a feast day. God must have been pleased to provide such luxury.

But at night, after eating a cup full of the stew and being sent to bed, the terror returned. Grey could not sleep. He hated to hear the Priest's slumber come on in deep, whistling breaths, for then it meant that he was truly alone with the spirits that came to tease and threaten him. Then he wanted his mother more than stew or milk. Finally, when the sky outside was turning from black to gray, he promised himself that he would go again to the spring and hide naked in the tall grasses, that he would find a way, every day, to have a little freedom. Freedom seemed the only thing large enough to replace the affection of one's mother.

The Priest added many things to Grey's list of chores, including a trip to the spring to fetch water for the Church's needs. When there was no one else at the spring, Grey took his clothes off. At first he just stood naked, looking around, feeling the air on his skin, pretending to stick his tongue out at the Weaver's son and himself watching from behind the holly bush. He was very aware of not paying attention to what was or was not between his legs. Then he sat in the grass, rocking back and forth, staring up through the branches, finally lying down and dozing off. On the fourth night in the Church, Grey was able to fall asleep with the Priest by following a plan he thought up to comfort himself. When the Priest was asleep, Grey moved his bedding to the space between the wall and the writing table, for he had gotten it into his mind that being exposed on all sides as he was, lying in the threshold, made him feel too nervous to sleep. It made him feel too easily the object of scrutiny and comment by any entities that passed by. Once he was snug and somewhat hidden, he imagined himself in the grasses by the spring and fell asleep. The Priest nudged him roughly with his foot in the morning, but was only surly about Grey's stirring up the fire in the hearth and said nothing about the change of his sleeping location.

In this way, the transition between old and new began to lose some of its pain.

His mother came to Mass, stooping humbly in the back of the chapel so as not to be noticed by the Englishmen—servants and free men who lived in or near the Manor. The Lord and Lady and their children had a private Mass said for them in the Manor, only rarely coming to the Church, and only with the certainty that others were not to be let in while they were there. They used the Church for private Masses and rituals to which only the clean and wealthy were allowed.

Grey's mother brought him some goat cheese wrapped in reeds. She was accosted by several people asking for payment for one thing or another, and she left in a hurry, running up to the road. Grey took the cheese to his bedding and unwrapped it, picking pieces of reed out of the moist, white lumps and licking his fingers. As he put a third bit of the cheese in his mouth, tears slid down his face, for he had become certain that the cheese the Priest gave to him was better. He threw the rest of the goat cheese into the fire, where it sizzled for a few seconds, and then he lay down on his bedding and stared at the stone in the wall in front of him. What spell was he victim of to throw food away? It was an insane, perhaps even evil act. He begged the saints to help him.

That day the Priest told him to go into the woods and gather wood, so Grey had whole hours of freedom. He pinched leaves and smelled them, threw pebbles into a pool surrounded by ferns and brambles, watched a fox roll in some dry dirt, tried to entice a blackbird to take a dead beetle from his palm. He stared at the rock by the spring, trying to focus hard and entice the spirit out of it, but he saw only the smallest wavering movement and quickly looked away. It occurred to him that Fiona's secret methods were not Christian, since the Priest never mentioned or appeared to use them.

It was on a midsummer morning that Grey finally looked long enough at a thing to see its spirit eyes open. It was a birch tree whose trunk had the form of a small and slender woman in its pattern. Grey sat a few yards from it and looked, sighing out all of his thoughts, all his lists and worries. In this way, he came through irritation and restlessness to sadness. Then Grey wanted to stand up, to go on with the day and forget about the effort to know the spirit of a tree. The Priest would not approve, and what of the saints? There were those saints who went away from Priests and knew God in waterfalls and thrush calls. He had heard of their lives as hermits who spoke to mice and befriended weasels. Grey stayed still, thinking of the saints on whom birds perched and to whom rivers spoke. So he sat still in the sadness and felt some calm. Then the spirit in the tree opened its eyes. They were kind eyes, with so much compassion in them that Grey took a sudden gasping breath that turned into a sob. He felt that the spirit's kindness would turn him into a tree as well, or lure him into a world of kind spirits where nothing in this world made sense any more. Before he went back to the Priest, he carefully touched the tree with his fingertips while all the forest was still and hushed.

"Are you God?" he whispered. There was no answer, no eyes, not even a sleeping face.

In a few weeks, the Priest expressed his pleasure at the silent diligence of his new helper. He had only had to strike Grey once, and that was for letting a cow wander into the Church and leave a steaming pile of manure near the altar. Grey had been at the spring and left the chapel door unlatched. Aside from this unpleasantness, the Priest was well pleased. He could work at his writing table, he could listen to the confessions of the Lord and all his family and be treated to the food on their table, without worry that the chapel boy was sticking a piece of Saint Augustine's thigh bone up his nose. If Grey tended to wander off, or to stare into space, so be it, as long as the pail of water was filled and the garden weeded. For the Priest liked his carrots and cabbage.

One afternoon at the end of the summer, the Priest sent Grey for the first time to the Manor. He was to retrieve from the Lady of the Manor a book of prayers that the Priest wanted to transcribe. "And ask for a bottle of ink, if they have some to spare," the Priest said, as though this was an afterthought, when really this was his main intention—to get more ink— and he had wanted Grey to be the beggar, not himself. Grey put the pail of water down by the hearth and scratched his forehead where a wave of hair tickled him.

"To the Manor?" he asked.

"Yes, to the Manor. Don't be thick-skulled when I've told you something plainly. Do as you're told. Now go on."

Grey was terrified that he would forget what he had come for, or that the huge dogs, which he had seen gamboling around the stables, would devour him voraciously. Or that the people inside would make fun of him in their language and laugh at his ignorance. His agitation was increased when Paddy's little girl, an eight-year-old with freckles, knocked against him as she ran past Grey, chased by two of the Flax Grower's girls. "Mind where you're going, you little witches," Grey called out, disdaining and perhaps envious of their carefree squealing. Then he climbed up the hill to the block of gray stone with its square tower, the Manor. The large wooden door was open, and three guards watched Grey stride up with his head down.

"I'm the Priest's boy come on an errand," he told them. But they did not speak Gaelic and made noises in demeaning imitation of the boy's words.

One of the guards nodded him through and Grey entered the large hall, where there was a lazy pace of activity and much that he had never in his life expected to see. Two, not one but two, tables were full of enough food to feed all of the village for a week. Breads, cakes, apples, grapes, cheeses, broiled lamb's legs—all of these things were simply lying out, flies buzzing around them and the people amazingly uninterested. One of the large dogs was sneaking a piece of stale bread from a table. Grey looked frantically around to see which human would rush to save the bread. But no one interrupted the slow gestures of amusement, pulling a needle through a piece of tapestry, turning the page of a book, reaching for a game piece, rubbing oil on a leather satchel, sleeping, talking, yawning. And all of the people were dressed in cloth that had no holes in it. The women wore head coverings that had jewels in them. The men's shoes were made of leather and strong cloth bindings. The food on the tables made Grey nervous, for the dogs seemed to nose it with impunity and take bits from the edges. He thought of what his family would do with such food. He thought how his mother and sisters would weep and bless God over and over as they filled their mouths. He had had no idea that people lived in this way, with so much food.

In the middle of his awe, Grey realized that he had no plan, no knowledge of how to make his request, how to find the Lady of the Manor and ask for the book and the ink. He looked at each woman trying to guess which was the Lady. He was loathe to make gestures and appear the fool. Walking timidly, as though silence made him invisible among the people, he forgot his purpose several times and began to search the faces for a reason for the good fortune of these people living in leisure and opulence. His own logic told him that surely they were all saints or wise beyond imagining for living in such ease and opulence, with so much food.

And indeed the faces did seem to him to have a holy serenity, a superior blankness and smoothness. And here he was, the Goatherd's son, a boy without a prick, daring to stand among them. His legs began to shake. Then a hand came from beside him, holding a small leather book, and the woman whose hand it was spoke English. Grey took the book and looked into the face, which was caked with powder and unsmiling. He stared, and the woman shook him by the shoulders angrily. What was she saying?

Grey nodded. It was all he could think to do, and this caused the woman to laugh, along with several people lounging nearby on benches covered with blankets and skins. One young man with red hair held his hand out for Grey to come closer. He remembered him from years before, the Lord's son called Red who had been naked in the clearing fucking a fairy. Grey could not speak or move; he could not stop his eyes from drifting to the man's crotch, covered in swollen pleated velvet. Why had the Priest sent him here to flop like a fish in a dry pail amid strange words and unimagined wealth? And then the man spoke in Gaelic.

"You are the Priest's new boy?"

"Yes."

"Good. You have the book, then."

"Yes."

"You'd better go back with the book now."

"Yes."

Were these the people he must fight and kill; were these the English that the Smith's weapons would mutilate, or were there some other English somewhere who were the enemies?

Grey remembered what Colin had said about ignorance and felt that before becoming a warrior and killing people and praying for one side or another, he needed less ignorance. He needed to know why some were well fed and others starved and how killing would fix that. Such wisdom, Grey guessed, had to come from something as great as God Himself or someone very close to God, a saint—perhaps one of the saints who lived and prayed alone with birds and foxes. The spirits who lived in trees, what could they give besides kindness?

Feeling as ignorant as his da, Grey turned and walked toward the door, aware that the dog who had pilfered the bread was now dragging a half-eaten leg of lamb off the table. In horror, Grey kept walking, and when he was at the door, he ran, running to the spring and holding the book against his chest. He lay down in the grass, breathing hard into the watching branches and sky. He could smell rain in some black clouds that were sneaking around above the tree.

The pictures of the food, the dog, the cloaks, the shoes, the powdered skin of the old woman, looked back at him from his own mind. Those people, he called them. Those people will never, ever starve. They will always have food. Always. The idea was like a blow to the forehead. Who were the people in the Manor and from where did they get all that food? He would dare to ask the Priest. He had known before that they lived in a bigger home and were somehow able to tell others what to do. But Grey had not, until that day, understood the astounding difference between his family's life, his people's life, and the life of those who lived in the Manor. From ignorance he had simply thought that everyone, all humans, shared the same hunger, that food was scarce for everyone. And now he knew . . . nothing. He knew another riddle. He would not keep silent with this secret. He would ask the Priest. He would ask, Why are some people given so much food they can't eat it all, and some are given so many hungry days they can't fill themselves? He would question the Priest when they were eating their supper by the fire.

But then he remembered that he had forgotten to ask at the Manor for the ink the Priest wanted. He groaned. He should kneel and beat himself, but let the Lord's son do that. Let them all do that to make up for what luxury they lived. Or if they were saints and knew God personally, let them have mercy on the poor. Grey shuddered a little, listened for some kind spirit or creature, and heard none. He remembered Fiona one day squatting and studying the cap of an acorn and holding it up and saying, "They wear these as hats, you know, sometimes putting tiny feathers in them." How sweet Fiona's spirits seemed, frivolous and kind. Grey began to weep. It was an angry weeping, mixed with shame, for he felt somehow that he had been a fool, that his family and all who lived outside the Manor had been made fools of. What had they done, the villagers—to be so punished by God?

The Priest was angry about the ink. He slapped Grey and brought up the incident concerning the cow. This cow would forever be for the Priest the reference for Grey's bad behavior. Whenever any other accident or carelessness occurred, that cow would be standing ready in his thoughts.

The nights were getting cold, and so Grey moved his bedding closer to the hearth and nearer to the Priest. He thought of his ignorant mother less and less, though she came to visit, always bringing some dirty bit of cheese, which caused Grey to feel hot anger toward her. "Pray for us, blessed child," she always said. "Put some notion in the Priest's head to speak to God on our behalf."

She told Grey the news from her part of the village. The Baker had lost one of the fingers on his right hand. The Plowman's grandson had been to

Tarmath and bought three candles. The lame Fiona was doing well with the goats after all, but Gregory fumed every day about his son. He saw no reason for a man's only son to be taken from him.

"You are fortunate," the mother said breathlessly to Grey, "so fortunate to live in God's house. Pray for us."

The phrase "God's house" brought to Grey's mind the tables full of food and the serene faces of those people, not the dank Church where he and the Priest ate bread dipped in gravy as they sat bent over in front of the hearth and stared wordlessly at the licking little flames. More and more he thought that his mother knew very little about the world, that his mother and his sisters, who lived by the whims of a half-wit Goatherd, were horribly ignorant. But it was also ignorant for the Priest or anyone to think that God would be confined to a dark little chapel instead of swirling about like the wind through the grass and trees and clouds and through fur and hair. If he were God, Grey would not spend very much time in the Church at all. He would eat with the rich and play in the woods.

11

I N WINTER much of the green color was drained from the world, squeezed out by the damp coldness, leaving grays and browns. The wind could bear down on all living things like a whipping. There were still the sporadic, dark greens of hollies and pines, some persistent mosses and mistletoe. Blood red holly berries beaded the forests, and frost veiled the ground like the discarded summer gowns of magical races that slipped into rocks and pools.

The bogs were frosted; the crows were irritable; the biting wind flew along the road trying to harass all travelers and hurl them into their homes. Families stayed by the hearth much of the day and slept more than they did in other seasons. They slept bundled together, dreaming each other's dreams of tunnels of ice and platters of green grass. Howling beansidhes begged to be let in with their mournful, crooked teeth and torn shawls.

One night, Grey dreamed of going to the spring underneath the rowan tree; it was summer and he could roll naked in the grasses again. But instead of water, dark red blood came up from the ground. He awoke with a pain in his lower stomach, as though worms were tying themselves around his flesh. There was only a little light from the embers in the hearth. The Priest slept buried beneath a pile of blankets, skins, and an old moth-eaten tapestry. Grey moaned with a new wave of pain. He hoped his moans would wake the Priest. Then he could tell him that something was very wrong, that he was ill and perhaps dying. But the man was well nested in dreamless slumber. So the boy got out of his own pile of rags, including an old cloak made of rabbit skin, and with a shivering hand put two small logs of oak on the fire. Pleased to have guaranteed his and the Priest's warmth until the end of the night, he stared at the rising flames, then looked down at himself and saw blood on his leggings.

Terror started as a sting and then crept up his neck and made his scalp tingle. He stared and stared between his legs, bending them and thrusting his pelvis toward the fire to see as well as possible in the intensifying light. Red blood, it was.

"Jesus, Mary and Joseph," Grey muttered as he had heard the Priest do. And he thought, I am dying, just like the last Priest's helper. He crossed himself and took up the old rabbit skin cloak. Putting it around his shoulders, he went to the chapel. By the light of the fire in the other room, he could see the long, solid shape of the altar. He knelt in front of it, afraid to look up at the crucifix the Priest had brought from England, at the blood coming from Jesus' wounds and the agony on His face. Crossing himself again, Grey said, "Please forgive me for speaking directly and in a language you do not like. Forgive me for not having the Priest intervene. Forgive me for everything that I've done that hasn't been right. Please heal me. Please don't let me die." He began to weep, feeling more blood come out of him, trickling a little down the inside of his thighs where the leggings were loose.

He glared desperately up at the little arced windows to determine if any light could be seen in the cracks of the wooden shutters. It was still night. Perhaps dawn would never come for him.

But he could not just bleed to death, alone.

Ideas came into his head. He wanted to live. He had to use his wits. He thought of all the relics in the chapel, of the hair, the thorn, the cloth, the bone. He quickly assessed the lot and determined that the most powerful magic must be in the bone. A piece of a man's bone, something that came from inside his body, must have a great deal of force behind it, especially considering that the man was a saint.

Grey grabbed the blue glass bottle with the bone in it from its niche and ran from the chapel, pulling the door carefully shut after him. The night was so dark he could not even see his own frosted breath, but he could feel the sharp cold in his lungs. And he could see the large shapes of his world, the empty line of road, the black lumps of houses. He pulled the ragged cloak around him, still clutching the bottle in his right fist, and ran up to the road. His plan was clear and intelligent; he would combine the best resources available for healing: the piece of Saint Augustine's bone and the skill of the Midwife.

The sweat on Grey's face was beginning to freeze as he stood outside the Midwife's hut and waited. Wind swirled. A black-and-white dog standing between neighboring huts was barking fiercely; white billows of breath were suddenly revealed by the half-moon that had come out of its bed of cloud. Grey squatted down, shivering, and called out, "Midwife" through the cow skin over the opening.

The answer came with startling clarity, as though the Midwife had been awake. But she was simply used to calls at night from husbands and children whose wives and mothers were in labor.

"It is Grey," the boy said. "I have to come in. I'm very ill. I'm bleeding to death."

The Midwife's hand came out and pushed aside the skin so Grey could crawl in. There was a brass pot holding burning coals in the middle of the hut, which was smoky and warm. The Midwife bent over the pot with a candle stub and got a flame on the wick.

"Where are you bleeding?" she asked, holding the light up. Her wild hair and wrinkled face made a dance of lines.

Grey held his knees tightly to his chest and rocked back and forth crying.

"Here, if you've come for help, then you have to tell me where your wound is," the Midwife said with some annoyance, for she determined that the child was not weak enough to be dying.

"I am bleeding from between my legs," he admitted.

The Midwife looked into Grey's eyes as much as she could determine where those eyes were. Grey looked away, sniveling, shaking, still holding his knees to his chest.

"You don't have to show me," the Midwife said.

"Am I going to die?"

"No. The bleeding will stop."

"How do you know?"

"I know. It will lessen and then stop in a few days, three or four. Use rags; place them in your leggings between your legs to catch the blood."

The Midwife blew the candle out. In the darkness, Grey took out the bottle and put it on the ground to readjust the cloak.

"Why am I bleeding?"

"Because you have no penis," the Midwife explained.

Grey's heart pounded like the fearful fist of a forgotten prisoner.

"Is there a wound there?"

"Yes, and it opens up for a few days each month, to let out blood, as in leeching. There is no danger. As with leeching, it is good to clean the body of its blood sometimes."

Grey thought for a moment as the Midwife lay back down and gathered her bedding around her.

"There is no danger," the woman said. "Tell me, are you content as the Priest's helper?"

"Yes," Grey said. He didn't want the Midwife to go to sleep. Clearly she was not interested in his bleeding, so he said, "I've seen the people who live in the Manor. Did you know that there is always food there? They always have enough food, even to feed the dogs." Grey whispered dramatically, "I saw dogs eating meat and bread."

The Midwife chuckled.

"Do others bleed this way?" Grey asked, almost ready to sob.

"Listen to me, my Grey, there is something you should know. You shouldn't worry if you aren't like other boys. It doesn't matter if you don't have their shape and such, hair on the face, that sort of thing. It doesn't matter. You have taken on the role of the Priest's helper and may someday go to the Monastery and learn to read and write and go on pilgrimages. You are as strong as any boy. There's no need for anyone to know your differences."

"I don't like the bleeding. My stomach hurts."

"There is no danger. It is a blessing, really, but you must keep it a secret." She took in a long breath and let it out in two melancholy notes.

"I am sick with secrets. There are too many secrets," Grey said.

"All creation is a great mystery, and there's not anyone can tell it full, though he may know it for a fox's blink."

The Midwife's sleepy voice came up from a lump of cloth, as though she had metamorphosed into a small hill. Grey began to doze off, his head bobbing forward. The Midwife said, "You'd best take the road home, now, Grey, before the Priest wakes and wonders if you've run away."

The road was colder now that Grey was not warm with desperation. He trotted along to hurry the journey and to generate warmth and because he liked to run. It proved that he was not dying. Dying people do not run when no one is chasing them.

When he got back to the Church, Grey got one of the rags he used to clean the floor and put it between his legs in the leggings. He lay down in the warm room, glad he had stoked the fire before leaving, glad that the Priest was asleep, glad that the Midwife was so calm. In comfort, he made a plan to go to the spring the next morning and wash the leggings and anything else the blood had stained. He would then make a diaper of rags to catch the blood and wrap a blanket around his legs while the wet things dried on the hearth. He would tell the Priest he had cut his leg in the night while putting wood on the fire. He thanked God for giving him wits. But he felt some discomfort still in his belly and in all his body, as though he were caught in some trap. He kept having the feeling that something was not right, that he was very, very alone because no one knew him, no one truly knew who he was. He was most afraid that he himself didn't know who he was, or what was right and wrong, and that as a result of this large kind of ignorance he would be severely punished by the God that lived in the sky and gave the people in the Manor all the food they wanted.

And then the spirit in the tree opened its eyes wide and told Grey that he had left the bottle with the piece of Saint Augustine's thigh bone in the Midwife's hut.

12

F AR AWAY from the Holy Land, far away from the profound center of
the world, of the Christian revelation of God incarnate, was Europe,
and farther away still, Ireland—a tiny, singing island, green and full of spirits. In these isolated outposts, what could the people touch, see, smell of
Christ and his saints and their miracles?

Relics. With great compassion, the Church allowed miracles to occur
in all parts of the world, pagan spirits to become saints, and Christian
relics to be housed in the most foreign of places. There were the last
breaths of saints, captured and corked in tinted glass bottles or caught in
little silver urns, sealed with ivory, jeweled with emeralds and rubies: the
exhalations of martyrs before their souls ascended to heaven. There were
the pieces of the cross, the remnants of the swaddling clothes of the infant
Jesus, the drops of sweat from the brow of a persecuted saint, and somewhere the chalice—the cup of the first holy transformation of wine into
blood. To touch these things, to smell them, to see them, was to be graced
by a little of the force that saved the human race from eternal damnation
and that promised eternal bliss in paradise, giving purpose to a life of fleas
and sores and heartbreak. The Flax Grower, the Smith's wife, servants
from the Manor, many slipped into the chapel to kneel near the Priest's
reliquaries, leaving the tarnished swirls of their fingerprints on the brass
or silver.

The Priest of Finnistuath himself had been on two pilgrimages in
the land of the Crusades, had seen Jesus' tomb, and had seen the sandal
worn by Moses when he came down the mountains and brought with him
the tablets on which God had written the Ten Commandments. He understood the power of these relics to both humble and exhilarate a man. He
wanted to give such an experience to the poor and ignorant peoples of
Ireland, as well as to encourage pilgrims to stop into the Church at Finnistuath to see some of the tangible evidence of Christian miracles. In this
way, perhaps he could sell a meal or two, or a warm and dry spot on the

chapel floor. In this way, Finnistuath might grow with devout Christians who came to see a piece of the thigh bone of Saint Augustine and stayed to raise some oats. They would attribute their good fortune to the Priest chosen by God to be the curator of his relics. The Church would be rebuilt, larger, more glorious, with more amenities, such as a bed for the Priest. But if there was no respect among the putrid villagers who pissed on altars and ransacked chapels, what order could the Priest keep?

So when the Priest discovered that the piece of Saint Augustine's thigh bone was gone, he felt a sincere urge to put his fist through stone. Grey heard him moan, like a calving cow.

The boy stood still by the hearth, cradling a log he meant to give to the fire. He could feel his own heart pushing against his chest. And then another moan from the Priest, and the words, in English, "This cannot be."

Grey stayed where he was until the Priest came in to him, bent over, steadying himself against the lumpy stone wall.

"Do you know what has happened to the bone?" he asked, struggling with his Gaelic, hardly able to lift his eyes to look at Grey, who just shook his head and stared back.

The Priest lunged at the boy. The log fell to the floor between the two, miraculously missing anyone's toes, as the Priest held himself up by grabbing Grey's lean shoulders.

"If you are lying . . . what do you know of this? It is gone! Gone! You must have heard or seen . . ." He started slowly shaking Grey in rhythm with his words: "What do you know of his?"

Grey continued to shake his head, in counterpoint to the direction his shoulders were being shaken.

The Priest gave up and was pulled down to his bedding by the weight of this tragedy.

"Someone in this unholy village has taken a Christian relic. Someone has sinned immensely, immeasurably, and will suffer unspeakably. Unspeakably."

Grey pushed the fallen log into the fire with his foot.

"Pick it up!" the Priest yelled. "That's no way to do it. Pick it up!"

Grey picked up the log and let it roll off his arms onto the smoldering remnants of former logs.

Staring coldly at the boy, the Priest said, "Whoever has done this horrible thing is cursed. I curse him. I curse him without mercy."

And then he brooded, staring at the flames, poking at the log with his foot.

"I'll get another," he muttered, and then louder, "We must secure the doors at night. And there must always be someone here."

Dismayed at the thought of any of his precious freedom being carved off for the sake of constant vigilance, Grey finally offered, "Perhaps God has taken the piece of bone."

"For what reason?" the Priest snapped.

"Well, in order to have all of the saint's pieces together—in Heaven."

The Priest scoffed at this and looked back at the fire.

"I tell you, the person who did this is now cursed, by my official word as a servant of the Church. I cannot have rampant defilement of my relics."

Grey spent many nights silently praying to any saint kind enough to listen, for he was now afraid to petition God directly. He asked the anonymous kindly saint—Patrick, or Brigid, or Saint Kevin, who loved animals but hated women—to spare him the Priest's curse. He thought of adding another example of rampant disobedience to the Priest's seething list by going to the Midwife's hut. But he was being watched studiously, and retrieving the bottled fragment from the Midwife would ensure that its disappearance be attributed to him.

When warm air came regularly to the little village, Grey had almost forgotten about the curse—and the Priest had regained his composure, assuring the village that he was soon to acquire a more precious fragment of bone. With some longing for times when his troubles seemed simpler, Grey went to the spring to rekindle the ritual that had been extinguished for winter. Mild shoots and plump buds were emerging in the world. The rains were warming. Grey, with the jumpy anticipation of a lover, hurried to the spring with the water pail clanging against his leg. The long grasses were tan and dry; among them were the short new blades. Grey happily removed his clothing, humming and shivering. He would be chilled, but how divine it would be to feel the breeze and the new grasses and damp earth directly on his skin. He felt blessed, graced by his awareness of this pleasure, and he wondered if anyone else secretly indulged in mingling their nakedness with the earth's textures. He understood why Red chose this place to expose his body to the unseen spirits. Grey was looking down at himself and wondering if Jesus had lived in a home that had plenty of food when he was stunned as though a leather whip had snapped against his bare back. Immediately, with heated horror, he remembered the Priest's curse, and there it was, manifested in the unnatural swelling of his chest into two subtle though plumping breasts.

He fell upon his knees, breathing deeply as though just emerging from underwater. He felt these growths gingerly, finally covering them with his hands.

He knew that now, without question, he must get the relic back from the Midwife. He pulled on the leggings and his wool shirt and put the billowing tunic over his head. He left the pail by the spring and ran down the road, pushing his arms through the tunic sleeves.

One of the English settlers was on the road, herding fifteen brown, bony cows northward. Grey ran down into the bog, leaping over soggy patches and gray pieces of wood. He ran, not stopping when he saw his mother and the two younger girls outside their cottage, pouring dried oats from sacks into baskets and sifting through them with their fingers looking for bugs or pebbles.

"Here is Grey," Caerla, a pale and thin child, called out happily. She had gotten weaker from the last winter and gentler in her nature.

"I am going to see the Midwife," Grey said, now striding hard past the crumbling cottage and up the hill behind to the huts.

The Goatherd's wife stood up and followed Grey for a few steps, calling out, "The Midwife's gone to help the Plowman's daughter-in-law who's having twins. Is there a birth at the Manor? Is the Priest ill?"

The Second Fiona came out, frantically dragging one of her legs, more crippled than before. Grey wanted to ignore his sister. He wanted not to look at Fiona or talk to her. He felt that if he opened his mouth and let any word out to her, he would tell horrible secrets that he could not take back.

Breathless with the effort to keep up with Grey, Fiona stopped and watched her brother stride away. And though she had only wanted to take his hand to ask what it was like to be the Priest's boy, Fiona was left behind with a cold disregard she had never felt from her brother. Grey muttered to himself, "Leave me be. Leave me be, Fiona." He felt anger at her for slowing him down with pity and guilt, and he kept walking toward the Midwife's hut. Once there, he bent down and crawled in. It was ashamble with odds and ends: herbs, pots, bottles, skins, blankets. In the dim light Grey looked through the small space, passing his hands over the ground beneath skins and cloth and baskets. There was no bottle that had the shape or the color of the one holding the relic.

He went outside and looked around, hoping to see the Midwife on the road, not looking toward his family's cottage, at the pitiful assembly of poor females standing around it.

"Here now, it's me son. It's me Grey."

His father was coming down the hill carrying a white kid who was bleating vehemently.

"I'm on an errand," Grey said. The Goatherd stopped in front of Grey, grinning toothlessly. The kid continued to bleat, closing its eyes.

"He's got two thorns in his arse," Gregory explained. "One's broken off so I can't get at it."

Grey muttered, "Jesus, Mary, and Joseph and all the saints," and walked around to look at the animal's haunches and saw in the coarse white hair the two thorns, one broken almost below the skin.

"Did he sit on them?" Grey asked.

"That he did. That is exactly what he did. Sat down hard, son, right in the brambles."

"Well, hold him, then, and I'll take them out."

"You're me son, then, aren't you, come to help."

"Yes, Da."

Old Gregory laughed. It seemed like a strange sound to him, his own laugh.

"Hold him still, Da."

"Don't speak to your father like that. That isn't right."

"Oh, hold him."

"He's kicked me good."

"Hold him hard. Here, here's the first one. The other's in deep and there's naught to get a hold of."

"You're me son and ought to be helping me."

"I can't get this one. I can't get it."

"You'd better stay here with me now."

"I've almost got it, if you'll hold him hard. There. Oh, that one wasn't so long. You can let him go now."

Gregory let the kid roll out of his arms and onto the ground. It landed on its feet and kicked its hind legs at the world for a few seconds before trotting up the hill and into the woods to find its companions.

Immediately the Goatherd grabbed his son's wrist and pulled him in the same direction the kid had gone.

"I have to go back," Grey said to his father's broad, determined shoulders.

"I have no more teeth," Gregory said, gripping the boy's wrist more tightly.

They came to the herd, scattered among some new oak in a sunny part of the forest. Gregory marched around, crunching leaves and dragging the boy along. He found a big enough rock for the two of them to sit on.

"You'd best let me go before the Priest comes for me."

"No. I won't do that."

Grey looked at his father's big face and said, "I've been cursed. You'd best let me go."

Gregory looked down at the boy.

"You'll stay with me and the curse will leave." He put his arm around the boy and held him close to his side. Grey could hear his father's deep breathing, steady and loyal.

He pressed his face against his father's side, smelling the goats, the smoke from his family's hearth, sour milk, sweat. Tears came up into his eyes and spilled down his cheeks. He was suddenly very tired. The goats trod near, crunching the leaves, staring at the two humans as the light faded and the rock and the man and his son seemed to fuse together as a rough sculpture hewn from a large stone.

Grey thought what a terrible disappointment he must be to his father and how badly he had treated Fiona. He felt worse about these things than about the Priest's relic, and he asked God's forgiveness for not putting his sins in the right order.

 **13**

*t*HE PRIEST heard from the English settler with the bony cows where the boy had gone. He ordered two of the settler's grown sons—the very two who had urinated on the altar some years before, now both with their own families to tend to—to go with him to bring Grey back. One took a club and the other a long iron rod. The Priest carried a torch fashioned out of a thick stick wrapped in waxed cloth. The three stopped briefly and loudly at the Goatherd's cottage, where they enlisted Mary to lead them to the place in the woods where the goats and their master were likely to be. Grey was asleep, his head in the crook of his father's arm; Gregory watched the torch and his wife and the men approach. Behind them were also the Midwife and several of the unfree laborers and their children, making up a crowd of fourteen people, not including Grey and his father.

"Give me the boy," the Priest bellowed.

Grey sat up and stared at the strange black-and-yellow gathering, ordering in his mind the details of the situation until he understood it. His father's hand gripped his wrist again. The Goatherd did not move.

"You're the village fool, a worthless soul. I will have you beaten away from that boy if I must."

"Don't harm him," Grey said. He stood up, still tethered to his father. "He doesn't understand."

"This is me son," Gregory said.

"He is in my service, or you will give me your herd and your home," the Priest responded. One of his helpers stepped forward and swung the club against Gregory's shin. The Goatherd howled and drew his legs up, but he still held onto his son's wrist.

Grey lowered himself carefully to his knees and spoke calmly. "Please, I beg you not to hurt him. He doesn't understand. He will want supper and forget his purpose with me."

Mary was holding her skirts up to her mouth, trying to stifle her whimpering with them.

"And I'll keep you from running away again," the Priest said to Grey.

"I won't run away."

"Leaving the pail on the ground, not doing your duties."

The other helper walked up to Gregory and started poking him in the stomach with the iron rod.

"Da, let me go," Grey pleaded softly. "Let me go." He could see his father's terrified eyes glisten. He was frozen in panic.

The iron rod came down hard on the Goatherd's wrist, breaking it so thoroughly that the hand dangled like a dead thing on the end of the arm. Gregory roared and stood up. His mouth, empty of teeth, was a round chasm, and from it now came howling sobs.

"Leave him. Leave him," Grey screamed. "I am loosed. Leave him. Tell them to leave him be."

People in the crowd called out, "Let him be."

But the Priest's two helpers kept pummeling the howling man, striking him until he fell to the ground, where they poked and kicked him. Three of his daughters and his wife had come around, falling on their knees and clutching the two men by the calves, imploring the men to stop.

Grey ran to the Priest and held him around the waist with his arms. He looked up at his face and said, "Please have them stop. Please. Please. Please."

The Priest said to the two men, "I've got the boy, now. There's no need to go on."

Breathing hard from their exertion, they looked up at the Priest, remembering the point of all the commotion. Then nodding, they walked down to the road chatting with each other congenially as though having just brought a stray calf back from the woods. The rest of the crowd moved away from Gregory and his family. Grey began to cry from the center of his body, bringing up sobs as though vomiting. The Priest guided him tenderly toward the road as the boy looked back at his family, who were turning into wailing shadows. The crippled Fiona looked up at him and they shared eyes and tears for one instant. He knew that tonight, in this terrible night, he was forever separated from them. And he would see them on the road or in the Church or on the bridge to Tarmath as a ghost sees the living, whom he cannot touch or eat with or laugh with.

The Midwife passed Grey and touched his shoulders.

"I'll tend to him," she said. And Grey wondered if the Midwife knew, hoped that the Midwife knew that she had in her possession a relic of healing powers. He was glad then that the Midwife had the miraculous piece of bone of the great Saint Augustine. If the relic could help to soothe his father's injuries and pain, then so be it. He would keep his deformities. He would suffer his own curse in order to let his father be healed with the relic and to let himself be healed of the guilt he felt concerning his father's beating. He just prayed, he prayed to Saint Patrick and Saint Brigid by name—for weren't they Irish and wouldn't they understand and love their own people and language—that the Midwife would understand the power that resided in the blue bottle he had left behind those many nights ago.

But now Grey was indeed the Priest's attendant, in the most thorough way. The Priest attached a bell to Grey's ankle, a dented brass bell that clanged mutely, but loud enough to give notice as to the boy's whereabouts. And now there was no separation between the two. But Grey was pleased to have the opportunity to study the Priest's every move. A new eye in his mind was opened, and he could see with it the world's falseness. For whereas the Priest spoke of blessings and of God's rule over men and of Jesus' commandment to love one's neighbor, the Priest used thick-headed thugs to cripple one of his neighbors. Even a man so close to God, with the duty of speaking to Him and listening to His will, was impatient and took matters into his own hands. The flow of God's will was apparently not fast enough for the Priest. Grey studied the man now, studied his face when he prayed and his hands when he lifted the cup of holy wine. He watched him eye the meats and parchment of the people of the Manor. And he watched him finger his relics.

Without complaint but with a simmering rage, Grey surrendered his solitude, going now with the Priest into the woods, pushed along toward the spring to fetch water, so that the pail clanged against the bell around his ankle and all Christendom knew the path of his errand.

"Have you gone daft like your father?" the Priest yelled when Grey just stood there swinging the pail and staring into the Priest's face. Grey had no response but thought instead that being considered daft might indeed alleviate him of a lot of responsibility. Perhaps a daft man would be let go to wander in the woods.

A few day's after the Goatherd's beating, the Priest made Grey follow him to a clearing in the woods, west and south of the new English cottages. He said to Grey, "Sit there on that rock and be idle while I do business too important for your meddling. Don't wander off where I can't keep you out of mischief, and if you see anyone coming . . . turn around and face the other way and tell me if you see anyone coming. Do you hear me?"

A cow had died in the clearing. The carcass had been stripped quickly of all usable items, including flesh, hide, and any large pieces of bone. A few small bones lay about. Grey didn't fully turn around but watched the Priest in the clearing pull out a dagger and carve out a fragment of bone from the cow's remains.

At that moment Grey understood many things without having words for that understanding. He could feel silence as both an end and a beginning. He stooped and picked up the discarded portion of the cow's cut bone before following the Priest out of the clearing.

A few days later, the Priest presented a new relic to the people of the Manor. Though Grey could not understand the words spoken about the item, he saw the eyes of the powdered Lady fill with tears and her bent fingers tremble toward the fragment of bone that lay in a small and intricately decorated silver box lined with purple velvet. It was a very white fragment of bone. It was, indeed, a piece of the right arm bone of John the Baptist. The story of how such a relic came to Ireland and to the Priest of Finnistuath through the Monastery of Tarmath was too profound, too convoluted and precious a story to be told in any detail. The Priest simply said that he had had discourse with a man in Tarmath recently, and that the man had a sort of glow about his head and provided him with the relic in exchange for the Priest's promise to say certain prayers about a certain matter.

During his cleaning of the chapel, Grey carefully dusted the box as he did the other boxes and bottles in the niches. He began to hum as he worked, more the idiot in demeanor, so that the Priest gave him less supervision. He hummed the songs Colin had sung, about thrush and alder and thistle and fox. Grey waited for word of his father and determined that soon, very soon, he would run away again.

In less than a fortnight the mangled Goatherd died in a confusion of fever and pain, his wrist crooked, the hand twisted into an unnatural geometry. Weakness from the blows to his torso deepened until, not understanding why, he became only weakness and pain. At the end he asked for his son. He asked that his son forgive him, and even he didn't know for what he should be forgiven. Fiona hobbled all the way to the Church in a moist gray wind to tell her brother how their father had died. Grey gave her some meat stew and watched her hands shake as she spooned the bowl's treasured contents into her mouth. The Priest was in the Manor and so the two spoke openly. Fiona told Grey that his father had asked his forgiveness, which made Grey stand up and pace before the fire.

The Priest came back, looking suspiciously at the two peasants speaking in front of his fire. He was still checking on the relics in the chapel when Fiona limped out.

Standing in front of the Priest, Grey put his foot on the stone wall and untied the bell around his ankle. Dropping the bell on the floor beside the man so that its clattering, muted ring got his attention, Grey quietly told the Priest that his father had died. "You must bury him in the cemetery near the Church, with a stone marker that has words on it," he said to the Priest, who laughed without humor. Grey continued, "I am not asking for the chapel floor where the Lord intends to be buried with his sons. I am not such a fool as to ask for that."

The Priest laughed again and said, "I'll be wearing a fairy's dress and dancing down the road before I do such a thing."

Grey sighed and said, "Then you'd best see the tailor in Tarmath. For if you do not give my father a holy burial, the whole village will know from what dead cows you take the bones of saints."

The Priest breathed deeply and said that Grey was grieved over his father's death and needed a good supper. He would then forget his bitter notions about the relic. "And who would believe a simpleton such as yourself, the son of a half-wit?"

Grey fell silent again, carefully placing the dented bell on the Priest's desk, and noting the sweat that was collecting on his master's blushing brow. Later, having had some hours to think over his plan, he spoke during a meal of boiled greens and oat cakes. Grey calmly explained his proof of fakery concerning the fragment of John the Baptist's bone.

"I have put the chipped cow bone in a safe place, for if someone were to find it, he would see how well your relic fits into it, making it whole."

The Priest threw his nearly full plate on the hearth and said, "And if you should die, there would be no one to know the place of the bone."

"The Lord's son knows."

This part of his lie came as a surprise to Grey himself.

"You are a devilish liar," the Priest hissed. "And I have treated you so well."

"I put the bone in a hiding place in the stable when the Lord's son Red was there. And I gave him notions, questions to ask were I to meet doom."

The muscles of the Priest's face fell slack.

"You can say that you are a good man and charitable, to lay your poor servant's father in the holy ground," Grey continued. "Or you can refuse, and the cow bone from which you carved the new relic that you pass off as a saint's bone will appear."

"Why would the Lord's son make deals with a goatherd's son?"

"I have seen him in the woods. I have seen him doing certain rituals."

"You will make trouble for yourself, boy. You will be hanged like the Smith. There are certain laws, a certain order in the world, and each man has a certain place in the order, a certain name and part to play. There are things you should not see."

"I will not look away from anything," Grey promised.

The Priest stood up, his fists clenched at his sides as he yelled, "A man's identity is fixed, boy! You are a boy; I am a man. You are a servant; I am a Priest."

"And out there in a silver box is the bone of Saint John the Baptist."

Wearily the Priest sat back down. He held his forehead up with the palm of one hand and said, with determination not to lose his control over this peasant boy, "I'll do this one thing for you, but don't imagine that you are a big rock that has fallen on my head. You and all your knowledge are pebbles. Pebbles. You haven't a flea's capacity for understanding that in fact a cow's bone can be transformed into the true piece of a saint. These are religious matters completely beyond your ability to think about. Completely." He waved his hand through the air as though whisking away the smoky illusions of an ignorant boy.

"I want my father to be put to rest as a good man, a man to be respected were anyone to pass by his grave," Grey said, and he let a few tears slide down his face.

The Goatherd's death made the world more unfriendly than it had been. Grey sensed that the mean spirits who had been repelled from the village by the presence of his muddled but vigilant father came around more often, unseen, mean, humorless. He sensed a new and cold silence everywhere. He felt it inside himself. He now needed to know who he was other than the Goatherd's son. He hoped he would soon learn what his identity in the order of the universe was. In the present, though—as he scrubbed the stones of the chapel beneath the flickering relics, and as he watched the Lord's son Red on the back of a black stallion galloping like a furious wind, and as he saw the Midwife stride up and down the road with her face lifted to the sky—Grey felt a horrible loneliness. He wanted the love that had passed through him and disappeared like a fog beneath the sun—the love of his mother, of the lads at the stump, of his father who had let him sleep so soundly against his large heart. The lack of affection felt like a thing that could choke him. He wanted some day to join his father, and anyone else he loved who would inevitably die, in some paradise, in Heaven. And this was all the more reason to go to a monastery and pray, as his mother had asked him to—for his and his father's soul, and anyone else's soul that he wanted to spend eternity with in a place with good bread and some honey dripping on it.

The Goatherd was buried a few yards away from the dead relatives of the Lord of the Manor, including several infants who had lived but a few hours or days. On the Goatherd's stone was written the English word, "Peasant."

14

THE PRIEST had persisted in wheedling attention from the Church authorities regarding Finnistuath's relics. Finally, as a miracle in itself, a monk from the Monastery at Tarmath came to visit the village Church and judge the merits of the Priest's collection, in order to write an informed report to the Pontiff.

The pilgrim was an Irish monk named Bartholomew, with mild authority and a well-fed frame. Bartholomew considered himself something of a philosopher, a man studying the materials of God's world. He adored travel and the opportunity to categorize plants and animals in his ledger, a well-worn brown volume, only slightly smaller than the Bailiff's ledger. But instead of names and numbers such as those in the Bailiff's records, Brother Bartholomew's ledger had sketches of leaves, blossoms, insects, even of some mammals. He also dabbled in the study of the Heavens and wrote down the position of the planets when anything odd or noteworthy occurred in the world that needed explanation. But he was more interested in the immediate wonders of the world that could be touched and examined closely.

Bartholomew's eyes often followed Grey around the room as the boy stoked the fire or served the bread. Grey kept his eyes down. He did not want to communicate in any way with this monk, who might ask him questions he did not want to answer. For example, concerning the origin of certain relics, the Priest had told Grey and other villagers that some of the relics Bartholomew asked about came from his own Monastery at Tarmath. Should Bartholomew not, then, already know their origins? Grey knew why there was contradiction in the Priest's words and the monk's questions. He knew well, and he was content to know and say nothing.

The wisdom of all servants is to keep one's knowledge a secret, or at least to use it when it reflects well on the master or when it can finally do the master in. But the blow must be fatal, for a wounded master is the most dangerous kind of all.

Bartholomew's interest in the serving boy intensified to the extent that the monk accompanied Grey on his trips to the spring to fetch water with the excuse that it was an area of interest to him in terms of its flora. But after unfurling the ends of a few ferns, the monk abandoned scholarship to take up the role of confidante with Grey.

"How you must weary of his tinkering with bottles and cases! You have been with the Priest a long time?"

Grey simply nodded. What was a long time? He didn't know; he was unsure if there were certain answers he was supposed to give, or if he was free to tell whatever truth came to mind.

"Where is your family? What is your father's trade?"

How odd that someone would want to know such things of a boy who had no apparent sway over anything. But Grey made a decision to tell what was so.

"My father is dead, killed when the Priest came for me, by men who were drunk on their ability to harm." Grey's eyebrows sank down as he looked at the monk who seemed to be searching the sky for a bird he knew.

Bartholomew took a long breath, held it, clasped his hands behind his back and then let the breath out.

"So he has gone to God," he finally said.

"My mother and sisters tend his goats. But I don't know if they are sound because . . . because they won't come near the Priest who killed Da. And I don't see as how a man who weeps over the way Jesus was put up on that tree to die stands by like a rook on a winter branch and watches a man who did no harm be beaten to death."

It was no use stopping now.

"My mother wishes me to go the Monastery and says that all my questions will be answered there, for it is a holy place full of God. And I wonder, sir, if there is truth to that, or would that be another story told to people to keep them from figuring things out on their own."

Bartholomew sighed and looked up at the muted sky again, laden with rain not yet fallen. Then he stretched and looked around him at the ferns. He picked up a fallen and dried leaf and crumbled it in his fist.

"There may be many answers to one question," he said.

"I want to speak with God myself, for I don't know as I can rely on the Priest to ask my questions without changing the words."

Bartholomew studied the boy.

Grey looked around at all the trees, who seemed to be listening intently.

"I want to become someone who is allowed to speak directly to God."

"I will pray for you," Bartholomew said. "And perhaps I can help you learn to petition God." Then he grabbed a clump of the grasses and let them sift through his fingers as he brought his hand up. "These are most succulent grasses."

Grey smiled and stepped awkwardly forward, grabbed the monk's hand in supplication, and said, looking down at its soft flesh, "You are kind."

Bartholomew pressed Grey's fingers gently and smiled. Grey pulled away and turned to begin the walk back to the Church.

Bartholomew grasped Grey's arm to stop him from lifting the pail of water.

"You are a clever boy, Grey. I have noticed your cleverness, how aware you are when one's plate needs replenishing, when the fire needs stoking, how to soothe the Priest or ready the writing table. How old are you?"

"I am thirteen years since birth, sir."

"And you have seen, then, that there are things which are unpleasant, even cruel."

"I have, sir."

"God is in the world around us, in the veins of the oak leaf or the sting of the thistle, which has learned to protect itself with thorn and poison."

Still holding Grey's arm, Bartholomew said, "So you know that there are many manifestations of suffering in the world and that perhaps they serve a purpose that God may reveal or not."

"Such as the suffering of Christ," Grey said, pleased to express some understanding of the monk's philosophies.

Bartholomew laughed.

"Even though you are an illiterate boy, I admire you. I admire also your fair face and strong, young body." He looked over Grey's loose clothing and at the firm young hand gripping the wooden handle of the pail.

A straggling smile came on his lips and he shooed Grey on by patting his buttocks.

The monk seemed in no hurry to return to the Monastery. He began to sleep copiously and became more and more friendly with Grey, even taking him with him to the Manor to discuss with the Lord's son Red his desire to enter the Monastery to become a religious.

When the Lord was sober, these talks went on unmolested. When the Lord had drunk several cups of ale, he interrupted the conversation between Red and Bartholomew.

"Monks are all milksops, flabby and pale, as impotent as geldings," he would growl. One night, when there was an angry wind outside, the Lord slapped the back of Red's head and said, "Why can't you be like your brother, Joseph, and find a wife with money and land and a ready womb?"

After such an outburst, the Lord would be contrite at the monk's next visit, saying, "I do like to jest, you understand. I mean no harm. If my son wishes to dedicate himself to God, so be it. And may he say prayers to save his pater's devilish soul."

In the Manor, Grey stared at the tables of food and at Red, for the Lord's son seemed devout and transcendent in all his efforts, which included reading small books full of charts and diagrams, tending to his mother, and talking to Bartholomew about his intentions to become a cleric as part of his mission to improve upon the world, which, he said, seemed a most miserable waiting station for Heaven. Red paid little attention to the food and wine on the tables, and less attention to his father's bellowing and laughter.

Grey's eyes were pulled to Red's face and his crotch, as he remembered about Red's fornication with a fairy. He liked the tanned skin over the Lord's son's high cheekbones and the golden threads of hair on his arms. When Grey realized that Bartholomew was watching him watching Red, he tucked his chin into his chest and looked down at the reeds strewn on the floor.

Trying to resist his fascination with Red, Grey stood ready for Bartholomew to instruct him to fetch more ink or pick up a fallen scroll, and when they were walking back to the Church the monk told him what the Lord's son said. The monk had firm doubts about Red's ability to withstand the lack of comfort in a monastery. And Grey responded, "But he is so fit and strong."

Bartholomew laughed and said, "You fancy the Lord's son?"

Grey's eyes widened in confusion and exaggerated innocence.

"I don't know what you mean, sir," he mumbled.

Bartholomew laughed again, ending the laugh with a cough as he often did. He put his arm around the boy's shoulder, hugging him tightly against his side in three friendly pulses. The physical affection felt fine to Grey. He had not been held so since his father was killed.

Bartholomew said, "I saw you studying him with fond eyes."

Grey feigned a yawn.

"You're a good boy, Grey. I am trying to educate you, to improve your station in life," Bartholomew said. And that night he asked for Grey to share his bed with him, since it had grown colder.

"We'll keep each other warm," he said against the back of the boy's head.

Climbing into the nest of bedding nearer to the hearth than his own, Grey was thinking that he indeed had a chance to see more of the world than Finnistuath and to do good for his family without having to be near his mother's constant sorrow. His friendship with Bartholomew seemed a strange and blessed thing.

And it was good to be warmed by another when winter was gaining entrance to the Church. Such were the sleeping arrangements when Grey slept against Fiona's back, but here was a larger warmth. Grey slept well, until one night when he felt Bartholomew's hand on his buttock, rubbing it with gentle affection. He moved and moaned as though disturbed in his sleep and the monk stopped.

In the morning, Bartholomew wrote out a letter to the Pontiff explaining once and for all the impressive and important aspects of the Priest's precious relics. The Priest beamed and admitted in secret to Grey that he was ready to have his room and his meals to himself again. "Perhaps he is leaving soon," he whispered, rubbing his hands together as though speaking of some nice gravy he was about to dip his bread into. "We will then build a pilgrim's hall and get payment for the food and shelter we offer."

When Bartholomew returned to the Church after his morning routine of relieving himself, saying prayers, and taking a walk in the woods with his ledger and charcoal at the ready, Grey was emptying the water pail onto the hearth so he could mop it.

"I will go with Grey to the spring this morn," Bartholomew said. "The sun is out and I want its warmth." The monk scratched the side of his nose and raised one eyebrow. It was the expression he had when a plate of good meat was set before him.

The monk and the Priest's boy walked in silence to the spring. The day was a jewel, blue and with some warmth in the breeze. When they got to the spring, Grey looked wistfully at the long grasses. He had had little time alone, little time to feel his own skin against the earth and his eyes against the sky.

"You seem sad," Bartholomew said sweetly. "Here, let me fill the bucket." He took the pail and held it against the rock to catch the water. Looking at the silver stream flow into the bucket, he asked, "And so, then, what do you think of our friend Red, the Lord's son? He is a handsome man, isn't he?"

"He is noble," Grey said. "I wish I lived in a place with all that food and warmth. Do you know they are never without logs for the fire or bread for the table?" He wanted to deflect the monk from a discussion of his opinion of Red's appearance, for he might be tempted to tell him that he had seen him naked years ago. It was no doubt unholy, the ritual of beating oneself and fucking a fairy.

Bartholomew set the pail down half full and stretched his back, sticking his belly out.

After a long groan, he said, "See, here, Grey. I don't intend to scold you. I, too, think that Red has a fine appearance. One man's admiration of another man's body is a good thing. God gave us our bodies, made them in his likeness. Men are strong and handsome in order to reflect God's strength and beauty. We are made in his image and cannot help but to love that image."

He stepped toward Grey and said, "You yourself have an admirable appearance." He smiled. Grey sighed and looked down.

"What is it?" Bartholomew asked. He was stunned when Grey lifted his head to show tears on his cheeks and filling his eyes.

"What is it?" he repeated with a gentler tone. He came closer, stroking Grey's arm.

"Oh, I am sick," Grey said, and sank to the ground. Bartholomew bent over, holding Grey's arm up as though to keep at least part of the boy's body from melting into the earth.

"Tell me. Tell me."

"I am deformed," he said.

Bartholomew removed his hand from the boy's arm.

"I have been cursed," Grey told him, weeping. "Cursed! And I'll tell you why, and then I hope I die right here on this place or am turned to a reed to wither and blow away. I have been cursed because I took one of the relics, one of the bones that the Priest had, which was no relic at all. But I took it and lost it. And he cursed whoever did it and now I'm deformed. For I believe the relic was false, but I believe that a Priest's curse may be real enough no matter on what lies it rests."

Bartholomew searched around for a patch of ground that was relatively dry and free of sharp sticks or rocks and carefully lowered his bulky torso to a sitting position. He reclined, leaning on one arm. Grey held his knees to his chest with one arm, poking holes in the dirt with his finger.

"I don't believe the relic was real, sir. I don't believe in any of the Priest's relics." Bartholomew's warmth, his humor, his curiosity about the world that seemed to transcend judgment of it—these aspects motivated Grey to speak whatever words came into his mouth. "The Priest has treated me well, but he let my father be killed, and he is a liar. And though I do not believe in his relics, I believe in curses; I believe that a man can curse another man if he wishes, if he knows secret ways. And Finnistuath is full of secret ways. This very spring, it is, I know this, it is a place where one is alone but not alone—I have seen . . . a man fornicating with a fairy here."

The monk held out his hand and waved his fingers at Grey so that he would come and lean against him as he had done with his father when they were goatherding.

"You are a handsome boy," the monk said calmly, with sincerity. "If there is a deformity it does not show. It cannot be significant. And there is goodness in you that is more important than a perfection of the body."

"You can't see it because I wear clothing that hides my deformities."

Grey started weeping. He was thinking of Fiona's crooked legs, and how he would trade his afflictions for hers. Fiona hardly walked any longer but stayed home with her legs wrapped in rags. This is what he heard from the Plowman's grandson.

"I am quite taken with you and want to comfort you, boy. Let us comfort each other in this world of sorrow."

Grey nestled happily against the monk's wool and flesh.

"Here, here, boy. You are so good." The monk was breathing heavily. He put his hands on Grey's thighs and stroked them. You are so good," he repeated.

Grey adjusted himself in the nest of flesh, feeling warm and eager to feel the affection the monk was offering.

"Grey," the monk whispered, placing his lips on the boy's cheek and closing his eyes. "Do you mind that I show you my affection?"

"No. I am glad of it," Grey answered. The warmth that had started on the outside of his body was now on the inside. He wanted the monk's hands to bless all of his body.

"Oh, you are so good," Bartholomew said.

The monk continued to stroke Grey's thighs, moving his thumbs along the line where the legs and the torso were connected. He breathed more noisily.

"I have been very lonely," Bartholomew admitted. "Tarmath is a lonely place, dark. I am sometimes in despair at its darkness, the windows shuttered, my brothers silent and full of doubts."

Grey listened, overwhelmed by this intimacy, feeling a hysteria in body and thought. His own breathing became hurried and he wriggled against the monk.

"I cannot tell you the things I have endured, the duties I have performed, tediously and tirelessly, in order to simply get a decent share of food. The vow of poverty is a respectable and holy thing, which I do not disdain, but God's world is full of luxury and flavors and aromas which I do not see as temptations but as blessings. I would far rather travel the world, to go to France and Italy, the Holy Land, than go back to Tarmath, though I have a dear friend there whose name I cannot speak without weeping with longing."

How odd it was to Grey that Bartholomew now seemed to be stricken with the urge to divulge his secrets and doubts. The closeness that two people could feel, two people who were not kin, was a miracle. If two could share body and soul, then there would be solace in the world of people, wolves, and wind while waiting for the world of angels. He listened to the sound of Bartholomew's voice through his chest, a softly booming and vibrating instrument. Grey closed his eyes and saw the face of Red, the Lord's son, a face with the strength and beauty of a warrior-saint, his chest full of swirling gold hair.

"I will tell you, Grey," Bartholomew continued as he embraced Grey more tightly, "I am loathe to go back. Loathe to go back, and especially now that we have become such good friends. I am so fond of the comforts here, though they may seem to you meager."

"Then why will you return?"

Bartholomew hesitated, his hand resting on Grey's thigh for a moment. "There is the one—one friend who should not endure the place without my companionship. I made a promise to him."

"I want to go with you," Grey said.

"To Tarmath?"

"I'd rather be with you there where there are friendships than here where there will be no companion for me. I don't want to stay here. The Priest was cruel to my father. I cannot forget. I will help you do your work."

"You want to go away from your village to Tarmath? To be my helper?"

"I know that I am too low and ignorant, that it is not my place to become a monk even though that is what my mother wanted from the beginning, that I should be a monk at Tarmath. I can go as a servant at first and watch and learn, until I am ready and . . . but the Priest . . ."

"Oh, that man and his cow bones!"

Grey sat up and looked into the monk's eyes, now dreamily focused on the boy's face. They shared a smile, and then they both laughed, Grey holding his face up as though feeling a refreshing rain on his skin.

Bartholomew began to rock Grey in his arms. "I will take you back with me, then."

Grey leaned back against the monk and felt the man's hands caress his thighs again, again moving up near his crotch. His whole world had changed, so quickly, so ecstatically with this man from another place. This time he would go away with him; this time he would not let him leave him behind as Colin had. He was older and wiser and aware of the role lust could play in a bond between people, between males and females of various species and between a human and an invisible fairy. Bartholomew, no doubt, had more knowledge to share on these and other matters.

"Tell me," the monk said breathlessly, "if you do not want me to touch you."

But Grey was intoxicated with the kindness and intimacy of the monk, spelled by the tender treatment he was receiving. He was full of joy that suddenly his life was transformed; his sense of who he was and what his life would be was altered; suddenly he would be out of Finnistuath and with a companion who did not labor from dawn to dusk to have his bowl of grain. He could learn to speak to God, and then God Himself would be his guide and protector when he was called upon to be a warrior and save men who were about to be hanged or beaten to death.

"Such a good boy," the monk said, closing his eyes and putting one hand under Grey's tunic. He found the top of the leggings and let his fingers slide underneath the wool to the skin. His hand plunged deeper, the fingers combing through pubic hair. And then abruptly they stopped.

Grey closed his eyes, waiting. His heart thumped. A little moan dribbled from his lips and he let his legs part more.

"*Deus et filius*," the monk said. He took his hand out of Grey's leggings and moved it up to the chest, gingerly touching the bottom edge of two plump breasts. As though it were bitten, the hand came swiftly out from under Grey's clothing.

"Stand up. Stand up," Bartholomew said furtively. It was the tone one used when a hornet was buzzing around the lip of one's mead cup. Grey's mouth opened, full of silence and confusion.

"Get up, I say," Bartholomew said.

Grey stood, looking down at his feet, standing very still, waiting for the blows, for the shame. The monk had discovered his deformities.

Muttering, Bartholomew stood, hardly able to keep his balance until he had caught his breath. With his hand laid on his chest, he looked at Grey.

"Your deformities," he said, "what are they?"

"My chest," Grey answered. He pulled his tunic up to reveal the full round bosoms his tunic had disguised.

"And . . . and what about . . .what about . . . down there," Bartholomew flicked his hand toward Grey's crotch.

"I have a badly shriveled prick," Grey explained. "That is why my mother thought I was destined to be a monk."

Bartholomew nodded, uttered a laugh, nodded again, turned around, and, humming, went about filling up the pail. Grey just waited, standing still and watching the monk, bracing himself for blows. After a moment, Bartholomew put the pail down on the ground and turned to Grey again.

"This is extraordinary," he said. "Quite, quite . . . Do you know? Do you understand? You are a female. You are not a boy. No, you are most definitely not a boy. You have lived an outrageous misconception. Or deception. Have you passed yourself off as a male? Oh, God in Heaven, that the world should be in such chaos! Have you lied to your entire village for the privileges of being male? Or do you fear marriage?"

Grey's face was so blank that it seemed that the features on it were disappearing.

"I am the Goatherd's son."

Realizing the startling truth he was facing Grey with, the monk gained some composure and said, "Now, see here. We will think carefully about this. We will find a way to . . . remedy . . ."

"No," Grey explained with some impatience. "You don't understand. I am a boy with no penis. And as I told you, I have been cursed."

"Yes, yes, I see. A boy with breasts and no penis. Yes, of course." Bartholomew picked up the pail, spilling water onto the ground, and strode forward, to the path that went back to the Church. Grey did not move, and soon the monk came back and put the pail down for the third time. He grabbed Grey by the shoulders.

"You are not a boy. You have been told a lie, an ignorant lie, and now I have no idea what . . . Do you bleed?"

"Yes."

"Well! Well, of course!" The monk threw his hands up and down twice. "You're a boy who has no penis, has breasts, and bleeds! Of course!"

"I do the work of a boy," Grey said. He was trembling now, as though it were very cold. He could not stop his body from shaking. "I am the Goatherd's son, brother to my sisters. I am the best hurler of all the lads of Finnistuath, and I can be a warrior. I can be a warrior and fight and be a hero in a song. If you take me with you, I can fight for the Pope. I'm not afraid." Grey's voice was shrill and impassioned.

"The ignorance of it all. The damnable ignorance. Well, surely your mother knows. Surely." He shook his head. Then said, as though asking to see a chicken he was considering buying, "Take off your clothes."

"But I am so cold now," Grey said. And it made him weep to think of how warm he had been only minutes before.

"Don't look for sympathy. I have had the blow of my life here. My hands have fiddled with a thing I thought I would never in my lifetime be obligated to touch. Now take off your clothes so that we know what we are dealing with."

"I am a boy," screamed Grey. "A boy!" And he ran away, down the path, not caring that he had left the monk, a man he was to serve, to carry the pail of water back to the Church by himself.

But Bartholomew was glad to be left, to calm himself and to wash his hand in the spring and pray to recover from what that hand had touched. He begged God's forgiveness and could hardly bring himself to address the Mother of God Herself, who stood for the untouchable sanctity of the female body. But he said to her in his best Latin that he meant no harm, that he would do penance, and that if she were to help him bring light to the Monastery at Tarmath, to somehow give him comfort there, he would return as he was supposed to. And he prayed to be given the chance to leave the Monastery for good—to travel as a scholar with his companion. If the rumors were true, Bartholomew said to the Virgin Mary, if the world were coming to an end soon, he wanted first to visit the Pope in Avignon. He would present the Pope with his studies of God's creations and perhaps achieve immortality, with his work copied and kept in libraries, in the event that the world did not end. He promised that he loved the Church with all his heart. He asked most fervently that the man who was dear to him be well and waiting for him.

How he missed the Librarian! It was the only reason for him to go back to the Monastery, to hold his friend again and communicate philosophies that they read to each other and whispered about with passion.

"I am devoted to Christ," Bartholomew assured the air around him, "to Jesus Christ the Son of God who died on the cross . . . who died . . . who died on the cross."

Perhaps the world should end, be cleansed as it was in the Great Flood; perhaps a world in which there were penisless boys and cow bone miracles should end. In the meantime, what was an intelligent man to do but to keep his eyes open and make his way as best he could. Let God decide the outcome of it all. Let man do his best to have warmth and food and not be overwhelmed by the chaos.

Nonetheless, Bartholomew shuddered once again at what his hand had encountered. He picked up the pail and walked back to the Church, occasionally shaking his head, occasionally laughing. If he were not compelled to keep his commitment to the Monastery, if he were not drawn back to it by a rich companionship with the Librarian and an inability to see himself as a fisherman like his father, he would have been a merry man. He would have laughed more. He would have strolled down the road and found a young man who was as lovable as Grey and had a good, healthy male's limbs and genitals. He would have gone on, far from Finnistuath and Tarmath like some druidic wanderer, for whatever time was left to the world, to eat, to drink, to love, and to see the living Pope. But circumstances being what they were, Bartholomew, a brother from the Cistercian Order of Tarmath, began to consider how best to take advantage of the absurdities of the world, including this Grey, this most handsome girl who lived as a boy. He prayed all the way back to the Church, continuing his conversation with the Virgin Mary, asking for some inspiration before he lost his senses and went back to his family in Arklow to ride the waves in a rickety boat and mend fishing nets.

# 15

WEARY, COLIN rubbed his eyes and squatted on a low ridge, watching the valley that spread out and ended on one side in blue-gray hills. He had been in those hills recently, with little to eat until a cow wandered up and let herself be milked. Perhaps he could have slaughtered it and fed well, but he had no stomach for killing what gave him gifts. The cow was one of many such miracles that kept his faith in the world's capacity for kindness warm in his belly.

He slowly moved his head and eyed the smoky air above a place in the distance where the town of Tarmath bustled. It was a place he could not stroll into in daylight without some risk, for he was known there as a thief. But he was too often hungry to keep to the woods. And like any man who wasn't a recluse saint, he wanted someone's touch, someone's back to lay his hand on during a howling night, someone's face to see close to his own, someone's ear to pour a joke into. Now alone, he looked at the valley and the Monastery that sat between him and Tarmath. In his recollection, the Monastery's stores were usually good, having in them what could keep a man alive for many weeks. And Colin knew that the winter was going to be long and cruel.

The Monastery at Tarmath sank into the valley between the hills and the town of Tarmath, hidden, like an ashamed or frightened old man. Smoke wafted from its multi-chimneyed roof. Trees and vines protected it, obscuring the large gate made of warped wood and rusting iron.

Inside was a yard in which a garden of spindly plants and withering greens neighbored a pig pen where three large black pigs spent their lives languidly waiting for slaughter.

The smell of the place was a sweet and pungent concoction. Sometimes wood smoke overwhelmed other odors. It was a sweet smell of burning oak and hickory; and there was a moldy dampness, mixed with the smell of urine and candles and bread baking. Occasionally the corpse of some bird who got trapped inside the flue or of a mouse dead and hidden behind the altar gave the honeyed stench of death to the halls.

And the sounds? During the day there was sometimes laughter, and, of course, chanting. There was chanting during all the Offices—an echoing piety that calmed even the hawks and their prey in the long meadow that stretched to the woods and stream to the south. Tools clacked in the yard and in the kitchen: shovel and hoe hitting ground, knife hitting the table through meat or bread or turnip, pestle grinding grain. Young men, new monks, provided most of the laughter and supposedly forbidden conversation. And they sometimes were responsible for the weeping, which often followed a loud scolding in the voice of the Abbot. Where two or more gathered there was muttering. Where the two or more included the Abbot, his voice vibrated beneath all others, invoking the names of saints or God Himself. The Abbot either whispered so that one had to lean in to catch each word, or boomed some scripture or admonishment. Sometimes he bellowed loud accusations that were followed by the soft, brisk slapping of worn leather shoes against the stone floors of the dark halls.

There were days in which the halls filled with the sound of a hard rain, or a strong wind through the trees around the Monastery. Talk subsided as nature commanded attention and made men's business seem small. There were nights when a scream came through the place like a flash of lightning. Things scurried; something fell in the kitchen; a quiet rain rustled the trees all around the place; a dog who had been banished from the village barked; a monk moaned—dreaming, masturbating, regretting, freezing.

Cold drafts blew in some places, which the older monks knew well enough when it came to seating assignments in the chapel. Thinking he had a choice spot in the chapel, against the wall on which he might lean and doze, a new monk quickly realized he was in the path of a wicked draft. The few cells, left to brothers who had some official duties—the Sacrist or Cellarer or Librarian or Prior—were particularly cold, with damp stones; some older monks preferred the damp coldness that reduced the number of bedbugs one had to contend with. The dormitory was a long room on the second floor in the front of the Monastery over the entrance hall; it had long windows, which gave some cheerful light from time to time but which were often shuttered against wind and rain and cold. Over the years, the monks who had to sleep in rows in that room devised methods by which to warm the place, stuffing reeds in the shutter cracks, draping old blankets over them. The effect was that in winter the dormitory was a dark and ragged tomb, fit only for the few hours between Compline and Matins.

Stiff and trembling with cold, well into the first of summer, the monks sat in the frater listening to scriptures, pushing warm bread into their mouths, gratefully breathing the steam that came up from their bowls of oatmeal. The ale was good. And sometimes there was a stew for supper, or a pig was slaughtered and there was a bit of bacon in the porridge. The vow of poverty freed some to come close to God and left others to consider the cruel suffering of human existence.

In the Monastery at Tarmath, the end of the world often seemed imminent.

And the Abbot spoke often of the end of the world, sometimes using the Book of Revelation as support and sometimes using astronomical charts that the Librarian prepared with help from the Pope's astronomers, who sent messages to all the Church's clerics about the position of the planets. The Abbot spoke of the reasons for the world's end: the wickedness of humans, their violence, their arrogance, their lack of discipline, their sexual longings and misconduct.

At first the new monks, the Irish lads who had the calling, were glad that the Abbot was a Norman Irishman, not English or French as some abbots were. But the Abbot of Tarmath had been schooled in England and therefore championed some of the stricter rules there, highly influenced by Saint Augustine. East of Ireland, in societies considered more civilized by scholars and clerics, celibacy was the standard for clerics: abbots, priests, and monks did not marry.

Soon enough, the new brothers longed for the fairies of their youth, which their mothers had warned them about—the spirits that laughed and played mischief, that understood human desires and pleasures. Fairies marked a man's body but only played with his soul. If they dared to enter that dank monastery, the fairies would pull at the Abbot's robe, hide his prayer book, come to him naked and beautiful in the night. Even the Abbot, the monks whispered while tilling the garden, could not resist a fairy woman whose body felt like silk, whose mouth was wet with honey, whose legs opened to reveal Heaven. He seemed to be a man made for fucking and fighting and reciting poetry at the same time. For they all knew that though the Abbot had severe moods, he was a man who could linger over the feel of a violet's velvet leaf, who could also hurl a leather ball with the force of a catapult, a combination fairy women were particularly drawn to. He held in his taut and muscular body the holy tension that made others feel unworthy with their petty concerns or merry moments. He asked for nothing from the monks that he did not do himself. When they fasted for three days, he began a day early. And when he decided to have an extra cup of ale with the meal, the whole community was given the same bonus. They loved him well for not being the man one would pick from a group of players to be the Abbot, but being one anyway, with fierce standards.

Colin saw the Abbot walk with a full stride out of the Monastery door, straight toward him, as though he had business with the distant figure. An instinct to crouch and slink behind the ledge he squatted on was outdone by a determination to be still, to let the Abbot come and interrogate him and threaten him with blows. To wrestle with this Abbot might be a fine entertainment, a distraction from hunger and loneliness. He had some anger still for the man who shoved him out into the frosted dawn for not being devout enough, for not respecting the Abbot's authority, for snooping about like a thief. Hungry or not, Colin would fight the man gladly and then let him live to remember who was stronger. He hated the man for his arrogance and envied him for his faith and discipline.

Colin stood up and the Abbot saw him, shaded his eyes, and looked right at him. There the two men stood, looking intently at each other and seeing many different things: authority, freedom, mockery, arrogance, the image of what they sometimes wished they were. The Abbot walked toward the stream, raising his eyes every few seconds to where Colin still stood. Colin moved along the ridge and then descended at a gradual angle. When the two men were close enough to each other to hear words shouted, the Abbot called out, "Ahh, the man who might have been a sainted monk were it not for his love of wine and sleep!"

Colin trotted down the hill now and came face-to-face with the Abbot in a flurry of pheasants rising up from a nearby nest.

The Abbot grabbed Colin's arm as though to fend him off.

"This is a brutal place without wine," Colin said, throwing the man's hand off of him. The two men stared at each other.

"It's brutal to those who don't have the strength to bear it, who don't know what's good for them," the Abbot answered.

"I know more than I should about this place and its misery."

"I'll agree with that."

The Abbot started to move off, to dismiss Colin, who said, "Do you still have the Pope's box?"

The Abbot turned and poked his finger against Colin's chest.

"There is no box. You and that sot drank yourselves into fantasies. You had him in your pocket because you gave him someone to drink with. There's no box except the empty one on your shoulders."

Colin laughed.

"The Church and its secrets, its privileges and manipulations, its gold hats and fancy robes . . . its jeweled boxes . . . The Pope's box it is, and makes you hungry monks who can't come up with an honest trade think you have importance."

"None of this is your business. You're a common thief who gives himself mystery so as to put his prick in maidens' cunts and then steal their brooches."

Rage came up into Colin's throat like vomit and he spit at the Abbot's feet.

"You've a foul mouth for one of the Pope's boys," he said and stepped forward. The Abbot pushed him back and Colin stumbled.

"Is it my freedom that gets under your skin so, Abbot, the fact that I wasn't obedient and in love with you like the other lads there?" He tossed his head toward the Monastery.

The Abbot now took a few steps toward the stream and without turning to Colin said, "If I see you lurking around here again, I will kill you myself, like a flea pinched between my fingers." He squatted down and splashed water on his face, groaning a little and rubbing water on the back of his neck.

"I have tossed your beggar's arse out once before and I'll . . ."

But when the Abbot stood up and turned around with his face dripping, there was no one there, no movement anywhere among the grasses and trees, no sign of Colin.

16

GREY SLEPT AGAIN under the writing table, away from Bartholomew, even though the winter was carved out of ice that year. Even
the air was made of solid cold, so that one was never free of chill. The two
babies born in Finnistuath that winter died, shivering and weak. The trees
wore white cloaks, but they shivered, too, and the crows puffed up their
feathers and hunched their shoulders. Half of the cattle froze to death.
The snow fell in sheets, making hills out of plows and wagons. Travelers
came through to tell stories of their companions frozen on the road. In this
misery, Grey wondered what poem Colin might have made of it.

Grey listened to the talk in the Church about the end of the world being
at hand, about the days growing darker and darker until there would only be
darkness. The solstice, many said, would come and go and the days would
continue to shorten, for God was taking the sun farther and farther away.
There would be no spring, people whispered—not ever a spring again.
Water was abundant, but dry wood was precious, and the guards from the
Manor went to every house, even the houses of the English settlers, and announced that the household had either to spend one day each week, from
sun up to sun down, gathering wood to be dried for the Manor, or have their
own store depleted. Several cottages were abandoned in order that two
families could share one hearth and the warmth of more bodies. And when
they were huddled together at night, the old Plowman said to the fire, "If
there be no more spring, it's because of the whore we've made of God's
earth, may He have mercy on us." The Midwife muttered about turning
people off the land and letting sheep tear up the grasses by the roots; the
grandfather in one of the Irish laborer's cottages grumbled about forests
emptied of trees to ship to England as lumber. The old ones remembered
stories of the chieftains who were elected and then were married to the
earth on which they ruled, promising like smitten grooms to protect and
honor what they wed. They told stories of a time when holy men shunned
finery and took up the sacred duty of poetry.

The Lord of the Manor had his own serious concerns and requested that the monk from Tarmath and the Priest come to the Manor and speak to him personally about their opinions concerning the world's end. He was angry; his wife was ill, suffering from some weakness in her limbs. She could not walk on her own, and the Lord was sure she would die soon. He wanted to be assured that the world would not end before he remarried, to a young woman from Kent whose father wished to have some investment in Ireland, and who wanted his fourteen-year-old daughter separated from a romance with her fifteen-year-old cousin.

Grey was taken along to the Manor, carrying a pail in which the Church's embers were kept and replenished. He would see that the embers did not go out and add to them from the Manor hearth. This was a gratefully accepted duty, since it meant staying close to a source of warmth. Indeed, the Manor itself was far warmer than any other place in Finnistuath, and it was full of the Lord's family and all the servants.

The dying Lady was wrapped in furs on a couch laid out near the large hearth. The Lord had gathered some chairs in a circle nearby and motioned for the two clerics to sit. Grey stood behind them, unable to understand all that they said since they spoke in English. He was glad to be warm, to be given bread. He was glad to have his private thoughts, which included some fear of Bartholomew, who was the only human being to share the secret of Grey's sin: the sin of wanton ignorance, the sin of having no clear identity with which to perform one's duties in God's Great Chain of Being as the Priest had explained it to him. He feared he was making a mockery of God's order. Grey had grown silent. He listened to the Latin and English words, falling like pebbles on wooden planks, without the softness of his own language.

Perched with straight back on one of the chairs, the Priest had a book of scriptures open and was reading from passages concerning the end of the world. As far as Grey could determine from the phrases he understood and the gestures he knew well, the clerics were staging a half-hearted debate concerning how soon the end of the world was to occur and whether or not it was to be evidenced by a horrific winter, such as the one the land was experiencing then. But the clerics knew, as Bartholomew explained later, that their part in this scene was to reassure the Lord of the Manor that there were signs that he would have time to bury the one wife and wed another.

Grey heard voices behind him and turned to see Red sitting beside his mother, holding her hand. The Lady of the Manor raised her head and spoke to Grey in Gaelic.

"Do you sing?" she asked.

Behind Grey, Bartholomew was leaning forward intently speaking in English, looking oiled and scholarly in his assurances that there would be great plagues and fires at the end of the world, not cold and ice. Bartholomew's words were directed at the Lord, but his eyes attended to Grey and the interaction with Red and the dying Lady.

"I?" Grey asked.

Red looked away, into the fire, and yawned. He hadn't slept much, so as not to leave his mother alone with her pain. Pain that he could not alleviate was an insult to him, a horrible indication of the powerlessness in him which his father laughed at.

"Yes, boy, do you sing?"

"No, my lady." His face sweated and he put the pail of embers down.

"I wish you did."

Grey looked back at the clerics. The Lord was calling a servant over to bring a pitcher of ale. Bartholomew stared at Grey, narrowing his eyes, studying his own thoughts.

Grey turned toward the Lady's couch and said, "I know a song from my childhood, that my sister taught me."

"Come sing it to me, then, for the end of the world is coming sooner for me than for others."

Grey stood before the couch, his back to the fire. Red pulled him by the hand so that he stood to the side, so as not to block the Lady from the warmth. Red kept holding Grey's hand, in an absentminded insistence that the boy do something to please his mother. Grey felt the touch as a firm kindness.

"Go on, then, sing," the Lady said.

Red let go of Grey's hand.

Grey breathed deeply, closed his eyes and sang,

> Sleep a little, a little little,
> Thou needst not feel fear nor dread
> Lad to whom I give my love,
> Son of the Goatherd, Gregory

Tonight the grouse does not sleep
Above the high, stormy, heathery hill;
Sweet the cry of her clear throat,
Sleepless among the streams.

The unwavering, high voice silenced the Manor, even the discussion among the clerics and the Lord. But the Lady sneered and said in English, "He trills like the peasants, curling the notes around in the Irish way. Oh, I miss England. Shall I die in this place?" Grey only understood her weeping and the words "peasant," "England," and "die." Then the Lady gasped for breath, and Red called on the Priest to come and say prayers beside her. Grey stepped back to the pail, and just in time, for the embers required stirring and replenishing. When he looked up from his job, he saw Red's eyes filled with tears. He looked away.

When the Priest leaned over, the Lady said, in English, "I hear that Pope Clement the Sixth sends all his unwanted filth to Ireland." The Priest straightened up, his face red. The Lady coughed. "Just say what you can to get me to Heaven."

Grey understood "Pope Clement" and "Ireland" and "Heaven"; and he understood the Priest's countenance as one that came before he struck blows.

"She is not herself," Red said sternly to the insulted Priest. "Give her comfort."

So the Priest bent over her again and whispered in Latin as she fell asleep.

In a few days there was a thaw. When the wind blew, it no longer snapped branches off of trees. Brown earth showed on the road in the footprints left in the snow. The Priest said prayers of thanks.

In fact, spring came early, and the warmth stayed, though there was rain and wind. And then a new catastrophe occurred. The river flooded, flowing over the new bridge, covering the eastern bog and the Plowman's fields with a sloshing mixture of water and earth that drowned plants. Inconveniently, the Lady of the Manor died while the river was still raging over its banks. Her body lay in the Manor as the Lord's son Joseph entered officiously as father of his own two sons and living a Lord's life near Dublin. He argued with his brother about her frantic death wish, to be sent back to England for burial in her family's church there, in a tomb near the font of holy water where some might be splashed on her from time to time. She had, at the end, clawed at all who sat beside her and said the same thing, "I will not be put to rest in this savage land." Joseph determined that there was too much expense in her whim. He said to Red, "You're willing to spend money when it isn't yours. Let father bury her here and have his travels to fetch his wife unimpeded."

"You would defy her dying wish?"

After conceding, Joseph said to his brother, "Have you no plans of your own but to leech from Father's stores? If you would travel to my land I could see what prospects there are for you among my wife's family."

Red left without responding. He rode his stallion into the woods and along the river as though hunting demons.

The entire village was put into service building a new bridge over the old one, so that the Lady of the Manor could be transported across the river and eastward to Dublin to be shipped to England. The Lord would take care of the business of burying his dead wife and collecting the new one on the same journey. Red would go with him, and on the return trip stay on the other side of the river and perhaps go south to begin life in the Monastery. His brother was making a speech about his hawks when Red interrupted him to announce his plans. Red was considering several images of himself as a religious, including becoming a mendicant Franciscan, a man who shed all indulgences and took only what was given for subsistence. He wanted, above all else, to reduce his own life to its simplest aspect, to find the basic material of his soul and of God's creation—the *prima materia* that gave order to all the cruel chaos, which, he had learned, even wealth did not assuage. For he had now in his mind a triptych that featured his mother's gasping and horrified face, his father's smirk as he watched his wife die, and the pelt of his childhood dog, now part of the mat of decay in the forest.

During the building of the bridge, Bartholomew spoke with Red about the religious calling. He listened to the Lord's son's confessions, stories of temptation and lust and pleasure that stirred an idea in the monk's mind. The ingredients for this idea had been collecting since the day his hands touched Grey's womanhood.

A week after the Lady's death, when Red was extremely agitated by the thought of her corpse swelling in a cart in the stables, he and Bartholomew sat outside on stools in a patch of sunlight.

"My mother died without the sensual pleasures she longed for, the sights and smells of her home. God takes us according to his own rules," Red said, tears standing in his eyes. "I think of her body's decay and think of my own body and its living sensations, its longings."

Bartholomew nodded, and continued nodding as Red added, "I have longings. I long to consummate my lust. I have . . . I have certain visions that arouse me, and I do not know if this is a sin that has any cure. I pray that I be . . ."

Bartholomew interrupted and said to the Lord's son, "In your troubles with carnal desires, perhaps you should consider that God speaks to you to celebrate His creation with sensual rituals. There are factions in the Church that believe most sincerely in such an approach."

"I want only to find the causes of disease and sin and pain and then to mollify them."

The monk replied, "Surely, the antidote to pain is pleasure."

Red looked down at the ground between his boots and shook his head.

"Is our own pleasure, though, pleasing to God?"

Bartholomew pretended to think hard on this and then leaned back and shook his own head vigorously.

"Well, you see, there is demonic vice and Godly pleasure."

Red stood up and stretched and then sat down again, laughing.

"I don't know of any woman willing to serve a man's devotion to God through her flesh, unless it be in marriage, and I have no plan to marry, for I have seen my mother and father's marriage as a Hell on Earth. Besides, Joseph has married and provided my father with heirs."

Bartholomew nodded now, as though understanding Red's dilemma. He pointed a finger at him and narrowed his eyes.

"You know, I do know of such a woman, a woman whose place it is to do just such service."

Red laughed again, nervously now, one side of his mouth up and the other down.

"You are speaking of a whore, then."

"Oh, no, no . . . not at all." Bartholomew sounded indignant.

"Is this woman here in Finnistuath? I know all the women here and cannot imagine . . ."

"She is available. She is nearby. That is all I can say."

Red leaned forward, his elbows on his thighs. He whispered, "Is she comely?"

"She is a rare and youthful beauty." Bartholomew's eyebrows went up in assurance of the marvelous truth of what he said.

Still affecting the nervous laugh, Red said, "And what must be done, what part must I play in this?"

Bartholomew closed his eyes and raised one hand and said, "Ahh, it is nothing more than tithing a coin or two. And a letter if you will, to the Pope advocating me as a scribe and scholar. For you see, I mean to travel the world and study its treasures. A letter from a nobleman . . ."

Red held up both his hands, palms toward the monk.

"I don't know, brother. I think that I should not . . ."

"She is a virgin." Bartholomew was now leaning forward.

"So she has no past in this service?"

"The solace she is ready to offer to you as God's holy creation is pure. I think some gold and that letter . . ."

The plans were made. Red would meet Bartholomew the next day at the spring, for once the decision was made to do so, Red could not wait long. He would need to leave soon to accompany his dead mother. And now that he had it in his head that he and some woman who was beautiful and willing would be together without moral restrictions, he could think of nothing else. It seemed the only thing to soothe from his mind the awful pictures of his mother's agony and then her silent corpse and his father rubbing his hands together as though in front of some fire just kindled.

That evening, Bartholomew pulled Grey from the hearth and pressed the onetime boy's shoulders against the outside wall of the Church.

"Listen, then, there is some business that you must play a most important part in, some business with the people of the Manor."

Grey wriggled a little and said, "I do not like going there, for the dead Lady still lies beneath a cloth."

"You are not going to the Manor. You are meeting the Lord's son Red for the purposes of . . . of soothing him . . . of relieving his grief."

Grey stared into Bartholomew's eyes until the monk was irritated.

"Have you heard what I've said? There is a service you must perform for the Lord's son and for God Himself."

"How will I know what to do?" Grey asked.

"It will come to you easily, I am sure." Bartholomew let go of her shoulders. "You must bathe well and comb your hair, and you must wrap yourself in some cloth. We'll take the cloth from the altar. Yes, that will do well. This must not be a low act. It must be pure."

"I am to wear nothing but a cloth?" Grey asked. Bartholomew waved his hand to clear the question from the air.

Grey persisted: "What will happen when my body is revealed?"

Bartholomew tapped his lips with his finger and then said, "We will put a veil over your head—the veil made of the lace in the chapel. He will not know who you are."

"What will he do?"

"He will touch you. He will be smitten with you, and he will fornicate with you."

Grey stared at Bartholomew without speaking. She envisioned one of the goats, mud hanging from its shaggy coat, mounting another goat, who continued to nibble grass as the male goat thrust into her.

"But fornication is a sin," Grey said.

"Not if it is in God's service. And what could be more in God's service than the soothing of a gentleman's painful melancholy? You have a woman's body, which God has made comely and able to give much solace. You cannot let God's gifts go fallow."

"What is going to become of me?" Grey said. "I haven't thought on the things that women do."

"I will pray for you. I will take care of you."

"How will you take care of me?" Now Grey was weeping.

"I will buy food for you. I will keep your secrets and support your ambitions."

"Will you give something to my sisters and my mother? Will you buy food for them?"

"Yes, yes. I will do that. I will pray for your mother as well, that she find some peace in this life and the next."

And that was exactly the right prayer to be prayed, Grey thought.

Bartholomew patted her on the arm and said, "I have had a revelation, and it precisely concerns your welfare and mine. And it will benefit both of us greatly. For now you are simply and quite briefly a man's fantasy, which means that you simply remain silent and give him pleasure. If you can do that, you will be well taken care of. Do you hear me?"

Grey said, "He is a rich man. He has authority over me and can do me harm."

"And you have something that has power even over a rich man, and that's the wondrous beauty of it!"

the whore

## 17

*T*HE MIDWIFE had survived the winter but sacrificed to it much of her eyesight. She was shaking out blankets and saw Grey's form coming up the hill to her hut. She recognized the gracefulness of the stride and the strength in the gestures of hurling. Grey was walking along in the evening, throwing rocks at various targets, hitting each one as intended. She had seen, down in the Plowman's field, the Plowman's grandson sitting on the stump with a few of the other young men of the village around him. They had turned to watch Grey, and the Plowman's grandson had stood and seemed about to summon his old friend, but Grey had raised a hand in stiff greeting and run up the road.

Grey stood before the Midwife and said, "I will ask my mother this question, but I ask you first. Am I boy or girl?"

The Midwife laughed, showing her good teeth.

"It doesn't matter, after all, does it?" she said.

"It must."

"Your father wanted you to be a boy and so you were."

"And now?"

"Now it is your choice. Perhaps you have uncovered a freedom the world did not know existed. Or perhaps it is an old freedom rediscovered. Women were warriors, you know. In my mother's family there were stories about the women who rode and fought and were wizards in these skills. It's the Englishmen like to scorn or pity us now, pretending we have always been weak when in fact we have always been strong."

"I wanted only to continue being a boy and be blessed with my deformities as my mother told me and grow up to be a fine warrior who can speak directly to God."

The Midwife shrugged. "You can be whatever you choose. I wish I had known such freedom existed."

"I will be stoned to death for deception."

"Why must the deception be revealed?"

Grey leaned forward and said, like a boy who is about to show a very large toad, "I am to be presented to a man for the purpose of fornication. Someone else knows that I have the features of a woman and . . . and arrangement has been made."

The Midwife stood. "Who makes such an arrangement?" She looked wildly around her as though the offending person might be hiding in her hut.

"I do not want to tell. I have agreed to it and . . ."

"Who uses your secret to make you a whore who lets her body be used for pleasure? And who is the man you must be whore to?"

"I cannot tell. I wanted only for you to tell me if I was born a male or female."

Agitated, the Midwife replied, "You were born with the body you stand in before me. And it is one neither I nor your mother can protect now. You must protect it yourself."

The Midwife squatted down, and Grey said to her bent head, "He is not a bad man. This man that I am to be with, he seems most good to me, and I would have him for a husband." These words sounded to Grey as though they came from another mouth into her own ear as a taunting consideration.

The Midwife spit out a laugh. "And I will tell you that most men want to make whores of their wives, for they get their pleasure without expense that way."

"You wouldn't be saying, would you, Midwife, that a woman has no thoughts of pleasure? For I think that I would forget my transformation altogether if I were to have to shun pleasures that men are taking. Don't women have pleasure, then?" Grey thought of her sister rubbing herself all over the servant from the Manor in the woods, but then saw her crouching in the corner, pregnant and abused.

The Midwife laughed to herself and muttered, "It was your mother who wanted this game to be played. She wanted it so your father would not kill you."

Grey's eyes felt hot, and she wanted then to strike the Midwife with a stick for her part in the sickening ignorance of her life.

"My father? My father loved me. He died for his love of me."

"That he did," was the quiet answer. "He loved you like his own true son."

"I am ignorant, a half-wit like my father, a fool for letting a Goatherd's wishes make my shape and place in life and my mother, too, with her talk of monasteries and me praying to God all night and day."

"People believe all manner of thing."

"I only want to believe what is true, Midwife."

Grey left, striding down the hill to her mother's cottage, trying to think of how a female would walk, would move her arms.

Mary came in with Caerla and Deirdre, both of whom had grown so thin they teetered when they stood and walked.

"I am your daughter," Grey told her before any other greeting.

Mary sat down on the stool. The two girls, silent and rickety, moved to the one bench and sat down, holding onto each other as though the force of emotions in the cottage might blow them into the sky.

The mother squeezed her hand into a fist, still lying on the table; she leaned forward, taut and angry.

"Then thank God you were a boy and leave my cottage. You can be whatever you like; your father's dead, thanks be to you. Be whatever you like and let us starve or freeze or whatever the heavens want us to do."

The cottage and all its contents, humans, pots, baskets, skins, wooden implements, began to fade as Grey looked at it, everything turning brown.

"I do love you, mother. I will do whatever I can to help you, to give you peace in this life and the next. And I loved my father."

"No," the old woman said. "Do not sing me that song." She let her fist blossom into a rough hand that protected her face from the words of her child.

The two daughters on the bench stared at Grey, their eyes as big as walnuts.

"Mother, bless me. I didn't mean for father to die. I made sure he was buried in the churchyard. If you want—" Grey had to pause so as not to sob "—if you want, mother, I will stay here and be Goatherd, or I will go to Tarmath, to the Monastery."

"The Bailiff, who comes to collect my debts, he tells me what the stone says. He tells me that it says, Gregory the Goatherd was a Fool."

The room became darker, empty of color. Mary turned to the hearth to stir it and blow into it. A small flame came up and she fed it a few sticks. There was a loud pop and a small fountain of sparks.

"I will leave now."

"Yes, leave."

"I will want to say good-bye to my Fiona," Grey said. Her fingertips were touching her mother's fingertips on the table. She felt their hardness and warmth for an instant and then stood and went to Caerla and Deirdre on the bench. She took their bony hands in hers until she heard Fiona come in, leaning on two sticks to walk. The two went outside and looked into each other's eyes.

Grey whispered fiercely, "We could go, you and I, and wander. I am no longer a boy and can make my way." She stopped and thought that she meant that she was now a young man, not that she was now a young woman. No matter. "We could do well, leaving this evening, and we could . . ."

Fiona let the two sticks fall and wrapped her two arms around one of Grey's.

"God forgive me, I am afraid to leave this cottage and the goats who feed us," Fiona said.

"Fiona," Grey whispered, "The Priest said that there are no fairies, but I think I have seen one."

"I see them everywhere," Fiona said, as though she were weary of fairies.

A pale star became visible in the sky, and Fiona said, "Don't be afraid, Grey, for you are well fed and have wit and strength to help you."

Grey leaned over and picked up the two sticks, placing them in her sister's hands. She placed her hands over Fiona's and held them there tightly, as though they needed the sticks and each other to bear certain truths.

It was early evening and Bartholomew stood outside the Church, the breeze blowing his robes as he waited for Grey to come closer. Grey was dragging her feet, dizzy and tired. She felt free of any form, invisible to the world, light enough to be blown like smoke by the slightest breeze.

Bartholomew chatted away excitedly about the preparations that Grey needed to make, reminding her to bathe and to be ready with the altar cloth and the lace by the spring at noon. Grey performed the duties the Priest expected, but left a serving of mush sweetened with mutton fat on her own plate. Bartholomew took the plate and cleaned it. He told her to pray to Saint Brigid and to know that if the Lord's son were to try to harm her, he would put a stop to it.

Standing by the spring, Grey tried to empty her mind of all thoughts except for observation. Any thought, she discovered, was barbed with confusion about the future or bafflement about the past. It seemed that she had spent many years in wasted thoughts, thoughts based on untruths. Better to observe than to think. Better to keep one's wits as sharp as a raven's beak. She held the altar cloth tightly around her naked body and then had to adjust the white veil, which was held loosely to her head with wild white roses and their thorny stems.

Red was led by Bartholomew to this vision draped in altar cloth and lace veil. He noted the slender arms and the fingers, dirty and rough. He halted a moment and glanced at Bartholomew. The monk nodded him forward.

Grey could see Red through the lace over her head. Sunlight made the hairs on his strong forearms sparkle. She breathed deeply and prayed to Saint Brigid for help. Bartholomew strode past them both and indicated that they should follow. Grey looked down at her bare feet stepping through grasses and thistles. The toes were streaked with dirt and there were fleabites around her ankles. A few yards from the spring was a blanket spread out between two bushes. It was festooned with tiny wild rose buds. None of the three spoke a word. A thrush called out from a nearby tree, and then again from a tree farther away.

Bartholomew bowed like a servant and backed away. Swiftly Red sat down upon the blanket and with agitated hands began to undo his clothing. When he was sitting naked, Grey, still standing, saw through the veil the familiar erection. She stood still, aware of herself as an icon, like one of the statues of the saints in the chapel, regally draped in holy cloth whose few golden threads sparkled when the sun moved out of the clouds. A breeze blew the lace around her head, and she saw the world as a gentle frenzy of patterns in green and brown, white and blue. Looking at Red, she felt like a saint, manifesting a great compassion for him and a strange power over him. He was old—almost thirty—and there were lines around his eyes, but his orange hair was still thick, tied back with a strip of leather.

Grey knelt down beside him and they looked at each other's eyes through the lace. Red reached for the veil and Grey jerked her head back. But then she unwrapped the altar cloth and was kneeling beside him, her torso naked. Red stared at her breasts and put his hand on her belly. Grey shivered and Red laid her down and covered them both with the altar cloth.

His hand kneaded her belly until she took it and placed it between her legs where Bartholomew had felt her. She wanted him to know that place, to feel it and know with certainty that she was a female made of warm fertile places. She wrapped her fingers around his erection, holding it tightly and feeling it move. In that posture, as Grey nestled more closely against

Red's side, he ejaculated. Grey removed her hand and pulled away. As she wiped the creamy liquid on her hand in the grasses, Red gathered her to him, breathing against her head and holding her as though she might unfurl wings and take him away into the sky and he must hold on to her or fall a long distance to the ground.

Grey finished wiping her hand on the cloth they lay on and hummed a song. As she continued to hum, she played with Red's hand, lifting it before her veiled eyes and tracing all of the fingers with her own, weaving their fingers together and apart. She went silent after she placed the hand upon her breast and he caressed it in slow circles. Red fell asleep, his hand resting where it had stopped in mid-caress. It was the sleep of great relief, like a pause in his life in a place where he felt no one's pain or scorn. Grey was loathe to move, to do anything that would end their bodies' closeness. There they lay until the thrush's notes were too distant to hear, and until Grey saw Bartholomew's face peering through the nearby bushes.

 **18**

BEFORE THE LADY'S casket was loaded onto the wagon, Bartholomew announced that he would finally be returning to the Monastery
in Tarmath. He eagerly prepared his satchel for the trek. He stuffed papers
and leggings and rope and wine skins into two leather pouches and a
woolen bundle tied with a leather strap. He wrapped leather straps around
his ledger, which had grown fat with pressed leaves and blossoms. The
Priest hovered around the monk with clasped hands as though in a perpet-
ual state of prayer.

"You must assure me that pilgrims will be directed here. I have already
engaged the Lord's promise to build a hall for them. I can acquire another
relic. I have heard that there is a piece of Saint Brigid's cape available."

Grey sang to herself in the chapel where she swept:

> *Ah! When Finn and the Fian lived*
> *They loved the mountain better than the monastery*
> *Sweet to them the blackbird's call.*
> *They would have despised the tonguing of your bells.*

In the doorway, Grey squinted toward the Manor, trying to see through
all the trees if there was any sign of Red. But he had left and was standing
behind the cart on which his mother's bloated body lay.

In the past two days, Grey had thought of Red with only brief pauses, no
longer able to give her mind only to observation. Now she was agitated by
thoughts of Red's hand on her breasts, and his face mystically mottled by
the pattern of lace and the shadows of trees. And if the thoughts were not
fixed on the brief past she had shared with Red, they were on the possibili-
ties of the future intimacies she would share with him.

Suddenly, Bartholomew was before her and took her by the shoulders to
speak softly to her.

"He is a Lord's son. You are . . . you are a Goatherd's . . . daughter," for he
recognized the countenance of infatuation.

He told her, "Your thoughts are in the Manor with your reason. You will come with me to the Monastery. Red is going there. You will see him there."

"What do you mean?" Grey stopped sweeping but gripped the broom handle harder.

"You are coming with me to the Monastery."

Grey looked all around her but found no clarification in the niches or cracked stones.

Bartholomew rubbed his head so that the tonsured hair stuck out in random tufts.

"And we shall see changes there, yes, you and I. To bloody, aching Hell with Finnistuath and its yellow-toothed Lord."

This made Grey smile. And Bartholomew shared the smile with her as a bluebird made an arcing dive from an oak branch across the doorway to a nearby bush.

Bartholomew farted and said, "Pardon."

Then he added, "I promise you that the plan that I have for you and me, a plan I believe that Mother Mary herself has inspired, will be full of holy pleasures."

Grey sighed. "I will take no pleasure but with Red, for that is my place in this life. And I will learn what to do to please God."

"All right, all right. But listen, you must continue as a boy. They do not allow females there. You are used to this ruse, and it will make matters easier to arrange." He lifted Grey's face by the chin. "Do you understand me? Hmm? We are brothers, are we not? Going to the Monastery at Tarmath, you to assist me in chores as you have done here?"

Grey nodded awkwardly, her head still held up by Bartholomew's plump hand.

He removed his hand to place it firmly on Grey's head, as a blessing and as an encouragement for her to discipline her thoughts.

"If the world will end soon," the monk said quietly, "let us taste every cake on the table and praise God for it all. And may God protect us."

"I must tell my mother," Grey said. "I must tell her that I will be going to the Monastery so she can be pleased by this news."

They could then hear the cart in the distance making a loud noise as its thick wooden wheels rolled with its dead over planks set over patches of mud in the road to the new bridge. Red was behind the casket, now on a horse that danced a little and tossed its head. He was thinking of the saintly fairy whore. He was hoping that she had the power to appear at random times and in secretive places. He told himself that his mother would have approved, probably without saying so directly, of her son being soothed as he had been, by a holy vision.

 **19**

FROM A DISTANCE, the Monastery seemed to Grey to be a ruin, overgrown with vines and trees. Bartholomew stopped on the hill above it and leaned on his staff, breathing hard. He sank down, squatting and bending his head over. They had passed by the village of Tarmath, which Grey had always imagined as a city full of goods and people and adventure. She could smell roasting meat on the breeze and could see a shamble of structures that far exceeded the number of dwellings in Finnistuath. She had given herself the courage to leave the only place she had ever known by telling herself she would finally visit the great and magical Tarmath. But where the road forked to go either into the town or up to the hill above the Monastery, they left the town behind. Bartholomew's pace was dogged and his silence deepened; a weight seemed to grow on his back as he got nearer to his old home. At one point, when the road had grown narrow and deeply shadowed by bushes and trees, Bartholomew squatted down, his sweaty hand sliding without will down the walking staff he had fashioned after crossing the bridge out of Finnistuath.

"Are you ill?" Grey asked. She squatted down, too, and touched his shoulder. They had been walking all day, the last few hours in silence, as Bartholomew's face got paler.

"I'm just remembering the reasons I was glad to go away from the Monastery. There are times when the Abbot's fierce and secret worries, when the lack of cream and discourse . . . Well, there are winds that come through the stones of one's faith and devotion, if you know what I mean."

Grey knew what he meant about faltering faith. She had felt the nauseating shifts in the world: first discovering that a man of God could pass a cow bone off as a relic and have an innocent man beaten to death, and then finding out that she had been completely duped as to her own basic nature. But at least that ruse had given her something to punish the Priest with.

The night before, as they walked out of Finnistuath along the thinning path that went to the bridge, they had spoken of the Priest's fury at having his helper taken from him. Bartholomew had finally and dramatically demanded that Grey reveal to the Priest that she was not a boy. On their journey, the two spoke for an hour of the expression on the Priest's face when two full, white breasts with pale brown nipples were exposed in front of his yellowed eyes. Then there was Bartholomew's threat to tell the Manor—so English in their sense of propriety and image concerning clerics—"that, you, their holy Priest with all his holy relics, have slept beside a young girl for . . . How many years now?" Thus the stunned Priest was convinced to lodge no complaint against the monk for removing Grey to the Monastery. Bartholomew added, kindly, that recognition of the Priest's relics would be forthcoming, and he would certainly suggest himself that pilgrims go to Finnistuath.

As they began their trek to the Monastery of Tarmath, Grey had asked Bartholomew about his faith.

"If you know that the relics are false, why will you support them? It seems an insult to the saints, who are so beautiful and noble."

"People need something to hold, to touch, to help them believe in God and the saints and in the sacrifice of Jesus. Even false relics are sacred in their ability to . . . to soothe fears. And as priests are able to change wine into Christ's blood, well then, perhaps a cow's bone into a saint's bone."

Farther along on their journey, just after crossing the bridge and hearing their cloth-bound feet thudding on the wooden boards, Bartholomew had stopped and told Grey how they must behave upon arriving at the Monastery. The monk had searched near the banks for a good stick, and while stripping it of cumbersome bark and notches he said, "Listen well, for I've thought and studied upon the matter well. You'll be presented as a boy, as my helper. I'm Second Prior, you know, and there are countless tasks to perform. No doubt, the First Prior is adding curses to his daily prayers for the burden left him by my long absence. But I have sent letters. Are you listening to me?" Grey nodded, though she didn't stop hitting at the stalks of bracken around them with a stick.

"And in those letters," Bartholomew continued, "I said that I would return as soon as I finished my assessment of the relics."

Grey laughed at the mention of the relics and said, "And then you talked many days and nights about the Priest's beloved pilgrim's hall, and the winter was too cold to travel in, and then the river was up . . ." Over a year had passed.

"That is beside the matter. You are my helper now," Bartholomew said.

"You will do as I say. If you do as I say, you will stay out of trouble. But if your deceit is discovered, well, I cannot say what could happen to you. But I will help you. And you will help me."

"What will you help me do?" Grey asked.

"I will help you to become a monk, to understand the powerful wisdom of the Church, the Church that God created to give us comfort and guidance."

"Perhaps I should instead become a nun, going to a convent. And Red would be pleased by me as a woman in two ways: that I give him pleasure and that I was pious."

"It is too difficult to explain why a nun cannot give pleasure. I will explain that and other matters later. You are entering a privileged world of men who are journeying with great concentration and devotion to the heart of the universe and its purposes. The fact that you are a woman presents a delicate and perhaps most blessed dilemma to be puzzled out. But a nun . . . no, that is contrary to the vision I have seen of how we will make use of such a strange phenomenon as your flickering identity."

Grey had few visions other than of her tryst with Red.

They walked along then, passing only a smattering of people, including a goatherd and his six goats and a woman pulling a cart full of pottery and two men with satchels flung over their backs. Perhaps sensing in Grey's silence her unfurling terror at leaving all familiar things behind, Bartholomew had told her, "I will take care of you. We will always be truthful with each other. We will eat well and you will learn prayers and chants that have more power than relics."

He had stopped again on the road then, letting a woman and her daughter pass, carrying baskets of bread. Grey had looked mournfully at the passing bread.

Bartholomew had held Grey's shoulders and brought her close to him. "In the leaves and feathers I collect I feel the warmth of God's hand. These are the relics that I love, and some day I will travel the world and study all the varieties of creatures and plants."

Now as they squatted in the road, birds twittering around them, Grey considered running in the other direction, away from the monk and his Monastery. Bartholomew was unsettling in his new weariness. He straightened up and nodded, watching three soldiers on horseback approach, nod, and pass by.

Bartholomew adjusted the satchel that was slung over his shoulder and nudged Grey to move on.

And then Grey and Bartholomew walked on in silence until they came to the hill overlooking the Monastery and Bartholomew hesitated.

In a fluttering voice, Grey began a song:

> The moon reveals a tidy nest
> And all the fairies see
> The magic thrush who's born tonight
> And sings so merrily.

She pointed up to the clearing sky, where an onionskin half-moon could be seen though it was still daylight.

"Your voice," Bartholomew said, shaking his head. "It gives you away. It is too high a voice for a boy so tall. You must not sing. And you must not speak, pretending to be mute. You must pass yourself off as half-witted and make as little response as possible."

Grey looked away, back up at the gauzelike moon so as to squint and keep her tears from seeping out of her eyes. But Bartholomew saw her misery, saw that the fear of the unknown was overtaking her. He was losing patience with her and his own emotions, the growing coldness, and dread of the Abbot's moods as he approached the Monastery. They walked down the embankment on a thin path between carpets of sedge and thistle, Bartholomew weaving his arm through Grey's.

Three monks were gardening the ground to the right of the Monastery door, which was also open. Behind it seemed to be solid blackness. All three gardeners looked up and nodded at Bartholomew. One of them came over to speak with him. This man smiled widely, showing brown teeth and genuine pleasure. Bartholomew stood straighter. He was gathering strength.

"Good brother, I thought never to see you again," the grinning monk said. He kept both hands clasped behind his back as though to keep himself from embracing and caressing too heartily.

"Brother Calvin, it is good to see you again." There were tears in Bartholomew's eyes. "Here is Grey. A boy who wants to serve God. I have brought him with me as a helper. But you look well. You look well, Brother Calvin. You were ill when I left. I dared not to hope to see you."

"The Prior will be glad to hear you've returned and with a helper, after he's boxed your ears. But I'll tell you, the Prior's laziness has been a boon to us, a few extra hours of sleep when he himself sleeps past Matins."

"What else is there to tell?"

"The Librarian is well and grown as fat as you. He looks up the embankment many days I think in hopes of seeing you tumbling down it. And there are new lay monks." He pointed toward the long ground-level dormitory where the lay monks lived to labor and be near godly men and their official devotion.

As they spoke, Grey felt a coldness creeping up her legs, up through her chest, to her head. She was at her new home, a place of strangers, unknown to her. There was no family here, no familiar place or sight. She wanted then to be with the Priest, just as she had wanted, when she was first with the Priest, to be with her mother. Now both Priest and mother scorned her for betrayal. She had no home. She was welcome nowhere and by no one, except perhaps by Bartholomew, perhaps by Red wherever he was. But her monk companion's attention was taken now by this brother, Calvin, and no doubt would be further taken by others here who knew him.

She took a deep breath and waited beside Bartholomew.

By the time they entered Bartholomew's cell, where the two of them would sleep together, Grey determined that all she would do at this place was wait for Red. If he were not yet there, she would wait for him, soaking herself in holy serenity, learning from pious clerics how the world worked, how one was supposed to behave, and the exact methods of arriving at last in a place where there was nothing but affection and comfort.

Bartholomew was standing in the gray, dim room, touching his fingers to the stones to gauge their dampness. A cross made of black walnut hung on the wall above a narrow platform covered with moldy hay. There was a stool and a bucket in the corner. A bench along the wall opposite the bed held a tin candle holder with the stub of a candle in it and a brown leather book of prayers and psalms. The book's pages were swelled and crenellated with dampness.

Grey pulled on Bartholomew's sleeve.

"I will get bedding for you. You'll have to sleep over here on the floor," Bartholomew said.

Grey said, "I may speak to you, may I not?"

"Yes. But do not speak loudly, for at this place there are those who press their ears against doors."

Some noises came from a distant part of the building, a crash and laughter. Then someone softly singing a sad secular tune passed by the door. Bells rang from another part of the Monastery. Doors creaked open along the hall around their cell.

"Tell me this, after your tryst with Red, you are still a virgin, there was no fornication, is this correct?" Bartholomew tapped his fingers on the walls.

"Yes," Grey answered. "But . . ."

Bartholomew brought his palms together and pressed his fingers against his lips.

"Then we can still say you are a virgin."

And Grey thought to herself that one can say one is anything.

 20

*T*HE NIGHT STAIR had thirty-three steps—the age of Jesus Christ when he was crucified. Grey counted the steps every time she went up or down them. In all her life before coming to the Monastery, she had never known of long stairways that took a person from one floor up to another floor. She had seen the Manor tower often enough, but only from the outside, assuming that the man whose head poked out of the high window had climbed a ladder. Perhaps there could be a place where one climbed many staircases, walking through cloud and passing at night into the realm of stars and into Heaven.

Grey used the night stair the most, for it went directly from the monks' dormitory and cells to the chapel, unlike the day stair, which the monks took to and from the frater where they ate: one, sometimes two meals a day, consisting mostly of cabbage, bread, and oatmeal.

Grey lingered on the night stair to listen to the services, to the chanting during Matins, Lauds, Prime, Terce, Sext, None, Vespers, and Compline. She whispered some of the words to herself, into the moist palm of her own hand, for these words might be more powerful than any others able to transform a person's pain into hope as they seemed able to transform the monks from flea-bitten, weary men to angels with soft, devoted countenances. "*Deus in adjutorium . . . Domine, labia mea aperies . . . laudem tuam.*" "*Deus, Deus, Deus,*" she breathed over and over again in the uneasy nights when her loneliness pressed hard on her chest. In those nights she touched her own breasts in remembrance of Red.

She peeked into the chapel, wanting to see the faces of the monks when they chanted so beautifully. She knew most of the brothers now, both the monks and the laymen, who did most of the hard labor there for the privilege of being closer to God without having to die of starvation in whatever ruined life they had come from. The laymen who labored at the Monastery and monks alike belched and picked their scabs, made lewd comments about bodily functions. But when the monks were chanting and when they came from Mass, they were transformed, no longer as they were in the garden or in clusters outside frater breaking silence to make a joke or sneer a complaint. After Mass, they seemed cleaned and simplified by the Latin words they spoke, and blessed by the saints whose forlorn faces were carved into the stones, many with chipped noses.

Bartholomew found Grey lurking in the chapel doorway one morning when he was entering late, and he pulled her backward roughly by the collar of her robe.

"You are not to attend the Offices or Mass," he hissed.

She looked at his face, so weary, the lines drawn more darkly since he came from Finnistuath. She mouthed the words with exaggeration, "But you promised . . ."

Bartholomew whispered sternly, "Be patient!"

The Librarian heard Bartholomew's whisper and knew it. He turned around and saw his friend in the doorway. They smiled and nodded to each other, Bartholomew's hand turning gentle on Grey's back as he moved to join his brethren in the chants. And Grey noted that the friendship between the Librarian and Bartholomew reformed Bartholomew's mood and made him tender just as the chants made men holy. Grey had no such friendship and could not open her mouth and speak, much less sing or chant. Perhaps she could play the part of a miracle, a boy who could not speak except to intone the psalms. She would try to shape the plans Bartholomew made for her in that way. She would lurk about as a deaf-mute as much as possible and learn what she could; she would ask Bartholomew questions when he was content and rested. And then, one day, when she was ready, she would perform the miracle of her own transformation, from illiterate boy to God-chosen cleric who knew the rituals and prayers.

One night as Bartholomew and Grey were lying on their bedding, their heads practically touching, their bodies at right angles, Grey asked, "What am I here?"

Bartholomew coughed. "You are a servant."

"Am I servant of God?"

"Yes. For you serve this house. And this is God's house."

"When you are in the chapel, do you pray for me?"

"Yes."

"But sometimes I listen for your voice saying psalms and you are not there. You do not follow all the rules that are set forth sternly for all."

"Sometimes I have business to do elsewhere. I am the Second Prior."

"Sometimes you have business with the Librarian, whose eyes soften your eyes."

"He is a good friend," Bartholomew said. "He knows other worlds besides this one, places where there are learned men who know the true names of all God's creations."

"Who is it who can know the true name of a thing?" Grey asked.

"Men who know the essence of those things," Bartholomew answered. "And the Librarian is a patient man who has traveled and listened well."

"Have we an essence, you and I, and is there a true name for us?"

"I am by nature a man, but in essence a monk, a cleric, the Second Prior, for my duties and actions reveal my essence as the actions of all things reveal their essences. See here, a bird is known by its call and the way it constructs its nest. So it is with men."

"I think that is like saying that the leaves that float on a pond explain the depth of that pond. It seems that you may drown a goat if you rely on such measurement of a thing's essence."

Bartholomew grunted. "You are no scholar. Do not debate with me as though you were, you who cannot read one word of scripture."

"What am I, then? What is my essence?"

"You are by nature a human with dark hair and blue-gray eyes that are too wide open, and your essence lies in what you do with your nature."

"Then I am a deaf-mute boy servant."

"Your real essence will reveal itself soon enough as a female human whose body serves in many ways."

Grey lay on her back and thought of how she had served the Lord's son, given pleasure and received it in the form of his intimate presence without the bondage of a household. To be a wife, it seemed, one must give up certain portions of herself, such as her ability to hone the skills of a warrior or take charge of the rituals in the church, or to meet with a man in the woods without persecution. But what was a woman called who did not want to be a wife? And how could she be both a woman and a monk?

She heard Bartholomew's sleeping breath and wished she could lie closer to him. If they were to share pleasure, perhaps he would let her hide sometimes during the day, instead of filling all her hours with duties; perhaps he would feel more protective of her; perhaps if Red did not come, Bartholomew would share pleasure with her and give her body a clear purpose.

Bartholomew passed Grey around to serve in all areas of the Monastery's business. He explained to those who wanted the boy's obedience that he was the only one who could communicate with Grey. And so Bartholomew made deals for her services, with the Refectorian, who had Grey hauling cabbages and fetching water and gave Bartholomew a loaf of bread to take to his cell; with the Kitchener, who had Grey set out the bowls on the long tables in the frater and who put two lumps of meat in Bartholomew's bowl; with the Sacrist for distributing the mutton-fat candles and the cressets, stones in which semicircular holes were scooped where fat and floating wicks made simple candles. The Sacrist allowed Bartholomew to take a few of these to his cell for forbidden reading during the sleeping hours. It was these cressets that the monks held in the palms of their hands as they walked the night stair for the predawn and evening offices, a procession of lighted faces. Grey stood on the stairway, pressed against the wall to be out of their way, but to watch them, to look at their faces boldly. Being a deaf-mute gave her license to be impudent in quiet ways. Some of the monks looked back at her, matching her audacity. Some smiled with charitable pity for a half-wit. Others ignored her.

There was a monk who sought her out, a crazy man who was also mostly ignored. This was Brother Dunsten, who had large teeth that crowded his mouth and jumbled his speech. His lips could never close over the teeth. He also suffered spells. The brethren sometimes found him lying on the ground staring at a rock or clump of grass. Or he would occasionally just stand still in the middle of the stairway, confused. He fell down sometimes when he worked in the garden. But he was not stupid.

He spoke incessantly to Grey when he came across her doing a chore.

"Listen," he said one day, striding up as she was pulling turnips from the garden and laying them in a basket, "I know you're not deaf, and perhaps you can even talk if you wanted."

Grey jiggled the greens of a turnip to loosen the bulb.

"Oh, yes, you could! I know." Brother Dunsten grinned, so that half of his face was made up of teeth, and he waggled his finger in Grey's face. She swatted at it and moved her head.

"Well, I'll tell you. There's something not right. The Abbot's face grows lines in the night. And he speaks when there is no other in the cell with him. He speaks to demons. He keeps a demon in a little box and lets him out to speak to him. He makes bargains with him."

Grey looked at him, studying his eyes to identify the seriousness with which he spoke, the certainty he had. She went back to the turnips, shaking them, placing them in the basket, ignoring the monk's firm refusal to move away.

Brother Dunsten continued talking. "And he knows how soon the world will end. The Abbot knows the exact day and hour. He knows. That's what's in that box, the hour and day when the world will end. Ha! And the Pope thinks by hiding it away he'll do what? Perhaps there is instruction in there, instruction to kill the Pope, to slice his throat!"

At night there were often the sounds of footsteps, of soft singing, of coughing, even whispering and sobbing.

Instead of growing used to the place and sleeping more soundly, Grey found that she had more and more trouble sleeping. There was a nervousness, like a constant humming or tapping inside her body—inside the body of the Monastery's structure—that intensified. At first she was bothered by the noises of the night, or by the cold, or by the bedbugs, or by Bartholomew's breathing, or by a piece of straw sticking into her skin. But there were nights when there was no excuse for not falling into a tender slumber, and she lay awake. The more she wanted to sleep, the more impossible sleep was. And then on an occasional night, mercifully, she would fall first into dreams that were mundane extensions of the present: dreams of lying on her bedding and talking to Bartholomew, or of getting up and going down into the chapel. These dreams would sometimes lead to deeper sleep. In one dream, she met a saint whose face seemed strong and kind though his nose was chipped. She asked him to embrace her. But in fact, the saints did not touch her or speak to her, though she looked into their kind and sad stone eyes. Jesus did not look up at her from the cross, where his head hung in sorrow.

"Love God," the Abbot always said as a fierce warning of the damnation that lurked in everyone's soul. And the monks tried mightily. They sometimes wept with their effort or suddenly smiled and spent days in a serenity that even a cold wind could not fluster. They kept silence, for the most part, puzzling out the exchange of love between God and man. Sometimes the Abbot spoke to them, and then their adoration found a place in his voice and strong arm on their shoulders. Sometimes strong friendships formed around whispered complaints. Weary of deciphering God's will, some brethren would sometimes meet in the barn to play a hurling game or tell stories of the girls they had fucked.

From time to time Bartholomew stayed late into the evening in the Librarian's cell sharing his booty of cressets and apples; they whispered their notions and longings about the world's learned places. The Librarian read the letters that Bartholomew had collected and counted the coins he had. They made lists of things for the Cellarer to buy. Grey listened at the door of the library to their fervid speech into which was placed, like mistletoe berries, their vows of admiration for each other. On these nights Grey suffered her loneliness as a physical misery. She had no distraction from examining the contents of her nature and the facts of her condition.

On such a night, alone in the darkness, Grey lay still, quiet. There were no noises in the hall. Then the heat of her fear arose. It began in the stomach and spread out, tightening her muscles, making her breathe more quickly. It was the heat that came with the first acknowledgment that she was not sleeping, that there was no rest from her awareness of her misery and that the hour would soon come when she would have to get up and do chores having had no sleep.

And then the notion occurred to her that she was like an animal, vigilant against danger. She could not sleep because there was danger. The world was going to end, and like a goat smelling a wolf behind the trees, she could smell the apocalypse.

She sat up and spoke aloud. "There is danger." But there was no one to hear her, no one that she could see, no smooth stone eyes or faces lit by cresset's flame. And she thought of the Abbot, in his own cell, awake, knowing the secrets of this danger.

Half dreams came like veils, and she saw herself as she had seen Red, through lace and shadow. She was a hungry young woman flickering between various roles: a boy in a Monastery where she could not participate in any of the soothing devotions or the distracting comradery; a future monk warrior or warrior monk.

Working in the early spring garden one day in a murky exhaustion, Grey stood up from culling stones to blow warm air on her frozen, red fingers that stuck out of the cloth that bound her hands. Just then a group of pilgrims came through the gates. They were dressed in rough brown mendicants' robes, and they wore wide-brimmed hats. Of the five of them, one was stunningly familiar to Grey. At first she couldn't place him, and then she realized that it was Red. It was the Lord's son Red, at last come with pilgrims to the Monastery. His beard was unruly, but he still had the muscles of a hunter and the thick, clean hair of a rich man. He stood out among the group in this way, for the others were more sallow and scarred. One man had one set of eyelids sewn shut, another had a dirty cloth wrapped around his hand as a bandage. Two were old men, one as thin as a corpse, the other slow moving. The slow-moving man spoke to Grey as the others, including Red, regarded her.

Grey looked the idiot, mouth open, face and hands streaked with garden soil. She stared, heart thudding. Red was still handsome, even as a mendicant. And no doubt he was kinder than before. She remembered him speaking to her, asking her to sing to his mother as she lay dying. She remembered his hand fitting over her breast as he slept.

"Look away," she said to herself as Red and the others waited for her to respond to the old man's greeting, and she just barely forced herself to turn away, to be the deaf-mute. The pilgrims went on, without insult to her. If Red knew her as the Priest's boy, he showed no interest in the phenomenon of her appearing here now. It was as though the face of such a person was not important enough to remember. And though she guessed that he would well remember her if she showed her breasts, it stung to know that the part of her that had been the Priest's boy—indeed, it had been the most of her and had sung to Red's mother—that person was no one to Red. Grey had to pretend to have struck her own foot with a stone to give reason for the tears that flowed down her face. So long ago, Finnistuath was so long ago, though maybe just a few months by the calendar. And she mustn't think of the spring or of the Second Fiona or of her father's hand dangling from his arm, which used to hold her tightly when she was his son.

When she walked through the main hallway, she heard the Abbot's scolding voice, not an uncommon sound, but she glanced over and saw that he was scolding Bartholomew. She only heard the Abbot say, "Your love of pleasure" and "false rumors" and finally, "should have their tongues cut off."

Grey hurried away.

That night she was on her knees, praying to Bartholomew to tell her all he knew of Red and the pilgrims.

"They are of those pilgrims who are looking for the end of the world." He seemed impatient, anxious. He bit at a callus on the edge of his finger.

"What do you mean? Why does one have to look for something that is coming?"

"In this case it is the actual place where the world ends and the heavens begin."

"Is there such a place?" She imagined the long and arduous but increasingly beautiful stairway that disappeared into cloud and stars. She imagined also her crippled sister, whom she would carry up those stairs.

"Some say so, that there is a place to the north where the earth and sky meet, where one ends and the other begins. One who is pure, who has purified himself, can find this place."

"I would like to go there," Grey said. "I am still a virgin and could go there."

After some thought, Bartholomew said, "Some say it is across the ocean to the west or to the north, where there is nothing but ice for hundreds of miles."

"Yes." Grey thought about the horrible winter in Finnistuath when people froze to death and everything turned to ice. She would walk through such a winter for years in order to find Heaven, and she would do so with Red, who would be kind enough to help her carry Fiona. Suddenly there was no other plan but this one. She could not stay in this place waiting for the apocalypse the monks sometimes whispered about, when the world would burst into flame, or tip at an angle so that all the people and creatures on it would slide off into eternal darkness.

"There are animals, cats that are as big as wolves and that eat men the way a housecat eats mice. I've heard this. They exist. And horses with long horns coming from their foreheads that can pierce three men clean through." Bartholomew looked at his fingernails under the flame of the cresset that sat on the floor between their bedding. "I'd just as soon stay safe and warm here than go limping around the world begging, starving, getting attacked by huge cats and such."

Someone screamed in a distant part of the Monastery.

"There are agonies here that I do not understand," Grey said, shivering. "I would rather be in search of paradise than settle for the bleakness here."

Bartholomew smiled and said, "You know, the Cellarer will be bringing back apples and cheese for us from Tarmath, and some honey cakes as well as the holy day cakes that are especially made for us with a cross of honey on each."

"But if one could find Heaven . . . You and the Librarian speak about going to Avignon, about leaving here to make a pilgrimage to see the one who is closest to God in all the world. Why not long for Heaven itself—to go to God without having to endure the agony of death?"

"In the meantime," Bartholomew said, "there are certain favors you will do for the Cellarer and we will have some of those cakes for ourselves, a bit of Heaven, I'd say."

He blew out the flame. They could hear hurried footsteps outside in the hall.

In darkness, Grey continued to speak: "I want to go with them. I am going with them, for Red has given up his essence as a Lord's son to be a pilgrim, and if I am a pilgrim too, then I have a right to share his meals." Grey spoke to Bartholomew as her friend, as a man who could understand the sacred nature of two humans sharing meals and longings. "You have the Librarian. You have him to give you comfort and companionship."

When there was no answer, Grey felt anger, a suspicion that Bartholomew saw her as a fool who had forgotten his promises. She said, her tone fiercer, "And when will you teach me to be a monk as you promised? I do not see you making a way for me to be anything but a deaf-mute while you find as much pleasure . . ."

Then in pitch dark she felt an object fall hard against her skull. It was Bartholomew's hand. Another blow hit her neck.

She scurried out of the bedding, kicking hay and blanket away from her. But he found her even in the dark, saying nothing, just pummeling her head and then shaking her, pushing her against the stone wall. Grey meant to say something. She meant to ask him to stop. But each time he pushed her against the wall she had no breath with which to expel the words.

Finally the beating stopped. Grey moved her back down the wall until she sat and felt the wounds throb on her face, on the back of her arms and shoulders. Bartholomew sat down, huffing from exertion. When he quieted, when he might have been asleep or might have disappeared completely from the room and the earth, Grey finally spoke.

"I thought," she strained to say between gasps, "that you were a kind man."

The black shape of a man now distinguished itself from the other black shapes.

It spoke in a growling voice that Grey had never heard before: "You cannot leave."

 **21**

O N THE DAY OF BATHING, buckets of water, heated in the kitchen, were brought up to the dormitory, where thirty-seven naked monks stood shivering. It was Grey's chore to carry the buckets, and she was cursed for not being fast enough, for the water was no longer hot by the time the monks dipped their rags in it. Some of them laughed and pointed at the naked genitals of their brothers, the shrinking scrotum or erect penis. One pale young monk with freckles and light orange eyebrows read scripture. He was newly arrived and given the job of Cantor, for his voice was pure. Grey kept her eyes down. The Infirmarer, a small but determined man with a studious expression always on his brow, paced the length of the dormitory to inspect the men for sores and signs of serious disease. No one wanted him to find any excuse for leeching or applying poultice.

As most of the monks were sitting on their bedding, shivering with their blankets around their shoulders, Grey was grabbed by the Infirmarer, who didn't bother to speak to her, but pulled at her clothing and nodded toward one of the buckets. His hands were surprisingly large and firm and seemed, like his face, to study what they held.

She backed away and he grabbed her tunic, gently but with the strength of a man who was used to the crazy resistance of a fearful soul not wanting to endure some painful but necessary medicinal process. She struggled, which amused many of the monks. She backed up and bumped against a thin elderly man still bathing himself. He squeezed her with both arms, holding her for the Infirmarer. A young monk with a lean and handsome body ran up to take off her leggings. She struggled more, trying hard not to make a sound. She kicked at the young monk and freed herself from the other, slipping quickly under the Infirmarer's closing hands and running down the night stairs.

Then she ran out of the Monastery, down the meadow toward the stream. She looked back and saw several of the monks leaning out of the dormitory window, laughing and calling out. She kept running. She ran to a copse of oak and stopped, leaning into the trunk of one tree, feeling her breasts against it and looking up into the branches where she wanted to go. She wanted to go up into the tree and sing, for she believed her voice was as sweet as the Cantor's.

Bartholomew was cross with her when she came back to the cell. He told her he had heard of the commotion in the dormitory, and that as a matter of fact she was lucky to have gotten away, but she did need to bathe.

"I have rose oil for your skin."

"Rose oil?"

"Yes, see what your labors can bring us?"

She held the little clear bottle and smelled around the cork.

"Roses!" she beamed.

"Very good. Now, go and get another bucket of water from the frater, but it will have to be cold. We have no time to heat it."

Bartholomew rubbed her with the oil, roughly jiggling her with his officious hands. But he had to admit that she had beauty. She had long legs; she had only a few scabs from bedbug and fleabites. She had clear eyes and a finely boned face. He combed her hair with his fingers and then he gave her a clean robe he had gotten from the Cellarer.

"You must put the hood over your head," Bartholomew told her.

"I am cold from the bath," she complained.

"You will be warm soon enough."

"In what way? What plan do you have? Your eyebrow is raised. You have a plan."

"Yes."

She bounced up and down nervously. "Oh, I am cold. What arrangement have you made?"

Bartholomew didn't answer but took a strip of brown wool and put it over her eyes.

"Wait," she said, pulling on the blindfold.

"You must wear this."

Grey trembled.

"I don't want to wear this."

Grey felt her hand get taken up by his thick fingers. Bartholomew led her out of their cell.

"Please," she said. "I cannot . . ."

"I thought you wanted this man," Bartholomew whispered. "He has called for you again. I thought you wanted to leave with him."

Grey stopped and Bartholomew pulled her along.

"Is it him?" she asked. "He has asked for me?"

"Yes."

"Then why must I wear this cloth over my eyes if . . ."

Bartholomew pulled her roughly in front of him, and with his mouth on her ear so that she could feel his wet lips move, he said, "He has shame."

The monk who was waiting for her in the library was already naked, holding his robes against his crotch. Bartholomew and Grey stood before him in the light of two large candles. Dark geometries frolicked on the books and scrolls on the shelves and tables in the small room.

Grey stayed still, breathing heavily as she heard the door squeal open and shut, as she supposed that Bartholomew had left her and the man alone. Now she was no saint, draped in holy cloth and lace. She was a thin and trembling soul. But she would soothe this man. She would make their communion pure and then suggest to him that they combine their ambitions to leave this world and find Heaven.

The man took the robe he was holding and laid it on the floor. Then he went to Grey and pulled the hood of her robe down. He rubbed his own face, thinking for a minute. Then he undid the rope around Grey's robe and lifted it over her head. He put that robe down with the other as she stood shivering and blindfolded.

The man again rubbed his face, harder than before. He looked at the naked young woman in front of him, a sight he had never again expected to see, much less touch. His hand went directly to her breast, making her flinch backward a little. But then she let both his hands grab her breasts and move them in circles. She could not match the roughness of this touch with the hand that had lain on her breast in the woods beside the spring of Finnistuath. He put his face into her neck, breathing like a man who wanted to be smothered. It was, she knew instantly, not Red.

In fact, he was the Cellarer, a tall and slender man, a little stooped and tired, who had control over all the goods of the Monastery, including the wines, before they were blessed and given to the Sacrist. He took Grey by the shoulders and pressed her down onto the robes he had laid on the floor. He was soon on top of her, wriggling so as to part her legs. His fingers felt between her legs. He could sense her body stiffen and waited without moving. He stroked her hair as one would stroke a frightened animal, as she had seen her father stroke a goat who was stuck in brambles. She was thinking of the men in the dormitory, wondering which one he was, if he were the handsome boy who playfully tried to pull her leggings down. He was all men, any man except for the one she wanted.

She took his erection in her hand, meaning to keep it from her, and then, responding to his moans, she gripped it. Her breasts jiggled as she stroked the man's prick. Her nipples were extended and hardened by the cold air. The man's eyes looked back and forth from them to her slightly parted lips. It took several minutes for her to feel the fluid pulse from the Cellarer's member, and then she lay back and waited, hearing his breathing slow. She rolled over and clutched the robes to her, holding them tightly and wishing the man would leave her alone.

He pried one of the robes from her arms. She heard him go to the door and lightly knock on it.

The door opened and closed and Bartholomew said, "Are you done?"

The Cellarer answered, "I will never do this again. This is a great sin. I must never do this again. I'll give you the cakes and oils you asked for and keep what I know to myself, but I'll not be making this bargain again."

"Was she trouble?"

"No. No." The Cellarer was insistent. "No, she is some kind of angel. I would run from this place with her, marry her. She is an angel or a fairy woman, and I should not be fornicating with either."

Grey tried to press away the smile that was creeping onto her face and sat up, holding her robe around her shoulders. In a few moments Bartholomew sat beside her and said, "He is gone. I will take you back now. Put on your robe. Put the hood over your head."

She did not want to talk to Bartholomew. She didn't take off the blindfold and even wore it to bed.

The image of the man was on her skin, inside her, left like the impression of a body or a fairy ring on a patch of grass where nothing could ever grow. She felt a cold irritation at Bartholomew and herself for the cruel hope that she was going to be reunited with Red. But she also kept smiling to think of the words the Cellarer had said, that he would run away with her. She touched her own lips and then her breasts.

Now what was she? She was a whore. She had been changed by mischief into a whore, and her own body's longing was part of the mischief. And Bartholomew had transformed from a confidant to a deceiver. She could smell honey cakes by the bedding but had no hunger for them.

Just at the edge of sleep, she jerked awake, certain that a stone thrown by the Weaver's son in Finnistuath had hit her on the cheek. She rolled over and thought that in fact she could throw far better than the Weaver's son could. She had proven that many times in contests with him and the other boys at the stump. And now she had a power that he could never have. She had a woman's body.

22

IN THE DARKNESS, rustling sounds. The sound of straw bedding beneath a restless body, of one sigh. The air is damp and slightly warm. Not fresh. If one thought about it, dwelt on the thickness of the air, the room would be suffocating. One would get up and run outside, stretching the face up and gasping for air, drinking the coolness. But the body doesn't follow the imagination. It stays, almost turned to stone. What is to come? What is to happen? Is everyone mad or objects of the whimsical games of fairies? What creeps around us and pulls us from our paths so that we awake in the middle of the night, lost?

The Devil.

A tapping on the wall beside her bedding, very light at first, becomes a long scraping. A finger—no, harder—a claw scrapes along the wall, on the other side, as though it is wanting to get in. What can suspend itself to the top of the Monastery to claw at the stones outside the cell of Brother Bartholomew and his helper?

Only the Devil. He is out there, suspended in the air, his long, clawed finger scraping at the stones.

A sheen of perspiration covers her skin. She is cold. But the air she breathes in is warm and heavy. She cannot breathe it deeply enough. The air is caught in her throat and won't go any deeper. The clawing continues. The Devil has chosen her.

Fear is not enough to move her. It has to be defiance. "I will not lie here and be frightened to death. I will not lie here for the amusement of any Devil. Saint Brigid, love me, protect me." If she thinks of Saint Patrick or Jesus, she would have to touch him, to embrace him, and he would cling to her like a lover or shame her as a temptress.

Is there soft laughter coming from the other side of the wall? Still the scraping, slow clawing, a pause, slow clawing again.

Grey moves the blanket off of her. Something tickles her arm, crawling on it. She brushes it off and sits, holding her knees to her chest.

"Am I awake?" she asks aloud. Then louder, "Am I awake?"

Bartholomew mumbles, "Yes."

The clawing continues.

"Do you hear that clawing?" she asks aloud. "Do you hear it?" She whispers directly into Bartholomew's ear.

"No."

Perhaps he does, perhaps this is his plan, to allow the Devil to drive her mad or to take her soul or to kill her. Perhaps Bartholomew has made a bargain with the Devil and will get honey and many hours of leisure in return, will be sent on fantastic journeys to Avignon, to the end of the world. And now the Devil is clawing through the stone. Slowly, patiently. He will claw until there is an opening, and he will sift through it like smoke.

She gets up and goes to the door, her legs stiff with terror. She cannot move fast. She dares not move fast.

The hall is empty and completely dark; she runs along it, passing her fingertips on the stones. Then she runs through the dormitory. The long windows give light. and she sees the men in humps on their bedding. The pilgrims are at the far end, in their own grouping, a bit distant from the others. They keep different hours, going to some of the offices, but often staying in the dormitory and praying in a clump like the closed petals of a flower. She sees Red and slows to a walk; his eyes are closed, and she wants to touch his face, to put her palms on either side of his face and kiss him gently on the lips the way she has seen the Abbot kiss the monks. She wants to bless Red and protect him from the Devil, stop him from beating himself. One of the monks near her sits up and calls out to her. It is Dunsten. She can see his teeth grinning.

"Grey, Grey, where are you going?" he whispers. She runs through before he can follow her, or before he wakes up others.

Out the other side of the dormitory are the day stairs. She can barely see them. And there is a narrow hallway that leads to the bell tower stairs.

She is shivering and breathing heavily, from fear. Should she go to the bell tower? The Devil could float up there, if he could float to the second level. And he could push her from the tower. In her mind she flies through the Monastery, looking for a small, secure place to hide from everyone, everything. Then she imagines herself asleep in the sacristy, safe and hidden among the robes, vestments, ornaments, altar cloths. She could sleep in a pile of cloth beneath one of the tables in the little room behind the chapel, the sacristy—so full of holy objects that the Devil will not dare to chase her there. She thinks, if only she could always go there to sleep. She would be able to rest there, free from the heat that spread inside her when she was trying to sleep in the cell with Bartholomew. She knows now that she cannot stay in the cell with Bartholomew. She will never sleep there.

She is about to go down the stairs when she hears Bartholomew's laugh. She stops, turned to stone again. His voice is coming from behind the doors of the library, which is on the other side of the dormitory from their cell. There is a light beneath the door. She opens the door and sees Bartholomew on bedding that is surrounded by low flamed cressets. He is lying on the back of the Librarian. He is mating with him; his sweating back gleams. He is pushing up and down and groaning, laughing. His orange buttocks jiggle and quiver. The Librarian is up on his elbows; his face, which he turns toward the door, has the expression of a howling dog, but there is no sound. Bartholomew turns and looks at Grey but doesn't see her. He is in a trance. Sweat flows down his face.

Grey removes her robe and her leggings and drops them in the hall. Then she is naked, standing in the middle of the monks' dormitory, just standing there naked until one man stirs and turns and his eyes open and he sees her and mutters a prayer, for he doesn't know whether he is seeing good or evil. And that man wakes the one next to him and they see a woman, her hands with fingers splayed in front of her face like thick lace. But her eyes look directly at them. And the second man crosses himself.

The bell for Matins rings, slow, full of resonance.

Grey backs away and runs. But somehow she is near her own cell again with her clothing in her arms. She opens the door and goes in. She can see nothing, but crawls on the floor toward Bartholomew's bedding, reaching out to feel for him. He isn't there. She lies down, pulling his blanket over her, over her head. Perhaps she sleeps. She doesn't hear the clawing anymore.

ᔔᕒᕒ 23 ᕒᕒᔔ

ONE MINUTE he was in the barn drinking from a barrel of ale, shush-ing the pregnant cow that lowed at him plaintively. He was afraid that the lay brother who was watching over the animal would think she had gone into a breech labor and come with help to turn the calf right. Colin knew enough about cows to know that this one was not in labor, but un-comfortable and not wanting anyone standing behind her. He took the dip-per of ale and moved to where she could see him. So, one minute he was in the barn drinking and looking a cow in the eye, and the next he was creep-ing around the chapel.

"There's nothing to steal here but souls," he muttered, annoyed at his muddled thinking and vision, and then he shushed himself, for if he had calculated correctly, it was near to Matins and the bell ringer might be up and about. But how had he gotten from the barn to the chapel, and how much time had passed?

He looked down at the wooden dipper still in his hand and then laid it on the floor and was transfixed by the red-and-black design of the tiles, a lion's face that was moving in a slow circle. Colin laughed, then steadied himself. Slowly standing up, he noted all the stone faces of saints looking at him and he closed his eyes again.

He was facing east, facing Jerusalem, and he thought for a moment that he would start walking, and walk until he came to the Holy Land. Ah, but there was the matter of ocean, and he would have to get on a ship as a sailor. The complicated nature of life, a fact that made the simplest, purest plan turn lumpy, nauseated him. He leaned over, thinking to vomit, but he prayed instead.

"Praise God and his son, Jesus Christ," he said, "and the beautiful Mary, who lost her only son." He felt himself begin to go weepy and cleared his throat.

"Ah, God, the suffering, the shit stinking suffering . . ."

He considered going to find the Abbot and beating the holiness out of him. That man, he thought, is a waste of muscle and sperm and a disgrace to Ireland with his English rules. "I'll beat the Jesus, Mary, and Joseph out of him."

He mumbled to himself about the self-righteousness of the man and his notions of the Monastery's importance. "It's that damned box," he whispered. "Damned box": the one the Old Abbot showed him, but would not open for him. "The Pope requested that we hide it here," the Old Abbot had said, "but it makes me ill. It is a curse." In Colin's opinion the thing gave the place airs; it gave the New Abbot a pompous notion of himself.

Once Colin determined that his mission was to relieve the Monastery of its hubris, he couldn't trust it to a drunk. So, he dragged the drunken version of himself outside and the two careened together down the hill. He finally lay down and went unconscious halfway down the meadow, sprawled on his back. When his eyes opened onto the constellation Orion, the warrior constellation, it seemed like a good omen. Colin sat up too quickly and had to put his head on his knees. Orion and Christ were the same, he thought, and he crossed himself. They were all the same. Every hero raged against lies.

Something had to change in his life, he determined. But he had no clear ambition. He was going to die of purposelessness and hunger. Why did he keep circling around this miserable Monastery? He had been attracted once to the vow of poverty, attracted to the transcendence of prayer and devotion in a world of merchants and soldiers and farmers and herders, attracted to silence.

In one sense, the Monastery had been a refuge for him, where he wasn't required to have a name, a town, or a father other than God. But he couldn't make a complete go of it, couldn't pretend to believe certain things, such as his inferiority to the New Abbot, who was his own age and with his own temperament if you scraped the piety and fear off him. Most of all, he couldn't believe in the virtue of shame. In the time of heroes and chieftains and women warriors, when Cuchulain made love to the daughter of a god, there was no shame of one's body and its appetites.

"Ah, that was a long time ago," Colin chided himself. "Let it be."

He had wanted Christ to be his hero, a man of great strength like Cuchulain, with a willingness to fight a doomed fight against the Romans rather than betray the truth. And Christ's truth, as Colin understood it, was that the ultimate man, the perfect man, used his strength in the service of kindness. And yet the Monastery, the Pope, and his pale clerics, it seemed, had more faith in shame than in kindness as a means of perfecting the world.

Carrying his own head on his shoulder like a wad of iron, Colin walked up toward the Monastery. He was sober enough now to do what he wanted to do; he wanted to take some of the pompous drama out of the Abbot. He waited until he heard the bells for mass and slipped in. It was easy to steal from men who believed they were holy, protected, chosen. The box was where it had always been, and he took it. It had a lock on it, but he didn't want to spend time looking for the key. The Old Abbot had never opened it, never revealed what was inside. There was time enough to work the lock.

He left the Monastery in a leisurely stroll, listening to the chanting, feeling both pity and respect for the monks; he respected their commitment to something. He wanted to be devoted to something, but it had to be true; it didn't matter if it was dangerous. It just had to be true.

The cow was still in the barn, but less agitated. She let the man uncover his satchels from a pile of hay in the corner. He barely remembered putting them there. The cow began to low again, and he put all his satchels over his shoulders and left the barn, jiggling and adjusting the weight as he walked under a clear sky.

He heard rabbits and ghosts in the grasses all around him. He stopped at the stream to wash his face and drink and pulled the jeweled box out to look at it, to assess its value. He emptied all the satchels, moving his hands over a motley and mangled array of candles, broken brooches, rubbing stones and knives, bundles of dried herbs. Then he organized and packed everything again and stood up, thinking that he would put the box somewhere, in one of several places where he buried things he didn't want to carry all the time, treasures and nuisances. He had made up a song to tell himself the locations of these secret stashes:

> *Start where briar on briar sits behind two trees,*
> *And rest where the spring in Finnistuath gleams.*
> *Follow Polaris across seven streams,*
> *A day to travel on a westerly breeze.*
> *Go where Kevin hid from the woman he drowned,*
> *And sit beside the Friar who sleeps in the ground.*
> *Always two stones separated by three,*
> *And the mark of Orion on the nearest tree.*

He had had trouble locating one of the hiding places, because in that location the tree he had put his mark on had been felled for use by a local barley grower along with several other trees around it, so that Colin had to
search the ground for five stones in a straight line. And he had wondered if
the stones had been kicked around by humans or animals, cursing his stu-
pidity for not being more clever. But he had found the spot and dug up a
satchel that had some jewels a woman had traded him for candles and a few
nights of devoted fucking. Two books he had buried there had rotted, but
Colin had read them several times and so only missed what he might have
been able to sell them for. One told of Saint Patrick's fight with a druid, a
fight that, most naturally, the druid lost. The other was about methods of
identifying medicinal herbs. They were both written in Latin, and the learning of Latin was one thing he could credit the Monastery for.

Weary of the maps and stories he kept in his head, wondering what he
would do with a jeweled box that was locked, Colin walked eastward, avoid-
ing Tarmath and thinking he might see some friends in Naas who always
welcomed and fed him until he grew tired of their talk of running the English out of Ireland. There was a woman there who said she loved him. He
wanted to love her. Dawn was a little orange, he noted, and his head felt like
it had been sewn on sloppily, with the needle left in it.

Grey saw the man with the satchels come out of some trees by the
stream. In the brief time he was revealed by moonlight, he reminded her of
Colin, with his packs and the way he walked, a little stooped but with a long
stride. Then she was sure it was Colin, and that's when she started after
him, dropping the buckets, which rattled and rolled behind her. Grey ran
and ran, crying out, no matter that anyone would hear the deaf-mute wailing. She called out, "Wait! Please! Wait!" But though she ran and he walked,
the distance between them spread like a stain.

"You!" she yelled. And a raven sprang still half asleep from an alder tree
and cawed in indignant irritation as it flew toward the higher trees by the
stream.

## 24

A DOOR OPENED and then closed. Then there was silence. Grey wondered if she had been left in a room alone. She heard what could have been the hem of a robe moving across stone, or what might have been a sheath of paper blown across a surface by a breeze. But she felt no breeze. There was light. She could see a patch of light through the dark cloth over her eyes. Then she heard a throat being cleared. It was not Bartholomew's.

Bartholomew whispered, "This is she."

No one answered, but she felt someone's warmth come close to her.

Then a man whispered, "She cannot hear or speak?"

"No."

"And is the blindfold secure?"

"Yes. But even if she were to see anything, she could not tell of it."

"I want her to be blindfolded. Always."

"Yes, I swear it."

"I want to tell you, I will not fornicate with her."

Grey almost stepped backward, but she determined that she would stay completely still, no matter what—that she would do nothing but endure whatever was to happen to her. If the man did not want to fornicate with her, she could not, did not want to, imagine what he planned to do with her oiled body.

"I only want to examine her, to study her," the man whispered, barely audible.

"Yes, of course. And don't worry, she cannot hear you."

"And you don't imagine that there are people who listen at doors in this place?" The man kept whispering, but she could hear the yelling in it.

Grey sensed that Bartholomew made some expression or gesture of agreement.

The man continued, "You will come back for her at the beginning of Nocturne."

That was hours away. Grey remained silent and still, her fisted hands lying against her sides.

"Now we are conspirators," the man whispered. "That suits you well, doesn't it?"

"Yes," Bartholomew replied, and she heard the door open and close.

There was silence for a few seconds. Then she heard the man's breath close to her. She felt some fiddling at her waist. He was carefully untying the rope belt. The robe came over her head. She lifted her arms clumsily and the man had to struggle to get the robe off.

The man noisily sucked in air, between his teeth, as though enduring some kind of suffering.

"You have hidden this secret well," he whispered. Did he expect her to answer, to hear? Did he suspect she could?

There was silence again; she sensed that he was distant from her. But his hand startled her, stroking her arm, taking up her hand and pulling gently at each of the fingers. It was indeed as though he were examining her. She stood still, refusing to flinch or cower, though she wanted to. Then she felt the back of his hand move up the inside of her thigh. The side of his finger stopped at the hair between her legs and then slid back down on the skin of her leg.

He stepped away. She knew that he was not near her, for the air around her became cooler. And then he returned and whispered something in Latin, a prayer, something she had heard chanted in the chapel. *"Domine ad adjuvundum me festina."* He whispered it over and over again. And he moved his hand lightly up her leg until it was on her taut belly, which quivered a little at the unexpected touch.

She grabbed the hand and pressed it against her more firmly. The hand itself became a personality, moving, stopping, confused. It slid out from her grasp and stopped on her skin just below her breasts, the fingers spreading apart and coming together again and again like the pulsing of a wing.

The man's hand moved upward and stayed over her breast, pressing it slightly, then cupped it and lifted it as though to weigh it. Its gentleness gave her a longing to see the man's face, to look into his eyes and read his intentions and emotions. His breathing was louder. She stumbled backward and he quickly braced her back with his other hand to keep her close.

"I will not harm you," he whispered again. Then he put his head against hers and said into her ear, "I will not harm you. Can you hear me?"

He said it as though pleading with her. She felt that in fact he was asking that she not harm him. She stayed still, until he took his hand from her skin and pulled her from the spot she had been standing in for what seemed like a long time. Her legs were stiff, her knees locked. But she shuffled carefully, blindly behind him, pulled to a large chair. When she sat on it, a leather seat sagged like a hammock. It was cold, but her skin was warm and moist and stuck to it. He gently pushed her backward until she felt another piece of cool leather slung across the back of the chair. He put both her hands on the thin wooden arms. She heard his knees crack softly as he went down on them. Then both his hands moved up her legs, as though pushing something carefully along her skin.

Suddenly, he stood up. His hand, shaking, now stroked her face. It glided down the side of her neck and then up into her hair. She wanted then to embrace him. He reminded her a little of Red, struggling with something, with some kind of weakness and longing while his arms were strong.

She put her own hand over his, which was still in her hair. For a moment their fingers wove together. Grey could feel the man's confusion as though he had spoken it with words. She could feel that something had occurred to the man's perception and intention. Their hands together had nothing to do with study. His loneliness is what she felt, the breath and touch of a lost soul. She understood that they shared at that moment an intense intimacy of loneliness. And she felt the thickness of his hands, a man's hands that could give protection.

She sat up and put her arms around his neck and lay her head on his shoulder. She turned her head toward the man's neck and smelled the skin there, perfumed by wood smoke and sweat. And there she meant to stay. But his hands moved her arms from around his neck and placed them on the arms of the chair again.

"That is enough. Enough," he whispered to himself. And then she felt him move away again. She heard the scraping of the door as it opened and closed. After a few moments of listening as hard as she could, she knew she was alone.

For many minutes she waited, and then the chill was too uncomfortable to endure. She crawled carefully along the floor to find the robe. She leaned against the wall and held the rough wool against her. She waited longer.

She spoke to herself for several minutes about the wisdom of removing the cloth from around her eyes, just to see where she was. But if the man returned and she saw him, what would happen? "Would he beat me if my eyes looked at him?"

She lifted a corner of the blindfold. It was tightly tied so that it hardly went over her brow bone, but with one eye barely open she immediately saw that she was in a room almost as small as the cell she and Bartholomew slept in. She saw the wood and leather chair she had sat in, a grand-looking thing, almost like a throne. Was the man the Librarian, she wondered? The thought sickened her. The Librarian had the face of a howling dog. She moaned and lay down, still holding the woolen robe against her. There was a table next to the chair on which there sat a good, fat candle, and a book. There were, in fact, many books in this room, and bedding on a wooden stand, so that a sleeper might avoid some of the things that could crawl on him. There were also curtains, velvet curtains along one wall to hide the cold stones and warm the room. This seemed like a secret place, where the stirrings and mutterings of the Monastery were distant.

Grey placed the blindfold over her eyes again and waited until Bartholomew came in and took her back to their cell.

"Will I go back and meet this man again?" she asked Bartholomew.

He laughed.

"He left without fornicating . . . and the other man did not want me again. Am I unfit or discomforting in some way?"

"In the name of Jesus and Mary!" Bartholomew hissed, "This isn't a brothel; it's a Monastery! Do you think the man who lives here, who has chosen to be a monk, is like a country lover?"

"Is it the Librarian?"

Bartholomew did not answer but rubbed his own forehead as though to remove the skin from his skull.

She lay down on her bedding and played with the cloth that had been over her eyes, pulling it through her fingers.

"Who is this man?"

Bartholomew sighed, "I will not tell you. I have made a vow."

"You've made many vows. I have seen one vow after another turned to smoke in this tomb. This seems to me more like where God is buried than where he lives."

"You don't understand God, His Church, and the weary and intense devotion that men practice to save us all, to protect our souls. Just don't become bold, or we will both get into most serious trouble."

"What did we get from the man?" Grey asked.

"Silence."

"Silence? That is what I give!"

"This man's silence is of much more importance."

On the stairs the next morning Grey sighed—a sound that drifted out of her just as the rogue Dunsten was coming down the stairs and could hear her.

She turned around, walking backward and whispered as loudly as she could, "Oh, Brother Dunsten."

When he turned sharply around and saw only her, she laughed again, out loud, and took the stairs, two at a time, not looking back.

25

O N A DAY that drizzled cold, Grey passed by a clump of monks talking in the pigyard beneath the bell tower. The small group was made up of the Librarian, Brother Calvin, the Abbot, and Brother Richard, the man she knew as Red. She wanted to stick her tongue out at them all, pull their robes, kick their shins. Sing a song—that one about the man who ate shit and drank urine that she learned as a boy. She stood near them, picking up stones in the garden and tossing them into a pail near the group of philosophers. It was Brother Calvin who got distracted by the remarkable skill of the deaf-mute to throw with casual and perfect accuracy.

She took no notice of Calvin but was there to be near Red, whose voice was getting louder and louder.

"I have heard many things, I tell you! I am sick with the deceit of the world—of nobles and clerics who say they are better than others. Why, that deaf-mute boy has more nobility and piety than the Pope and the King together."

They all turned toward Grey, who just then tossed a rock directly into the pail with a side motion. Their discussion was suspended for a moment.

Ah, how well she knew now that there were other men in the world besides Red, though she felt a bitter longing for him to at least recognize her as the Priest's boy. Well he would know his fairy lover, she thought to herself, know and desire.

Then the Librarian rubbed his hands together vigorously, nervously. "This discussion should not take place. You are not part of our order and have no right . . ."

"I have no right?" Red responded.

"You should leave for your journey before winter is on us," the Abbot said, quietly but sternly.

There was a silence among them, and then for no apparent reason, the Abbot laughed, his eyes as merry as a king's, and he looked down and shook his head. It was exactly as though a player had forgotten his line or had broken out of character for a moment. For after shaking his head, the

Abbot looked up sternly again, pursing his lips, which had been errant in laughing.

"You are full of impudent and impious outbursts," Red said angrily, "and insults as well. Why are there communications from Avignon so regularly? What does the Pope care about a little monastery in the middle of nowhere? What is here that concerns him so much?"

Brother Calvin moved away from the group, walking quickly inside. The three men who were left looked down at their feet.

"I will leave," Red said. "I am looking for God, not men's intrigues. I wish that there would be an end to this world, a purification."

The Librarian then left, as briskly as Brother Calvin had.

The two men left alone, the Abbot grabbed Red's arm, squeezing it so that when Red tried to pull it away, he could not.

"Here, then, let go of my arm," Red said.

Grey pretended to be silently scolding the pig, which lurked too close to the garden fence, her finger waving in front of its wriggling snout.

The Abbot said, "You are still an English Lord's son, aren't you, arrogant and bold? You dress as a pilgrim but act like a King's soldier with his conquered people, even here. You are privileged wherever you go, aren't you—privileged like a conquering Lord to demand answers, to pry, to speak your mind, as only an Englishman can."

The Abbot tossed the arm away roughly and Red stood straight, looking hard at the Abbot's wild eyes, unable to find anything to say.

The Abbot walked close to him, backing him toward Grey.

"I wager your father is pompous, too, and that you think you are better than he because you have taken the religious road—both of you pompous. Well, you'd better move quickly from here, because there are things beyond your little arrogance and your little notions of truth."

They were no more than boys or village laborers about to fight.

Grey watched them openly now, holding the empty pail's handle with both hands, her mouth hanging open like a true half-wit's.

"The only truth I am interested in is the way to diminish suffering, and I fear that there is too much ignorance here."

"Perhaps you have learned that at such a place your wealth does not increase your wisdom or decrease your suffering." The Abbot kept speaking, spitting his words. "You do not know what I have suffered, the burden I suffer here, what I must protect and what battles my soul fights every day while you ponder and study and praise yourself for a hunger you can end any time by going home to your Manor. In fact, you know less than any Englishman I have ever met, and that is very, very little indeed."

The two men stopped walking, now so close to Grey she could feel the small breeze the hems of their robes made.

Her eyes closed, Grey heard Red hiss, "We have your backsides in carts, then, don't we, we English, you and all your filthy, barefooted half-wit countrymen."

The Abbot laughed and said, "You have no idea what I know, and it would make your testicles wither." Then he walked away.

The bells rang; Grey didn't know for what Office.

 26

BARTHOLOMEW usually went to the woods to empty his bowels. The particular spot he preferred was behind a knot of briars where a slim birch tree had fallen partway across the stream. He could perch on it with his feet resting on some stones. He sat with his leggings around his ankles and his robes twisted around his waist. He was thinking about how there were some physicians who studied a man's feces to discover the source of illnesses both of the body and the soul. He was willing to glance at his own shit dissolving in the stream when he got up, but could never consider studying it closely or letting anyone else do so. What if something moved in it? What if he saw worms?

Since he had returned to the Monastery, his mind often wandered into strange, dark nests. He was far better off studying some new place, distracted by foreign flora and fauna, pressing leaves into his book. He hadn't even looked at the book since he came from Finnistuath.

He needed to travel again, to leave the Monastery, to speak directly to the Pope in Avignon about financing his scholarship, which would of course be in service to the Church.

Bartholomew slid forward to wipe himself on the tree before standing up and pulling on his leggings. He let his robe down, shaking it a little. Briefly he looked toward the brownish-orange feces on the other side of the log and then strolled along the stream. Without knowing why, tears began to come from his eyes, and he sat down on the edge of the stream and sobbed, his belly jiggling. The world was not as he had hoped it would be.

He had loved the Abbot so much once; it was the love of that man that caused him to commit to the Monastery and devote himself to serving it. But he could hardly muster that admiration now, after seeing in small increments the human weaknesses of the man: his temper, his lust, his lack of calm in the face of any troubles.

For several days there had been rumors of a spirit walking about at night. This spirit was a woman, naked and beautiful. The rumors eroded the holy silence until a fight between two monks piqued the Abbot's wrath. One of the monks, with orange eyelashes and freckles, said that the vision was created by the Devil. His companion, bulkier and darker than he, said it was the Virgin Mary appearing.

"Oh, certainly," the orange monk scoffed, "the Virgin Mary herself, naked as a pig standing in the middle of a group of men and not speaking a word but showing her woman's parts to the world. You wouldn't be suggesting that the Virgin Mary is displaying her cunt for the purpose of stimulating our spiritual devotion, now, would you?"

The other monk replied, "Well, she is so beautiful and gentle."

"Oh, you should turn around and bend over so I can hear you better, man, because you must be speakin' out of your arsehole! Do you think the Devil's going to send a temptress looks like yer toothless grandmother? And do you think the Virgin Mary has nothing better to do than to traipse around naked, leaving Jesus her robes and shawl to hold while she's at it?"

Bartholomew had been about to run outside and hush them, but it was too late; the Abbot was upon them like an uncle on a thief. "Silence!" he yelled. "Your own lust and ignorance is behind your mad visions. I'll not hear another word about the Naked Woman or I'll have leeches put on your testicles!"

That was enough instruction for the two monks. They parted like the Red Sea, one going to the barn to supervise the cow tending there, and the other gliding inside to take his seat in chapel, positioning himself in fervent prayer and pious solitude.

The Abbot, Bartholomew understood, was a hypocrite. And now the disenchanted monk plodded heavily back up the hill, looking up to see the threads of smoke coming out of the Monastery chimneys as though the place were a seething god.

There was a new crisis now, which obscured the interest in the Naked Woman, and which some said was a direct result of her visitation and the subsequent stir. A young monk had fallen in the garden and had been bitten by one of the pigs. The bite festered and the monk had to go to the infirmary, where he had moaned and yelled in fever for two days and nights. The Infirmarer had lanced the pussing wound and poured scalding water on it. Masses were given for him. The Abbot prayed with the Infirmarer by the dying man's bedside. The man was afraid of death. He whined about many sins for which he knew Jesus would not forgive him. At night Grey heard the young voice cracking as the dying man called out to his mother, called out to Jesus. She saw the Infirmarer on the night stair, weeping into his cupped hands, his strong man's back bent over, and she touched him briefly, touched his back with the tips of her fingers.

Even the Abbot was disheveled. He interrupted the monk reading scripture during the meal and quietly said, "Just help the man with your prayers and your own piety."

A pall, a black cloth, covered the Monastery. Some cursed the monk who had the carelessness to be dying loudly of a pig bite. The Kitchener threatened to smother him and send him on to wherever the Lord saw fit to put him. Finally the young man died. There was silence and a funeral. Grey stayed in her cell, crouching in the corner with her chin on her knees. She thought of her father's cruel death, of the bleakness of life and the ways in which men tried to name things and order things and know things; they seemed to take some comfort in words and reasons, causes and explanations. But in pain there was only pain; in pleasure there was only pleasure. Both came and went despite the theories or rules or laws. It seemed reasonable to seek as much pleasure as possible.

Grey lay on her bedding one night thinking of where Red and the pilgrims might be. Perhaps they would not find Heaven.

She was alone with Bartholomew, who had just come into the cell. He whispered something under his breath and crawled onto his bedding. She could barely see him in the light coming through the little window.

She lay for a while, thinking of how she might return to Finnistuath, how she might see her mother and her sisters again, and the Midwife. She would stop first in Tarmath and clothe herself as a woman. The cloth would be red, perhaps a velvet or brocade like the Lady of the Manor wore. She would perfume her hair and wear silk slippers.

When Bartholomew began to snore, Grey rose up from the bed; her back was hot. The space around her was square and dark, geometrically cold, stark. Winter was coming on. It was seeping into things and darkening the world. There was no comfort. The ceiling in her cell was so high and cavernous that many spirits could hover in the air above her and look down at her, scrutinizing her, judging her, teasing her.

The night stairs were soaked with shadows. Grey had to place her hand on the stone banister, on which decorative peaks rose every few feet like sentinels, minor stoic gods. Her fingers, though work-worn, could feel the rough texture of the stone. Someone was whispering, laughing in the hall below. She swept through the arched doorway into the chapel, which was full of emptiness. The pews and altar and the cross on the altar were all dark lines. Her hand slid along the back of one of the benches.

Grey had not yet learned to speak to God. The men who sat and prayed in these pews believed. Their faith made their flesh solid, as did their purpose, this desire for perfection, for holy perfection and purity in the eyes of God. Few reached such a state; some gave up, secretly or openly. But they moved through life with that purpose as their guide and ambition. Even those who made fun of the holy ways or were cynical had days of piety. They still fasted and hoped. And even their despair, though heavy and mean sometimes, had religious meaning: it was sin, transgression, the doubt of Saint Thomas.

But what did she have? She was disappearing in a restless metamorphosis.

Grey crossed herself in front of the crucifix and stared at it fiercely. Jesus' eyes remained downcast with exhaustion and remorse.

The little wooden door to the sacristy had the shape and humility of a door to an enchanted elf's house, deep in the woods. Fiona had told Grey once that there were doors in the bottoms of big trees that opened up into beautiful little rooms, and stairways that led down to halls filled with banquet tables. Grey pushed down the iron latch and the door whined open into a fully black space, no windows to give light. Grey's hands moved around the darkness as she took small steps and finally found a low table on which a pile of smooth cloth, linen robes sat. This was all she needed to find. She filled her arms with the linen and squatted down. Then she leaned under the table and laid the cloth on the floor there—a layer of robes against the wall and then a stack of robes to hide her. Into this nest she went, like a fox going into a cave. She lay there telling herself that no one, no one in the entire world knew where she was. It was as though she could disappear, like a fairy, and appear again whenever she wanted.

She fell asleep and slept as deeply as she had ever slept, past Matins, which drifted into her dreams as the sound of compassionate angels. She did not fully awaken until Lauds, when the door burst open and the wiry Sacrist grabbed one of the robes still on the table and left without seeing Grey. Then she sat up, full of clarity, and waited until Lauds was over. The Sacrist returned, in as much of a hurry as he had previously been, and left the robe he had taken. But he saw the disarray and the robes lying on the floor and gasped. Under the table, Grey pressed herself against the wall. The Sacrist breathed out exclamations that grew in intensity. Then he left.

Grey emerged from the chapel as a lithe no one. The spell of invisibility was broken when the frater cat, who had been hunting mice in the chapel, rubbed against her legs. Then Grey was seen on the night stair by two monks who were in silent thought passing by in the hall below. They nodded at her, one motioning with his hands for her to hurry up the stairs, hurry to her cell. Bartholomew was enraged.

"I have had several disappointments," he hissed. "And the Kitchener has threatened to have you thrown out of the Monastery for being useless. Where have you been? What nonsense have you been up to?" Bartholomew rubbed his face as though trying to eradicate something from it.

"I have only been asleep. I have been with no one. I have been alone."

"There is a delegation coming from Avignon in a few days. Do you hear me? Do you know the significance of that? There will be monks chosen from here to go back with them, perhaps. They are sometimes given escorts, and I hear that one of the delegation is ill and may need replacing. I want to be chosen."

Brother Dunsten came along just then, poking his head into the cell.

"They say that something walks about at night," he said, "making mischief. They say that something has been in the sacristy defiling the holy items there."

Bartholomew lunged for Brother Dunsten's throat.

He slipped away, laughing, and added, "But the world will end soon. That is all we are doing in this miserable life, waiting for the world's end. And then what will matter but the purity of our souls?"

"You are a rodent's ass!" Bartholomew bellowed, and Dunsten scurried away, his shadow and his giggling bouncing along the stone walls.

"I am not going to be a monk, am I? I am not going to be allowed to speak to God, am I? Tell me the truth, Brother Bartholomew."

Bartholomew opened his mouth and then closed it without letting any words out.

"Then answer this question," Grey said. "When men touch my body, do they move closer to God or do they forget Him?"

He had no answer to this either.

## 27

GREY RECOGNIZED the odor of books and the satchels that hung on hooks and held scrolls. The room smelled like trees and leather. There were many books and scrolls in this room.

"I don't want to be seen here with her," the man whispered to Bartholomew. He sounded angry.

"I will stand outside the door," Bartholomew said.

The door opened and closed. She could hear her own breathing and felt the slightest movement of air as he came close to her. He took her hand suddenly, which made her start. He waited a moment and then led her across the floor. He turned her around and pulled the woolen robe over her head so that she was again standing naked in the cold room.

"You are cold," he whispered. He put both his hands on her shoulder and pushed her down. She was again in the leather chair. She felt the woolen robe fall over her shoulders. Through the blindfold she could see patches of light, of candle flame—three dispersed around the small room.

The man muttered in Latin. Grey adjusted herself in the chair and sat straight, her hands lying in her lap. Then she felt the man's hands move up the inside of her legs as they had done before. The hands stopped and moved around her hips so that they were holding her buttocks. Then the man's head came down onto her thighs. The weight surprised her, as did his stillness. She could feel his warm breath on her skin.

He turned his face into her flesh. And then her own hand lifted and came down on his head. She could feel the tonsure and a fine border of hair.

The head lifted up. She felt the man's torso come between her legs. He was on his knees. Hands, very warm and wide, lay on her breasts. Then roughly he lifted her up by the waist and they were both standing. She was held against him tightly, his hand pressing her head against his chest.

The man breathed into her hair, whispering Latin words, English words, Gaelic words. When he spoke Gaelic she heard him say, "You are enchanting me."

She put her arms around him and leaned against him, her mind empty of words and thoughts, her body full of wanting to lie down with this man. She began to move against the wool of his robe, pressing her breasts into him so he could feel them, imagine them. She clung to him, grabbing the back of his robe in both fists and weeping freely. Who was this man who shared her loneliness and to whom she could not speak? She would penetrate his loneliness and hers with the force of her senses, hurling her body with unrelenting accuracy into the core of that loneliness.

He picked her up as though she were a child and set her back in the chair. She let go of his neck and sat straight and still, sat with dignity, her head held up though the blindfold was still over her eyes and tears slid from under it. She almost spoke; her lips parted, but the man kneeled before her and took up both her hands. He placed them together and held them there in the gesture of praying as he whispered the Lord's Prayer in Latin. Then his hands left hers and she felt him wipe the wetness on her face with a woolen cloth; perhaps it was her robe, which he then put around her shoulders. She heard the door open and close as she slipped the robe over her head.

Seconds before she was going to lift the blindfold and look around, Bartholomew came in, grabbed her by the upper arm and pulled her out.

When they were in their cell, Grey kept the blindfold on, touching it lightly with her fingers as she lay on her bedding.

"You are smitten," Bartholomew said solemnly.

"Yes."

"There is nothing more tedious than a companion who is smitten. All decent conversation ceases."

Grey sighed.

"But it is a grave mistake to be smitten with this man or any of the men I will deliver you to," Bartholomew said.

"I want him to know me. I want someone here besides you to know that I am not a deaf-mute."

"You must not speak to them or look at them or try to discover who they are, for I will go to Avignon and will not let scandal ruin my plans."

"Do you intend to take me to Avignon with you?" She lifted up one side of the blindfold and looked at Bartholomew.

"I cannot say. It will depend upon your usefulness, your reason."

"And if I do not want to go there?"

"Where will you go?"

"I will go to Tarmath."

Bartholomew patted her arm.

"We will see. In the meantime, we will look after one another."

Grey pulled the blindfold back over her eyes.

She touched her own breasts beneath her robe, letting her thumbs pass over the nipples and feeling them bloom. She passed one hand down the length of her body and combed the hair between her legs then smelled her own fingers. Behind the blindfold she saw the monks of the Monastery bathing. She wondered what it would be like to take this one's hand and weave her fingers in with his. She wondered what this one's lips would taste like. She wondered how firm and lasting the embrace of one strong young man would be. Would someone small and sinewy like the Infirmarer be able to carry her over his shoulder to a nest of hay in the barn and cover her body with his in a passionate promise of devotion and protection? She imagined turning in the arms of the man she had just been with and meeting his eyes, perhaps green, perhaps a light blue. He would feel her breasts against his chest and she would transport them both beyond the Monastery, beyond fear into sensual ceremonies that only her woman's body could perform.

28

THE WINTER was wet but not unfairly cold. Only a thin sheet of ice covered the stream, so Grey didn't have much trouble breaking through the ice with a big stick when she had to fetch water. Early one morning she trotted down the meadow to a mulberry tree and dropping the empty water pail, climbed up into its leafless branches, the loving tree's sturdy arms.

The tree's branches had impressed her many times as providing easy climbing. They were thick and close together. She went up and up, grabbing and pulling herself higher, feeling like a cat, exhilarated, smiling. She sat down on a high branch, almost at the top of the tree. She could see the roof of the Monastery, the ugly sooted chimneys like rows of blackened asparagus. She could see the embankment, crawling with brambles and thistle. In the other direction, she could see the snake of stream moving miles to the southeast. She could see the forests of gray sticks and green feathers spread out endlessly to the south. She spoke to the tree as she had wanted to speak to the man. "Let me stay here with you. Keep me."

When she returned with the water, the Kitchener boxed her ears. This was the first time her ears had ever been boxed, and it was a horrible blow— two fists crashing against her ears as though her skull was being crushed. The ringing did not stop for hours, and her fear of ear boxing was permanently affixed.

She complained to Bartholomew, saying, "I am treated roughly by the Kitchener. Beat me again, if you want, but I am weary of being a servant when I can be with men whose hands caress me or when I can leave this place and make my own way."

"You cannot cause trouble now. You cannot. The delegation from Avignon is a few days away. You must help with the preparations. There are thousands of chores to do, thousands."

"I don't want to work for the Kitchener anymore. He boxes my ears."

"It occurred once. It is not his habit to box ears."

"He has proved that he is willing and most able to do it. And that is all I need to know. I want to work with the Sacrist, with the robes and cloths in the chapel."

"The Sacrist," Bartholomew scoffed. "Indeed."

"I am fond of the sacristy."

Bartholomew sighed. "Why do you assume that these choices are yours—a goatherd's daughter from Finnistuath?" And then there was a tap at the door. Grey had heard it many times, one slow tap and three quick. It was the Librarian.

He let himself in. Bartholomew greeted him with the usual "Blessing to you brother." The Librarian ignored Grey. She sat on her bedding, sullenly pulling a piece of straw through her fingers. Then Bartholomew and the Librarian left together. Grey waited a few moments and then stood up and looked out the little window and saw the two men walking side by side. They were strolling in the field outside the Monastery, going toward the stream, appearing to be two monks in religious contemplation.

Grey sat back down on the bedding. Soon she would have to help serve the day's meal; at meal time she often looked at each man and tried to pick her lover from them. It had to be someone with influence—not any novice—perhaps the Cellarer, the man who oversaw the Monastery's economic life—its stipends from Avignon, its purchase of goods and services, its selling of relics and prayers. It was he who had the freedom to go regularly to the village and arrange for prayers to be said for the sick and dying or the sinful. It was he who had the privilege of handling coins. Bartholomew could get coin from him and then give it to whomever could arrange his journey to France. Or her lover could be the Novice Master, but he was very fat—clearly not the stature of the man who had held her as close as one holds a blanket during a cold night. Or perhaps he was the Prior or the Sacrist or the Abbot or the Infirmarer. There were some comely young men, but Bartholomew would not have bothered to deal with them, for they had nothing to offer but their lust.

At that day's meal she listened intently as the Abbot read the scriptures at the meal, wiping his brow often. His voice soothed Grey though she understood only a little of the Latin, such as *Deus*. What if she suddenly interrupted him, fell down on her knees and said, "Jesus, Mary, and Joseph, I am cured of my afflictions! I can hear and speak! It is a miracle!" She laughed to herself, twisting up her mouth so as not to make a sound, but Brother Dunsten saw her and squinted his eyes in a dramatic expression of annoyance. She narrowed her eyes back at him and then felt a cold ache fall from her head to her stomach. What if her lover were Brother Dunsten? She shook her head. A few of the monks nearby saw her and fit her demeanor into their belief that she was a half-wit. But Brother Dunsten cackled. This made Grey even more distraught, and she dropped the bowls she was carrying. The Abbot stopped abruptly in his reading. In the brief but deep silence the orange-and-white frater cat mewed, the younger monks chuckled, and the Abbot sternly resumed the reading.

She begged Bartholomew to tell her that the man she had embraced with such abandon was not Brother Dunsten. He laughed at her pale face.

"I'll not play guessing games with you on this matter."

"I can disappear. I will disappear," Grey said.

She stayed many days in the mulberry tree and nights sleeping in the sacristy, sneaking bread and cheese and apples from the frater. The Kitchener asked for her; the Prior asked for her; the Abbot asked for her. But Bartholomew could only say that she was suffering a spell of madness. He even asked the Infirmarer for any herb or method he might have for helping with madness. The Infirmarer suggested fennel for mental vacancy. And Bartholomew said, "What about the opposing ailment—a plethora of thoughts?" The Infirmarer said that fennel was also good for folly, which Bartholomew said was precisely the problem.

Once, from the top of the mulberry tree, Grey saw Bartholomew and the Librarian sitting by the stream laughing and embracing. She looked away.

When she came back into the community as a visible entity, Grey asked if the man had requested to see her again, and Bartholomew said that he had not, but that it was only because of a great deal of preparation being done for the visit from the Pope's emissaries.

Later than expected, in late spring, the delegation from Avignon came with six men, one of them very ill. But Brother Peter, the head of the delegation, was a hardy man, a farmer in frame and stride. He was Irish, one of the few who had risen in the ranks and been assigned to Avignon. He laughed heartily but had a blunt mouth and was openly displeased. He was greatly displeased at the condition of the Monastery, at the infestation of bedbugs. Brother Peter blamed the Abbot for running the place too much as his own kingdom, and screamed at the Infirmarer for the unhealthy habits of the brethren. Quiet and concerned, the Infirmarer nodded when Brother Peter spit out recipes for concoctions, instructions for leeching, and warnings about walking outside at night when the planets were in certain positions. He explained that bathing was an ignorant Irish habit, not done in civilized places. The four healthy men beneath Brother Peter were silent and clearly intimidated. They did whatever he told them to do, including sleeping together in a corner of the barn. Brother Peter occupied most of his time in the library, sitting in the leather chair of Roman design, reading, studying, calling various people to speak with him, including the Abbot.

Brother Peter had outbursts, some of them at the meal, some of them late at night. He lectured everyone about Pope Clement VI's position on the end of the world, which was that it could occur soon, and that the most important thing to do was to be prepared in all areas of virtue, cleanliness, and obedience to the Church and its wise advice. As several days went by, Brother Peter became more and more agitated, as did everyone else.

Bartholomew got into the regular habit of pacing and rubbing his hands. He repeated thoughts and phrases over and over until Grey wanted to live forever in the mulberry tree, whose leaves now made a rich, green veil around her.

"The Abbot does not jump to Brother Peter's orders, and I admire him for that, I admire him for that, I do indeed. But it has gone too far. He has become too arrogant. If the Pope requests the return of the box, then there is no reason . . . no right . . . the Librarian, who knows all about the matter, has said as much."

Grey dozed on her bedding listening to Bartholomew's dreams of going to Avignon, of going with the Librarian. He went on and on about the cleverness of the Librarian, and the power he had, the secrets he knew.

The next evening, blindfolded again, she heard the door shut and separate her from Bartholomew. There was silence in the room, a different room, not the one with the leather chair.

She knelt down, bowing her head against her folded hands. She was immensely weary. Then she heard feet shuffle across the floor. Something was wrong, crooked, out of balance and about to topple. A stinging panic sprang up in her stomach and spread quickly to her heart. Then she felt the man standing above her, breathing. She shivered violently. It was not the same man. It was a different man.

She stood up and stepped back. She shook her head. She heard laughter and a hand shook her shoulder.

"So, you are a female. Let me see." He did not whisper. He had no fear of being found out.

He grabbed the woolen robe and pulled it over her head awkwardly, catching it for a few seconds and roughly yanking it away.

"Very good," he said. "Very good."

She stepped back. It was Brother Peter. She knew.

"Ahh, little muted idiot," the man said. "I can do whatever I like. I can do whatever I like."

She folded her arms over her chest, holding herself together, possessing herself.

"Yes," he said. "Oh, yes."

He pulled her arms down and mashed her breasts with his hand. Then he pushed her down to the floor, which was made of packed dirt. She struggled against his hard hands. He parted her legs and put his prick against her crotch. It would not go into her.

"Come on," he said as though trying to get a cow through a gate.

He went away from her. She could not smell him or feel his heat. But she heard him speak to himself from across the room. She stood up.

"I suppose she still needs coaxing like any woman."

She was pulling at the door, trying to find the handle without taking off the blindfold, because she knew that if the man thought she could hear him or see him, and worse, could speak about what she heard and saw, he would dispense with her as easily as twisting the neck of a chicken.

He came back and pushed her down again. She felt two fingers massaging her between her legs. His other hand patted her cheek. She wanted to scream; she felt the day's meal climb up into her throat.

"Come on, now," he said.

His fingers went away. His prick returned, jamming into her, ripping. She squirmed backward. He pulled her back roughly, growling and laughing. The stinging continued and she beat her fists against his back. He held her wrists and pushed her hands away from him, still laughing.

Three strokes and he said, "Ahhhh, you little deaf-mute," and fell out of her. She sat up and held herself between the legs with both hands; warm moisture slid out onto her fingers.

She said over and over in her head, "Go. Go. Go." It was a prayer. She wanted to be able to take the blindfold off and look at herself, to see if she were dying. She wanted to scream at him to leave her alone. But he stood up and talked. He kept talking, even though she was a deaf-mute.

"This is a filthy place," he said. "This is a dark and filthy place."

"Go. Go. Go," she thought.

"It should be burned to the ground. It should be wiped from the face of the Earth."

"Please go. Please go. Please go. Please, Saint Brigid, please make him go."

She heard his feet shuffling around the small room. She leaned against the wall and patted the floor to find the woolen robe. She put it on as he continued to talk.

"I should put a torch to it."

Then after a pause, "Damn that swollen toad. Damn him and his ignorant defiance. He doesn't know what he's doing."

He was silent for a few moments and then suddenly near her again.

"Stupid thing," he said. And then he left.

She took the blindfold off immediately. To hell with Bartholomew. If he got angry, so be it. It didn't matter what Bartholomew did any longer.

There were four candles lighted in a small empty cell. There was no bedding. Just a crucifix on the wall and a bench with an old wooden bucket and a faded vellum Bible on it. It was a room off the chapel where a single monk was isolated when he had committed some sin during the Offices: the sin of sleeping or talking to his neighbor. It was a room for reflection on one's flaws and smallness.

Grey got a candle and hunched over with it to look between her legs. There was watery-looking blood on her pubic hair and on her hands. Liquid still slid down the inside of her thighs. She walked stiffly over to the door, feeling the soreness between her legs, and sat down, leaning against it and looking around the room. What would she do now? She was going to be sick; she was going to vomit up the last hour. Had the man she had been with before known about this liaison with Brother Peter? Did he know? She bent over and vomited a small amount of tan oatmeal. A string of it and her spit hung from her lips as she began to weep.

She wiped her mouth with the back of her hand and then held her knees, putting her chin on the right one and closing her eyes. She squatted, groaning in response to renewed stinging. She fell back. Slowly, hardly able to force herself to move, she stood up, staring down at the floor.

She looked around and finally went to the open Bible. Words. She looked down on all the marks that meant nothing to her. And then she wiped her hands, the pale blood and yellow liquids streaking the faded lines of scripture.

 **29**

NEAR THE TOP of the mulberry tree in a pouring rain that thundered on all the leaves of all the trees, Grey sat. Rivulets ran down her shorn head, on which a half an inch of thick hair had grown out like a covering of moss.

On the morning after he raped her, Brother Peter had been screaming about lice. He had ordered that everyone have his head shaved. Everyone. He ordered that all clothing and bedding be brought outside to be shaken, beaten, and blessed. He ordered that everyone fast.

Into such a day had Grey wretchedly crawled, snatched up on her way to her cell by the Kitchener, who was rounding up everyone and taking them outside. There, each resident of the Monastery was set down on a stool as the Kitchener wielded a sharpened blade. And each man rose with shorn head and a few bloody nicks. When Grey stood up from the stool, there was an instant of silence as the community saw the beauty of her eyes, no longer behind the tangled, thick veil of her hair. The bluish gray color was deep and unusual.

While the Kitchener continued his chore, Grey drifted into the frater and took a knife there, a dull-bladed knife for use at meals; but with a strong and accurate thrust behind it, it would do well to remind a man of the dangers of trying to steal her body. The she went to the barn and made a strap for it, which she wore as a belt beneath her clothing.

Now Grey looked as far as she could across the stream and toward the southern woods until, at some point in the distance, the rain dissolved everything into a white mist. She could hear some creature's constant high-pitched rattle—insect or frog. And at some distance a bird called out, one long, one short note. Everything was being drenched, everything echoing through the constant noise of the drumming downpour.

An animal, a large bird, screamed. Grey closed her eyes. She was perhaps hearing the death of something, its death cries. But the sound came again and was, after all, a declaration of anger and annoyance. Grey lay down on the branch like a cat, arms and legs drooping down. No tail, though. She turned around to see—no tail. She put her head back down on the bark and closed her eyes against the water running into them. She was free there, from Bartholomew's plans with Brother Peter, and from Brother Dunsten, who winked and nodded whenever he passed her. Now that his head was shaved, his teeth seemed even bigger than before. She was free also from the constant hissing of rumors in the Monastery: that it was to be closed down, that Brother Peter was going to exorcise it of fairies, who were fornicating with the monks, that the world had begun to end already at the hands of a flood or a fire or a scourge that had already begun in France.

Even with all the rain, Grey could hear Brother Peter's voice rise up and spread out from within the Monastery. He was in the frater, giving a sermon while the monks ate a paltry soup of water and cabbage to break their fast. In this weakened state, they listened to shaming admonishments about their Monastery and their Abbot. It had become more and more clear that Brother Peter detested the Abbot.

"He has betrayed the trust that was given to him by the Holy Father; he has been entrusted with a treasure, with one of the Pope's treasures, and will not return it."

The Abbot left the frater and the lecturing cleric to walk in the rain; he took a fistful out of a loaf of black bread as he passed by the end of a table on his way out. He left while Brother Peter was still making references to the disobedience of the leadership at the Monastery and to the possibility of the whole place being shut down. The Abbot let Brother Peter see him leave and grab some bread on his way out. And many of the monks saw, too, and admired their Abbot more.

Dunsten nodded vehemently at everyone. Hadn't he told them about the Pope's box and how it contained information about the day and hour that the world would end and the means by which it would end? Hadn't he?

In the rain the Abbot walked in long strides, his hands—one still holding the bread—folded against his back. He strode and strode, with no concern for the drenching he was getting. When he stopped beneath the mulberry tree, he did not know that Grey was looking down on him, her imaginary tail switching back and forth. He dropped the clumps of sodden bread and bowed his head. Grey watched, considering dropping a leaf or twig on that head. These men in this Monastery, she determined, regarded themselves with far too much solemnity. Maybe it was grace that she could not be one of them.

The rain abated, growing softer, moving off to wash another place, other leaves. And the Abbot looked up and saw Grey way over him, high up in the trees, a dark shape woven into all the green and gray, with a head that moved, with eyes that looked down on him. At first he believed this to be a spirit, perhaps a dangerous one, but then he recognized Grey. He backed up to see her face with less disruption from the leaves, and then he called out, "Come down from there." But he said quietly to himself, "Why bother to speak?" Then he lifted his arm and motioned with his hand, in large movements that rocked the upper half of his body, for her to come down.

But she was a cat now. She was not going to come down. She was not going to let anyone control her, grab her, pull her tail, feed her fish heads. The Abbot walked away, back up the incline to the Monastery.

Later that evening, listening to the bells announcing Compline and standing naked in the middle of the cell, Grey watched as Bartholomew spread her leggings out on the floor. He was being fastidious, cleaning everything, like everyone else afraid of the judgment of Brother Peter.

"They will be dry by tomorrow. Keep the robe because you've a duty to perform tonight."

She stepped backward, covering her breasts with her arms and lowering her head. More and more she forgot that she did not have to be the deaf-mute with Bartholomew. More and more she was the deaf-mute all the time, or at least the mute.

"You don't have to play that part with me," Bartholomew said.

Then there was a loud knocking on the door, a vibrating banging, and the Librarian barged in. He was panting, which made his long face seem even longer. "I'm going to go to Avignon—with you." He smiled and panted, standing ready to be embraced. Bartholomew stared at him.

"Yes. We are going! We are both going to Avignon! Tomorrow!"

Grey grabbed the robe out of Bartholomew's limp arms and put it on.

"What did you say? Why did he change his mind?"

"I told him what I knew. I told him directly, with no equivocation."

Bartholomew looked at Grey and then back at the Librarian. He finally embraced him, turning him around and around.

"Oh, tell me, tell me, we are out of this place."

"We are indeed, my friend. We are on our way to France."

Still holding onto the Librarian, Bartholomew said, "Did you say anything about me, that I know anything?"

"No, no. I simply said that you were the most qualified to arrange and oversee the journey, for you had already made a vocation of journeys and knew well how to deal with innkeepers and shipowners. I said that I would trust no one else to provide safe and efficient passage. He seemed most ready to comply."

"Oh, this is very good. This is very good." He left the Librarian and paced the floor.

"I had to tell you. But I'd best be going. I'd best be going. Oh, I will not sleep tonight. I will dream, but I will not sleep."

Grey turned and looked out the window at the night.

Standing in the doorway, the Librarian leaned in and whispered, "I will ask the Pope directly, my friend, about the matters here. I will find out the truth; he will explain the contents of the box, for Brother Peter himself said that there was an explanation that the Pope himself will tell me."

When the door closed, Grey said to Bartholomew, "He knows about me, that I am not a boy. He saw me standing naked here and showed no surprise."

"He knows. Of course he knows. He was sore as a beaten dog that I had a companion in my cell. I told him the truth. He is a good man with secrets. He has discipline. When he makes a vow, he keeps it. He has not even told me what he has been warned not to divulge about the Pope's box, about the contents of it."

"Is that what the Abbot will not give to that man, that ugly man from Avignon?"

Jovial, Bartholomew waved his hand at Grey as though to say, "It isn't important."

"You will leave me here, with whatever it is that scratches at the walls and makes holy men do unholy things. I am not fulfilling your bargains any longer. I will not be handled by that man again. He is rough and horrible. I will no longer be a part of your plan. You have gotten what you want. I have nothing. I am nothing."

She sank down onto her bedding and tried to shrink into a ball.

"It is the other one tonight. The one you have been with twice."

Bartholomew turned to the door, but Grey leapt up and her hand grabbed his forearm. "Wait. I will go to him, if it is indeed the one . . . the one with the leather chair."

When the Office of Compline was over, the last note of the Kyrie Eleison still shimmering in the dank air, Bartholomew flew through the dormitory clapping his hands for all to be in their beds. Then he returned to his cell and blindfolded Grey. He took her down the night stairs and then made her spin around and around so that she was completely disoriented and unable to tell in what direction she was being led. She had to hold onto his arm with both hands to keep from falling from dizziness.

"Slow," she whispered.

When they reached the room, Grey could feel the man's presence and she could not keep her mouth from smiling.

Bartholomew left the room, the door making a breeze against Grey's face as he shut it. She was inclined to step toward the man to go to him and touch his face with her hands. But she didn't. She waited.

His hand first perched on her head, feeling the thick carpet of hair there, stroking it kindly. She smiled. Did he see her smile? Was he smiling as well? Was his hair shorn? Was it perhaps the Kitchener himself checking his work? Could a man box a woman's ears and also embrace her? Thank the rain for softening and washing away the scabs the shearing left. She smelled good candles, warm and pure wax, not the lowly cressets.

The man then embraced her, rocked her tightly against him so that his own hands almost met each other against her solar plexus. She could barely breathe, but she wanted him not to let her go. She put her arms around him and lay her hands, fingers spread out, on his back. He loosened his grip but continued to rock her. Her face lifted, she could smell smoke on the skin of his neck. There were dark places on the blindfold where tears had soaked through.

Then there was a knock on the door, so startling to both of them that they froze, and then the man pushed her away, grabbed her hand, and pulled her away from the door. She could feel cloth against her arm, the heavy cloth of a velvet curtain, and then she was in a darker place, in warm, stale air. She heard the door open and the voice of Brother Peter.

"I am up preparing for the journey. And I thought I would share a cup of wine with you."

The other voice was very quiet, and she could only hear a few words of it, but Brother Peter replied loudly, " Do you know of any reason why we should not simply have this place destroyed like a weed in the garden of the Church?"

The only word Grey could hear the other man say was "loyal."

"Then give it to me. Just give me the wretched thing that was never yours. It was a mistake to place it here in the first place, a mistake to risk it getting lost or stolen."

Grey could not make out any words in the calm low tone of the other man. But she jumped when there was a sudden banging noise.

"Your stubbornness will get shoved up your ass with a poker."

Grey grabbed the velvet cloth with her fist, then quickly dropped it, realizing that the men on the other side could perhaps see the curtain bunched when she held it.

They did not speak for a minute, and she imagined them both looking toward where she was. But then Brother Peter said, "And who are you but a minor nothing, a minor little servant in a minor little monastery in a poor and worthless land in the middle of nowhere?"

Slowly, methodically, Grey undid the strap around her waist so as to make as little movement as possible.

"I will pray for the Pope," the other man said in the same growling whisper. "I will return his property to him myself in a few months."

The strap fell loose with her hand squeezing the knife. She pulled the knife, trailing the strap, away from her skin and let the robe fall back. Her hand sweated around the handle of the knife.

"The Pope must not be troubled by this any longer. He hears when the rumors spread from those who leave this Monastery. It has made him ill," Brother Peter said, more irritated and weary than angry now.

"I will pray for his health," she heard the man say hoarsely. And then he cleared his throat.

Then Grey heard the door to the room open. She waited. But she heard nothing else. She guessed that the man had gone out with Brother Peter, but then a hand closed around her wrist. His hand was colder than before and pulled at her. Grey transferred the knife she held into the other hand and dropped it behind the curtain as she was pulled out, coughing to hide the little thud of the knife and its strap hitting the floor. Then she put her hand over his that held her wrist and rubbed it, warming it.

He led her to the door and then stopped. She knew that he meant to send her out, to take her back to Bartholomew, or just to leave her in the hall like a cat put out to mew for its food. It was Brother Peter who had ruined her tryst.

With both of her hands still wrapped around his one, Grey pulled back from the door. She shook her head. The man sighed.

Then he led her away from the door until her ankles touched the edge of some bedding. He pulled her hand downward as a sign, and she sat on the bedding. There was cloth on it like the velvet of the curtains she had touched. She ran the palm of her hand over it. It was perhaps the smoothest thing she had ever touched. The man was kneeling in front of her. She reached out and could feel that he held his face in the palm of his hands. She stroked his head. He whispered, "Forgive me." And she smiled and lay back carefully, in case there was a wall behind her. But there was none, and her shoulders were still on the bedding, her head lifted so it would not fall back onto the floor. He put his hands under her robe, moving them up along her legs as seemed to be his habit. He held her hips and pulled her toward him so that her head could lay back on the bedding. He moved the wool cloth up and lay his head on her naked belly.

She could feel his weariness. She could feel the sadness and weariness in his head, and she placed her hand on it. She moved her fingers over his cheek—moist warm skin, smoothed with a pumice stone—over his eyes—hard moving curves beneath warm lids—over the bony bridge of his nose and down to his lips—the lower one soft and wide. She pressed the fingers against his lips as though to shush him, as though to quiet the thoughts that were bothering him. She was seeing him now with her fingers, which he took, and he touched their tips with his tongue, tasting her.

And then he moved slowly up and lay on top of her. She waited for a moment then reached down to take his cock, but he moved her hand away. Then he stood up. For a moment she didn't know where he was, but soon he lay back down on top of her, naked. He pushed her robe up until it was above her breasts. She put her face against his shoulder and felt the angle of his collarbone there. She took in the odor of wool and smoke. She put her lips on the skin of his neck as he was entering her. When he went inside her she felt as though she was rolling fast down a hill in a cart, thrilled and frightened at once. All her sensations were between her legs and on her skin. He was slow in moving in and out of her; he was careful not to lie too heavily on her. He pressed his cheek against hers. He stroked her arm with the backs of his fingers. He lifted one of her legs, bending it against his side so he could thrust more deeply. Heat went through her body from between her legs, radiating, flashing, and illuminating her from within, the way the clouds and mulberry leaves sometimes looked at sunset. This ecstasy of fornication, it was a piece of the world that had no pain or worry or humiliation. It was a moment of pure feeling and pure affection and the careful use of power. For this man did not hurt her, and she did not hurt him. She could. She could be difficult or pretend that he repulsed her. She had power, too. The more he went in and out of her the weaker her legs felt; then it was as though nothing existed for her but the heat and the feel of him lying on her. And then she throbbed as she had once done in a dream from which she awoke to find herself breathing hard and moving her hips against the bedding. She clung to the man who was now breathing as loudly as she, with the same rhythm. He was whispering, beginnings of words, pieces of prayers. And then he held himself in her as deeply as he could go, propping himself up on his elbows. He let out a moan, almost a growl. And then he lowered himself carefully back onto Grey. She put both hands on his back, holding it, calming it, cherishing it. He rolled over, lifting her onto him. There he lay, catching his breath, slick with sweat, and she tangled her fingers in the hair on his chest and listened to his heart. What a strange and large heart it seemed. He held her head in his hands and said into her ear, "How cruel this place is; how pathetic a man's attempts to be holy. I wish that you could speak and hear. I would confess to you. Or perhaps you are a better confessor as a deaf-mute."

She lay still; she was thinking quickly, imagining the next few minutes and how they might be played; she was about to say, "I can speak and hear." Almost. But she could not speak. She wanted nothing to change or disturb their closeness. If she spoke, there would be words, there would be promises, there would be misunderstandings, there would be philosophies and accusations and discussions. She stayed quiet, playing with the coils of his chest hair, spreading her fingers through them, plowing through them up to his neck and then coming to smooth skin and going over his shoulders, where she felt a delicate chain. With two fingers she traced the chain to a place just below his throat, and there she felt a small, hard key. He moved his hand from her back, where he had been sweeping his fingers over her skin. She quickly let go of the key, but he took her hand back to it. He held it there, the key buried in the two layers of their two fists. She fell asleep this way for several hours as though she were in the sacristy in a nest of holy items; the next thing she felt was Bartholomew shaking her, and she awoke to find herself on her back, holding nothing.

30

BROTHER PETER and four of the men who had come with him from Avignon walked across the sloping valley toward the path to Tarmath like the vanguard of some mystical, dark army. The sixth man had never fully recovered and was, in fact, dying in the infirmary. He would never see France again, but he was grateful to die with the Infirmarer's face near his—for it was full of a genuine desire for an end to the suffering, and his hands were not afraid to touch the sick.

Grey stood at the window of her and Bartholomew's cell. She watched Brother Peter. Brother Bartholomew and the Librarian were with them. All the luxuries that Brother Bartholomew had accumulated as a result of his use of Grey were still sorted and piled in the cell: sacks of apples, bottles of oil, scrolls tied with silk twine, and baskets of cheese. But his ledger of notes and drawings and pressed ferns that he had brought back with him from Finnistuath was gone, and Bartholomew had not said good-bye.

Now he walked, a little behind Brother Peter's group, chatting with the Librarian as he tapped on the ledger. Brother Peter stopped and turned to face the two monks behind him. Grey watched as he snatched the ledger from beneath Bartholomew's arm and flung it away, spinning it hard so that it flew apart and landed in the grasses. Birds flew up from a nearby tree and swooped in a flock to a more distant perch. Grey opened her mouth to yell out, waiting for Bartholomew to run to save his work, his years of work, the seeds and ferns, the patches of fur from Finnistuath's woods near the spring. But she saw one of Brother Peter's men push Bartholomew along. For a moment the Librarian stood still, his arms raised, calling out. But Brother Peter yelled and motioned at him to hurry.

Grey could see Brother Peter laugh as his group turned eastward on a path near the stream. She watched Bartholomew's back as he walked stiffly, not looking back, and she spoke to him. "You will have another ledger. God will give you another."

She sat back in the corner. She was a deaf-mute again. She had no one to speak to. The Monastery hummed in low tones that evening, the bells ringing slowly as though they suffered with each stroke. The shadows dragged themselves up and down walls. Grey became a shadow, part of a box of darkness that smelled like Bartholomew. The warped prayer book sat on the little bench like a dead rodent.

Outside, the pages of Bartholomew's ledger blew open, freeing the leaves and blossoms, a futile liberation, since they were dead and flattened. But they fluttered around the meadow, some caught on grasses, some tumbling all the way to the trees by the stream.

That night Grey fled, as soon as the Monastery was silent, down to the sacristy. She threw the robes under the table and burrowed into them, curling herself into the smallest possible ball. She lay there, determined never to leave. It was dark and silent, warm. She hummed to herself the Kyrie Eleison. The whole Monastery smelled like blood—like goat's blood, or Jesus' blood, or her blood.

The Sacrist came in before dawn. He saw the piles of robes on the floor again, and this time he squatted down to investigate this blasphemy, this desecration. He saw first the head, and he was afraid for an instant that it was a creature of metaphysical substance and power. Then he thought better of it, that the head he was looking at had apparently been shaved as recently as his own.

"Who's here, then?" he bellowed and found a shoulder to shake.

Grey looked up at him.

"You, you little rat. Get up. Get up." He pulled her by the crook of her arm, bumping her head on the underside of the table. "Come up. I'll box your ears, I will. That's probably how you got deaf in the first place, you little rat."

Grey regretted that she was again the focus of one willing to box ears. She covered both ears with her elbows as the Sacrist, small but strong, pulled her through the door, through the chapel and in front of the Abbot's chambers, monks watching at various stations in their procession.

"He'll do more than box your ears," the Sacrist said. "He'll throw your arse out just in time for winter."

He knocked and was called in.

The Abbot was on his knees in front of a black walnut cross that hung low on the wall in his room. There were also in the room a table with some scrolls on it, a cot, and wine-colored velvet curtains to soften the chill of one of the stone walls. The Sacrist's demeanor changed abruptly as he entered the Abbot's cell. He spoke softly and with deference.

"Forgive me. Forgive me for this interruption. I have brought this little mischief maker to you."

The Abbot looked horrified. Sweat popped out on his forehead.

"What do you mean?" he rose slowly to his feet, pressing on his knees with his hands to slowly straighten.

"I found him in the sacristy, defiling the robes, nesting in them like a rat."

The Abbot's mouth hung open. He rubbed his eyes with the thumb and forefinger of one hand. Those eyes had clearly not seen enough sleep.

"Leave him here. Leave him with me. I'll take care of this."

Grey stood with her elbows still protecting her ears. The Abbot just watched her for a moment. He looked darkened and beaten, so that Grey thought he might fall onto the floor. He seemed about to give up everything.

Then he sighed loudly and stood up straighter, laughing a little to himself.

Grey lowered her elbows but backed out of reach of his hands. He shook his head and looked down, then rubbed the stubble on his face.

He looked around as though he didn't know who or where he was; then he went back to the cross and knelt in front of it. He turned to Grey and motioned for her to do as he was doing. She moved cautiously, knelt down and put her hands together in prayer, keeping an eye on his face for any signs of imminent violence. He began the Pater Noster and stayed there for a while after the prayer, his eyes closed. Everything was silent until the bells rang morosely for Prime. The Abbot stood up. Grey was still kneeling, bracing herself for a blow on the back of the head. But he just sighed and went to a little stool on which there was a meal knife with a leather strap tied to it. He stood before her, letting the knife swing in front of her by the strap. He dropped it, and she picked it up and held it pressed between her breasts.

The Abbot leaned over to help Grey to her feet. She saw then the little key that dangled out of the top of his robe. She quickly looked away. He moved her gently toward the door and pushed her out. For a moment, before the Abbot closed the door, they looked into each other's eyes. But this time, it was he who looked away quickly; he stepped back and closed the door, which scraped softly against the stone floor.

Grey went back to her cell and sat in the corner, rocking and thinking, looking at the knife lying on her bedding. The Kitchener's novice came to get her. He nodded toward the door, and she followed him down to the frater, where the Kitchener was standing with the empty water pail swinging from his fingers.

31

I drank my fill of wine with kings,
Their eyes fixed on my hair.
Now among the stinking hags
I chew the cud of prayer.

IT WAS A SONG Colin had taught Grey when she was a boy.
She sang it as she passed the chapel door. Out of the corner of her eye she saw something sitting on the altar. A large body and wings, crouching, almost obscured the candles and crucifix. She looked straight at it until it was a configuration of light and shadow.

Grey stopped singing and walked on to the Abbot's cell.

The door was open, but the room behind it was dark except for one sputtering candle, the wick almost drowned in a pool of melted wax. Clearly, the Abbot had not meant to fall asleep before putting out the candle and closing the door. It surprised Grey to think of the Abbot as asleep. It seemed to her that he, like her, was often awake, wandering around the cavernous Monastery, or listening to the demons scurrying within the walls. She went in and tried hard to see in the dark. She had, after all, made her way in the room blindfolded, with his gentle guidance, of course. After standing still and looking hard at the darkness, she could see the larger shapes and finally made out the Abbot lying half on his bedding, his cloth-wrapped feet on the floor and his hand perched on top of a scroll. She stood over him. She squatted next to him. She put her fingers just above the skin of his face. She ran one finger along the side of his neck and down to his chest, insinuating her touch and her smell into his dreams.

Then she stood up and left the room, running up the stairs two at a time.

That night in the dormitory, the vision of the woman reappeared to the monks. This time, she was wearing a black lace veil, one of those used to cover the painted statue of the Virgin Mary on Good Friday. The veil covered the vision's face but was swept back over the shoulders. The naked woman slowly walked the length of the room, holding a cresset in her hand.

Three monks immediately awoke and shook others, but most only got a glimpse of the vision leaving, the veil swelling out a little behind her in the breeze of her shadowy movement.

One man jumped from his bed and ran after her. Grey dropped the cresset, which cracked on the floor. There was yelling now from the dormitory, and the man was close behind her. In a moment, someone was ringing the bells, not for Office but as an alert, and soon there were flickering cressets throughout the dark Monastery and a few large torches lit. The quiet had erupted into all the noise of suppressed desire and confusion about the nature of the world.

The man chasing Grey, a stout, dark fellow, reached out and grabbed at the veil. Grey tugged it away and wrapped it close around her head and kept running. Ahead were three monks, including the Infirmarer. She turned back toward the first pursuer and rammed into his chest with her head, pushing him against the wall. Then she ran past him and into the chapel. There was no one there. She crouched naked between the benches and waited. She could hear no one coming, just distant yelling, and saw one light passing by in the hall outside. It was cold, and she was shaking terribly, holding herself, putting her head down on her knees and feeling the scratchy fabric of the lace against them. She cursed the men, cursed them for not just letting her be a vision.

Imagining the warm robes and cloth in the sacristy, she dared to move. And when she stood up, she saw a darker aspect of the room shaped like a man in the doorway. Neither of them moved.

Grey could feel her feet, glued mortally to the stones.

The man walked toward her and she could see now that he was the Abbot. And he could see now who she was.

There was a tiny pinging sound of something dropping on the floor near the altar.

Grey said quietly, "I am neither mute nor deaf."

He said nothing.

"I can hear and I can speak," she told him again.

The Abbot nodded, as though he were hearing a confession from one of the novices. Then she stepped forward and grabbed his hand and put it underneath the veil against her cheek. She turned her head so that her mouth moved into the palm of his hand. "You are not speaking," she said. "I am speaking and now you are mute."

She was shivering and so he put his arms around her and pulled her against him. The veil slid from her head onto the floor.

The bell ringing changed to mark the time for Matins. Grey looked at the Abbot and then wriggled away and went into the sacristy. She grabbed a robe and slid it over her head. There were five monks in the chapel with the Abbot now. He was sternly putting two fingers over his mouth to quiet them as they went to their places.

Grey came out of the sacristy, her head bowed. The Abbot grabbed her wrist and pulled her out into the hall, where several monks were whispering on their way into the chapel.

"SILENCE!" the Abbot bellowed; it was a sound that stopped the bells and left the air trembling. Everything ceased, including movement, until the Abbot lead Grey by the wrist past the monks and the two could hear the chanting begin behind them.

He pulled her into the library and closed the door. He walked her backward until the back of her legs touched the edge of the leather chair and she sat down. Standing over her, not touching her, he asked, "Why do you go about showing yourself, shaming yourself like a whore?"

"I am your whore, then, aren't I?"

The Abbot held her chin between his thumb and forefinger and lifted her face roughly. She looked into his eyes and repeated, "I am your whore."

The Abbot leaned in close to her, daring her with his enraged eyes.

She sat up and ran her tongue along his neck and then gently bit at his lip where his words had come from. She felt for his prick and held the erection with the cloth of his robe.

It comforted Grey to feel the lust that she inspired, but it made the Abbot angry.

"You are a demon who knows my weakness and preys upon it like a wild beast." He took her hands away from him and held them by the wrists before throwing them from him and straightening his back.

Grey stood up and walked to the door, but he was there in an instant, turning her around and hissing into her face.

"You must serve me, serve me only."

Tears leaked into Grey's eyes and she said, "I came here to learn to be holy, to have the privileges of the clerics who pray and sing to God."

The Abbot puffed up his cheeks with air and slowly let it out as he closed his eyes. Calmer, he said, "You must not play with these men's lust."

Grey put her arms around his neck and rested her head on his shoulder.

That Abbot said to her, "You are a comfort to me, the only thing that thoroughly distracts me from . . . from my troubles, worries, doubts."

He passed his hands gently up and down her back. He pressed himself against her, holding her head in his hands as though it were a treasure.

"I am either doomed or blessed that you are no deaf-mute."

"Would you rather that I did not speak but just fucked?" Grey asked.

The Abbot did not answer but said, "Are you not afraid that the world is coming to an end, and you and everyone else in the world will be consumed by the mouth of Hell because of God's disdain for us?" He stopped holding her and took a step backward to look at her. "Disdain for *you*. You have lied. You have deceived men of God, pretending to be a deaf-mute. You were not a witless woman fornicating. You heard and knew and could speak to refuse. Do you think when the world is destroyed your soul will go to Heaven?"

"And what of your fornication?"

He laughed at her ignorance. "I am a man!"

"Do you not want me as a wife? It is not fornication if I am your wife and keep only to you. I will not show myself again to another man."

"What will you do for me?" he said. "What will you do for me if I do not reveal your tricks and have you flogged in the barn and run out of this place?"

And she said, "I will do anything for you."

The Abbot stepped close to her again, pressing her between himself and the door. She could feel his hard erection against her hip. He ground it against her and one hand went carefully to her breast. With the other hand, the Abbot lifted her chin and put his lips on hers, just placing them there.

"You are an angel," he whispered, "a whoring angel."

He lifted his robes with one hand and lowered a pair of linen trousers that were cut roughly off at the knee. He took her hand and put it around his cock. The feel of it made her legs feeble. She wanted it inside her. She lifted her robe and took down the wool leggings she wore though winter was gone. She pushed them down around her ankles, still holding on to his erection with his hand gripping her hand, moving it up and down.

"Yes," she said against his neck, rubbing the skin of her torso against his, stroking his penis. "Yes."

He squatted against her and held her up by her buttocks. She wiggled her legs, ridding them of the leggings; then she lifted her legs and put her knees against his sides.

"Is this what you want?" he asked as his cock touched her between her legs.

"Yes."

He put the tip inside her and asked again, "Is this what you want? In God's house, in a holy place?"

"In God's tomb," she whispered and immediately regretted it. He would throw her from him for saying such a thing. But he laughed, gently, with appreciation for her body, her innocent wit, her willingness to fornicate though she could speak and refuse.

She smiled at his laughter.

He let her slip down so that he was entirely inside her. They stayed still for a few seconds, breathing into each other's ears. She put her arms around his neck and he thrust hard into her, banging her against the door, banging her hard, over and over. The heat between her legs began to overwhelm every other sensation.

"Do you like this?" he asked her breathlessly.

The world vibrated like taut threads on a loom, vibrated with purpose, a myriad of purposes in a chaos that God's eye could see as a beautiful, infinite pattern. The world inside her shook and her legs trembled. She moved her shoulders back and forth and felt her breasts rub against the Abbot.

And he thrust deeply, as though he couldn't stop even when he had ejaculated. He kept moving in her until they were both calm.

For that moment he was her Abbot, enchanted into being her ally, her affection, her man's body. He was able to provide protection in a world that proclaimed women weak.

They were almost lost, almost without separate vision. But the Abbot's arms grew tired. And Grey had a faint memory of a story that Colin told her a long time ago, when she thought she was a boy; it was the story of a man who was taught to be a warrior by a woman. As the Abbot set her down and they both pulled up their underthings, she wondered when women had become weak and why. She turned around and leaned her back against the Abbot's chest, pulling his arms around her, aware that his agitation had moved from his prick back to his mind so that the intimacy between them had dissipated.

"You have to leave me now," he said.

"What will you say?"

"I will say that the deaf-mute Kitchener's boy was terrified, cowering in the sacristy again, terrified of the commotion and of the vision he saw."

"He saw the naked woman. And who is she?"

"She is a mad-woman from the village, a Devil-possessed woman whose family I will speak to. I will suggest that they go on pilgrimage, to Saint Brigid's well for a cure."

Grey opened the door.

Later that day, when she was in the frater putting out platters of warm bread, the Kitchener's novice was breaking silence, asking the Kitchener what all the banging was on the Abbot's door in the dark hours of the morning. The Kitchener shrugged and suggested that the Abbot, who was a fine carpenter when he had to be, was doing repairs or nailing a cross to the wall.

"Perhaps what he was nailing to the door was that woman from Tarmath!" the novice grinned.

It was a good joke that had the two men laughing and shaking their heads for a while.

"If she comes again, I'll do some work on her myself," the young man continued. His laugh was cut short by the Kitchener's large wooden spoon cracking against the back of his head.

Grey the deaf-mute said nothing.

32

tHE END of the world began in earnest, in a subtle way, slowly, so no one really noticed. It was the kind of beginning of the end that one could look back and recognize and say, "That is when it all started, and we didn't realize what was happening."

The Kitchener and his novice and three monks who had been hoeing in the garden stood just outside the Monastery gate, watching a man in white-and-red clothing walking up the slope from the stream toward them. He had a flowing gray beard and seemed, by the bend in his back, to be very tired. Twenty yards away he waved at them and showed the few yellow teeth left in his head. He bent forward with his head down and trudged on until he was standing right before them, his beard blowing in the breeze.

Meanwhile, Grey was on her knees in the chapel.

"Sweet Brigid," Grey began. "I am afraid. I'm becoming a male again. There is less pain in becoming a man than in becoming a woman. There is no pain and bleeding in this transformation." She put her hand over her abdomen. "There is no bleeding. My bleeding has stopped. For four fortnights there has been no pain or bleeding."

For the changes in her body had tormented her, filled her with panic all day and all night. She had been praying constantly to Saint Brigid to stop this metamorphosis, to make her womanhood a permanent thing. She had pulled away, running and hiding when the monks tried to drag her into one of their hurling games. For they liked her aim and strength.

She heard someone outside in the hall and sank down and whispered. "Sweet Brigid, Mary, Jesus, and Joseph, I'm afraid to look at what might be shrinking and what might be getting larger. Sometimes I sense that there is a swelling between my legs. But I am afraid to look. And my breasts are very sore. My nipples burn. Perhaps that is part of the transformation. Please, Brigid, tell me what to do. *In nomine de . . . Deus et . . .* Please, Brigid, I would rather die than become a man." The chapel was quiet in response, but she could hear voices from the hallway.

Grey wandered out into the hall, drawn to the whispering commotion.

She stepped softly up to the group of men, now standing in the hall. "I'd like to speak to the Abbot," a stranger with a wispy beard was saying breathlessly in English. The Kitchener understood English and asked what his business was. Grey looked at the Kitchener and then back at the nervous old man; she had understood "speak" and "Abbot" and concentrated on what he said next to decipher his purpose.

"I am willing to pay a great deal of money." He lifted up a leather pouch and shook it so they could hear the coins inside.

"Where are you from? We have never seen a man dressed as you are." The Kitchener crossed his arms over his chest. There was a red dye in the man's vest that was unfamiliar in that region.

"I have just come from Dublin, and then from a place across the sea many days away, on a ship."

"And what is your business here? This is a remote place, far from the sea. I have not even seen the sea myself."

The man laughed. He said, "Well, it is just a great deal of water, friend. A lot of water."

"So I am told."

Grey could understand only a little of what was being said, but she looked hard at the man's eyes and noted a terror in them that did not go with his casual laugh.

"May I then speak with the Abbot?"

"This is a closed community of the religious, open only to members of the order. We do not take payment. We vow poverty here."

The man smiled, but his facial muscles were taut with growing impatience.

"I don't think your Abbot would like your turning away a man with so much wealth to offer this place. It seems in need of some amenities."

"We are not concerned with earthly amenities. We are concerned with our souls and the salvation of mankind."

The novice whispered in Gaelic to the monk standing right next to Grey, "I have never heard the Kitchener have such a pious tone." They chuckled softly.

"I am also concerned with salvation. Please, brother, let me speak to the Abbot."

The Kitchener thought for a moment longer, as a cold breeze that smelled like rain pushed through the grasses and came into his face. He uncrossed his arms and nodded for the man to pass through the gate.

Later that evening, Grey saw the man sitting at a table in the frater, furtively eating with the monks, his eyes darting around. He seemed no longer jovial but quite agitated. At one point he stopped eating and rubbed the skin on his forehead as though he were shaping clay. Then he stood up and spoke, in broken Gaelic, "Pray me. Pray me. Pray everyone." His voice shook, and he left as the monks looked at each other, some of them laughing. But the two new monks from Tarmath did not laugh. "He is from England," said one who had a scar that imitated the arc of the eyebrow below it. The Kitchener came up behind him and smacked him in the back of the head. "Do not break silence," he said.

"He is English," the boy repeated.

"Get out and pray all night in the chapel for forgiveness, for breaking silence or go join the lay brothers and clean the cows' arses!"

The boy stood up and said, "You are not the Abbot. You cannot give me penance."

"No, but I can give you this." The Kitchener smacked the back of his head again and then made two fists in the air as though he were about to box his ears. The boy's friend pulled him by the arm out of the frater.

A few nights later, Grey was treading quietly through the halls, going from her cell to empty a pail of her urine, the smell of which was irritating her fiercely, when she heard a strange weeping. At first she thought someone was being funny, making sounds like a chicken. Then she thought perhaps it was a chicken that had somehow gotten caught inside, or a pheasant. She had vivid images of a lost and mournfully cooing fowl prancing slowly about. But the noise had a willful cadence to it that was human or humanlike. She stood like a tree.

She put the pail down and moved along the wall, feeling it with her hands behind her back. The noise was coming from the dormitory. She slid around a curve in the wall and saw the foreigner—the man with the beard—illuminated, completely naked, white flesh hanging from his bones, standing over a candle in the corner just outside the dormitory. He was bent over so that his beard brushed against his distended belly. He was examining his groin, intently feeling with his fingers the inside of his leg where it connected to his torso. His limp scrotum trembled from the shaking of his legs.

The next week, the foreigner died in the infirmary, bathed in sweat, black boils cracking his skin and oozing blood and puss. He spoke to the Infirmarer in Latin mixed with English. "It is our greed, our greed that has done this. The merchants brought this scourge back on their fattened ships." He asked that someone take down his words, that someone write down what he said. He said, "They are blaming the Jews, because they hate our acumen with their money. They pretended they were too pure to handle money and let us be their bankers, and now when their greed has turned to a horrible plague they point their fingers at us. But we are dying, too! We are dying of the same plague!" He grabbed the Infirmarer as though to pull him into his conviction. "No one dare place the blame on the rich men whose goods the world has become addicted to. No one dare admit that their consumption of these goods, the addiction to spices, spawned the disease, that the plague came to us in a frenzy of greed."

The Infirmarer nodded kindly, though he didn't follow the man's logic, for he had never known a rich merchant or Jews or greed for spices.

His patient looked at his caretaker's furrowed face and smiled a little and said, "Perhaps I have come to the right place to die."

In the end the foreigner vomited blood. His flesh was like rotten meat, stinking and swollen, with blackened pus running from sores. The Infirmarer was greatly shaken, for he had never seen such a death, and a Mass was said for the stranger.

A few days later, the orange cat was found dead under one of the benches in the frater, its mouth open and full of bloody froth.

Grey was weeping in the Abbot's arms while he spoke: "He begged to stay. He begged. He said his life depended on it, that the world was coming to an end. He said that I must lock the doors and let no one in. He said that he came because he knew few others would come. He said that I must seal up the Monastery and let no one else in."

"But he has died anyway," Grey said.

"Yes. He has died anyway."

Grey moved away from him to look into his eyes.

"Is the world ending, then?"

He pushed her gently off him and stood up, holding the back of his neck and looking around on the floor for some wisdom.

"Is this punishment for the thing you would not give back to the Pope?" Grey asked, sitting back down in the chair.

The Abbot squinted at her as though to make out some detail that was hard to see. Then he lifted the chain from around his neck and threw it past her onto the floor, where it clattered and lay with the little key on it. After a few seconds, he growled and fiercely rubbed his face with both hands.

"I have lost it, you see. That's the truth of it. I have lost it."

Grey reached out to touch his wrist, but he jerked backward and looked at her with wild anger.

"It has vanished; it has gone, and I don't know where. It was gone long ago, before the men from Avignon came. If they knew I had lost it . . ."

Grey sat and listened, her hands contained in her lap.

"And now the world is ending," he said.

 **33**

FIRST THE INFIRMARER, then three of the monks in the dormitory—there was no abatement once the disease became present in the body. No hope. Simply an assurance of terrible agony that lasted three or possibly four days. It would have been better to be ignorant, not to know what lay ahead without comfort: the flesh rotting on one's living body, the stomach bloated with blood that in the end came up into the mouth. One young monk drowned in his own blood, lying on his back, unable to roll over. Others had the first signs, the pea-size swellings, the headaches, but hid them, denying even to themselves the inevitable. Time was running like a beast with a spear in its gut, dragging people with it; life was changed; everything had suddenly changed.

Grey lived in her secret places, trying to smother fear and sorrow with solitude. It was the death of the Infirmarer that was a blow to her chest. The death of their healer seemed to leave the place bereft and hopeless, a cruel and ironic loss. How many deaths had the Infirmarer attended, and how had he kept his faith after witnessing such suffering? The Infirmarer seemed the most devout, touching the wounds on his patients as though they were the wounds of Christ. Sorrow for the absence of his ways came up into Grey's throat and eyes. He had been a good man; she had liked to bring water to him in the infirmary, where he squeezed out rags and wiped the faces of the sick. And his own death was full of rasping and thrashing. He must certainly now be in Heaven, but he was not needed there as he was in the Monastery of Tarmath and in all this world of disease and pain.

God was angry or absent or weak, and the Abbot could not fix the world, which was trembling on some brink, perhaps about to fall into Hell's gaping, infinite pit of flames. He had an intellectual rapport with the idea of the world's ending, but the process now seemed insane, something the human heart could not endure. Intermittent, unexplained drum beating from the distance, from the village of Tarmath, made the Monastery walls and floors tremble and caused the birds to go completely silent. Now that the signs were upon him, the Abbot wanted to find a way to get around the world's terrible end, to bargain with God. He had not reckoned that it would be so pathetic and repulsive; he had thought more in terms of dramatic and huge events—fire, flood—while the devoted and stoic among clerics were given unimpeded passage to Paradise. But one man dying at a time, in his own filth, calling for his mother—this was too tedious and cruel. And if the Infirmarer was not spared apocalyptic horrors, why would he be?

"We must stop all sins, including fornication. We are being punished." The Abbot was sweating, closed up in the sacristy with Grey, holding her upper arm and pulling at her although there was nowhere to go, as though trying to pull her through to another world or into his convictions. Sweat slicked his skin; his fingers were making indentations in her arm, but she didn't care about that discomfort. Instead, she was feeling terribly dizzy, sickened by the close warm air filled with the thick scent of wool and linen vestments and the oily cressets that were lit. She was suffocating.

"I cannot stand." She began to let her legs collapse, but the Abbot would not let her cave in; he held her up by the arm from which she drooped like a puppet.

"You will stand, and you will hear me. You must leave me alone. You must stop coming to me. I think of fornication when I see you. We must pray to God to forgive us."

He let go her hand and she leapt for the door and opened it, breathing in the cool air from the chapel. The Abbot strode past her as Grey sank onto the first pew.

"I know what has been loosed in the world," he said, "what I let slip out into the world. But perhaps that was my part to play, just as Judas had his part."

That evening the Kitchener's novice fell in the frater and had to be dragged screaming to the infirmary, where seven other monks were lying on the floor, praying, laughing, weeping, moaning, left unattended in rank ethers to die. The bells rang constantly, for Offices and deaths.

Two new boys from Tarmath who had recently asked to be let into the Monastery ran away that night. Grey saw them from atop her tree, two shadows fleeing toward the village of Tarmath, clawing their way up the vine-knotted escarpment behind the Monastery, stinging their hands with thistles.

She felt bad; she was sick, unable to eat much while her belly was growing. She was afraid to die. She stared hard into the leaves of the tree, the configuration and shades, stared to wrest the spirit from in there. And all she could finally see was a faint and transparent angel that said nothing, just put his chin on his knees. She had to close her eyes to feel other entities, hear their whisperings, and feel little hands touching her back. The stream spoke to her sometimes, shushing her softly, so that her thoughts were a little quieter.

One day an English soldier walked panting into the main entrance and fell on his knees. There was fear among the monks that there would be some violence or some order to vacate. But the soldier would not move or speak until the Abbot came to him, and even then he did not get up from his knees but spoke English into his hands, which grasped each other.

"Abbot, you must let me in. I want to dedicate my life to God. I want God's protection."

"There is death here, sir, not protection." The skin around the Abbot's eyes was dark.

"There is death everywhere," was his reply. "Everywhere. It has been brought by those demons, the Jews, who worship money and hate the purity of the Christians." The high-pitched, terrified whine of the soldier's voice made the Abbot know, as not even the deaths of his monks had, that the whole world was in a state of insane upheaval. When an English soldier who did not have a blade pushed against his heart was pleading like a child to an Irishman, then there was no recognizable order any longer.

"Is this plague in the village as well?" The Abbot stood above the man with his hands folded behind his back. He allowed the sweat to collect above his lips and drop onto the stones near the soldier's knees.

The soldier looked up, his brown eyes dull, opaque, empty of hope.

"This plague is throughout the world, Abbot. Everyone is dying."

The Abbot felt relief, a great and wonderful relief that his sins, that the sins of the Monastery, were not to blame for the hideous suffering he had seen. He was not to blame. He felt a great deal of compassion and gratitude toward the soldier now. He lifted him up, holding him by the arm as he had held Grey's arm.

"Come now, man. Get up and sit in the frater and have some water. Tell me what you know. We are ignorant here."

The soldier said that he preferred to have wine, and so the two men sat in the shadowed frater at the end of a long empty table with heavy mugs full of red wine in front of them. And the soldier leaned in and confessed to the Abbot how ugly the world had become. He explained that the village had had to dig pits to bury its dead. He explained that men fled their wives and mothers their children who got sick, there was such fear of the methods of this disease.

When he was speaking, Grey watched his mouth and recognized the overbite and the full lips; she knew that mouth from a vision that she had not been able to banish. He was one of the English lads from Finnistuath, one of the lads who had beaten her father and made him die; he had defiled the altar in Finnistuath years ago and had wielded an iron rod against her father.

Now he was a runaway soldier, and he stayed in the Monastery and prayed constantly in the chapel; he was there at every Office. And Grey could stare at his face and see the human fear, the awful and desperate desire to deserve God's love and not His punishment. She wanted to put her hand on his arm and say, "I forgive you," but who was she, an illiterate peasant, to forgive anyone, even in a world so upside down as this one?

After the two boys, many others fled from the Monastery; there were fewer and fewer monks, until the Monastery seemed cavernous and haunted. So strange were these times that the Kitchener stopped in his work one afternoon, boiling peas, and embraced Grey. He said nothing. At meals, before empty places at the tables, the Abbot read from the scriptures, reading about scourges and miracles, sins and punishment.

The few monks that were left talked openly in the frater while the Abbot read. He told them to be quiet, to abide by the rules. One said, "For what purpose? The world is over."

Brother Calvin spoke up, saying, "Respect the Abbot."

"What can we do?" someone asked the Abbot.

He looked down and wiped his brow with his hand while shaking his head.

"I do not know," he said. "We must wait and pray, I suppose. We must hope that after the torment we've seen men go through, there is mercy, there is God to judge us with mercy and a better life, a better place."

Then he looked at the few faces before him, the helplessness in them, and said, "Perhaps if we endure the suffering, if we do not give in, if we do not make any bargain with the Devil who may offer us comfort . . ."

They waited.

"Perhaps Jesus Christ our Savior understands the temptation to believe we have been forsaken."

"There are children, baptized children who suffer with this plague," a monk said bitterly.

"'My God, my God, why have you forsaken me,' Jesus said, and then . . . perhaps he did not have enough faith, and we must show faith. For Jesus saw the men around him die, as we have; he saw them hanging on the crosses around him, bleeding to death in agony, thirsting for water, for more life, for some comfort or a quick end . . . all around him on the hill."

Now the faces of the monks were enchanted by the Abbot's ramblings, forgetting their concerns and wondering what he was talking about, why he sweated so and was speaking more and more loudly.

"How could we expect him to endure? And God, being accused of forsaking him . . . didn't Job have more endurance, more faith, more obedience?"

Brother Calvin stood up, and after him another monk, both crossing themselves and leaving.

"If the Devil were to offer us comfort, some end to this suffering, would we refuse him? It is so easy to feel forsaken," the Abbot said, finally bending over to place his head in his hands.

On one warm morning that brought the faint smell of the village corpses to the Monastery, a message from the Pope arrived, dated two months before, tossed into the Monastery yard tied to a stone. The messenger who threw it rode past on a dark brown horse without stopping to enter the place.

The Abbot read it to himself as all of the twelve monks who were left stood around him in the yard, and Grey lurked in the doorway behind them. The Pope would save them; they knew this. The Pope would tell them what to do, how to get out of this horror; he would explain to them what was happening, if they were to build a boat, if some of them were to survive, if they were to say certain prayers, if they were to build a ladder to Heaven. The Abbot finished reading and looked up at all the faces around him, some of them young and some of them old. The Kitchener held his large wooden spoon. A red-haired man was coughing gently but relentlessly. Grey put her hand over her stomach, where she felt a soft fluttering, as though a moth were trapped inside her. The Abbot smiled and shook his head. But he said in a comforting tone, "The Pope has summoned scholars in Paris to discover the cause of this plague. The result of their study is this: the plague is due to a particularly unfortunate conjunction of Saturn, Jupiter, and Mars in the sign of Aquarius that occurred one year ago. Apparently, this conjunction caused hot, humid conditions, which caused the earth to exhale poisonous vapors."

There was much silent thinking as the Abbot continued to look at their faces.

One monk asked, "Then this is not a punishment from God?"

"I cannot say."

Another asked, "Is there any remedy?"

The Abbot looked back at the parchment and translated, "No poultry should be eaten, no waterfowl, no pig, no old beef, altogether no fat meat. It is injurious to sleep during the daytime . . . Fish should not be eaten, too much exercise may be injurious . . . and nothing should be cooked in rainwater. Bathing is dangerous."

One man held his head with both hands and screamed, "This is lunacy. Lunacy. Was there not a few days ago a rumor brought from Tarmath that bathing and much sleep were curative? Who does one believe when the scholar declares one thing and a fortnight later another declares the opposite. This is no science; it is guessing; it is wanting something to be so and therefore declaring it so; it is wanting to appear to know when they know nothing. We are all dying. The world has become foul with sin and filth."

"We are in Hell," one man whispered, and he lifted up his robes and showed the black swellings on his groin. "Look, I am going to die. Look."

They all did, as though they had no will not to. The Abbot said, "We must pray constantly. There must be prayers said and penances done every minute of the day and night."

The monk dropped the robes and said, "I'll fuck a witch before I pray again to God, who has made this punishment."

They all crossed themselves. The Kitchener struck the man in the back of the head with the spoon. The Abbot hissed at him, "Get out. Get out of my Monastery and die in the road."

The monk laughed. "You'll all go down that road. And you know it. So you spend your last days praying to Our Father who art up my arse. I will die with a belly full of ale or wine or mead, or whatever I can drink from a maiden's cunt."

Several faces turned away in shame.

The Abbot read further from the letter. "He also states that rumors placing blame for the plague on the Jews are in error and must not be further spread."

"The Jews killed Jesus," the red-haired man stated.

"Jesus was a Jew, you ignorant . . ." The Abbot tossed the letter on the ground and said, "Go pray. Everyone, go pray! NOW!"

Grey stepped back and went to her cell. She lay down and then remembered what the Pope's message had said about not sleeping during the day and quickly sat up. She had been sleeping much during the day. She lifted her robes and looked down at her belly, glad that the swelling there had not turned black.

# 34

IN A FEW DAYS there were four bloated, blackened bodies lying on top
of the rows that had been hoed to prepare the garden, rows now grown
over with weeds. The eight remaining monks, including the Kitchener,
wore linen cloth tied over their faces to dull the stench, a sweet emetic odor
that saturated every part of the Monastery. The Abbot locked himself in the
library after the monks died and would not come out. He was in there for
many days, until Grey heard the Kitchener suggest that he was dead.

"He was too young to be Abbot," the Kitchener said to the novice left
to help him. "I always thought so. But he was sincere. He was young but
sincere."

The Kitchener took over the running of the Monastery, what was left of
it, and suspended all Offices except for Lauds and Vespers, telling everyone
to pray to themselves and recite the psalms constantly into their own hands,
as though God, like the fairies, had been reduced to a being that could sit
in a man's palm. "Though I walk through the valley of the shadow of death
. . ." He put the few people left in the place to bringing out all bedding and
burning it and to digging a large grave beside the four rotting corpses. When
they pushed them in, large chunks of flesh came off the bodies. The pigs
had to be kicked away. So angry was the Kitchener at their greed that he got
a knife and killed one of them. Everyone stared at the dark red blood
spreading out over the weedy stones. Some minds were silent, numb. Some
minds wondered how the world had changed so quickly and so horribly.
There was talk of signs that had been ignored—stars that had burned up in
the night sky. Brother Calvin remembered one day when he clearly saw the
sun reverse its path for an hour, moving from west to east. Brother Dunsten
laughed at their intellectual machinations. He said, "We are all just ants in
the shadow of a boot."

Grey kept waiting for the headache, the chills, the boils, and the blood
coming into her mouth. She was no longer concerned that she was becoming a boy but suspected that she would soon be dead, that her breasts and
stomach were swelling as the groins of the men swelled.

And then she wondered if, instead of becoming a boy, instead of dying of this disease that took others in no more than four days, she were not growing a child inside her.

She was carrying a child put there by the Abbot. She was amazed at how one's life could evolve and change without one's control or understanding, as though one's body were not one's own at all. But if she were carrying a child . . . why would God give her a child to carry if the world were ending?

She went to the library door and spoke against it.

"It is me. Please let me in."

There was no reply, no sound.

"Please, you must let me in, because I have news for you. I have to tell you that the world may not be coming to an end."

She pressed her ear against the door. There was a small sound that could have been the movement of a mouse across the pages of the Bible, or a bird entangled in an altar cloth.

She saw flickering light come through the crack at the bottom of the door.

"Let me in," she whispered. "Please."

When the Abbot opened the door, Grey backed away, first from the smell of fecal gases and old urine that burned her nostrils and then from the appearance of the Abbot. There was a pile of excrement in one corner beside a brass urn apparently full of piss. Strong gases emanated from the Abbot himself, whose robes and skin were damp with fetid sweat. The skin around his eyes was almost black, and his new beard and hair were shiny with oil and sweat. As soon as he opened the door, he let it go.

"I have something important to tell you," Grey said quietly, to calm the Abbot, to soothe him.

He smiled and lifted his eyebrows. "Come in, then. We can pray together. That is all we can do, now, pray."

"It is so foul in there."

"I cannot leave this room," the Abbot announced, quickly losing his smile. "I must keep myself cloistered so that I can pray. That is all I can do now. That is what must be done by all who are left to do it."

"Then I will tell you from here that I am growing a child inside me. I think this is what has happened."

The Abbot looked down at her belly. She touched it.

"How can the world be ending if there is a new child to be born?" she challenged.

They looked into each other's eyes. The two vertical lines between the Abbot's eyebrows deepened.

"We have to leave here," Grey said. She reached her hand out, but he would not take it.

"You have to understand that I have done evil. You should leave me. You should have nothing to do with me. I am a careless man and a fornicator."

"We have to leave," Grey repeated. She touched his hand. "Come on. We will go together to Finnistuath, where I can get help from the Midwife."

"Listen," the Abbot whispered, holding her arm hard. She remembered that whisper.

The room was warm and close; Grey sat down on a splintered stool, and the Abbot let her go as she bent over and put her head on her lap.

"You offered yourself to me. You knew well your effect upon me. And you knew well that I am the Abbot."

"But there is affection. We are like a man and his wife. You are my child's father!"

"It is all a bargain with the Devil. Everything." He tried to laugh, but had to rub his face instead.

He looked at Grey from an angle, his hand still rubbing his chin. "And this child, how do I know that it is mine?"

There seemed to be no air in the room, nothing that wasn't fouled.

Grey sat up straight and said, "Because that is whose it is. I know how a child is made, and the time of my last bleeding."

The Abbot looked down, thinking. Grey touched his shoulder and said, "I do not want to endure what is happening alone. I do not want to go away without you, but I cannot stay here. I need the Midwife."

The Abbot knelt down in front of the chair and said, "Jesus Christ the Son of God—you have heard that he asked why he was forsaken." The Abbot lifted his face up with his eyes closed, saying, "My God, my God, why hast thou forsaken me?" He looked back at Grey. "And do you know what God said?"

A moment of silence spread between them. The Abbot raised his hands and held them out to her as though he were a magician who had made something disappear.

"Nothing," he whispered.

 35

*T*HOUGH HE had been often called upon to help build walls out of
heavy stones or defend his family's honor with his fists, the Abbot
had been determined to be a cleric since he was a boy, since his father had
left him and his three brothers and not come back. His mother wept and
raved and held her son, then called Niall, close, saying over and over that
he was her only comfort because the eldest boy was already married
and the younger brothers were ignorant of a woman's sorrow. She drank ale
often and told him what she missed most about his father, his lovemaking.
The mother never touched her son as a woman touches her husband, but
she gave him images of intimacy that were disturbing to him. They obsessed his mother and reduced her to sitting at the table and letting
the chickens wander about around her feet. He wanted to get away from
her and felt great guilt for such a desire. He would serve the Church, the
greatest mother of all.

And now he must leave the Monastery, for to end the world there would
be too horrible. He did not want to be alone in his death. If Grey left, there
would be no one to take his hand, to stay with him through the horrible
transition from Abbot to fetid corpse. The woman carrying his child had a
beautiful face and a strong will to go that he could not undo. He had a sense
that if anyone were to end up sitting at a table weeping and letting chickens
wander around, it would be him, not Grey. As long as he had no authority in
the Church to bolster his sense of his strength and autonomy, he would
have to settle for the authority of a husband. He didn't want to wither alone
and impotent, knowing God's capacity for abandoning those who suffer.
"Why are you called Grey?" he asked as they sat by the stream. And every
question now seemed to him full of poignancy, for behind it was the phrase,
"Before we all perish and the world ends, tell me . . ." They spoke as though
they had just met.

"I am called Grey, named for my father, Gregory."

They looked like two monks contemplating scriptures by the stream, a leather satchel on each of their shoulders. "What is your father's trade?" the Abbot asked.

"He was a goatherd, but he was killed." She didn't tell him he was a half-wit. She shivered, thinking of her father in the grave in Finnistuath, of the Smith hanging by his neck by the river. It did not take a plague to bring death, but the cruelty of men was not as hard to take as the cruelty of God. She touched her belly. More than two weeks had passed since she had told the Abbot that she was growing his child inside her. In those two weeks he had cleaned the library, sat with the Kitchener, and given him orders as to how to close up the place if he did not return from his journey.

"I am going on pilgrimage," the Abbot had explained, "with the boy to serve me."

Then he had gone through the chapel, a dark and silent room full of the artifacts of a pious life: benches, crucifix, the statues of saints. He had touched their faces, cupped the cheek of the Virgin Mary with his hand.

Now, sitting by the stream, he could not look back at the Monastery. But Grey turned around, and the Abbot wondered if she were going to turn into a pillar of salt.

On the road there were many stories. In every story there was some theory, spoken or unspoken, as to the meaning of the pestilence. Strangers behaved as though they were kin, for the world had grown small enough, it seemed, to be one family, and one live man saw another as his brother; for he didn't want to be related to the thousands of dead. Still, there was a great deal of caution; a man did not stand in front of another man to speak, for people understood that deadly ethers traveled in the warm currents of exhalation. Still, frightened and weary people could not resist company. Together they heard the beansidhes wailing at night, the fairy women who mourned the suffering of the world in awful and exquisite keening.

Travelers did not comment on the corpses they passed—humans, cats, dogs lying in ditches; most of the humans were covered with tattered cloth, piles of old clothes, or blankets strewn with camphor leaves. There were fires along the road to warm the living and abate the smell of putrid flesh, so that at night the world was a large expanse of silent blackness and with random flickering orange flames that illuminated a patch of road and brush or the solemn faces of a few keeping vigil by a mother's or child's or grandfather's corpse. Few traveled into the villages; the road itself had become an elongated village of sorts. On the first evening, just to the south of Tarmath, an old man and a young woman who was his daughter let Grey and the Abbot sit with them. The old man explained that the bundle in the ditch was his wife, the young woman's mother, and that they were waiting for the gravediggers, who, they were told, were a few days to the north.

The daughter said nothing but tended the fire with wild eyes. She fed it cedar and lavender, so that the smoke made a warm perfume.

"There is naught in Tarmath," the old man said when Grey and the Abbot said that they were going there. But they went anyway to find bread and cheese to take with them on the road.

In Tarmath Grey and the Abbot saw a cart with three corpses in it; one seemed to look directly at Grey with wondering blue eyes. It was a woman her own age, her face still pretty and framed by foaming red hair. Ghost faces peered out of dark doorways. Though it was well after dawn, no one was out in the street except for a bread man who threw loaves into those dark doorways after coins or jewels or a silver cup was thrown out at his feet by the wealthy merchants of the town or by those who had stolen from the empty homes of the wealthy. The Abbot gave the man a bookmark made of gold threads for a loaf, and he and Grey hurried through Tarmath to eat the bread on the road, beneath an oak tree. Grey recalled that years ago she had wanted very much to see the town and all its merchants. She had seen the smoke of Tarmath's busy life and imagined people bargaining, not crouching in dark homes.

Soon three young men came by. The one who spoke first had straight black hair that he tied back with a strip of leather. His skin was very tan and dirty, which made his eyes seem too white. He said, "We don't have any money and our parents are dead. We're hungry and want some of your bread."

The Abbot was sitting with one knee bent and his arm over that knee. He remained casual and said, "Sit down, then, with us and we'll share our bread."

"Just give us the bread," the dark one said.

A tall skinny boy with not much of a chin and dark red blemishes all over his face chided his companion.

"We can sit with him. He's offered to share with us."

The third, a silent boy, smaller than the other two and with curly fuzz for hair, sat down, and the Abbot tore off a chunk of bread for him. The other two sat as well, and the Abbot addressed the skinny one, the one who wanted to join them.

"You don't seem grieved that your parents have died, that they have suffered this terrible plague. Do you pray for them?"

The bony shoulders went up and down in a shrug as the boy stuffed bread into his wide mouth.

"My father's been dead for a long time, before the pestilence. He fell off the roof."

The other two boys chuckled and the boy telling the story laughed, too.

"And what about your mother?" the Abbot asked.

"Oh, she got the boils and died a few days ago."

They were all silent. The skinny boy picked up a twig and threw it against the trunk of the tree.

"She was a dog. She treated me badly. She deserves what she got."

The Abbot gave him another chunk of bread and said, "Pray to God for forgiveness. Pray for your mother's soul."

"I don't believe in God." He looked up with eyes that were supposed to be mean but which were made out of sadness. "My mother was a pious woman, and it made me sick. She loved her saints and relics. She cared more for them than for me."

"Did she beat you?"

"I'd have beaten her if she tried. I'd have cracked her skull if she tried." The other two laughed again, prompting the boy to laugh after them as he had done before. He seemed to wait for them to let him know whether what he said was funny or not.

He continued. "She was after me all the time, like a fly—wanting me to do chores, not allowing me to drink ale, going through the village looking for me when she wanted me home. And when I was home she chided me for doing nothing."

He looked at the ground where he was digging little trenches with his long, thin fingers.

"When she got sick she wanted me to do everything. She wanted me to bring her things all the time. Then she told me that I was the dead one. She told me that. She said that when I was a babe she doted on me, but I had become cruel and lazy, that the boy she had loved was dead."

He stood up.

"She's the one who's dead now, and I say damn her soul to Hell. We whose parents are dead are lucky, and if there is a God, I praise him for setting me free."

The other two boys nodded and stood as well.

The black-haired boy said, "Do you have any coin?"

"No," the Abbot said.

"You're a liar," was the reply.

The Abbot stood up and said, "I'm bigger than the three of you put together if you'd like a go."

Grey watched him and understood for the first time that the man who had fathered her child had not always been an Abbot. He had been a boy, had worked with his thick hands and put his strong shoulders to repairing walls and digging wells.

"Come on," the tall skinny boy said to his companions. He was hunched over and weary looking, though trying to appear uncaring and casual. He addressed the Abbot: "We're grateful for the bread. We're your friends. We'll look after you if you ever need some help."

The Abbot put his hands on the tall boy's shoulder and looked up at him. Tears put a sheen on the boy's eyes and he turned away. The other two boys walked away as though they would have left their friend forever without thinking about it much. Their tall companion nodded and whispered quickly before leaving, "Will you pray for my mother, Father?" And the Abbot nodded.

"You must have faith in something, boy," the Abbot said.

"What should I have faith in?" Grey asked as they watched the boys leave. What if her child became like those boys, mean and faithless, or struggling to be?

She was making circles on her belly with the palm of her hand, wondering what was growing inside her, wondering if she could ask the Midwife to give her a tea or a poultice to make the thing shrink, go backward, becoming tiny and then wink out. Perhaps it was best if there were no humans left on earth, only black and blue and brown birds, foxes, wild horses, wolves, cows and pigs gone feral, and trees and herbs, everything singing or rustling, raindrops tapping.

She did not want to think long on the world into which her child was to be born and the way it would harden its child's heart. If all the world was dying, what would his short life mean? Perhaps it would mean that she could give birth to innocence that would not be stained before its life on earth was over. Then it would go to Heaven and be taken care of by angels. And perhaps she would go there, too. And perhaps this, this place right here of plague and stench, was in fact Hell, where fires illuminated wide-eyed corpses and where the flesh rotted on the living.

The next day, like the one before, made it clear that the human race was diminishing. Furrowed fields were overgrown with tendrils. The corpses of sheep and cattle lay about in meadows near empty houses. There were occasionally people huddled around fires; gardens untended and swirling with weeds and birds; and small groups, sometimes single people on pilgrimage. Most were going to Kildare, to the well of Saint Brigid, which went deeper than Christian times, into the center of the earth where the pagan spirits still lived and where Brigid was still a goddess in a time when the land did not warrant the punishment of a plague.

One pious Christian woman, a bulky merchant's widow, wanted to talk and walked beside Grey and the Abbot. She was heavy and waddled and panted between words, but she never complained or stopped to sit down, so absorbed was she by her own story.

The Merchant's Widow's Story

My husband were as rich a man as the English allow the Irish to be, God be praised. He did business in Dublin with our son, Edward, named for the King. For my husband was in court and saw the King many years ago. He were a sickly boy, my husband told me. But he were the King. My husband's hands touched all manner of goods that most in Ireland know nothing about: potions, ornaments, and such as I could hardly list without expiring first. And he made good bargains, getting sometimes ten times what he paid for an item. He were a good man and knew Lords and Counts as you might know a cousin. I had the servant of the King's brother, the Viceroy's man, come to the house. I gave him some ale and he said it were the best ale he'd had. We brewed good ale, we did. Most in this region knew our ale to be of the finest quality.

My husband were the first man in Tarmath to be stricken by the horrors. Some say that Mary the Weaver were, but she were a lowly woman, all the time sickly. No, it were my husband who had it first and died first of it. We had no notion of what had struck him and he wailed an awful wailing, saying his body was full of worms causing him to ache. He called for all the ale we could bring him and shivered something terrible so that I called for the Priest and paid him a good lot to pray over my husband and exorcise the demons. But four days from the one when he said he felt poorly weak, he died, his groin as black as that storm cloud and his neck swollen so that he were fit to choke on his own spit.

The morning he died, he stood up. He stood right up and said that he were feeling a mite better and would go to his storehouse and make certain there were no thieves picking through the bolts of brocade he were so proud to have. But I seen that he could hardly walk, having to move his legs side to side because of the swelling. And sure he fell on his knees, and blood and ale spilled from his mouth like he were a broken pitcher. And I said, "Husband, get to your bed and be not walking about like a sick animal." And he looked at me and said, "Wife, you must call for a priest, for I am so sick that I will die soon and I am asking God that I die."

By the time the priest came he were dead, still lying in the hall, for I could not move him but covered him with a blanket. And when the priest came, I saw that he had the swollen neck, too, and I said he'd best go and pray for himself. Soon after, he died, and then my son and his wife and children, all three of them, and I am alone as I can be now and hope to die soon, but not by those methods. Before I sleep, I pray that a thief bash my head and I wake up in paradise, and that is what I will ask Saint Brigid. I will ask that I die by any method but this scourge, which lays a man's life out so cruelly for him to watch slip away with no hope and growing torment, making us all believe that the world is cruel and comfortless.

I have much money in my pockets, and I have had my husband well buried and my son and daughter-in-law and grandchildren, too. It is only now that there are not enough priests or gravediggers to do the work, and I thank God that my kin died before the worst.

When the woman left them at the bridge to Finnistuath, Grey spoke for the first time since the Merchant's Wife had joined them, for she was still in the habit of being a deaf-mute to the world.

She said. "Perhaps we, too, should go on pilgrimage to Saint Brigid's well."

The Abbot did not respond but sat on the steps of the bridge and gave himself and Grey a chunk of bread, picking the blue circles of mold off and throwing them into the brown water. He pulled out the chain and gripped the key in his fist, bending his head forward as though in prayer or nausea. Grey looked at his hand and felt sadness for him, for the burden he had given himself with his ambition to be Abbot. It was then that the Grave-digger passed by, whistling, his shovel over his shoulder. He nodded at them, glad to see people who were sitting up and had nothing to bury. He stopped to offer them some cheese in exchange for some bread.

The Gravedigger's Story

Yes indeed, I will tell you this, I will—there's no man too rich to rot! Ha! Death makes a peasant of every man.

I've seen a man covered in furs, gold coin in all his pockets, the grease of a pheasant on his lips, who once gave men like me his shit to carry to the river; I've seen such a man lying beside a weaver's corpse, his eyeballs being pecked at by the same crow as ate the weaver's.

I've just come from the Manor up at Hannagh, where all but two servants died, and the flies feasting on all the good meat and bread left on the table. Ha! There was no cure in all that good food and wine nor in all the coin and silver. The plague as likely will choke a man on French cheese as on stale bread, that's what I've seen. Why, I've dug graves for the peasant and the Lord, and they all fell the same way when I shoved them in with me boot.

But the rich man goes in the churchyard, and his gold goes in my pocket. I never dreamed that I, a poor Irishman with no trade but what I can put me back to, would have a Lady in silk slippers kneel down to beg my services. What a world! I praise God, from whom all blessing flow!

It was Adam brought this scourge on the world, fallen from grace, and God's angel Lucifer. And the world is coming to an end, and Adam will rise again and lead us all into the garden. Those of us left alive are preparing the way, cleaning up Lucifer's mess.

I've seen Jesus on the road, walking just as plain as that man there with the red hat. That's how plain I saw him, and Noah, too. I seen Noah and Jesus walking together. You don't believe me? Well, I tell you, it's sure they're inspecting things, looking over the work of those left, which is why I do good work. I'm not careless with the way I dig a grave, and when I saw Jesus and Noah walking along I kept on walking toward them, with no fear nor shame, and they passed by me, as close as I am to you, and nodded, like this. Just nodded, because they seen who I was and what good work I've done. And they'll be back around, and I consider them me friends.

The Abbot felt compelled to tell the Gravedigger who he was, that he was an Abbot and that he had knowledge of the inclinations of Jesus. And he chastised the Gravedigger for having the audacity to speak of religious things in such ignorance. "There are things which need the care of learned men," he informed the Gravedigger, who shrugged. And the Abbot knew that the man could see him in his cleric's robes, blackened and dead like any other plague corpse.

Grey listened but was more intent to study a rash that had formed around her right ankle. This and every bump or ache was cause for panicked scrutiny. Was this the beginning? Was this the first sign of the black and hideous death?

The Abbot guessed her fear, and when the Gravedigger moved on to the south, he said to her, "It is nothing, just a rash from some thistle or poison weed. It is nothing. Come, let's sing psalms and stop picking at yourself."

And then Grey was glad to have the Abbot as a companion, but still wished more every moment that there was no child inside her to come into the dying world. She was cheered to see the familiar lay of the land of Finnistuath and prayed as hard as she had ever prayed that the Midwife was alive and could help her endure the burden of motherhood or help her avoid it all together.

After crossing the bridge and walking for an hour along the river, they heard the thread of a tune, a cheery tune made of drum and flute. It was a dance tune, merry but distant, coming from the Manor house, which Grey could see only a little of through trees that had grown larger and fuller than they had been when she was the Priest's boy.

"There's the Church, through there, where I was the Priest's boy."

There was no sign of the Priest. Indeed, the only person they saw was the Bailiff, still in his wide-brimmed hat, briskly walking down the road from the direction of the Plowman's feral fields toward the Manor house, a large ledger under his arm. He did not recognize Grey but stopped to speak to the Abbot, to ask his intentions in Finnistuath, to ask if he was passing through, visiting, or involved in some litigation concerning an estate. Having written the response in his ledger, that the Abbot was looking for the Midwife, the Bailiff sighed and was glad to tell a stranger all that he had been through.

The Bailiff's Story

No man has had the burdens of this one, save perhaps Abraham, who was asked to sacrifice his own son, or Noah, who was responsible for building a ship and gathering up every beast on the earth to be put in it. It is I whom God has left to fend off chaos.

In this book is written by my own hand, the only literate hand in this village, the names and properties of every being, alive and dead, the dates and circumstances of all deaths, and the legal standings of all inheritors.

In some cases there are none left to inherit, and so all the goods and properties go to the Lord of the Manor, but he has sequestered himself and his family and dogs and horses and servants in the Manor house and does not give his seal to these documents, which cannot be official until he does. And I must speak to him through the door, for the guards he set out have died and were left until the gravediggers came. And now there are shutters on the windows and the doors closed and sealed, and I must speak through the door, sometimes getting the ear of a servant, sometimes hearing nothing but the music that's played day and night. Even now you can hear it when the wind blows our way. There are four tunes played, and I know them all, each one.

There have been twenty-seven dead in Finnistuath of the plague. Most of them lived in the houses around the Manor, for a merchant had come to sell the Lord's household fine things and threw death into the bargain. There are six who show the symptoms still, and as I have indicated here, seventeen left, not including those in the Manor who throw out purses of coin and set me to the task of getting food for them. But fruit rots on the ground, and the deer and pheasant are as numerous as ants with no one to hunt them, for I am not a hunter, nor a butcher. But some men come in from the woods, where I know they make up a band of outlaws—I do not count them as villagers and do not want to go among them to record their numbers. They sell their services and some meat, so there is food enough, but never time enough. I need seven men to do my work.

I must go on, now. I can't be idle and beg your forgiveness for my haste.

Go there, up the road, past the Plowman's house, which is only inhabited by one of the Plowman's daughters and her two little sons. Then keep
going, past Mary the Goatherd's hut, which is empty, and then up the hill
behind there and you will see a few huts, one of which belongs to the Midwife, who is a surly witch and sightless, but with whom I must consult concerning the vital statistics of this place. We are partners, in that sense,
though she is lowly, and I am related on my mother's side to the King. Once
I asked her to be my wife, but now I see how foolish I was, for we must all
prepare for the end of the world without frivolity. And clear and precise
records must be kept of all who lived and died, and of the efforts they made
toward prosperity.

Prosperity is the mark of God's grace. I am his servant in counting coins
and measuring the size of a man's field. God spares me to do this work, for
if there be no one to keep the records of these large changes, there will be
no order to the world's end. The Devil loves chaos. And he would make me
say that you were a boy I knew, but no boy swells with a child, and so I will
keep God's order and let reason stand.

When the Bailiff was striding away, creating his own frantic wind, Grey
said to the Abbot, "I no longer know this place or who I was here."

36

eXCEPT FOR her blindness, the Midwife had hardly changed. She had one less tooth, but the teeth remaining were well fixed and clean. Her hair was still wild and thick, and her features strong though filigreed with many lines. She had no less calm than she had years before. The plague to her was cleansing and sad at the same time. There was not so much trouble from the English any longer, especially since the Lord of the Manor had sealed himself and his household up. And for the time being, there was a little food left in the stores. What would happen the next year when there would be no stores because many fields had been neither plowed nor sown? The Midwife didn't worry about things that hadn't happened. She was also, as were many, not certain that there would be a next year. So why waste time sowing a harvest when no hands would reap it?

Despite her detachment—what some called coldness—the Midwife felt a surprising joy fill her when Grey called to her from outside her hut. When Grey and the Abbot were in the hut with her, the Midwife admitted that she was greatly relieved to know that Grey was one of those who was still alive. She laughed to hear that Grey had a child inside her, and laughed harder when she learned that an Abbot was the father.

"Is he the man who is here with us?"

"Yes, he is the Abbot of the Monastery at Tarmath, or he was that. And I was the boy who tended goats and a priest, as you know. And though my face is not so changed, I am hoping that others will be more blind than you as to what I was, and let me be what I am now, which is a stranger."

Then Grey said, after coughing when she didn't need to, that she was afraid to have the child, to bring it into a world as horrible as this.

The three sat in silence as summer insects droned outside.

The Abbot got up and left the hut, saying, "I am in need of solitude so I can pray. I want to pray for my child."

When he was gone, Grey said to the Midwife, "Tell me of my mother and sisters."

"All dead." The Midwife sighed and bit at her thumb where there was a hair-thin thorn that had been worrying her since morning.

"The Abbot has a weakness in his mind. Some days he is good and strong. But his reason has been whittled by various certainties that have become uncertain. He has bitter moods."

The Midwife was not interested.

Grey asked, "How much time before I have the child?"

"From what you have explained, it will be about six fortnights." The Midwife's hands felt the air until Grey leaned forward and let them touch her belly. There was a murky light in the hut and many skins and blankets. Grey sank into the nest these things made and let the Midwife comb her hair with her fingers until she slept. She stayed there a few nights, hardly moving but to piss in the woods and eat a bowl of porridge. When the Midwife came in one afternoon with a bowl of dandelion greens, Grey stood up and said, "I'd best go to the Church, for I know that the Abbot is there."

After she was on the road, Grey began to trot and then to run, toward the spring. She was holding her belly up so that it didn't bounce uncomfortably as she ran as fast as she could, thinking of the comfort of the spring.

She passed by the silent, dark Church and turned up the path to the spring. But she soon saw that all had changed concerning the place where she had lolled in the grass for the amusement of fairies.

The spring had been engineered into a well. A round of stones enclosed it, and a wooden lid went over the top and was locked with an iron lock. The trickling stream that used to take the spring water to the river was a silent, black earth trench, with dry stones and new grasses in it. Words were carved into the wooden lid that Grey could not read. But the Lord of the Manor's seal was also there.

It was a ridiculous vision: a beautiful free spring, locked up like a prisoner. Grey had never dreamed of such a thing; it was as absurd as someone claiming to own a river or a cloud or a tree. She grabbed the iron lock and shook it. She shook it violently, trying to make the rattling louder in her head than her Fiona's weeping. Fiona, her lame sister, was weeping and miserable in the rotting odor of her own death. Grey imagined spirits locked up in the well with the water, mournful and suffering. What a sad, empty world without Fiona and her stories of acorn-capped fairies and crows wearing capes and singing poems. And what of her mother, made obscenely helpless as the babies she had begged God to spare died around her, calling for help she could not give. Forsaken—all of them, and Grey was alive, no longer able to seek forgiveness in her mother's face.

Grey laid her cheek against the wood. "How has this happened? How have you let this happen?" She could hear the tiny and sad song of the water dripping inside the well. She wondered if the sin of trapping spirits, of walling them in and making them property to be owned and hoarded, was cause for the plague.

One of the tunes she had heard over and over since coming back to Finnistuath wafted out of the Manor on a breeze that was getting harder and colder.

"Fiona," she called out, as though everyone she loved were trapped inside the well. She called out again through weeping, "Fiona, you should not have died." Fiona was meek; she was supposed to have inherited the earth.

While Grey had slept in the Midwife's blankets and skins, the Abbot had taken up residence in the Church, since the Priest was locked up in the Manor with the Lord's family. In a frantic swirl of inner dialogues that he sometimes spoke out loud, he found some solace in clerical duties. Grey felt no familiarity with the place, especially since its appearance had been altered by a proliferation of relics. There were relics on every surface, and in piles in the corner: bones, things wrapped in cloth, little cases and chests, a shriveled human hand, swatches of cloth, gilded items, crosses made of glass, bottles with blood or fingernail clippings or hair in them. Grey touched some of the items and then found the Abbot in the Priest's room, tending a fire.

Grey glanced underneath the writing table, where she had once slept. Then she looked back and saw the key dangling and sparkling before the fire that popped and grew.

"Why do you bring your burden with you here when you can shape yourself as anything?" she asked the Abbot, who looked as though he had gotten little sleep.

The Abbot considered this and fingered the key.

"I was charged by the Pope . . . If I find the box . . . if ever it is returned to me . . ."

Grey looked at the Abbot's shadowed face.

"I am afraid, Abbot," Grey said. "How could God be so cruel as to deliver his son to be nailed to wood and to deliver children into plagues and cruelty?"

"This world is the realm of challenges and tests of the strength of men's souls. With faith we can endure; and when there is no faith, there must be discipline, then God will lift us into his arms for eternal nurturing."

"I am afraid and need nurturing now, for I feel that all the spirits are as sorrowful as we. I have no family here and wish to know that I belong to you, that the child and I and you, for however long we will live, will nurture each other. It is the only comfort I can conjure."

"How can we take comfort in anything but God? How can we take comfort in what can be gone tomorrow, rotting and dead?"

The Abbot picked up the iron poker leaning against the hearth and threw it across the room, where it clanged like a sword against the wall and fell.

"I will pray for you," he said.

That night, the Abbot put his hands on her stomach and felt the movements of the child.

He felt that the child was pulling a part of him that was a danger to his faith and discipline. He tried to fit the tiny life that had his blood into his scheme of the world, where God's will must be puzzled out and obeyed. He had made mistakes, he knew that. And though reason told him to, he could not feature the being growing in his lover's belly as a mistake. But he had so little time to right things before he was called to Judgment, before the caverns of Hell would be before him. His sins, his mistakes, had to be absolved. But was his bond with this woman and his child sin or grace?

He and Grey listened together to the strains of music that came from the nearby Manor. Like the Bailiff, the Abbot now knew the tunes very well. Grey imagined the people inside the Manor dancing and singing and feasting, while the world outside came to an end in suffering, starvation, and boils. The people enclosed inside with food and music could wait and wait. And when the end of the world came, they would dress nicely for it, come out smiling, and march up to paradise accompanied by their music.

"Where might we find comfort?" Grey whispered into the Abbot's ear, but he had no answer.

The music continued, sometimes feebly, even in the night, and the sound became a torment to Grey as the Abbot breathed in heavy sleep beside her. She stared at his orange face in the firelight. She rubbed her child, locked up inside her like the spring locked up inside the well. Then she leaned over and carefully, quietly asked if he was awake or asleep. He was silent. She was afraid, mostly afraid of the sorrow that was overtaking her in the lonely night. She thought of those who were dead and who might be dead. She kept imagining a large and tattered angel in the Monastery, lonely and forsaken, guarding the body of the Kitchener, who had kept the Monastery in order in ways far more potent than the Abbot's authority. For the Kitchener's authority used bread and cabbage, which spoke with much more force than any scripture.

Grey sat for several minutes, staring at the chain around the Abbot's neck, with a key on it that unlocked nothing.

After a few weeks Grey went back to the Midwife's hut and told her that she was afraid of the pain she would have when the baby came. She was also afraid that it would be born with boils and ruined flesh. The Midwife didn't bother to reassure her, but told her not to think about anything that had not yet happened.

The Abbot began to conduct Offices in the chapel, though there was no one to attend them but himself.

## 37

O NE DAY on the western shore, somewhere southwest of Atherny, where the Bruce had waged a battle against the English, Colin had taken a stone that fit his fist and pounded the box lid open as the crashing and silence of the waves continued in an eternal rhythm. There were two shriveled items, rank and frightening, which Colin put in his palm and stared at. He turned them over by shaking his hand a bit, and he realized what they were—the severed tongues of two humans. He closed his eyes and laid them on the ground, behind him where he could not see them as he examined what else was in the box.

There was a scroll tucked into the Pope's jeweled box. And there was writing on the scroll, unfamiliar, curled writing, some of it faded so Colin could not read it. It was neither Latin nor Gaelic. And so he had meant to put it away and find a fellow who might be able to decipher it for him. But being a thief and knowing many ways of hiding gems and gold, he found the false bottom of the box and pulled it out. There was a codex, folded and un-folded many times, that had words written in Latin. These he read, sitting hunched over, the two shriveled tongues clucking behind him on the ground.

What Colin read on the Pope's scroll was not in any gospel that he knew of. It was a translated epistle, a letter from some unknown to a man named Apphia. It said:

> I write to you, fellow soldier, whereas I have the witnessing of a cer-tain man who lifted up unto Our Lord a reed, upon which was fixed a sponge filled with vinegar. Christ called out, "My God, my God, why hast though forsaken me," and there was with the people a great pity for him in the stillness after his words. This man who gave our Lord the sponge upon the reed has kept himself in a great fear and has therefore told to me of the strange events he witnessed when standing close by to the Son of God as he suffered upon the cross. It is the vinegar giver's account that a voice which spoke to Jesus on

the cross said, "Oh, Son of God, I have not forsaken thee, though God has left you to suffer and die in agony." And the vinegar giver felt fixed to the ground like a stone that had grown roots, and he heard Our Lord say, "I have no want of fame or power and tell you again to get behind me." He also proclaimed that all he wished for was to die forthwith and endure the pain no longer. The vinegar giver listened well and moved not, and he heard this same voice that vexed Christ offer a bargain. He would give Our Lord a swift end and in return Jesus Christ would rise from the dead and show himself as risen. And Jesus answered, "Finish this agony." And the voice said, "It is finished."

All that are with me greet you. Greet them that love us in the faith. Grace be with you all.

Colin sat for a long time with the scroll in his hand; he read it over once again, very slowly. Then he thought back to conversations he had had with the Old Abbot, the obsessive repetitions in the man's drunken rants about the damned box. "The Devil knew," he had kept saying while laughing bitterly. "The Devil knew what men would do in his name if he were to be a god." Colin had thought he meant "if the Devil were to be a god," but the Old Abbot was saying that the Devil knew what men would do in Jesus' name if *Jesus* were to be a god. And what was that? What evil would people do in Jesus' name if he were to be a god, an immortal untouched by death and not just a man? Colin's head fell between his knees and he shook it. If Jesus made a deal with the Devil, if his resurrection fit some evil plan, then what was Jesus but a man, a human being? And if Jesus were just a man, then despite all the good that he had done, all the times he had called himself the Son of God, he was just a man. And that meant that any man could be that good, could be God's child.

Colin stood up and grabbed the hairs that flew around his face and pressed them to his head with both hands.

"If Jesus had not been made into a god by his resurrection," he said aloud, "then all men would know that they could be like him. Humans would try to be like Jesus. But with the Devil's bargain, we can just muck about, kill each other, steal from each other and say that Jesus was a god and we are just humans, just sinful humans. Is that it?" He yelled out over the sea, "IS THAT IT?" And then he walked around in circles, staring at the ground, thinking.

"Who even knows what the truth is?" he muttered aloud.

He made a decision to purge himself somehow of all notions of the truth, of all hope that anyone could tell him how the world worked and on what convictions a man should act. He went east and north, walking several days to Lough Derg. The island in that lake was a wild place called Saint Patrick's Purgatory, where bird cries skipped across misted waters and the most devout and mystic of the pilgrims came in silence, fasting for days to prepare themselves for the immense and awesome submersion into solitude. Colin had knelt in a state of hunger and fatigue inside the cave there, praying constantly for one day and one night to nameless and formless beings.

As was the tradition on the pilgrimage to Lough Derg, Colin lay down inside the tomblike cave. He made himself into a corpse with his arms folded over his chest. There the pilgrim was to experience his own death, dwell in it, pass through the terror, and try to find the vast and benevolent state of grace in which God allayed all fears. Colin wept, not certain if what he was feeling was God or a surrender to not knowing and perhaps never knowing. But there was calm and relief in the purging. And when he stepped out of the cave, all the world was gray, the lake, the sky, the trees, everything shrouded in gray mist. He knew that the place was holy, that it had been holy all along, before Saint Patrick, before any human, and that perhaps everything, including Saint Patrick, was holy. Holiness was something that could not be contained in one creed or one hero. The words in the box he carried and the words that would be written to dispute those words, they weren't the truth. They were symbols of symbols, ideas about ideas, threads in a great net in which a man could get entangled and ensnared until he died exhausted from his struggle. And during such a struggle, he missed the fact of a morning's mist, the taste of cooked fish in his hungry mouth, the ability of his arms to embrace and his feet to dance.

On the slow and quiet boat ride back to the shore, he let the jeweled box slip out of the satchel, freeing himself of a futile burden. It sank into the lake, and the other passengers were oblivious to anything but the oars passing through the silver water and their ordinary lives waiting like trees on the nearing shore. They all looked like souls being taken to Tech Duinn, the realm of the dead.

And so it was, because many who traveled to the east found a dying land of corpses and disease, a sweeping of the land more thorough than any army could manage.

Unaware of any great changes other than those in his own mind, Colin headed for Naas.

There was a woman he could try to love there, and others who had mighty notions of revolution coming out of their bearded mouths. He missed them and their convictions and wanted to join them and turn their smoky words to fire. He wanted to burn away everything that got in the way of freedom and dignity and stand with those he loved in the warmth of it. He didn't care that he might be a fool.

Colin had determined that a man had to act without waiting for an image of himself to form, for it was possible if not likely that any such image was based on lies other men told about how the world was ordered. He must have no authority but what he sees and feels, for anyone with wit knows what causes suffering and how to be courageous. Colin went back to the east, back to meet his friends in Naas and tell them he was with them, he would do whatever he could to rid the land of the English and furthermore their lying priests and foul monasteries. And he now understood well enough that the English had made cruel use of their wealth and their religion in constricting the freedom and mangling the lives of others. Colin gathered talismans and feathers and carried pouches of stones and dead chieftains' rings. On his journey eastward he stopped in remote villages and drank ale, and he said, "The Chieftains will return some day, they and the women who make them bold and teach them to use wit and sword. They will take their place in Tara." There were still chieftains who held power in the western lands, where a man was elected King by virtue of his integrity and his skill with horse and sword and where the King was married to the land, to whom he pledged love and protection. "Not like these in-bred weasels, pale English boys whose uncles rule behind the throne with corrupt cruelty and carry blindfolded hawks."

But as Colin got closer to the pale, to the lands occupied and controlled by the English, he heard rumors of a scourge worse than colonization. He heard that a curse on the body had come to Ireland, and it put people into a boiling fever that erupted as black and pus-filled bubbles on their skin. These were no folktales, for the eyes of the tellers did not sparkle but seemed as dead as the corpses they spoke of. People shuffled hurriedly along the roads, looking up wildly. The world had started to unravel.

By the time he arrived in Naas, Colin's pontifications about the English were weakened remnants of convictions that could no longer be spoken by any protagonist. Now the world's stage was dominated by Death, who laughed at all convictions. Colin listened to his friends, who were terrified of the infection and pain they had seen in Dublin. They described the relentless and unstoppable course of the disease so as to make death by sword or hanging seem a mercy. In such a world, where a man's cough or a swelling was the stamp of an unavoidable terror to come, the evils of the English seemed almost irrelevant. Colin listened, sitting in dank and murmuring inns where men and women spoke of the meaning of this purging, of this new flood, not made of water but of disease. In this new order, people were divided not between the English and the Irish but between the living and dying, and then between those who were turned to stone by terror and those who walked among the sick to offer some kindness in word or deed or a drink of water. The latter were rare.

With a meekness he did not know he had, Colin asked the priests who visited the dying if they could make use of any of his goods, and they picked through his satchels, taking candles and some pouches with herbs in them. The woman who loved Colin said that she would plant some of the seeds he had collected, even though others told her she was a fool to waste time on planting when the world was ending. One of the priests in Naas who drank at a table with Colin and his friends poured black ale into himself to dim the hellish visions he had of the outskirts of Dublin, where he had gone to give last rites. He said that the most important thing to do was to plant the seeds of salvation and to remember how Jesus endured suffering in order to save the souls of those who followed him. Colin stared at him with such intensity that no one spoke, and then he said, "What's needed is not salvation but an end to ignorance. There is a way to reason out what is happening and what needs to be done, even if it be a way to end suffering quickly, to shorten a man's misery in this horrid death. The Church peddles no cures. The Church peddles the ignorance that locks us all in misery."

The fair woman who loved him said then, "Ahh, so Colin is onto another of his rants, I see." The ale had set her bitterness free, for she knew he did not love her, though he was kind and had a good touch in bed.

The priest leaned over the table to say to Colin, "I thought you were going to purge the land of English, O mighty Chieftain. I thought you'd come back from the Underworld, Cuchulain himself to fight for freedom." Colin stood up, pushing against the table so that it touched the priest's chest. He said nothing, and then he leaned over and put his hands on the priest's shoulder and nodded.

Later, as he lay in bed with the woman who loved him, he told her that he was haunted by the thought of those children, orphaned and terrorized by the disease that made corpses of their mothers. He wanted to do something; it was no good to live without trying to do something. The woman said that she had made a good garden near an old farmstead in the next valley, a plot of cabbage and peas and carrots that she tended herself against the ridicule of those bitter about the world's end. They could care for some children there.

Some of Colin's friends in Naas spent their nights plundering abandoned manor houses and told him to join them and not to let himself be swallowed in this Armageddon and its horrors. He dismissed their warnings. He built a cart, keeping to himself, not talking to anyone who might waste his time, and then he went to Dublin. Pulling the cart around the tortured city, he felt a deep silence seep into his head, while on the outside there were the terrified calls of the dying, hands lifted to be taken somewhere else, to be taken where there was not vomit or blood or screaming. He concentrated on finding children who were alone. He lifted orphans from homes stinking with their parents' death. He loaded children into his cart, giving them apples to eat. Gravediggers fought with him to use the cart for their business, but Colin could find a rage in him brutal enough to fend off anyone who got in his way. The children he found squatting in the street or sitting in doorways sucking their fingers were quiet, always so quiet, just standing in place, waiting to be put by Colin onto the cart. And most of the gaunt and dirty faces believed at first that they were indeed being placed on carts for the same purpose their dead parents were put on them. Colin whispered to them, smiling, reassuring without denying the horror of it all. He said things to them that he now understood he had wanted to hear years ago, by his parents' graves: "It's a horrible sorrow, it is, for sure a horrible sorrow, but you'll be taken care of. Don't worry. You'll be cared for and won't be alone, and there'll be new playthings and bread enough to eat." The children watched the man's back as he pulled the cart, sometimes turning around to point out a group of deer bounding off or a badger digging its hole. He stopped and rubbed his shoulders, and while he rested he sang songs. The children just stared, maybe one small boy reaching out to show

Colin a pebble in his fist, or a girl, snot glazing her face, smiling when he sang about rabbits.

They traveled back to Naas, where some of his friends guided by the woman who loved Colin cared for them at the old farmstead. And then Colin went back for another load of children and another and another. The cart broke one evening, halfway back to Naas. One wheel split in two, and a three-year-old girl with red curls was crushed against the side of the cart and died. Colin buried her there in the woods and walked the others to the farmstead. There were twenty-four children there, three of them dying of their parents' sores.

At dawn, the woman held Colin's arm to stop his work as he was sorting through wood to fix the cart with.

"We have no more room, Colin. There's no more room for another child, God willing that most of them live. We've not food enough for another child. There's no sense in bringing more."

He kept rummaging through the pile of wood and the woman kept speaking.

"You'd do better to go with the others who find food and things to barter with in the rich people's homes. We don't have enough here. Leave off the children; you'll only be bringing them here to starve, man, aren't you hearing me?"

Colin said, "It's better that they die here with some notion that they're cared for, if that's what's to happen, if they're all to die."

"Use your reason, man," she said gently. "Use your reason." And he dropped the piece of wood he had lifted and stared at his own empty hands. The woman put her hand on his back and said, "We can help the ones here. You can go and hunt and find what you can to trade for food."

That night the two lay in bed together, Colin feeling the woman's lips on his neck and her arm cradling his head. He stared up at the ceiling with his hands behind his head.

"I don't want to bring any more children into this world," he said.

There was a silence between them, so that their closeness became awkward, suddenly painfully inappropriate.

Slowly, the woman got up and found her clothing. Holding it against her she said, "And where would you be thinking of going now, Colin?"

"You were right. The food will run out here," he said. "We've got to go farther afield to get more stores. We ought to have some cattle here as well, for milk and meat. Rory has been about to see what there is to take."

When Colin sat up and tried to touch her, to give some affection though he knew he had ended it between them, she drew back and put on her clothing, not looking at him.

The next day, Colin walked with a few of his comrades, down to Finnistuath, where he had heard that the Manor was getting ripe for the picking. He made no speeches but led the men by virtue of his knowledge of the place.

Now outside, waiting in the woods of Finnistuath, he gave quiet answers while the members of his encampment asked questions as they stared into the dying embers of their fire. He believed that he was still alive for a purpose, and he hoped that the purpose had to do with the creation of a new world where some of the old spirits reclaimed the land and its philosophies. He knew that he had some clarity, that his own mind's clutter had been greatly reduced, by the words he read from the Pope's box, and by the pure and simple force of relentless death and terror. Staring into the fire, he worked himself into a frenzy. He mumbled to himself, "I will not be beaten; I will not be too bitter or too frightened to fight or love," and hoped it would be true. Colin wondered about people he had known, about how they had been reshaped by the sweeping cruelty of the plague. Who was dead and who was still alive? He wanted to tell them all what he admired most about them, what gifts they had given him, even the Abbot, whose passion, infuriating as it was, inspired him to find his own passion and express it. And that boy who was a girl with those beautiful eyes—that strong girl. Was she still alive? She would be a young woman now. Ah, what man would take on such a woman, who knew how to be a boy? He would have to be a man who was not prone to being muddled, who could reason calmly and love passionately.

Colin spoke to his comrades fervently, saying, "Our error was in keeping our petty feuds between tribes and not banding together to oust the English, whose soldiers have limp cocks and coward's hearts. You remember the raid at Leinster, how the English made no attempt to fight." His comrades did remember, from the times he had told them. He also told of the great cattle raids of Ireland's heroes and how the Irish had either beaten or absorbed all invaders.

"The English have been more devastated than the Irish by this plague. The plague has mocked their entitlement and left room for great changes for those who survive."

The Plowman's son of Finnistuath was one of the survivors standing beside Colin. He had run into the forest months before, driven there by grief and fear. He lived like a fox, eating the seared flesh of small animals and lapping water from shadowed pools, until he had shuffled into Colin's camp one night, as humble and brazen as a beggar, and taken up the group's ideals.

And when he said, thinking of the Priest of Finnistuath's words, "But the learned men say that this is the end of the world," Colin answered, "Use your own eyes and ears and reason, man. There is no need for anyone's authority or teachings, for lies come in words; the truth comes in a man's work and a woman's touch, in rain and seeds and bird call. I'll tell you this, it's better to listen to a crow who lives in the trees than to a learned man who lives only in ideas."

the mother

38

THE ABBOT often walked in the woods praying, talking to himself. He had conversations with the Pope, who insisted that Jesus Christ was always meant to be a god, part of the Holy Trinity, and that the Church must correct certain truths and protect the ignorant masses. The contents of the box, though they were lost now, perhaps copied and distributed, could be explained, could fit into the Church's order and authority.

"And what of the passages in Saint Mark when Christ prophesized his own resurrection?" the Abbot said.

The Pope adjusted his hat and nodded.

The Abbot continued. "Perhaps Jesus did have a very understandable but unfortunate moment of weakness in bargaining with the Devil. The Church's duty is to help Jesus do what he was destined to do, form the institution that would civilize the world and bring God's law to everyone through the good priests and occasionally a few pious soldiers."

Sighing and shaking his head, the Abbot pleaded to be given a faith so deep that he would understand these paradoxes and not be beset by demons.

"Who is to say," the Pope said, as he faded away with one of his hands raised, "that the Devil wasn't lying to Christ, that Christ would have risen anyway. Who is to say that the scroll itself wasn't forged by heretics or agents of Satan?"

The Abbot stared at the ground, not seeing the earth or his feet as he walked back to the Church, but seeing his mistakes. He should not have left the Monastery; he should not have abandoned his duties. He should not have looked into the woman's eyes who now had his child inside her. Many had died; he had lived. Surely he had not survived to be an errant cleric siring children in a dwindling village.

Grey told the Abbot, when he was with her again in the Church, that there was a rotting smell on the wind when it came from the south. The Abbot said crossly that the world stank of death now. The music from the Manor continued, sometimes thin and slow.

"I don't know where the graves of all the people, of my family and my sister, are." Grey asked the Abbot, "If I find them, will you say prayers there? Will you bless the ground where they lie?" But there was no longer even the marker she had made the Priest put on her father's grave. And they had both seen the pits dug for the graves of the poor. In Finnistuath, the Abbot had heard of people being put into the river.

The Abbot told Grey that he wanted, more than anything he had ever wanted, to travel to Avignon to speak with the bishops there, even the Pope himself, about the burden he had carried for so many years. He wanted to confer with the Pontiff about other matters, for example, the purpose of surviving the end of the world. He must analyze, think, understand. "There is a burden in my soul," he told Grey.

The Abbot continued to talk, as he wondered who was left alive to speak with. "If there is no one left alive to talk with, I will go to Rome." He dreamed of the libraries there, which could perhaps help him untangle the theological riddles that grew in his brain like a tumor. He didn't sleep well but stood outside at night, often looking into the sky, waiting for the clouds to clear and reveal some pattern in the stars that had some rational explanation for the world's chaos. Occasionally, he saw someone slip from the Manor and go into the stables and then return.

Grey wondered if men had to create things to carry in their minds because they couldn't carry a child in their bellies. Perhaps they needed to pretend that they were as important as women who bore children. But why were they not satisfied to be able to tell people what to do, to pull plows and start wars?

When Grey went into labor she told the Abbot, "Something is wrong. My back is being kicked with such force, it cannot be the small child inside me." Terror tightened her body. The thought that the thing growing in her would have to come out was a distant notion that Grey had not allowed herself to consider directly. The pain was sickening. She perspired and clutched the Abbot's arm, begging him to pray to Saint Brigid for her, because she could hardly put words into her head. She went into the forest and paced, waiting for the intensifying waves of pain, leaning with her arms against the trunk of a large beech tree when the wave came. The Abbot paced with her, praying, and when she told him to stop praying and do something, he stopped and did nothing.

"God forgive me," she wailed. And some of the ocean poured from her in rivulets down the inside of her legs.

"We must go now to the Midwife."

The Abbot helped Grey up the road, pausing with her when the pain was bad and letting her clutch his arm and bend over.

The Midwife was in front of her dwelling when Grey saw her and yelled out, "It is coming; I need your help."

The Midwife said, "Come in, then, and have the child here. You'll see that the child will take its time. There's no hurry." She turned to the Abbot and said, as she had said scores of times, "There is no room for you."

"No hurry, you say?!" Grey screamed. And the Abbot backed away.

Grey passed into the dark space of the Midwife's home and watched as candle flames bloomed and illuminated the pillows and jars and boxes and bowls. For whom? Only for Grey or to give the Midwife a vague sense of the geometry of the space. Grey wondered if the Midwife's sight was now what Grey's was with the blindfold on when she visited the Abbot in his cell and could see the light of the candles. In those days she had felt the mystical union of fornication; now she felt the outcome of that pleasure—to create more humans, more souls. She, perhaps as all humans were, was blind to so much.

Grey lay down and howled, bending her legs and begging the Midwife to removed the child from her.

She moaned. "I did not mean to bring a new life into this dying world, so full of misery."

The Midwife sat on a low stool and took up a brown dress she was patching. She hummed a tune, a tune mercifully different from the one that had constantly been played in the Manor.

"There is a fee for my services," the blind woman said.

"I will pay. I will pay you anything to end this."

Grey breathed a few times and sat up to say, without any pains to distract her, "I am sorry Midwife, but I am not fit for this and wonder why there is such pain to endure."

"It is Eve's curse," the Midwife explained. "Whereas Jesus pays for the sins of man, women pay for the sins of Eve."

"What did she do? What did Eve do that I must lie here and be beaten inside my body?"

The Midwife laughed. "She wanted freedom from God, freedom from ignorance and obedience. She wanted something good to eat without having to ask permission."

Grey moaned.

As the pains became more frequent, and Grey more exhausted, she asked the Midwife questions: "Will I die? Will the child die? If it has the plague, will you smother it as we sing a soft tune to soothe its poor little soul?" She fell back weeping, with the thought of so much death and with the onslaught of a fierce pain.

The Midwife gave Grey some tea to drink and placed a knife under the pile of blankets on which she lay to cut the pain. And to distract her, the Midwife told her stories of the people she had seen slip from the womb and how their first acts had portended their lives.

"There was the Barley Grower's girl who pursed her lips for kissing when she first was born and ended up married to a rich merchant in Tarmath who said that her kisses were enchanted."

If Grey was between pains, the stories lulled her, but if the Midwife prattled along during a searing contraction, she wanted to stuff the woman's mouth with rocks.

When dawn was an hour old, Grey asked, "How much longer must this go on?" Minutes later, the child fought its way through to the open air. The Midwife cradled the infant in the crook of one arm and passed her hand over the infant's swimming body; she said, "It is a boy and has no deformities."

Grey's body, sore and stinging, yearned for the infant. The Midwife showed her how to suckle it and helped her to remove the soiled robe that Grey wore. She wrapped the afterbirth in it. She gave Grey the brown dress she had mended during the night.

"I feel that it is not mine to keep," Grey said, looking at the smooth, red child. "It is as though it is a creature given into my protection, but it does not belong to me. It has a strength of its own."

The Midwife had held too many babies to want to notice anything special about this one. She had seen them come and die within days, or grow into ungrateful children or beaten children or hungry children. Over half of the babies she had delivered had died, some as adults, of the plague. There was no reason to become attached to a human life, not even one's own.

She left the mother and child, letting them sleep, saying the routine prayer to protect the infant from its mother's madness or carelessness, and from spirits, both visible and invisible. She stepped outside to stretch her aching back. The sun was moist that day. There was dew on everything, which soaked the hem of her skirts as she walked carefully with a walking stick into the woods with the bundle of afterbirth. She had a particular pool around which she buried such bundles.

Grey floated on sleep with her nameless child. She felt its confusion at coming into the world, saw its eyes try to make out what kind of a world it was and what it was supposed to do in it. She knew it was her duty to protect the child's body while its soul grew independent and strong. No damage must be done, no lies told. She pressed her cheek against the infant's warm forehead and smelled his skin. It was the smell that imprinted itself on every mother who smelled her child's warm, sweated hair when it slept. Without words, without any document or seal or proclamation, she had been given a solid identity that saturated her and shaped her, put milk in her breasts: she was mother. Awed at the thoroughness of her transformation, she was desperate for the Abbot to help her, for in this role she was not willing to make any error. The child's needs frightened her, because she could not dismiss them, but she also could not be certain of her ability to fulfill them.

39

THE ABBOT WAS in the middle of Nones when the Bailiff interrupted him without apology, his ledger, a permanent attachment, under his arm.

"There are men from Avignon at the Monastery in Tarmath, I am told," he informed the Abbot, thinking that the news would be welcomed, something of importance he could have his hands in. "I have been to find the Plowman's relatives there. His pathetic estate, which is not much more than a plow, is in some question, and there was a daughter in Tarmath. But that's of no concern to you. These men from Avignon are inquiring about you concerning some item missing from the Monastery. They fear that thieves have made off with something of great value. And there is good news: the Pope is still alive and not afflicted, proving the protection he gets from God."

"Are they coming here?" he asked.

The Bailiff consulted his ledger and said, "I have no notion of that."

But the Abbot could surmise that now these men would know where he was. The Bailiff was like a wind of information that could blow in all directions, so that a man had to run to grab the parts of his life that might be blown away.

The two men stood in officious silence for a moment until the Bailiff looked up with a pale and frightened expression and said, "The music has stopped."

They both listened. Then they went outside and stood among the trees, waiting for the wind to pause.

"Indeed," said the Abbot. "It has stopped entirely. No, there is one instrument, the harp. I can hear it playing lightly."

The Bailiff took out his ledger and opened it, then closed it. He looked at the Abbot for a metaphysical explanation for the chaos of the world, or for spiritual guidance, which he admitted he had been too busy to consider, but the Abbot's face was shining with perspiration and an agitation that was not comforting. The Bailiff touched the frayed edge of his hat and ran off toward the Manor. The Abbot went back inside the Church and got the leather satchel from beneath the writing table. He jammed cloth and candles and books into it and slung it over his shoulder as he strode to the road.

He saw Grey and the Midwife stepping carefully through the Plowman's overgrown fields. He didn't ask what they were looking for, staring at the ground as they walked like fishing cranes, but went and peered at the face of his son, who was cradled in a sling lying against Grey's side. He had known the child was born and was told by the Midwife to stay away for a few days while the mother healed. She knew that occasionally a man made his wife fuck him as soon as the newborn slept; the Midwife didn't know the Abbot well but didn't want Grey to have to endure his lust if he were the kind who thought he had to reclaim a woman's cunt as soon and as often as possible.

But the Abbot seemed gentle with Grey, putting his hand on her head in a gesture of blessing. He then touched his son's cheek and said to Grey, "You are well?"

"He has no name," Grey said to him.

"I will think of a name."

"Where are you going?"

"I am going to Kildare. I am going to throw this into the well there." He held the key out from his chest. "There are men coming from Avignon. If the Pope's men see that I have the key, they may think that I know where the box is; I am afraid of their methods."

"Brigid's well is many days from here."

"I will be back."

The Midwife had wandered away and was uprooting a turnip. Grey walked a little to the stump that she had hurled rocks at with her companions, the boys of Finnistuath. She sat down and adjusted the baby.

"He is strong. I am glad of the Midwife's help, for tending to an infant has no finish. There is little rest."

The Abbot took up the child, holding it against his shoulder, where it continued to sleep. Grey stood up and stretched.

"I will go back with you to the Church."

"I just told you that I have to go to Kildare and give this burden to the well there."

Grey carefully lifted the chain and key over the Abbot's head, making sure that the baby was undisturbed. The Midwife, using a black walnut stick to test the way, walked past them and up to the road. The Abbot took a step forward and then watched, let Grey do as she wanted; the child she had produced from her womb, the milk filling her breasts, gave her an authority he had not expected.

She walked with the key down to the river, a nearly impassable spot she had to crawl under tree branches and brambles to get to, near the same place that Colin had emerged from years before. There were boulders in the river there, and deep brown eddies and currents flowing hard around them. As children she and her friends had been told that the eddies were made by witches who stirred the water with large spoons, mixing potions and poisons. Grey looked behind her and saw the Abbot with their sleeping child stop before having to navigate the thick trees.

"You don't have to go to Kildare and the water there," she called out above the noise of the rushing water, not even sure that the Abbot could hear her. "It's just as holy here."

And she threw the chain and the key into the roiling water.

40

THE WHOLE ORDER of the world was in question, all but the desire to survive. The fragile order of men and their intentions had been revealed as nothing compared to the order of seasons or the movement of water or the calls of birds.

All those who were in the Manor were finally dead. A few days earlier, the yellow-toothed and aged Lord had stumbled out to the stables. The Abbot, watching from the door of the Church, thought he meant to mount the horse there and ride away, but instead he took the animal, its nostrils steaming, back into the Manor. A few days after the Lord sequestered himself again in the Manor, there had been a wretched smell, and then began the ceaseless, hellish howling of one of the dogs still trapped inside.

The Bailiff returned to Tarmath and sent word by official document to the relatives of the Lord and his wife that their estate in Ireland was in need of attention. He hired gravediggers to take care of the corpses in the Manor. But the gravediggers did not come until the howling of the dog ceased and the odor weakened. The gravediggers helped themselves to whatever they could carry easily, for they had no rivals and therefore their duties were priceless. The three men took the bodies out and opened all the doors and windows. The black horse, the Lord's favorite, was still alive, roaming about the hall with round and unblinking eyes. It had gone mad, and when the doors were opened, it fled with an arched tail and pounding speed into the woods. The Bailiff counted twenty-four corpses, for he followed every move of the gravediggers and assessed all the property. Among the dead, there were servants and some of the English from the cottages around the Manor who had fled there to escape death, which they had always associated with poverty. The servants were taken in a cart to the river and put in the water there. Most of the others were given places in the churchyard. A few, including the Lord and his new wife, were placed in sepulchers readied for them in the Church months before. Their bodies lay beneath stone replicas of their best selves, free of blemish or disproportion, stone eyes closed, stone hands folded peacefully over their breasts instead of clawing at the sky. The Priest of Finnistuath was also among the dead, and his body was put in the churchyard, where the Abbot prayed over him fervently. It took one week for all the graves to be finished, and a stonecutter came from Tarmath with his family and decided to stay after carving the grave markers, taking over the Baker's old cottage.

The Bailiff was now in a fervent search for Red, who had not been seen since he had left the Manor as a mendicant before God's punishing plague struck. Joseph and his family had all perished weeks before in another manor house to the north. If there were to be survivors of this purge, and if Red were one of them, then it was the Bailiff's duty to secure the Manor for him.

He was trying to nail a notice on the door of the Manor, struggling with it as it kept curling up, when he saw Colin and two men step out of the trees and stand, with staff and clubs with blades attached to them. One of the men was the Plowman's youngest son, a man who had lost all his family but his sister and her children. And he knew the purpose in his survival, for he had years ago taken and hidden the weapons made by the Smith.

The Bailiff tossed up his hands and let the notice curl into a scroll and fall.

"I'll not have a tussle here. I'm a reasonable man and there are laws to abide by."

The Plowman's son held up his crude sword and said, "This is the law now, Bailiff, and we are its carriers. We'll take over the Manor now."

"You'll not. It belongs to the Lord's family, and they haven't been properly notified."

Colin laughed and said, "We'll be sure to notify them," and the other men laughed, too.

"Now, run along," Colin said. The third man, who carried an old plow blade, turned back toward the woods and gave a whistle, and others came out of the forest, but the Bailiff wouldn't move.

"This would be a sad battle, indeed, Bailiff, too sad to undertake. Go on, now, and find your own soldiers and have at us later, but move aside so you don't get hurt, man."

Colin and the others walked forward, and the Bailiff fled.

"It is ours," Colin said quietly as the group stood and stared at the great block of stone.

"I never would have believed . . ." the Plowman's son said.

"Listen," Colin said as the group began to feel the agitation of impending celebration, "we must secure it first. There's no telling who the Bailiff can raise in Tarmath or elsewhere."

"It is ours!" shouted the Plowman's son, and the others cheered, and Colin laughed and sang,

> We'll open all the doors and make way for spring
> For a bridal bed is a fragrant thing.

It was the only song he could think of for the moment, and it fit the lusty mood of the group. The troupe swiftly and thoroughly occupied the Manor, placing strong bolts on the doors and laughing behind them.

There was a muffled and frantic noise as the Bailiff came back the next day and pounded on the door, threatening that Colin and his friends would all be hanged, that they would starve when there was no more grain. And the answer was that he should go to Hell before them, because everyone would be dead before the year was out.

Grey stood near the entrance of the Church.

A wind stirred up the trees and blew the sun free of clouds so that sunlight swam in large blotches on the infant's face. Grey, who was watching the Bailiff, moved back into shadows and pulled the blanket more securely around her child's tiny shoulders. Between the trees she could see three deer walking, two does and a buck. She whispered to the child to look at them. Everything in the world had become wonderful to her through her child's eyes. Grey wanted to put the child's hand on the deer's soft coats, but the animals moved nervously ahead and finally out of range. So Grey went to the spring where the lid had been splintered so that anyone could get water, making a ruin of the site and a dark pool just below the spring. The stones that had made a well were scattered on the ground. An oak leaf fell into the pool and spun slowly. Grey looked around to see the Midwife nearby, asleep leaning against the trunk of the tree. A bowl was resting in her lap. Grey carefully took the bowl away and placed it on the ground.

The Bailiff was gone from the Manor when Grey laid the child in a cradle the Abbot had made in the Church and set about to make some supper for herself and the Abbot. She mimicked the Kitchener's preparations, making a meal of meager stores: withered cabbage and oat porridge. She could hear someone inside the Manor pounding a drum and another stroking the harp a few times.

The baby awoke and fussed, so she sang one of the songs Colin had taught her:

> *Birch tree, smooth and blessed,*
> *delicious to the breeze,*
> *high twigs plait and crown it*
> *the queen of trees.*

> *The aspen pales*
> *and whispers, hesitates:*
> *a thousand frightened scuts*
> *race in its leaves.*

> *But what disturbs me most*
> *in the leafy wood*
> *is the to and fro and to and fro*
> *of an oak rod.*

Grey bent over the cradle, and the child blinked into the large luxury of its mother's face. There was no thought in her mind but the child's eyes and face.

That night, Grey lay down on the bedding next to the fire, where the Priest used to sleep, and slept with her child beside her. The Abbot fell asleep with his head on the writing table but later came to lie down with his family after adding wood to the fire. He caressed Grey's shoulder and breasts from behind, but she wriggled forward, away from him. He rolled away to be as he was before. She understood now that sharing pleasure with a man satisfied the man's lust easily but never completely, and with no price paid by the man. But a woman's body and life could be transformed in those few minutes. The geometries of the shadowed room shifted and swayed in dizzying whim. Transformations occurred every moment; in millions of ways one died and was reborn as emotions came and went, as certainties became doubts, as boys became women and women became mothers, as wives became widows, as a leg went lame, as a flaccid prick became an erection. In this swirl of metamorphosis, where was there rest?

41

"WE CANNOT FORGET," Colin spoke firmly. "We must not forget that the plague can finish us all, whether we plant cabbages or not. If we have a few days left or years, how are we to choose to live them? For there is no more bondage to the conquerors. It is our choice." He looked around the room and saw the idle people around him, arguing over the rules of chess, smelling empty, uncorked bottles, discussing the need to take some of the Manor's goods and see who was left in Tarmath to bargain with for food. Colin admitted to himself and his comrades that there was not much to send back to Naas for the children there. But if they could bargain for goods in Tarmath, they could share them. He sent one man to Tarmath and another to the woods to hunt.

Standing inside the hall, gently bouncing the baby in her arms, Grey listened to Colin and wanted to say to him, as a student who timidly considers a point her mentor has overlooked, "Is it not clear that we must first have food to eat, and then one must have love for something?" Colin moved on to each man and woman, trying to engage someone in a plan to free the trapped spirits of Ireland's past and fend off bondage to foreigners. Grey looked around the room at the others, who seemed to want no more than amusement. She had thought that Colin would make a beautiful temple of the place, a version of Paradise that her child would some day frolic in, free from hunger. But there was an aimless and tattered imitation of the old Paradise that had been there. She wondered, had Red found his Paradise? Was he safe and free of the plague-infested world?

She imagined that Red and his fellow pilgrims had escaped the plague; that he had escaped his human legacy as Lord of the Manor, gone beyond all of it and found that place, shown on maps, where earth stopped and heaven began. There was no better goal, Grey believed, than to find paradise for the children and to protect them from the bitter realities of greed, violence, and pain. There was no better goal than the kind of freedom that came from a sinless world. That is what she wanted for her child now, more than she wanted it for herself, though the Midwife had said, "The child is not a year old yet. It may well die as many do. The plague is a bully who takes children and elders."

Grey had said quite plainly, "The child's death will be my own, for I will follow it into death if that is where he goes."

Now she rocked him as she stood and studied the condition of the Manor to see if there was any food to spare for her.

One of Colin's men found a bolt of fine linen dyed blue and started running all over the hall drawing it from couch to couch as though he were making a huge, ungraceful web. There were bones, dried manure, and dog feces on the floor, for no one wanted to play the part of servant. Everyone wanted to be equal, but as nobles, as privileged men and women. A fight broke out around a bench full of candles that had burned down to pools of wax; one had ordered the other to sweep the floors, and the man refused. The two men wrestled on the floor, tearing the cloth and tipping over cups of water and bowls of meal. At one point a young man with disheveled yellow hair leapt backward to avoid being tripped by the rolling fight and fell into the harp. When the crashing echo ended and the man's wriggling to stand up caused some twanging, Colin walked over and stood over him. "When did you learn to play the harp with your arse, Orpheus?" The man didn't understand references to Greek mythology, so Colin sighed and gave him a hand and lifted him up. He heard a woman's laughter and met Grey's eyes before she looked down.

Then Colin looked around at his sheepish comrades and thought, not for the first time, that he should move on, be on his own again to bask in solitary freedom, passing through Naas whenever he had something of use to leave with the children there. Perhaps he could be chieftain of orphans and teach them to teach their children not to be slaves to any king's or priest's creeds, but instead to worship what fed their stomachs and their minds directly: what gave food and knowledge.

Colin walked past the long table strewn with picked-over food and grabbed a basket with some wilted leaves of cabbage in it. He thrust it at Grey and shrugged, as though to say, "There is really nothing we can do but give each other cabbage, is there?" Grey smiled and nodded a thanks as she readjusted the baby and left. When she was back in the Church she spoke with the Abbot.

"Do you remember the beggars with the Lord's son, Red? They went from the Monastery before the plague came. They went to find the place where earth and heaven meet. Perhaps we could find that place for our child."

The Abbot stood up and looked at her as though a frost had covered his eyes and his heart. "I will do what God tells me, what my duty to the Church is in these final days. I cannot wander out on the road, not with men from Avignon at my back, not until I have had a chance to explain to them. I am Abbot and you are a peasant girl. Order must be restored. I have learned obedience to order and do not want to bring any more suffering on myself or others."

"I was never a peasant girl. When I was a peasant, I was a boy. And now I can live in the Manor if I choose. There is nothing to the names we give each other."

The Abbot laughed at her without smiling. He came close to Grey, his hands in fists. She stood still, defiant.

They both looked down at the baby, asleep in a nest made of blankets and cloth from the Old Priest's robes.

The Abbot rubbed his face as though to erase his features and thoughts. He saw himself years ago, young and eager—an excited scholar, devoted to serving God to alleviating all the misery of the world; he saw himself bent over the box, reading the brittle scroll. He saw himself those years and years ago, suddenly emptied of strength, his finger shaking as it followed the text. "'It is finished.'"

"You are ill," Grey said, for the Abbot's face was now as pale as a cloud. She put her hand on his arm. "Are you ill?" A moment before she had wished the Abbot were dead, and now her heartbeat choked her breath as she wondered if the plague had finally come for her child's father.

"No, no. I am not ill."

He took a deep breath, puffing his cheeks out to exhale, and then said, "Let us not think, not wonder or think, just for a while. The world is changed."

They looked into each other's eyes and then Grey slowly closed hers. She moved about the room, touching the walls, passing her palms over the surface of the writing desk, crouching down and feeling along the floor, until she found an old linen smock. Sitting down, she tore a strip of it off. She tied the strip around her eyes and lifted her dress above her head. The tunic she wore beneath it was stained with drops of milk that had leaked from her breasts, which were aching and full. She pulled the tunic over her head and lifted one breast with her hand.

She soon felt the Abbot's mouth around the nipple, a penetrating, wet warmth. He gently drew the milk down into the nipple and out into his mouth, playing his tongue over the dimpled skin. He lifted his head and held her to him, one hand untying the cloth around her eyes. He let it fall to the floor and looked into her eyes.

Grey took off her leggings and sat on the stool while the Abbot removed his robe and leggings, freeing his erection. She pulled him to her, and they both watched as he went inside her, standing between her legs, which spread apart like angel's wings, her feet perched on the rungs of the stool. They watched his cock going in and out, felt the smoothness and heat as his movements drew liquid from her.

"You must not give me another child," she said. "I do not want another child."

"But the world is in need of more children. It is so empty now. Let me put another child inside you. How healthy our son is."

He lifted her by her buttocks, then lowered her again. Lifting and lowering her, he sank himself deeply inside her.

When he was finished, Grey draped her arms and head over the Abbot's shoulders, still wanting him, still hungry between her legs. But he was at peace and lifted her up and carried her to the bedding.

"We must put on our clothing," she whispered, "so as not to be feasted on the whole of our bodies by mites."

The Abbot told her tenderly, "You have become very sensible as a mother." He then said that he wanted to return to the Monastery at Tarmath. He held her from behind and spoke into her ear that he wanted to be the Abbot; he was the Abbot. That is who he was. Grey laughed.

"Are you an Abbot or a father or a fornicator? Which are just words and which is the truth of your nature?"

They were both silent until they drifted into an afternoon sleep.

They were awakened at dusk by loud shouting and banging from the Manor. They stayed where they were, afraid.

While they had been sleeping, four men, two clerics and two ruffians made into ragged soldiers, had come pounding on the Manor door. The Plowman's son opened the door to them, a little drunk and not afraid. One of the clerics, a very thin man, spoke in French to the other, who said in Gaelic, "We are looking for the Abbot."

The Plowman's son grinned and said, "Why, I am the Abbot!" And he was run through with one of the ruffian's swords.

Standing still as the blade was pulled back out, he watched blood rush into the palm of his hand, which he cupped beneath the wound. The blood spilled over his hand and the Plowman's son fell.

It was Colin who jumped first, snatching up one of the Manor's fine swords, which he had adopted. He swiftly leapt over the body of his friend and with a sweep slashed the ruffian's chest open. The ruffian bellowed and staggered backward. Others in the Manor ran out and clubbed one of the clerics to death. The skinny one ran hard and escaped them. The other ruffian turned and pleaded to be spared, and though Colin yelled, "Spare him!," the young man pursuing him split his head with a heaving blow from a plow blade.

Then there was silence, and Colin went down on one knee, breathing hard, shaking his head.

He turned and yelled at the panting group around him: "Go dig graves, then! Finish the work!"

They stood still for another few minutes, one of them pushing the corpse of the cleric with his foot.

Grey and the Abbot held one another tightly, listening to the noises coming from the Manor nearby, and waited for hours until there was some assurance that whatever had happened was over. Then they slept again, until morning, when they would creep out and discover what new horror was in the world.

The Bailiff came to the Manor the next evening and stood under a brilliant yellow moon with a warning.

"The family of the Lord of Finnistuath still owns this Manor," he called up, with a hint of inebriation in his tone, though no one had ever seen the Bailiff lose his control to any intoxicant. He continued, holding his arms up but not waving them. "Their claim includes the lands around it, the well, and the fields to the north that have been left unattended. It is only a matter of time when you will all be expelled and hanged."

"The world is ending, you fool," came a shrill reply.

And then refuse came at him through the windows as projectiles of dried dog feces, moldy oatcakes, and broken pottery. In this way, the Manor was finally being cleaned. But the Bailiff was not defeated. He had learned years and years ago to suffer humiliation without his sense of duty being in any way diminished.

He could hear the Abbot's baby crying in the Church and shook his head. It was only a matter of time, he thought, before such barbaric and heathen practices as a cleric having a wife and child would be wiped out of Ireland entirely. If the world did not end soon, Ireland would be tamed and civilized, because men like the Bailiff would not give up. By God, they would not give up. And if they were spared the ravages of the plague, then that was more reason for them to take up the cross—"Take up the cross!" he said aloud—and teach this wild place propriety, culture, and order. "I have it all right here!" he yelled, slapping his ledger book. "It is all here, the truth!" Yes, men like him would keep the records, no matter what; they would keep the records and the laws so that no matter what plague occurred, the world's order would be restored with lists of goods bought and sold, of lands owned and inherited, of crimes committed and punished.

The Bailiff's shout woke up the Abbot, who noted that Grey was gone. He looked at his sleeping son, who was beginning to fret. He admitted to himself and to God that the worst thing he could endure now was to see his son suffer, to see this child of his die before him. He wanted his son to be as safe and thriving, as full of possibility as anyone could be. It would be better to be separated from the child than to watch it suffer; how could a man of God, responsible for the souls of Christendom, tend to a child and ensure that it did not go hungry? Grey was a good mother but could not provide what his child should have, and certainly could not teach him to become a scholar. Where could he find an apt guardian or a nunnery left to care for an orphaned child with an Abbot's blood in him? He wanted the peace of knowing that he had not brought a child into the world to starve or to be an ignorant peasant. He also wanted to reconcile the horrors he had seen and the great doubt his faith had endured with his need to be devoted to God. The Pope's box, the plague, the predicament his own lust got him into, there was no salvation in the face of all that, other than a bargain with either the Devil or God. And true enough, the Devil's bargains were clear and immediate, whereas God's bargains were as subtle as a stranger's smile and as immediate as eternity. What did God want him to do? How could he be forgiven?

Then the Abbot heard in his head, perhaps in one of those subtle ways that God communicates, that reconciliation, that peace and grace were not a matter of men being forgiven by God but instead a matter of God being forgiven by men. He felt in his gut that he had to forgive God—for the plague, for the suffering, for the silence. He also had to forgive Jesus. Yes, perhaps Jesus had made a mistake in bargaining with the Devil, but he descended into Hell before taking his place in Heaven, and he had lived as holy a life as he could and endured as much suffering as he could, as few men could. Men, even saviors, had to make minor bargains in order to endure and transform suffering. God waited, ready to embrace those who forgave themselves and others.

## 42

THE ABBOT became more clerical, more devout and insistent in his role as Priest. He constantly spoke about his urge to return to the Monastery. But Grey was full of her child's discoveries, taking him with her to the spring and letting him lie wide eyed to look through the fluttering trees into the sky. There were days of weariness when his discomfort or restlessness kept her away from sleep. She was full of peace when he nursed at her breast, nuzzling the nipple first before sucking it in with pure need. As she felt the milk make her breasts heavy and then release into the baby's mouth, she knew who she was.

The village of Finnistuath was sparse and silent. Only the Bailiff reminded anyone that there was any order or significant human history there. Colin and his people came out from the Manor to hunt and root through the forest for food. He and the Abbot nodded at one another, in a strange truce, a sheepish acknowledgment that they were on to a new game, that the old posturing and shoving made no sense now. Not wanting to insult the other, each kept his pity of the other to himself. To the Abbot, Colin was a pathetic failure as a hero, a man trying to wrest from the dregs of the Earth some dignity that was doomed to be squashed by one's own mortality. To Colin, the Abbot was an impotent man whose faith was based on desperation; the Abbot's only merit was in having as his mistress the most interesting creature in all Christendom, a woman Colin had known as a boy, a woman with a raw and beautiful disinterest in conformity, almost an ignorance of it.

The Midwife lived in Finnistuath, but she traveled sometimes to Tarmath, where she said there were people coming from many of the ghost villages in the region. Her services were required there. Grey saw her with her walking stick walking as boldly as the sighted toward the bridge and coming back days later with bread to sell to the smattering of people left in Finnistuath.

People seemed to be waiting for death to take them as it had all the rest, but when they did not die, they began to wonder if they should have planted after all. There would be no harvest that year except for the small patches of garden that some of the women could not help but grow. Plague legends were spread, stories of angels appearing to the dying and making their swollen sores disappear; cures being handed out by Saint Peter in some port town; a cat saying the Lord's Prayer; a man gathering children in carts in Dublin, which he and his band of Satanists garnished with roasted apples and ate. The stories increased as the dying tapered off.

Grey's child was still unnamed, for she didn't want to fix him yet in some sound or title. He was on his feet and swaying in a persistent effort to walk. As Grey lunged for him before he fell one afternoon, she noted how stiff she felt, how unable to move her head comfortably. With one hand holding the child's wrist, Grey felt her neck with the other hand. There was a swelling there, beneath her chin. And then she felt immediately weak, and both hands fluttered to hold onto her child.

"Pray for me, Abbot," she said, because she could not leave her son in this world to go to another, no matter how beautiful and perfect the other world was, for it would be hellish without her child's warmth in her arms.

In her fever one day, Grey noted that the Abbot and the baby were gone. She saw the shadows in the room slide from one place to another quietly, so as not to disturb her. Spittle came from the side of her mouth as she lay, sometimes sleeping. She could not swallow without a sharp pain, as though there were a thorn stuck in her throat. She sat up once and crawled to the pail in the corner to piss. Her head throbbed, pumping pain and nausea into her body. Falling back on the bedding, she was in the sacristy in the Monastery, nested in the clerics' robes and altar cloths.

She wondered if the Abbot and her son were in the Monastery now, and she called out for them.

Then there was night and a fire. She heard the Abbot's voice in the chapel, saying prayers, chanting in Latin. She saw his candle wandering and making large shapes that moved across the walls and floor. She heard her child's cries and crawled to its cradle and put her hand over the edge, letting the child suck on her fingers and play with them.

Then there was a hand in hers, a familiar hand that grew very large in hers, as large as a mountain. She held it, knowing that it was the only thing that kept the aching in all her bones from intensifying. Tears came to her eyes, and she wiped them on that hand and felt another placed on her soggy hair. "Water," she said. And the hand put a rag soaked in water to her lips.

The kindness of the hands overwhelmed her, separated her from her illness, though the illness still raged. She sometimes knew that they were the Abbot's hands, but then wondered if they belonged to an angel or to the Midwife or the Kitchener or Colin, or to Brother Peter. One's enemy could take one's hand and no longer be an enemy.

In the morning, there was a light so bright that it seemed to crack the stones of the floor. The Abbot was staring down at Grey with disdain for her and her illness.

"The baseness of human existence," he thought to himself. But the baseness was the result not of a lack of knowledge but of a lack of pious obedience. Grey had seduced him into that baseness, taking control of his life. And now she was sick and needed to be cared for and had let her hand be held by Colin, a worthless stranger, a man he had booted out of the Monastery years ago, who now spoke knowledge as the salvation of the common people. The Abbot had met Colin at the spring one day and told him, confided in him, that he was a man burdened by the devotion of a whore who was now ill and perhaps dying. Colin's hand curled into a fist, but instead of slamming it against the cleric's tight jaw, he went to Grey's bedside and held her hand.

Grey looked with narrowed eyes at the light and slowly sat up. The Abbot walked out. She took her hand away from Colin's to hold her head, which felt much heavier than it had been before the fever. But there was no longer a sharp pain in it. "Where is my child?" she asked. And Colin nodded to where the child was asleep, its plump mouth open. Grey knelt and bent over to smell his sweet hair and warm, moist neck.

She stood up, swaying a little, and then moved slowly, touching the walls for security, to the chapel and then to the door of the Church.

"Stay with the child, please, until the Abbot or I return," she mumbled, and Colin nodded.

The bright light was only the midmorning sun, which was in a cloudless sky. But it seemed as though it were a new sun altogether. Grey went to the spring, dragging her feet on the path. Her hand lay over her heart, which pounded hard. At the spring she sat on the wet ground and washed her face, and then her hands fluttered around her neck and finally perched to discover that the swelling had subsided. Weak on her knees, she moved her hands from her neck to the pail on the ground, which she filled with water that had blue and yellow and white dancing lights in it. She stared at the water and saw many little spirits winking at her. She perched the pail on the pile of stones and lifted water out of it. It shimmered and winked in her palms. She put her lips to it and then drew the liquid in and swallowed. There was an aching in her throat, but no sharp pain, no sense of it closing and suffocating her.

"So, I will live," she said.

She lay down and slept until the now constantly irritated Abbot, his hair in ridiculous unkempt tufts, came to find her and carried her back to the Church.

 43

EIGHTY-SEVEN COWS, all brown and bony shouldered, clattered across the bridge with three soldiers as cowherds behind and two leading them on horseback in front. And before the cows was a man on a large horse, the same brown color as the cattle. The man's red beard was forked and well combed. He wore a red velvet cap and jacket and had leather boots dyed green.

A few yards behind the herd was a contraption, a cart with four poles on it from which hung a green velvet curtain that swayed and shuddered. There was a slight opening on one side of the curtain through which two women could be seen sitting on large tapestried pillows.

One woman in the cart was Lady Constance, a former widow, recently remarried. She was traveling with her new husband, called Richard the Red, to reclaim lands his dead family had in a small village. In the cart with her was her maidservant, a pockmarked English girl who was terrified of the Irish heathens. The two women were juggled about in the sweltering cart with a cedar chest in which there were things more precious to Lord Red than his new wife—glass bottles and vials, brass containers with bulbous bottoms darkened by soot, oil lamps for heating up the brass containers, some small bowls and platters, little gold boxes and linen sacks full of herbs and metal ore, and corked tubes of various liquids. At the bottom of this chest was a leather book written in Latin, entitled *Prima Materia*. When the rattling and clomping and lowing entourage had crossed the bridge, the Lady leaned out and retched, leaving a little pool of aristocratic vomit along the road.

Colin saw the Bailiff trotting down the road toward the river later that afternoon and climbed the tower to see what his business was. From there he saw the cattle, the cart, the soldiers, and the man with the red forked beard on the horse. He watched the procession get closer and closer to Finnistuath and knew that he and his people would either stage a battle and die or leave the Manor like thieves. The Lord's son, who had been a mendicant, was reclaiming his rights and his lands. He, as his father might have said, had come to his senses, and thus the old order was returning.

This did not surprise Colin. He had wondered how long it would be, with the Bailiff keeping records, sending out communiques, traveling to Tarmath, before some relative of the dead and decaying Lord would come and make his claim. And he had thought out in his own mind the two plans: fighting or running. From the tower, he was assessing the strength of the entourage. The four soldiers were well armed with metal weapons, things they could swing from their horses, and they were armored, and no doubt the Lord himself carried weapons.

Many fresh deaths would occur, Colin knew, if there was a battle. Then there would be sorrow and intensified bitterness. What a world this is that goes on when we thought it was over, he thought—what a world where our gratitude and relief at not being murdered by the plague is barely upon us and we begin to kill one another.

But he could not just run into the woods. He could not be so easily weakened in his own eyes, allowing the world to drift back to its injustices without a fight. He knew, for example, that no man had a right to so many cows when others starved.

He then sat down and leaned against the wall of the tower just beneath the little window. What could his store of wooden spears and rusted blades and arrows do?

He closed his eyes and leaned his head against a stone. He was tired. He was older than his years. There needed to be a new Colin, a young man with rage in him. But the plague had quenched his audacity. He could see the faces of the children, too silent, staring at the road ahead. He felt the same inclination, to simply stare at the road ahead as someone else directed the cart. But there were predators, arrogant and privileged, who waited, patiently, grinning, waited for the truth tellers and the justice seekers to tire, to give up; they waited and then grabbed up whatever they could and hoarded the world's goods, laughing at the fools who had spoken with such lovely ideas and then fallen asleep in the road.

Colin stood up and looked out again, leaning out with his hands pressed against either side of the window: a herd of cattle. How many could he take? One, easily, but why not more, why not five or six? The cycle of cattle raids that had gone on since the time of Cuchulain would continue with Colin; and yet in the new times, influenced by the hero Jesus, the cattle stealing would be not just a matter of pride but also a matter of justice and charity. There would be milk and cheese and butter and meat for the orphans of Naas.

When Colin's mates in the Manor heard of the coming of the new Lord and his men and cattle, a few stood and took up spears, which they had been using to tease and poke each other with. They wanted battle. But Colin stood in the doorway and yelled out, "Don't be fools! If you fight your ragged fight, you'll just give the soldiers an excuse to murder you all."

They grumbled, and Colin told them, "Take what you can to bargain with. You, Orpheus, you go back to Naas and start building a wall for cattle." The others stuffed bags and satchels with whatever they could find: cloth, candlesticks, silver platters, needlepoint pillows. One of his men waited behind to piss on one of the couches. And then the Manor was silent again.

 **44**

Lady Constance swooned to see and smell the condition of the Manor so that her maidservant had to unwrap her headpiece and take her to a couch by the window. But as she was combing out the Lady's long brown hair, the maid herself was horrified to discover that the couch was wet and smelled of urine. She could not think of how to tell her mistress and so kept combing the hair and telling her how well the Manor was being righted and filled with their things.

"Won't it be wonderful when the tapestries and furnishings arrive from England—your bed, madam. It won't be long in arriving."

The five soldiers were coming in and out with baskets and trunks. The Bailiff was scurrying about, talking to the Plowman's daughter and the Stonecutter's wife, whom he had brought in to sweep and clean. Like bovine counterparts of the humans, the cattle wandered around outside, getting into the graveyard and lowing around the Church. Grey passed among them, touching their warm, taut haunches. The child stood in the doorway of the Church clutching a piece of bread. Grey and the Abbot were hungry. They had hardly eaten in several days; Grey had begged bread from the Midwife and given it to the child.

"What do you call the child?" the Midwife had asked.

"I cannot name him," Grey said. "I fear a name will be something that will bind him."

Now Grey was lurking about, wondering how to pull one of the cattle off into the woods and slaughter it. She looked back at her son, unwilling to risk execution for cattle stealing. But Red might remember her, might have pity. There were no stores of food for the winter.

"Who is that rough woman standing by the door?" the Lady asked her maid, in English.

The maid replied, "It is one of the natives, a half-wit, it seems." She added after a casual pause, "Perhaps you should move to another couch. I believe this one is soiled."

The Lady looked down at the moist stain and rolled away, almost falling to the floor.

She went to her husband and leaned her head on his back. Grey watched.

"It is horrible here," Constance told him.

Red turned around to hold her and comfort her. Grey slipped out and walked back through the cows, which stood around stupidly. She found her child sleeping over the Abbot's shoulder as he continued to write at the table.

"We will starve to death," she said to him. He did not reply. "I have been in the Manor and seen the new Lord and his wife. We must get food." She got the pail and walked out again to fill it at the spring. And when she had done that, she brought the water to the Manor and set it in front of the Lady, who was lying on another couch. Her maid was supervising the placement of a large trunk of her mistress's clothes, which two soldiers were carrying. The Lady eyed Grey haughtily but with some curiosity. Red hurried over with a glass bottle and filled it with water from the pail.

"Thank you," he said to Grey in Gaelic. He hesitated before going back to the paraphernalia at the table.

Grey said, "Did you come very close, sir, to the place where the Earth ends and Heaven begins?"

Red's smile melted on his face and his hand dropped down.

Lady Constance was shaking out her skirts.

"I am on a different quest now, one with less myth and more science. The *prima materia*," Red said, "is the basic material, the one element out of which everything is made—everything." His eyes sparkled with the certainty of a speech he had made many times, which had impressed many people. "It is what God Himself is made of and what He made everything from."

"Why do you speak to this woman in her language?" his wife sang out.

Grey said to him. "I have no quest other than to feed myself and my child."

"If I find this element, there is no end to what can be done. The manipulation of it can cure illness, give immortality."

"I want only a little more mortality, Lord, and need the miracle of food for that. Do you have food to spare? I will fetch water for you and the Lady."

Lady Constance then said to her maid, who came to sit on a stool beside her and do some mending, "What liberties she takes! She must be mad. I will not have her going about so freely, as though she had some rank or title. She looks like a wild spirit, someone who sits on men when they sleep."

The maid covered her mouth and giggled. Grey understood that she was being judged and that the word "wild" was part of the judgment.

Red waved his hand at a nearby table. "Take what you need, and bring water everyday." Then he said, "Your face is familiar to me. You had kin here?"

Grey looked down and nodded, then said, "I am grateful that I can serve you and feed my child."

When Grey brought the baby, a few months past a year old, into the Manor one day, to give him a piece of bread from the table, the Lady stood up and pointed, saying to her husband, "This wild woman comes and goes and takes food from our table. I want her out." It was the first time Grey had heard the Lady scream so loudly, and she dropped the bread, causing the child to wail. Red went to his wife and calmed her. She whispered something to him, and he looked up at Grey and the child.

"Come here," he said to her. "The Lady wishes to see your child."

Grey gave the boy the bread and carried him to the couch. Red was smiling kindly.

"He is a healthy boy, though lean," he said, as his wife played with the boy's hand.

The Lady whispered in his ear again, and Red said, "May she hold the child?"

A tingling in her scalp made Grey hesitate. Then she passed the boy onto the Lady's lap. He sat contentedly looking at his mother and feeding himself the bread. The Lady cooed at him and rested her cheek on the top of the baby's head.

"She has had many miscarriages," Red explained.

She lifted her eyes and looked at Grey.

The Lady held the boy under his arms and turned him to face her. He squirmed and twisted around to see his mother and reach out for her. Grey touched his hand.

"Tell her that we will keep the child," the Lady said, and Red stared at his wife and did not speak. "Poor thing; he is in need of food."

She noticed her husband's silence and looked up to say, "Tell her we will give it a good home. He will eat well and become a Lord some day. Oh, tell her. She will be so glad." The baby's mouth trembled and he reached out for his mother. But the Lady pulled him away.

Grey stood and pressed her hands between the Lady and her son, trying to pull him away.

"Give me my son," she said above the child's wailing.

But Red held her by the arms from behind and pulled her back.

"Give me my son," Grey screamed.

"Listen, listen," Red said, turning Grey around and bending over so as to look closely into her face. "We will take care of the child for a while, just for a while. We will see that he is fed well. Look at all this food. We will give you more food for yourself."

"I want my son. I will feed him. His father is the Abbot of Tarmath. We will feed him. What are you doing? What are you doing with my child?"

She moved toward the baby, who was now distracted by the Lady's dangling a bright brocade belt in from of him as her husband made the argument for a thing already sealed.

"You are poor. We can raise the child as a Lord. Think of it, your child, a rich man!"

Grey struggled and fought to get to her child. "I am his mother," she called out, pleading, terrified.

One of Red's soldiers came in and grabbed Grey by the arm, pulling her to the door.

"NO!" Grey screamed. "NO! I am his mother."

She fell on her knees, and the soldier grabbed her hair and pulled her, sliding her across the floor. She grabbed at his hand, remembering her father being struck by the Priest's thugs. She looked up at Red and put her hands together in prayer.

"Please, he is my son. He is my life. I will do anything you ask. Please . . ."

The Lady and her servant took the child to the back of the hall into one of the curtained beds.

"PLEASE," Grey howled.

Red said to the guard, "Lock her up in the stables and guard her. Give her some meat and ale."

"Don't you remember that I was with you by the spring, that I was your fairy lover?" Grey pleaded.

Red turned away, and the guard took her as Grey wailed. The child needed a name now, she thought, a name for her to call out.

# 45

GREY ATE the food given her; she ate it like an animal who is determined to remain strong. She asked the guard over and over to let her go, promising that she would not cause trouble. But he didn't speak to her. She lay on hay and heard the horses snorting and stamping during the night. She slept little and wept.

In a few days, Red came in and stood in front of her.

"Once I was a mendicant."

Grey sat up, straws stuck to her hair, and nodded.

"I wandered through many places after that, looking for the world's end, for passage to paradise, and that is when the plague began and I saw instead Hell all around me. It seemed a terrible thing to seek for Heaven for myself when there were so many tormented people who had no means or strength for pilgrimage. At first I thought that the wickedness in the world was the cause for all the horrors people suffered, but what could I say about a child weakly mewing in pain, with no comfort from its dying mother? What God would allow this suffering?"

Grey was shaking, thinking of words to soothe, to cajole with—words that had the power to get her child back. She would bare her breasts and let him touch her; she would be his fairy lover; she would serve him as she had the Priest, washing the stones on his floor.

Red continued speaking:

"That is when I left the pilgrims and removed my mendicant's costume. I went to England to take advantage of my family's position there and eat and drink until I died with the rest of the world. My wife's husband was a Lord in Brighton who had contracted the disease and was allowing every kind of debauchery in his household. There were whores and wine sellers and musicians there day and night. I fornicated and drank myself to distraction, and was well past clear thinking when I came across the man's wife and her brother in a private room. The Lady's brother, Henry, was dying, and Constance did not drink or whore or neglect him. She lay beside him and held him. She looked up at my drunken face and showed me the shame and sadness of all that the world was suffering. I slipped away and could not loosen from my head the vision of her and the boy, like Mary holding the crucified body of Christ. When her husband died, I threw all the derelicts out of the household and closed the place. I then waited and prayed with her by her brother's bedside. But he also died. Her sorrow was quiet and deep. She prayed to die also, but after a few weeks there was a pause in the disease in that region. I then suggested that we come here, where I could discover the health of my family and estate and where she would have no reminders of her tragedy."

Grey listened; she listened because that is what he wanted her to do and she would do it as her heart beat and she thought of her child, of what cajoling would be required of her to get him back. She carefully stood up, as though not to scare a wild animal away, and let Red finish.

"It is my desire to relieve suffering," Red said.

Grey spoke, softly, calmly. "Please let me have my child back. He is a peasant, too low for you and the fine Lady."

"He only needs to be given a name, and that is what he will be," Red said. "The boy's father agrees. I have given him money and provisions to return to the Monastery. He wants the boy to stay with me, to be my own son and heir. The child will be baptized. His father understands the boon this is, the miracle."

"The miracle." Grey's head, in a rush of dizziness, could not focus on the image of the Abbot's hand receiving coin for their child.

"You are lying," she said. "The Abbot loves the boy well."

"Yes, he loves him well enough to leave him where he will have the best fortune."

"You have killed the Abbot, or let him be killed by the men from Avignon."

Grey was pulled down by a leaden fear to her knees. Then she changed her tone.

"You are a kind Lord," she said.

She kissed the top of Red's boots, tasting the dust and leather.

Red stumbled backward and commanded that she be released.

In the darkness of the Church, only a few embers burning in the hearth, Grey could see the papers on the writing table that the Abbot had left behind.

Her breasts were very full; she ached for the child to nurse from them, and this ache went beyond her breasts into her stomach and her head.

In the morning she left a pail of water just inside the door of the Manor, peeking in to see her son. He was crying fussily but was soon swept up into the Lady's arms. Grey closed her eyes and turned to leave. A torrential rain began to fall outside. The child began to wail. The Lady cooed to him, calling him Henry.

"Your child is to be raised as the son of the Lord and Lady of Finnistuath," she told herself. "He will never be hungry." And he had been given a name. He was called Henry. Grey walked into the forest, letting her clothing and skin get soaked. She wandered like a spirit, mournful and chained to the Earth, but not belonging to it.

 46

GREY LURKED AROUND the Manor and the Church, spending
nights in the stables. For she had no desire to stay in the Church
watching the empty cradle. She spoke to Red's black stallion, stroked him
and fed him grasses. She told the horse about her love for her son, and sat
upon its back, lying down and weeping into its mane.

Finnistuath had now been reduced to the Manor and a few houses to the
north, where the Midwife still lived. Of those who had survived the plague,
seven had died of starvation and others had left for Tarmath and other
larger towns where some trade might exist.

One day there was a great commotion among the people of the Manor,
and when it was over Grey saw Colin tied to a tree between the Manor and
the Church. From a careful distance she watched him and the tree. Others
were watching openly: some servants, including the Lady's maid, and the
Lady herself, bouncing Henry in her arms and pointing at Colin as though
he were an amusement.

Colin was secured to the trunk of a beech tree by ropes around his chest.
His legs were bent beneath him and his head sagged onto his chest. A wind
blew his long, disheveled hair, but Grey could see no more movement than
that and feared that he was dead. A soldier, who held an iron spear and
stood by the tree, allowed the people to observe the man and even answered questions. Darkness came like a lazy yawn, and in its softness Grey
moved closer to Colin, and the small group drifted into the Manor. When
the soldier seated himself, Grey waited a moment and then came around to
sit beside Colin so that she was hidden from the soldier by both the tree
and its prisoner. She put her hand on the prisoner's calf and felt that it was
warm and tensed a little at her touch.

"Tell me what to do," she whispered right into his ear.

His eyes opened and he looked wearily in front of him, not knowing the
source of the voice.

He slowly turned his head toward her and studied her face in the meager torchlight afforded by the windows of the Manor.

Grey begged him, on her knees, as though she were the one imprisoned and needing help.

"You must tell me what to do."

He carefully moistened his lips with his tongue so he could try to speak, and then he said, "Tell the story. Tell how I took his cattle, six of them."

But Grey was not interested in constructing a hero's tale; words had not worked to help her get her son back.

"Your comrades, where are they?"

"They are long gone, back to Naas."

She waited with Colin until night, when she saw that the soldier was fast asleep on the ground, curled around his spear as though it were his favorite toy. Grey sawed at the ropes binding Colin to the tree with a dull blade from the stable; the effort took an excruciatingly long time, so that the moon rose and moved in a slow arc over the Manor.

"I might as well be using a stone," Grey said. She thought she heard something and stopped to look up into the tree, hoping that some fairy or angel were there and would help. When do the spirits choose to help and when do they leave humans to suffer alone?

Finally, time spent sawing at the ropes and the weight of Colin tore the last shreds, and he fell forward onto the ground. Grey held her breath and watched the soldier to see if the noise of Colin's fall had sifted into his slumber. No one moved.

She squatted down and said, "You must get up and come with me." She passed her hands over the ground and found a stone that felt right in her hand.

Colin slid up to his knees, his head hanging down.

"You must stand up," she said.

She lifted him, her hand under his arms. He said, "Hold, hold. I cannot walk."

"You must walk," she said.

A few yards away, the soldier suddenly stood up. Holding Colin, Grey let nothing in her body move.

The soldier looked around, dazed, and then turned away from the tree and began to urinate with his back to Colin and Grey. The two moved a few feet, Grey wanting to go as fast as she could before the soldier was finished.

"You are an angel, you are a warrior angel," Colin said, drunk with pain and exhaustion.

The soldier turned around quickly, stuffing his penis into his leggings. He grabbed his spear. Grey let Colin slide out of her hold and lifted her arm. She paused, then hurled the rock.

It hit just below the soldier's left eye. He fell back, whimpering, touching the crushed bone and yelping. He had no more concern for the prisoner.

With aching effort, Grey dragged Colin away until he was able to hobble a bit and they made it to the spring, where Grey helped him to sit on a pile of stones and washed his scraped skin. He drank water from her cupped hands, which were steady.

"Where can you go?" Grey asked.

They were silent for a time, until Colin said, "Can you give me the knife?"

Grey put it in his hand. He stood up slowly and was about to say something when they heard two soldiers running down the path toward them. Colin, dragging one leg, hurried away as Grey tried to scramble up the tree.

One of her bare feet was on the bark; she could feel the coarse comfort of it on her sole. Her hands were reaching for the first branch. But other hands found her ankle and pulled violently, so that Grey fell, hitting her chin hard against the tree trunk. The hands dragged her down to the ground. She twisted around and kicked as the man who had her grew more ferocious and pinned her down with his whole body. His breath was warm and vinegary. Grey turned her head away and he stood, lifting her up by the collar of her dress. Her chin throbbed, and when she inhaled, a dull pain billowed in her side where she had fallen and been dragged.

The other soldier came running back and shook his head. The three went back down the path, Grey hanging her head and thinking that at least Colin was free.

The Lord of the Manor had been asleep, and with a large dog he met the two soldiers and Grey at the door. "I don't want my wife and child to be disturbed," he said, and so he spoke in whispers and patted the head of the dog, which was at his side and on the verge of barking.

When the soldiers finished telling him their story, he asked Grey, "Did you do this unlawful act?"

"What is the law?"

Red closed his eyes.

"You have let go a thief, a man who stole cows from my herd."

Grey looked up at him. The light of the torch by the door made him a black shadow, not a man of flesh.

"You have stolen my child."

"I am the Lord of this Manor. And I will not have my property taken by a man who celebrated the death of my family and defiled my father's home."

"Once you were a fairy's lover and then a mendicant. Whatever you are, I am begging you to let me go," she said. "Let me take my son, for he grew in my belly and has my nature. He cannot be the Lord of the Manor. He will be trouble for you."

He laughed and the dog wagged its tail. In good humor he directed the soldiers to take Grey and keep her in the stables. There she stayed in the corner with the new Lord's new black horse. The two soldiers stayed outside the door and thus the night passed with only the horses sleeping soundly.

One soldier said to the other, "Why are there two of us to guard a woman?"

The other one did not answer for almost a minute and then said, "Perhaps she is not truly a woman or even a human, but a witch."

There were many fleas in the stables. Grey was bitten all over, even on one eyelid, which swelled up. She emerged into the open air, pulled by a soldier, to see the Bailiff walking from the Church to the Manor. He lived in Tarmath now but came once a month to the Manor to do business. Grey was taken inside the Manor after receiving permission to squat down and urinate.

Lady Constance and the maid were sewing in one corner, with the child in a fine walnut cradle beside them, chewing on a strap of leather. Grey's breasts were dried of the milk for him, but she wanted to lift him, hold him to her. The Lord was sitting in a large chair by the hearth, which had a small fire in it. There was one wide and well-upholstered stool beside his chair, and a discordant group of chairs and stools were set up facing him. The Bailiff went to the wide stool and sat with the ledger opened on his lap. His face sagged drearily. Grey was pushed down onto a stool by the hand of the soldier, which stayed on her shoulder.

She heard these noises keenly: the baby making sounds that were almost words; the maid singing a soft little child's song in French; the scratching of the Bailiff's pen on the ledger book, which was tattered now, with soiled pages falling out of it; the ticking of the fire; the open-mouthed breathing of the soldier; a fly buzzing over a spot of spilled honey on the floor. Sometimes a harder sound occurred: the scraping of a stool or chair leg on the stones, the clearing of a throat. Red spoke heatedly as the Bailiff nodded. Then the Bailiff made patient references to his ledger. When the speaking stopped and the two men stood up, Red spoke to Grey in Gaelic.

"It has been determined that you are a half-wit and therefore will not be executed."

"So it is written in words that I am a half-wit?"

"Yes, for it has been disclosed that you have the features of a half-wit. This is a matter of scientific knowledge, a measurement here and here." Red spread his forefinger and thumb apart and touched them to her face.

"Yes. I have noted the likeness between you and a certain half-wit goat-herd's son. It is now written thus in the ledger," the Bailiff said.

Grey stood up and said to Red, "So, do you fear that your son is a half-wit, for his face has my features?"

Red looked over to his wife and saw the child's toes sticking out above the top of the cradle.

"The trait must come from the father. I have studied such matters."

"I see that the scholar is like the priest and can use knowledge to fit his needs. But I am a half-wit and do not understand your wisdom."

Red told her, "It is also determined that Henry is my son and will inherit this Manor and be Lord here."

"There is no village left. Finnistuath has only ghosts," Grey said.

"But there is still good hunting in the woods, and good land."

"But there is no one to plow or sow."

"These are no concerns of yours," Red said.

"I wish that the world had ended," Grey said, "for I cannot endure a long life without my child. My child conjured a love that is like the sun itself, giving warmth, a thing of Heaven felt on earth."

Her voice grew weak and trembled with the tears that shimmered in her eyes. The new Lord said, "As half-wit you are to be given charity."

He looked away when he added, "But you must not come near the child, or you will be killed, mercifully and swiftly killed."

47

tHE VILLAGE of Finnistuath died that year. There was only a Manor house and the ruin of people's lives. Colin bought those in the Manor their goods from Tarmath, and Red continued to play at alchemy. Grey wandered, imitating a half-wit well. There were always leaves in her hair, for she spent many hours in the woods by the spring. There she had various objects hidden, things pilfered from the stables, including a long iron fork for lifting hay. When she was in the stables at night, she conspired with the black stallion. Grey sat upon the horse, talking to it, soothing it, singing to it. She seemed mad to the soldiers who worked around her when they had business in the stables. But at night, she was alone with the horse. A half-moon called her out one night and told her to bring the horse. She sat upon it without saddle or stirrups and rode in slow, walking circles around and around. No one saw. And then she rode the horse farther into the woods, finding meadows where she could sing aloud, songs about her love of Henry and how fine a man he would be. When the horse first trotted with her, she fell off hard. She got back on and fell off again. The night when she learned to hang on, to bend low and hold hard with her legs, she rode until it was almost dawn. She heard voices as she neared the Manor and slid off the horse. She pulled it slowly along until she could see a soldier sitting on a stool outside the stables talking with another soldier who was leaning against the stone wall. They were laughing and nodding.

"Damn them," Grey muttered to herself, her skin hot and her heart pounding. And then she let the horse go; she grabbed its head and whispered into its ear. "I hope you'll understand what I'm about to do and not hold it against me in the future."

Then she went behind the horse and smacked it hard on the flank, sending it toward the men. It bolted forward and into the clearing in front of the stables. The soldier who had been sitting stood up and yelled, "Whoa there! What's this?" He called out to his friend, "Stop him, block him in, man!" The other one grabbed the reins and the horse reared up a little, but without much resistance, and was easily calmed. Grey went back into the woods and waited for a few days before going to the stables to sleep. She slept in the Midwife's old hut, where a small fire gave small warmth. Then cautiously she returned to the stables, apologizing to the horse and taking up her nightly rides again.

In the spring she played with the iron fork, jabbing at the trees with it, learning to have a firm grip on it as she beat it against a stone. One day, as she was throwing the fork into the base of a dead oak tree, she saw Colin standing to the side of the tree as part of the forest. He smiled at her, and she stood still to decide if he was a spirit. He spoke, saying, "I have you to thank for my life."

She nodded and said, "I hope you are glad of it."

He said, "I am," and walked to her and embraced her. This embrace caused Grey to weep. She fell against Colin and wept against the rough and oily cloth of his tunic. He smelled like a deer, like a creature who lived always in the woods.

Colin asked no questions about Grey's weeping. He stroked her tangled hair, picking leaves from it. She let the iron fork fall from her hand and stood in the woods, surrounded by holly and oak and fern and rowan. She stood entwined with Colin, who said nothing. And they only breathed.

When she parted from him and still had her hand on his shoulder, he told her that he was glad that she had not been punished more severely.

"What game do you play here?" he asked.

"Every game I play is for my child, who is now called Henry."

Colin nodded, and she asked, "Will you play this game with me?"

"Tell me the rules, and I will play."

"I think they are a mother's rules and may seem unreasonable to others, but there are common warrior's skills that are needed."

"I owe you my life, and I will serve your passion if you serve mine."

"I am drained of all passions but the one for my child."

"Then I will use the skill of waiting," Colin said. And then he added, "I remember you as a boy."

"Now I am a half-wit, for words in a book say so."

Grey picked up the fork and threw it at the tree, where it stuck well.

"What is your plan?" Colin asked.

"To play the game well," Grey answered.

## 48

COLIN TOLD GREY the stories of Mughain, wife of Conchobar, who led the women of her kingdom naked into the road so as to diffuse the battle frenzy of the great hero Cuchulain; of Scathach, the woman who taught Cuchulain his battle skills and gave him his weapons; and of Morrigan, the goddess of battles, who was scorned by Cuchulain and used her wrath to destroy him. He told her that Creidne was a champion among the Fianna, the elite warriors who guard kings. Then in the ninth century the Catholic Church, built upon the holy scriptures, wrote a rule that women could not be warriors.

Colin said, "But there is no reason to adhere to such rules."

Grey nodded, "I do not believe that because something is written down it is true. What I desire to do and what I am able to do is all the truth I need."

She would take her son back, for she had studied the facts and behaviors rather than words and theories. Her son wailed and cried more often in the Manor than he had with her. He had reached his hands out to her when she passed him, and when she had secretly touched him and told him that he was a good boy, she felt the understanding that passed between them that she and her child were still bound together.

Colin waited in the woods, where Grey brought the stallion to him, and they tied the beast to a thin birch tree. From there they walked at dusk to the Manor, Grey holding the iron fork and Colin carrying a club. They walked in silence, not just to be undetected, but in order to burn into their whole being the battle frenzy that they would need, a fierceness that could pass through any fear and sharpen their awareness to a needle point. Grey prayed for faith in herself and her purpose and for help from all powers that she could neither see nor name. She and Colin exchanged one glance before Grey shed her clothes and strolled from the woods, naked. Colin, watching after her, whispered to himself, "The poor lads are doomed for sure."

She stood in front of the two guards, who laughed, but uneasily, as they spoke to each other in English. She held up her breasts and smiled, motioning to the woods with her head to the larger guard. He shrugged and looked at his comrade, who nodded enthusiastically, and the couple scurried into the trees, where the guard was swiftly clubbed over the head by Colin. While Colin was bent over, making sure the man was still alive, Grey went back to the other guard, who immediately straightened and pointed his spear at her; he was not such an idiot as to be unwary when the woman returned alone. She stood in front of him, speaking her foreign language with soothing tones, saying in Gaelic, "You are an idiot with a pig's eyes and a worm's brain," making it sound like, "Your friend will be here soon, but you certainly are handsome." She took his free hand and put it onto her full breast to induce him to forget any other matter. He was stepping toward her to feel the whole of her body against his when the club came down on his head and he fell, almost knocking Grey over.

While she was putting on the man's tunic, Colin said, "I've tied the other one up, but we'd best just hurry in and take what time we have while this one is deep in it."

Then Colin and Grey passed into the hall. Immediately she knew that the task was too easy. Red was working at his table of potions with his back to the doorway; the dogs were sleeping by the hearth. The Lady and her servant and the child were snuggled together in the curtained bed off to the side of the hearth, one side opened to the fire. There were no other servants there. Grey trotted to the bed and grabbed Henry, who barely woke up but draped himself over his mother's shoulder and fell back into sleep again. The servant awoke, screamed, and shook her Lady. Constance drowsily took in the situation. Red turned quickly and grabbed a sword from a pile of dusty blades lying on the floor. He lunged toward Grey, who was backing out of the door with the boy, holding up the iron pitchfork. Then Red was grabbed from behind by Colin, who had stuffed a sack full of bread and meat from the table.

Now there was a great deal of noise. Red yelled in English, "Get off of me! Men! Men, get in here!"

The Lady Constance shrieked, "She has taken Henry! She has taken my child!"

The servant was wailing, "God help us. God help us!"

Grey made it through the doorway and ran into the woods. Now Henry was awake and crying, but not hard. And Grey said to him, "Shhh, sweetling. It's your Mum and we're off on an adventure!" He quieted and she found the horse, which was pulling hard at his tether, ready to crack the small tree in two.

She put the child down and thought a moment, hoping that Colin was going to show up soon. She piled stones while talking softly to Henry, who helped by putting rocks and twigs and dirt on the pile she made. Then she took up the iron fork in one hand and Henry under the arm, untied the horse, and nudged it over to the pile of stones. She carefully stood on them. It took several tries to get the horse to stay still long enough for her to throw herself over its back and sit up with the child sitting between her legs and the weapon still in her hand. And still Colin was not there.

She wrapped the reins around her free hand and guided the horse toward the Manor at a careful trot. Henry was silent except for an occasional question: "Go? Go?" He spoke in English.

"Yes, go," Grey said in Gaelic.

A few yards from the Manor door, Grey saw Colin, the sack of food slung on his back, fending off Red with his club. Red still had the sword and had already pierced Colin's side with it.

"Get up on the horse behind me," Grey yelled. But Colin had only enough strength to swat at the air with the club and keep Red at a distance. The horse pranced around, hard to control. When she could get it still enough and close enough to Red, Grey pointed the pitchfork at him and said, "Let him go or I will kill you."

Hardly able to speak through his breath, Red said, "You are not a killer."

"That's right. I am a half-wit, for that is what is written. Now put your sword well down on the ground, man, or I will put this fork in your chest."

Colin had taken the opportunity of their conversation to back away, closer to the horse, but it made the horse skittish, and Grey lost her control of it so that it moved farther away from Red. Red raised the sword and leapt toward Colin, who weakly lifted the club. Grey aimed the fork and threw it hard just as the horse pranced backward. She meant for the tongs to go into his chest. She meant to kill him and call out that the same would go for anyone who killed innocent men and stole children. But one of the fork's long blades pierced through the soft suede of Red's fancy boot and nailed his foot to the ground.

Growling and yelling, "You whore!" Red tried to lift the fork, and in that time Colin staggered to the horse and lifted himself up and onto it so that his head and feet were hanging over its haunches. Grey pulled the horse away and headed for the bridge.

"Sit up! Sit up!" she called back to Colin. "Sit up and hold onto me, for we must ride fast." Colin moaned and grabbed her around the waist, leaning against her back.

Now Henry was wailing, frightened and wailing and pressed against the horse's back as Grey lay on him to keep him secure while she kicked the horse into a gallop.

"Take it north, north!" Colin called out.

Grey responded without question and the horse went on the road north, away from the bridge to Tarmath, past the place where her father and mother had tried to make a living and a home, past the place in the road where there had once been a felled tree blocking it. They rode until there was nothing but marshy fields and patches of sodden road.

When the half-moon had risen through a veil of clouds, Grey slowed the horse to a walk. She whispered to Henry, who was silent but awake, "Are you well?" She lifted her son and held him, weeping and shaking.

"My boy, my boy," she said over and over.

She could hear Colin moan a little, and she turned to him and said, "You are badly wounded."

He nodded. "I am badly wounded."

"I was going to go to Tarmath for the night."

Colin shook his head. "We cannot go into that town. The Bailiff lives there, and his eye is too sharp and official."

Grey said, "But I will go to the Monastery. We'll go to the child's father and get help there."

"There's a small bridge up ahead to the left. We'll have to get down and take turns, one of us walking the horse across," Colin said, and he put his arms around Grey so that she could feel the wet of his blood soaking through to her back. "Then we keep going east and circle around the other side of Tarmath to the Monastery. It will take us two days because we will need to stop and tend to my wounds."

"We will do it. Lie hard against my back to slow the bleeding," Grey said. "We will stop soon and feed ourselves and rest."

And Grey felt like one of the women in his stories, free now to feel that way with her son against her skin. Her father would be proud, and Fiona, too. There was some honoring of everyone she loved in her own courage.

 **49**

*t*HE MONASTERY was a disheveled and dark mass of stone and untended plants. In dim moonlight it looked like a beast holding itself
in a frightened ball. It was filled with darkness, but a thin and curling
stream of smoke came up from one of its chimneys. The horse jerked its
head forward and champed on grasses; Henry squirmed to get down; Colin
was fallen against Grey's back.

She lowered Henry down and said, "Move far away from the horse, lad.
Go on. Move away or you'll be trampled."

The boy toddled backward but stood staring at his mother astride the
black horse. Colin stirred a little. Grey slid forward slowly so that Colin was
let down gently, now lying on the horse's back, and then she slipped down
over the horse's head. The animal jerked his head up and stepped backward, and Grey held his mane.

"Here, now, stop thinking so much of yourself," she said to the horse,
patting it firmly. "Come here, lad. Come on, then, Henry." The boy heard
his name and went to her; she grabbed him up and then led the horse with
Colin on it up to the Monastery door.

Inside there was emptiness and darkness. The horse clomped in and
then stood still as Grey helped Colin off. As she lay him down on the floor,
she heard someone coming.

It was the Kitchener, holding up a flickering cresset and still holding his
wooden spoon as his weapon.

"Here now!" he yelled. "What is this beast doing in our hall? Out with it!
Out with you!" He swatted the air in front of the horse, and Grey watched
as affection filled her chest. Here was the Kitchener, alive, much thinner
than before, but alive. She said, "Kitchener, we are here to see the Abbot.
This is his son, and this man is sorely wounded."

"Who are you, who know I am the Kitchener?"

"I am an old friend who passed through before the plague."

The Kitchener held the cresset up to Grey's face.

"It's the deaf-mute boy!" he said, grinning at the ridiculousness of the world.

"Yes."

Taking a closer look he said, "But here, you are not deaf nor mute nor a boy. You are a woman!"

"Yes."

He crossed himself. "Jesus, Mary, and Joseph, did the plague do this to you, then?"

"No, Kitchener, my mother and father did it years ago, and I have since done a number of refinements. But here, this man is a friend, and he is dying of blood loss. Is the infirmary still above?"

"Sure there's an infirmary, but no Infirmarer and no infirm."

"Will you help me take him there and wrap the wound and give him water and whatever else may help him to heal?"

"Well, then, I suppose . . ."

"We'll leave the horse here and I will tether it outside when we're done."

"See that you also clean up what it leaves behind. I'll not have horseshit in my hall."

Grey squatted down and got Henry to climb on her back. Then she and the Kitchener carried Colin up to the infirmary. Grey carried his feet and the Kitchener his shoulders, saying over and over, "You're a female, then, for Christ's holy sake, and all that time . . . Mary and Joseph!" The cresset sat on Colin's stomach, lighting their way.

Grey remembered the stairs. She remembered the infirmary and its bedding and jars and pots of herb. She remembered the screams and moans and smells of the dying men, filling the room and begging for mercy. Now it was an empty room, everything taken out and burned.

"Lay him there and sit with him. I will be back." She put Henry down and kissed the top of his head.

Then Grey ran down the steps and into the chapel. She saw no one and heard no one. The crucifix was still on the altar, as though nothing in the world had happened. The sacristy door was wide open. Grey scooped into her arms a pile of robes and altar cloths and took them back to the infirmary. There she made a bed for Colin. During the night, she washed his wounds and bound them with strips of cloth.

Colin awoke near dawn and smiled at her face and said, "If I am to die, it's good to have your face to look at."

She looked down, studying his hand, which she held firmly in hers, afraid to look at his eyes.

"I think I remember this hand," she said.

Colin nodded, remembering, too, that the Abbot had called Grey a burden and a whore. And thinking of finally pummeling the piety out of that man gave him reason to fight against death.

He closed his eyes, and though he didn't wince, Grey did, guessing that he had spent his strength for the moment and was focusing now on pain. She had no talent that could save him from his wound, not as a boy or a mother, not as a whore, though she wanted to kiss his lips.

"It's this place," she whispered. "It's this place makes me think like that."

But she put her fingers on his lips, gently, wishing him to keep breathing.

Meanwhile, the Kitchener pulled the resisting stallion out into the yard and tethered him to a post with a bell on it that he had used to summon the monks to their meal. He rang the bell once, just to spook the horse a little.

Grey put on one of the robes from the sacristy and lay down beside her son and slept a few hours before dawn. When she woke up she took Henry outside and they squatted together to piss and watch the sun come up. The Kitchener was already at work making oatmeal for the morning. The chapel, the dormitory, and the library were empty of monks and purpose; the day's ecclesiastic schedule was ignored. Grey and Henry sat at the table eating the oat porridge as the Kitchener stood by and shook his head.

"I don't understand what the world has come to," he said crossly.

Someone was coming to join them, and the Kitchener got a third bowl and set it on the table. Brother Dunsten staggered in, rubbing his face. He looked at Grey and grinned. Henry snuggled closer to his mother and said, "Big teeth." She nodded and patted his arm.

"Is there anyone else here?" Grey asked the Kitchener.

"Only the Abbot," he said, not looking at her.

"Will he come for his porridge?"

"He keeps to the vows; he eats only the one meal and keeps the Offices."

"By himself?"

Dunsten chuckled.

"There's too much to do here, and there are only myself and Brother Dunsten."

Grey nodded.

"Will you see to the man I brought in?"

"He was here some years back, I recall, pilfering wine and drinking with the Old Abbot." This was a new thought to keep the Kitchener comfortably annoyed with the world.

"Please look after him. I am going to find the Abbot."

"Does the Abbot know you are a woman?"

"He knows it well," Grey answered and lifted her child.

The Abbot's cell door was open so that Grey could see the leather chair he'd moved from the library. She walked in, but he was not there. When she sat Henry in the chair, he promptly slipped out and went around the room trying to grab things. As she was taking a candle out of his hand, Grey heard the Abbot come in.

"What are you doing here?" he asked.

The words and tone made Grey's bones cool.

"I am here with your son, whom I have taken back. He is ours. He is mine to love and I have come here for your help."

The Abbot glanced at the boy and then closed the door.

"I am the Abbot here."

"What does that explain? Does that explain that you are not the boy's father?"

"I cannot be a father to this boy and Abbot of this Monastery."

"You say you cannot, but you are! Do you think your words will change what is?"

"I have chosen to keep my vows, to serve the Church."

"You have chosen to betray your flesh, your son, whom you loved and protected?"

"He was doing well to be a Lord's son. Why did you take him?"

"Because he is not a Lord's son. He is my son and your son. You cannot change what the body has done. And I cannot change what my heart knows, though yours is content with lies."

"Where have you learned to use your mouth this way?"

"As a boy I was raised to believe in my strength; as a deaf-mute I listened well to how others made their way around suffering. As a whore I learned about falsehoods and lust; as a mother I have let all the words collected in my head come out to protect my son. He is your son as well. Will you give us protection?"

"The world has more dangers than you or I can protect against, little mother. And you cannot stay here. A woman cannot stay in a Monastery."

"Ahh, so you say, and yet in truth, a woman did stay in a Monastery, didn't she, so it seems to me that she can!"

"I am Abbot here, and I say that you cannot stay. Leave the boy and I'll raise him to be literate and devoted to the Church. I'll tell him that he is an orphan."

Grey touched the top of Henry's head and shook her own, incredulous, stupefied.

"You would raise your son in a lie? He is no orphan. What has happened to you?"

"The world needs order. Lies are necessary to preserve order from time to time. You could not possibly understand."

The Abbot stepped forward, his enraged eyes close to hers.

"Get out of my Monastery. Get out. And take the boy."

"I will tell him about when you carried him in your arms, about when he slept as an infant on your chest. I will tell him that his father chose an image of himself and secret ways of getting pleasure, chose an idea and words and fantasies over his own flesh and blood."

"I have faith. There is nothing but chaos and fear without faith."

"Look at you! It's not faith that you have, man; it's fear. And it seems to me that true faith has no fear."

"I am telling you to get out."

"And where will I go? Where will I go with a child and dying man?"

"The man in the infirmary?"

"Yes."

"He can stay here. We will look after him. He was once a . . . he has been a monk here."

"Will you sell him to the soldiers who will be hunting him?"

"No. I need as many men as I can get here. And if he lives he might be humbled, finally ready for devotion and obedience."

"Why should I trust you, you who are a betrayer and a coward, a man of fear who sold his own son in order to escape a world he could not control?"

"These are harsh words for a woman to speak to a man she opened her legs to."

"I opened more than that, and well you know it, though you seem to have locked yourself shut again. You hate your own desires and yet you seek to satisfy them. This is a terrible weakness. You would do well to leave this game and come with me as my husband and as the father of your child."

"I have made vows here, long before you entrapped me with your body's mischief. I need God, as do all mortals. You'd do well to remember that."

"I have faith in something that I cannot name, that has no name, that words ruin. I see you and others full of fear. It's fear drives your faith."

"You are ignorant, an ignorant peasant."

Henry grabbed onto his father's legs and looked up at him. The Abbot stared down at him and then looked away, covering his eyes with his hand.

Weeping softly, he said, "Take him away."

Grey picked up the child, and as he grabbed her nose she said, "I am sorry that you are so thoroughly a coward. But I take back what I said. I'll not ruin the child's need for a good father. I'll not soil your image in his mind, but I'll not lie either. I'm done with lying."

She left, her heart pounding and her limbs filled with trembling. She left Henry with the Kitchener and went to Colin, who was feverish and muttering. He grabbed her hand and said, "I am near to death."

"I have to leave," she said. "I fear for my boy here. I don't want him brought up in shame."

"Then I will die alone."

Grey knelt down, folded in on herself, and wept into her palms.

"You must not be weak," she said. "Please do this one thing for me and be one person who is strong. Please do not die."

"Death is stronger than anything," Colin said. "It finishes everyone."

Grey slid onto his chest and felt the frightening heat of his body. His hand, fingers splayed, rested on her head, and she sobbed.

"All right, then," he said. "Go on. I'll survive this to beat the piss out of your Abbot."

The Kitchener had a bundle prepared for her that included cheese, bread, barley, apples, and a small knife. She didn't know if he had given her this help on his own or if the Abbot had told him to; she didn't want to ask.

She got on the horse with Henry in front of her. The Kitchener put a honeycomb in his hands, and the boy delighted in making a dripping sticky mess on himself. It amused him to dribble the honey on the horse's coat and smear it around. Grey rested her lips on the top of Henry's head, the smell of it mixed with the smell of horse and honey.

50

FOR A WHILE Grey took the horse eastward, and then she remembered that the man who brought the plague to the Monastery had come from the east, from near Dublin. And so she sat by a river, alone with Henry, and tried to reason out the path she should take. Many times she thought about returning to the Monastery to try again with the Abbot. If she thought too much about her desire for his protection and solace, she would fall into a misery that she did not want to impose on the child, who was concentrating on digging little trenches in the dirt with a stick. She joined him, and side by side they busied themselves with serious intent, Grey occasionally pointing out a bug. When a fox came to drink at the bank across the river, she and the boy stopped and watched, Grey motioning him to be quiet so as not to startle the beautiful animal. Then she decided that the most reasonable plan was to ride west, beyond the pale, to the lands where it was said that there were still chieftains in power and where it was said that the plague had not cut its putrid swath. But those were lands and places not of her people, not of her past: strangers.

She and Henry got back atop the fine horse, too fine a horse for any peasant, but in those times, many a peasant sported a Lord's dress or ate with a Lord's silver. Grey amused herself and the boy by making up a story about the fox—its adventures and friends.

They spent the first night just south of Finnistuath, close enough to see the square tower of the Manor house above the trees in the distance. There was only a little food left at the end of the second day when she saw a village of about twenty houses. Smoke came from three of them. She walked the horse slowly through the town, and one man with curly black hair and eyebrows that met over his large nose came out and asked, "What is your business here?"

He was not friendly, and so Grey said, "We are passing through. I am a widow with my son."

He looked her over. "And why do you wear a monk's robe?"

"I have just had help from an order that gave me charity."

"You'll not get charity here. We are full of sorrow and burdens here."

"Do you have food to give us? We are in sore need of your kindness."

"There is nothing in our cups here to give away."

The man stepped aside to watch Grey and the boy pass through. He even followed and watched from the edge of the village until the road went downward and took them out of sight.

Toward evening, Henry fussed, using simple English words, such as "no" and "want." If he were in the Lord's Manor, Grey thought, he would have a full belly and good prospects. She soothed him in his true language until they came to a wide stream where the road stopped and the water was shallow enough to cross through. On the other side was a man cleaning some game that he had trapped. Grey got down and walked the horse across, with Henry clutching onto the mane.

"We are hungry and have no food," Grey said to the man, who was hardly out of boyhood. He stood up, holding a half-skinned rabbit by the back legs.

"Then start up a fire and we'll share this."

After an instant of disbelief and gratitude, Grey started to gather wood, and Henry helped, throwing small sticks onto the pile.

"Who are you?" the young man asked, tossing hair out of his face as he sucked on a bone across the fire from Grey and Henry.

"I am Henry's mother," she said, " and a widow."

He nodded and then asked, "Where are you going?"

"I'm looking for a friendly village, a place to do some work and find some lodging."

"What kind of work?"

"I can tend goats and do all manner of service for a household." She added casually, though not looking at the man, "And I can fight."

The young man thought for a moment and said, "There's a village to the south, over those mountains. There's a good pass there, though it's not well worn and there used to be a scourge of thieves regularly harassing people. But I've been through last year and saw no signs of them. You go up there about half a day's ride to the pass marked by a cairn and then another half day through and down into the village. I can't say as there's any work or lodging. But it's the nearest hope you have."

Grey followed his gestures to the dark shapes to the south that she had seen as blue-and-green mountains that day. She nodded.

After some time of looking into the fire the man said, "I must be going home, taking the rest of the meat to my family. You can come with me if you'll share my bed."

Grey answered, "I thank you for your kindness, but I'll stay here the night with my son."

The young man shrugged and wrapped the meat in a cloth to put in his satchel. But before he left, he gave the meat to Grey, saying, "I can tell them I had no luck." Then he said, "Farewell," and took long steps into the night. Watching him walk away, she thought how subtle a saint's disguise could be.

The next day, Grey and Henry walked the horse into a village called Rosconen. It sat on the other side of the mountains on the edge of a hill, beneath a single round tower belonging to the Chieftain of those parts. The Chieftain's house was a stone structure like many of the houses in the village, the tower being his fortress and claim to leadership. There were many sheep in the town, for the people traded in wool and mutton. Grey could smell meat cooking and saw small gardens, well tended. It seemed that this village was from another land and time, making the horrors of the plague seem now like a story. A woman dumping out a pail of water stood up and greeted Grey with a two-tooth smile.

"It's a nice still afternoon, eh?" she said, looking up at the sky.

"So it is."

"I can smell the rain coming though, there from the west."

"Could I bother you for some help? My son and I are alone in the world and trying to find our way."

The woman studied them.

"That's a good horse," she said. "Are you come from a rich man's house?"

"We come from the east. I am widowed."

"And what of your people? Why are you not with them?"

"There has been a disease come and kill my whole family."

The woman shook her head in sympathy.

"We've heard of it, but no one comes here much from the east. You should stay here for comfort, poor thing, you and your son. What is he called?"

"He is called Henry."

"I've never heard such a name as that. And what is your name?"

"Grey. I am Grey of Finnistuath. Where can I stay?"

"You'd best get permission from the Chieftain. He lives up there in that stone house. Go on up and tell him that Old Mary will let you sleep at her hearth."

"I thank you with all my heart," Grey said, and she led the horse up to the Chieftain's stone house.

There were sheep standing all around it and lying about on the ground inside the tower. A young man was leaning out of one of the narrow windows at the top of the tower as Grey left the horse outside and stepped on the threshold of the Chieftain's house.

It was warm inside, the fire in the hearth full of yellow flames. In front of the hearth was a portly man stretched out on a bench, his hands under his head. Two women were at a table, culling through oats in a big wooden bowl. One was the daughter and the other the wife, an older version of the first, with thick black hair and a long straight nose. They wore fine woolen bonnets and cowls without capes, caught at the neck with silver brooches. When Grey stepped inside, they looked up and nodded. The Chieftain glanced at Grey holding her child and then stared up at the ceiling and spoke.

"Come in then and tell your story."

"Thank you, sir."

Grey walked in and sat on a stool. She put Henry down and began to stare at a black dog that was near him and whose tail thumped happily when the child roughly patted his haunches.

"I am Grey of Finnistuath, a goatherd's daughter and now a widow, with my child, Henry."

"Finnistuath? To the west or east?"

"To the east."

"And who is Chieftain there?"

"There is no Chieftain. There is an English Lord."

This caused the Chieftain to rotate his body and sit up in one firm movement.

"And what business do you have here?"

"There has been a plague, sir."

"So I have heard. A severe punishment come from across the sea."

"Aye. Severe it is."

"And you and your boy have found Rosconen." He scratched his head and laughed.

"I need to rest awhile, my boy and I."

"Can you card wool?"

"Sure I can learn what I need to learn, and Old Mary said that I could sleep at her hearth."

"Did she, now?" This amused the Chieftain and his wife and daughter, as they all exchanged glances. "Well, it's Old Mary who is the real chieftain here." The women laughed. "So, I have naught else to say but welcome to you." He lay back down on the bench and picked at his nose, wiping what he had extracted on the underside of the bench.

Grey stood up, and the man did have more to say, for he had heard the sound of snorting and hoof tramping just outside. "I'll ask for the horse as a tax, for it sounds like a fine animal, such as a Chieftain should have, and it'll give me something to distinguish my authority from that of Old Mary." The women laughed again. "You'll have him back if you leave," the Chieftain said and winked at her.

"All right, then," Grey said, and she stepped outside. The man in the tower still looked down on her, but now he waved, and Grey waved back.

"Oh, Henry, we'll be all right, then," she whispered into his hair. "And your mother loves you so."

Henry pointed back into the house and said, in Gaelic, "Dog? Dog?"

 51

*T*HE ABBOT stood with a cresset over Colin, who was swimming in a fitful sleep, his head moving from side to side slowly. The Abbot wondered if Grey had had sex with the man, and he wanted then to fall on him and strangle him. Instead he prayed that Colin would die, and then he despised himself for making such a prayer and resolved to beat himself later with a stick he kept for that purpose in his room. The Abbot understood how evil he was, but everyone was evil, though most were too ignorant to fathom their sins.

Colin's head stopped moving and his eyes opened to see the human form of darkness standing over him behind a flickering flame.

He shielded his eyes and asked, "Who is it?"

"I am the Abbot of this place."

"Ahh, yes, the Abbot. I thank you for letting me stay here. I'll soon be well enough to leave."

"Why not stay and become a monk? Perhaps a second effort . . . We need new blood."

"I have little of it left to give," Colin said, perching himself on his elbows. "And I have done with clerical ambition."

"Can you read scriptures?"

Colin laughed, letting his head fall back. "That I can, and that I have. I have indeed read scriptures."

They shared a silence as the Abbot nodded his head and suddenly felt an odd and painfully clear notion passing through him like freezing water.

"And if you have read scriptures, why do you wear pagan symbols?"

Colin sat up further, feeling strength in his head spreading down into the rest of his body.

"Because I don't want to be counted among men who would put a child into a woman and then call her a whore."

The Abbot said, "You sack of shit," as he pulled him up by the shirt with one hand so that Colin's back arched until he got his feet under him and stood up. "I saved your thieving arse," the Abbot hissed.

The cresset flame flickered more, and Colin understood that the Abbot's hand was shaking.

Colin said, "I am grateful that you have given me a place to recover. You have shown me kindness when you could have thrown me out on the meadow to rot or made some coin with the Lord of Finnistuath. That kindness has more weight than any scripture I have read."

"What have you read?" the Abbot asked.

"The same as you—of suffering and of the human pity of it."

The Abbot pulled Colin closer to him roughly and held up the cresset as though to burn Colin's ear.

"Where is it? What have you done with it?"

"I don't know what you mean. What have I done with what?"

"With the box?"

"I have many boxes."

The Abbot spit into Colin's face with his words. "What have you done with the box?"

"Is that all you are concerned with, a box with words in it? You have abandoned your son and the finest woman in all Ireland and you want to know about the safety of a godforsaken box of words?"

Colin pushed forward, thinking that the Abbot had a clear physical advantage over him, but he smelled cowardice and shame and walked him backward. He took the cresset out of the Abbot's hand and put the flame against the knuckles of his other hand, which immediately let go Colin's tunic. Colin put the cresset down and said to the Abbot, "I wouldn't mind dying after getting in a few blows on your arrogant, fat head."

"Get out of my Monastery," the Abbot said, sweating.

"I'll tell you where the box is, Abbot. But before I do, you'd better understand that there are other boxes, hundreds of other boxes, with thousands of other words, all over the known world and into the Otherworld. You and the Pope and all the priests in Christendom can't secure all the boxes there are that tell the stories that you don't want told."

"The Church is our only comfort. You are too ignorant, too bull-headed to understand. The Church is all we have to comfort us." The Abbot lunged at Colin, grabbing him by the throat and pushing him back. "You stinking dog," the Abbot said. "You would take a blanket from your mother's dying body in the name of truth."

Colin had never told the Abbot about watching his parents starve, burying a mother lighter than her own boy's body because she gave all there was to eat to him. The accusation of a dying mother's being deprived of solace by him created such a battle frenzy in Colin that he burst out of his pain and weakness with a strength neither man expected. He pulled the Abbot's hands from his neck and pushed him backward, then followed with a fist into the stomach. The Abbot folded over, and Colin shoved him onto the floor and kicked him in the back of the neck. The Abbot rolled over and grabbed Colin's ankles, pulling him down. They wrestled on the floor, each trying to pin the other down, until the Abbot's back rolled over the cresset and put it out. In the surprise of sudden darkness, Colin had a chance to get loose from the Abbot's grip and stand away from him, for he was quickly coming to the end of his ability to fight.

They could only hear each other's panting, until the distant bell rang for Matins, like a mother's voice telling her sons to stop their nonsense.

"I will pray for your rotting soul," the Abbot said.

"You do that." Colin bent over in pain, but tried to make his voice sound strong.

"You will endure the torments of Hell for an eternity."

"I think we've made a good hell of this world, Abbot."

"I must go to Matins," the Abbot said, standing up and feeling for the wall.

And Colin said, "Go to your rituals, Abbot. I will be gone before the second psalm is done."

5 2

SOON ENOUGH, the town of Rosconen had discovered that Grey was not a good carder of wool. She pulled it too thin or ended with many of the short fibers sticking out, giving the wool an undesirable fuzzy appearance. Old Mary let her stay at her hearth, though, and Grey took part in the village routines. There was a small chapel near Mary's house, where a priest who was also a herdsman gave Masses and officiated over funerals and christenings. Grey went to the chapel and listened to the Priest's Masses; she pushed Henry forward to sit and kneel and say the words he was supposed to say. But she crossed her arms over her chest and stared at the turned-down face of Jesus on the crucifix. She believed that Christ was too ashamed to look her full in the face after all she knew of his Father's house and the goings-on there.

As soon as she had a dress to wear, Grey was courted by two men in particular, one the Cheesemaker, who had been widowed for three years, and the other the man who had looked down upon her from the Chieftain's tower. He and the Chieftain liked to play chess, called fidchell there, a game of wooden pieces that were led by a king. Henry watched them play the game and began to learn the rules for the movement of the pieces by the time he was four years old. He played at hurling with the Chieftain's four grandchildren, especially liking the naughty one, Seamus. They came from the other side of the hill, where two of the Chieftain's sons had settled with their herds of sheep.

By that time, Grey no longer even tried to be a wool carder but had shown her ability at the skills of weaponry. In a few idle games of tossing daggers, she had shown the Watchman that she exceeded his skills, and then the Chieftain gave her his duties. And so Grey became a chieftain's guard, which in that village meant that she tended to the sheep that lay about on the ground floor of the tower and kept the stock of arrows and spears in the tower sharp. She practiced with them often, throwing them from the high window of the tower at piles of discarded wool she had set up as targets, which Henry called woolly soldiers. And she rode the horse and taught Henry how to tend to the animal. The previous Watchman continued to climb the narrow stone steps of the tower, saying that he didn't trust a woman, even one with her skills, to come through during a real danger. In fact, he wanted Grey to be his wife. But Grey couldn't see herself as anyone's wife. She had borne the Abbot's child and fixed cabbage and bread for him from time to time, and that seemed enough of being a wife. And Rosconen needed no whores, since, as in most villages, their services were supplied by adulterous wives.

People came and went in Rosconen, mainly from the west, having some trading to do. They brought oats, barley, candles, and such in exchange for the wool and mutton Rosconen was well know for. There had been a lull for two generations of Rosconen chieftains in the rivalry with other villages to the north, south, and west. No one came from inside the pale, from the east where the English rule was thorough, and no one traveled there. When rumors of plague had spread, there had been even more isolation. Grey had nightmares of someone coming over the pass, coming and taking her son. In waking hours, the nightmares were fears that fluttered for a moment in her stomach, of Red or his soldiers finding her and Henry, having years of frustration to fuel their rage and unyielding determination to take her boy away or worse. And one day, Grey and the Watchman saw a stranger come from the mountain pass to the east. She grabbed a bow and placed an arrow on it. Standing to the side of the window, she aimed at the man, moving the bow slowly to follow the man's progress. The Watchman crouched down and peeked over the edge of the window.

"Get back," Grey said. "If he hurls a stone at the window, your forehead will stop it."

The Watchman moved aside and picked up a spear. But just then Grey lowered the bow and leaned full out of the window.

"Hey! You there!" she yelled out, and then she laughed loudly. "You there! Hey, Colin the Cattle Stealer!"

The man stopped and looked toward the tower. He put his hand up to his forehead to block the sun and walked slowly forward.

"Hey there! It's Grey!" She leaned out dangerously and waved her arm. "Grey!" she repeated. "Henry's mother!"

He stopped and stared up.

Grey ran down the steps, passing Henry, who was playing fidchell with the Chieftain. She ran past them to hear her son say, "My mother can run fast."

And soon she was at Colin's side, her arm through his, walking him into town. He had a limp now, a hesitation to bring his right leg forward for the increase in pain the movement caused the years-old wound in his side.

"Why, you look fine," Grey said. "Many a night I lay wondering how you were, and if you'd lived or been caught by Red."

"What are you doing in this place, aiming arrows from a Chieftain's tower?" Colin smiled hard, making the permanent rays around his eyes deepen. "This place seems like an enchantment outside the world. Have fairies brought me here?" He didn't tell her how many travelers to Naas he had asked before he got rumor of where she lived, the widow with a boy, a woman who had an aim better than any man and rode a fine black horse. It was the horse that was identified most surely.

"I am raising my boy in peace and well I like it. And I've come to know what work I'm fit for. And are you still a wanderer?"

"From time to time still," he answered. "I spent these years in Naas mostly. But I'm not needed there now."

Colin put down his pack of goods on Mary's hearth. It was a lighter load than years before, and when it slid from him and Colin straightened slowly, Grey could see the burden of his pain. He sat down to a mutton stew with Grey across from him, her hands against her lips staring at him. When Henry came in and saw him he said to his mother, "Is this my father?"

"No, son," she said. And then she asked Colin, "What news do you have of the Abbot?"

"He is thriving," Colin answered. "He has gathered fourteen monks now in these past five years, and there's still the old Kitchener and Brother Dunsten. He has been to Avignon. That is the news I heard a little over a year ago."

The image of the Abbot glad to have his Monastery and his charge of monks stuck into Grey's chest like a needle. She could not think long about it.

"And Tarmath? The Midwife, do you see her?"

"I stay well away from that town, for the Bailiff still lives there, and there are others who know me and know that I am enemy to the Lord. But I have heard that he has left the Manor and gone back to England with his wife. I have only heard this and cannot say it is true."

Henry ate the stew and asked his mother, "Will you play hurling with me?," for it was something they did together often. But Grey said, "Oh, Henry, I am just seeing my old friend and want to talk more with him."

Henry pushed his bowl of stew away. He went out.

"Where are you going then, young man?" Grey said at the door.

"To the Chieftain's," he answered.

"And it's home before dark or a stick on your legs."

He waved without turning around, both of them knowing that he would be back and that there never had been and never would be a stick on his legs wielded by his mother.

"You and the boy are a pair."

Grey stood up to poke at the fire with an old, broken-tipped sword. "He is seven now and thinks he's a man. And the days go more swiftly, like a runaway horse with me bouncing around on it."

Colin sat up straight, combing through his hair, which he let loose in thick gray waves from the strap that tied it back. His forearms were thick with the memory of various loads, the packs and weapons and children he had lifted. He looked at Grey and laughed, and then he grabbed her and pulled her to him so that she fell onto his lap. He was smiling with such joyful mischief that she had to laugh. She looked into his eyes; so close was his face that there was nothing else to look at. His eyes glistened summer green; there was a little weariness there and sadness, but no bitterness.

He kissed her then, bending her back and holding her head with one hand. It was a full celebration of touch with no desperation or fear of sin.

"What is this, then?" Grey asked, still bent back with Colin's face close.

"I have wondered for many, many years where you were and how I might be a husband."

"And whose husband were you thinking of being?"

Colin kissed her temple and then whispered into her hair, "Be my wife. Only a woman as strange as you can share my life."

Grey laughed and bent her head toward her shoulder against the tickle of his words. "Strange is it? Strange compared to what?"

"I'm good at building things and repairing what's broken and might be thrown out."

"If it's work you're asking after, you should speak with the Chieftain."

Grey stood up but let him take her hand in both of his, which were large and more freckled than she recalled.

In a softer voice she told him, "I have my own life, and I feel that I am blessed. My child and I have lived through the plague. We are well here. He plays fidchell like a chieftain's son and knows horses. I want nothing to interfere with our blessings."

"What if he were to have a father? Would that not add to his blessings?"

Grey slid her hand away.

"I'll tell you straight, man, that whoever is my husband must know that it is Henry whose welfare is my first concern. If you are looking for a woman who will put her own child away to have a husband, you must look elsewhere. For I know such women exist, and I call them evil."

"Such a speech, woman. Such a speech."

Colin stood up and took her wrists and pulled her to him.

"Let me be the boy's father and your husband."

"Go up to him then, and court him first. For if you win him, you can have me as your reward."

Old Mary came in and saw them there and said, "Ahh, the Cheese-maker's heart is broke now, and we'll have no cheese for a week." For the Watchmaker had found himself a woman to marry, leaving the Cheese-maker the hope that biding his time without rival would unhinge Grey's resistance.

Colin began his courtship of Henry, and it was hard on him. He played at hurling with the boy, and Henry taught him the rules of fidchell. But the boy did not soften and asked his mother one day, "If you were to have Colin as your husband, and we were both of us dying of the plague, who would you tend to?"

"I would tend to you, Henry, for you are my son."

And this was true and firm in her mind, though she liked more and more to feel Colin's hand slide across her waist as he passed her. He traded all his goods, knives and bowls and pots, for four of the Chieftain's sheep and so transformed from a traveler into a herder. He built a house for himself, and Henry came to help him one day and then the next. It was the first house that Colin had made that could not be blown down in a strong wind. When Colin winced, Henry asked him about the wound and was told about the night Grey saved his and Henry's life.

"I tried to be the same afterwards," Colin explained. "But I soon learned that I couldn't travel with a heavy load on my back any longer, and I couldn't stop thinking that of all the women in Ireland, your mother was the most . . ."

"Beautiful?"

"Well, yes. But I was thinking more of, well . . . she was the most worthy of a man like myself." He lifted his chest and chin dramatically.

"You could be right of that," Henry said, shaking his head.

Grey helped Mary make some good bread and brought it by to Colin as he and Henry worked on the house, mixing buckets of mud and getting it in their hair and all over their clothes. One day while Henry was helping the Chieftain's grandson with the sheep in one of the northern meadows, Grey put Colin's hand on her breast. He laughed at her and moved both his hands to hold her face.

"Sit you down here with me," he said, and they sat down on a fallen tree he and Henry and the Watchman had dragged from the woods to make some lumber from. He held her there, her head on his shoulder, and he said, "I will tell you, before I take you as wife, that I have lost faith in the God of churches altogether and think naught of the rituals and words that go around that faith. But I will keep to the habits of priests, the churchgoing and such, because I understand that the people need those habits. And what bother is it to doze on the church bench instead of the bench at home."

"I have no devotion to priests," Grey said. "You needn't make this speech to me."

"But if a man is to make a place for himself in this land he must acknowledge the comfort the Church gives and be glad of the old wisdom that can't be drowned in baptismal fonts."

Grey shrugged.

"Will you teach Henry to read? I don't see the use of it for myself, but I want him to know everything."

Colin turned his head and kissed her lips. She moved to straddle him, to sit across his lap with her legs on either side of him.

"I am a free man in some part of me, always," Colin told her, holding her waist hard.

"I think you should be free in all parts," she said.

Colin laughed. "You have ways that might frighten a man, like a wolf that will not run away when you raise a stick. But it isn't hunger that makes you bold."

"I'll not pretend to be weak," she warned. "Or pretend that weakness is good in a husband, for I see how some women treat their husbands as though they were one of the children, and I'll not do that."

Colin nodded, then lifted her up in a sudden movement so that he was standing and holding her slung over his shoulder. He waited an instant, but the pain was sleepy and so he kept her there.

Grey laughed and wriggled but then let him carry her into the woods. They looked at each other as they stood apart and took off their clothing, Grey hurrying to be rid of whatever cloth lay between their bodies. Then Colin sat up against a tree and Grey straddled him, fixing herself to his lap with his erection inside her. Almost immediately she felt her body soften into mist as his became harder and stronger.

"I'd be glad of it if you were to keep your skin's affections for me," Colin told her.

"Would you, then? And what will you keep for me?"

Colin grabbed her buttocks.

They entwined themselves, using tongues and fingers and eyes and thrusts in passionate affection, each one thinking what a miracle it was to be with the other. Colin coaxed an orgasm from her with his fingers before he plunged deep into her to let loose his own unencumbered lust. And when he held her firm against him, he could feel her slip into sleep, and he wanted to let her rest always there on his skin, where he could make sure that no one disturbed her.

When they put their clothes on again, Colin kept staring at her. She asked him what he was thinking, and he said, "We have to keep secrets, my girl, from each other when the details of our thoughts or past lives would do naught but cause pain."

Grey thought of Bartholomew and the secret they shared.

"I agree with that."

"And we have to keep secrets from others as well, our shared secrets."

"What secrets are they?"

"That though we say certain words, and though the world says how a man and his wife should behave and what kind of household they have, we make our own way."

"I see that you may not be desperate for a woman but you are desperate for freedom."

"Yes, that could be said. But I want as much for others. I want the same thing for you, and I think, from the way you threw that spear and rode that horse with me and the boy, you'll not be trapped into breadmaking and concubining for any man."

"I agree with that as well," Grey said. "And agree that should you need to treat me as a wife when there are others present, that we know that that is not all I am."

"All right, then. We have made a bargain, and so will keep it until it causes suffering, and then we'll make another one."

An insect rattled loudly, and it seemed to be a signal that a ritual was completed and a covenant sealed.

Grey and Henry and Colin made a household together, and the Priest sanctified the arrangement with a wedding that the whole village attended, though there was some grumbling about these new members of their clan not being rooted to the place. The villagers didn't like mystery and so had concluded that they knew the family in Finnistuath that Grey came from: someone had once had a cousin there. And Colin, he was no doubt of the MacRaignaills, to the west. He played a drum with the Wheelwright, who played a flute, and people danced with partners or looking at their own feet. There were oatcakes and lamb and cabbage with butter on it, and the Chieftain got too drunk to walk home. The Cheesemaker kissed the bride and ended up fucking the Chieftain's daughter in a cart out behind Mary's house with a dog sniffing at them. The Watchman, with his ever pregnant wife sitting on his lap, was the loudest in compelling Colin to recite poetry, which then began a riot of poetry reciting and composing and blessings given and cups raised.

When it was still night but almost dawn, the party finished. Old Mary put a bowl of ewe's milk out for the fairies and told Henry to go on home where his mother and father were.

"I don't want to go home," he said.

"Don't you like your new father, then?"

"I like him well enough," Henry answered. "But he's not my real father. My real father doesn't care for me."

He never spoke of this to his mother, for he didn't want to see his pain in her face. But he had kept all these years in his pocket a piece of a monk's robe his mother had used as a rag. He knew that it came from where his father lived.

Still, it was hard for him not to like Colin, and one day, when he was nine years old, his fondness for him was fixed when his mother found an empty apple crate in the wood-lined hole that served as pantry beside the hearth. She yelled out for her son. He was playing fidchell with the Chieftain and heard his mother's call. He climbed up to the tower, where a pile of old and often-repaired arrows lay and the Watchman slept soundly. He hid there until Colin found him asleep and lifted him up. He awoke, and his stepfather said into his ear, "It's best that we hunt rabbit for a day or two, don't you think?"

Henry nodded. He said, "I fed them to the horse. He's more loyal when he has an apple to eat."

"I understand," Colin said. The boy was generous, that was certain, and mostly with animals, whose cause he took up often. They seemed to him to be helpless in this world and apt to lead a sorry life determined by human whim. He didn't even like an old cur to be called ugly.

Grey fumed alone in the house for those days, telling Old Mary when they met by the well that her son was becoming unruly and disturbed her thoughts at night when she should be sleeping. She worried that he had no discipline and that he didn't put himself to hard work enough and gave away what little he got for his labors.

Old Mary listened. She also listened when the Watchman's wife, pregnant with their third child, used the pretense of concern to mention that Grey was an odd mother and an even odder wife. "Well, as I see it, she lets the poor man fix his own gravy while she dotes over the boy. Treats the boy like a Lord, she does. It'll make him as wild as she is, such treatment, and her poor husband having to take the leftovers. She's too lazy to discipline the boy as she should. Well, I don't mean any harm by it."

It was easy enough for Grey to compare herself to the other wives and mothers and feel odd, to see how they put forth one child after another and spent their days covered in flour from the breadmaking or dirt from the gardening. And they scolded and made their sons and daughters say prayers to various saints. Grey fretted about the way she was raising Henry, for she had rules for him, and she let him know when he was taking too many liberties, but she was his friend as well. And she wondered if she was depriving him of a good mother when she shared a joke with him, or raced him to the tower. She liked to listen by the well to the complaints of women, having to do with mealworms, herbal remedies, and giving birth, nursing one child while taking a knife out of reach of the other. But she also liked to walk with Henry to the woods and play the game of story telling. He would give her a subject—a fairy and a ram, for example. He would try to think up the most unlikely pair of items he could, and she would make a story, ending with the fairy using the ram as a steed and riding him up into the sky to graze on clouds, or a stick and an oatcake becoming partners in a clever robbery. There were places in the woods that they gave their own names to: a thick tree fallen across a stream that had owl droppings on it one day was always called "Owl Shit Bridge"; and though there were many waterfalls, Henry and Grey knew exactly what the other meant when he or she said, "Let's go to the waterfall." That's where they stood next to the roar of water and yelled out things as loud as they could.

If other mothers did the same, they didn't talk about it at the well.

But the Watchman's wife always asked after Colin, saying, "He's got strong shoulders, like a hero's," and invariably adding, "I'd look after him well if he were my husband, I would." And Grey invariably said, "He's a grown man. I'd say he's to look after himself." Then there was little else to do but for the women to wander home thinking their own thoughts that they might tell to their husbands in the darkness, about how odd Grey was. And it was good they couldn't see the look on their husbands' faces when they brought Grey to mind, especially the Watchman's face, for Grey had the kind of oddness that made them wonder, the way a man might wonder if he could tame a particular horse he had seen running wild in a meadow a few miles west.

On the hunting trip, Colin caught Henry trying to steal a knife from his satchel. Colin spoke that night to him by the small fire they made.

"It's a heartbreaking thing to betray a friend," he said. "For I know that I am your friend and not your father, but I would be a good friend."

Henry nodded and wept. But he kept the knife because he felt that it evened things out. Colin had his mother as a wife, and he had lost some of her attention. Colin let him keep the knife, understanding the trade, and understanding that he would probably give the knife to his friend Seamus.

"My real father worships the Devil," Henry said as the two walked back to Rosconen the next afternoon, carrying two fat rabbits over their shoulders on sticks.

It was a statement that stunned Colin. "Is that what your mother has told you?"

"No, but it's what I feel."

And Colin took the boy's head and held it firmly against his chest. Then he let go and looked at the boy and saw some of the Abbot in him, strong legs and thick eyebrows. It did not make him like the boy less, but made him like the Abbot more.

"My mother tells me that time is running faster with her life and that what seems to have happened yesterday happened years ago."

Colin nodded and said, "That is how it is to be as old as we are." He made a circular motion in the air with his finger going around and around faster and faster.

"To me yesterday seems a long time ago and I am always restless for tomorrow," the boy said.

53

ENRY, THE downiest shadow of hair above his upper lip, poked one of the arrows into the wooden planks that made up the floor of the tower. His mother stared at him, getting more and more irritated with his careless disregard of the weapons she carefully tended, feeling that time and her son were moving much too fast for her to control.

"Stop your fidgeting, son. That's an important thing there, not some toy to idle with."

"There's no enemy ever comes here anyway."

"Not yet."

"There will never be anything to do in this tower."

"Most of a watchman's job is watching."

Henry threw the arrow against the wall, near where his mother was leaning.

"Here, now! You're driving me mad with your disrespect."

"I want to DO something," Henry said.

"Then clean the arrows. You can oil the tips so they don't rust."

Henry made no move toward the arrows or the box of oily rags.

"You're lazy!" Grey said, shaking her head.

"Well, you're just sitting there."

They fumed at each other. Grey kept shaking her head, and finally she said, "Why don't you go on, then, and play fidchell with the Chieftain?"

"He's with his son," Henry said. "They're getting ready for shearing."

"Will you be shearing again this year?"

"Sure," Henry said. "And I like it well enough. But . . ." He looked up at his mother, who seemed almost old to him, with one tooth missing on the left side, just behind her smile.

"I want to go on to something else. I don't want to be a shearer all my life."

"You have to do what's needed," Grey answered. "What do you think needs doing that you could do?"

"I think what needs doing is having adventures." Henry had been idling around Old Mary's when the ale was in, taking a few drinks offered him and listening to the stories told by the Priest and the musicians who came through. "I want to travel and have adventures, to go somewhere and come back to tell stories that no one has ever heard."

"And who'll take care of me when I'm old and withered?"

"I'll come back from time to time and see that you've got a crust to gnaw on."

"You're a fine son," Grey said, tapping his leg with her naked and dirty toes, "and you know I love you well and hard, don't you, boy? Now, don't go looking away. How can you be a strong man and you can't even look at your mother when she says she loves you?"

"I want to see strange and new things. I want to be a warrior."

"What will you be fighting against as a warrior?"

"The English and whoever else tries to do harm," Henry said, as though it was an annoying thing to have to explain something so obvious.

"Sometimes harm is not done by an enemy but by things in the world that come like a wind from nowhere, an invisible wind carrying all manner of suffering. You can't fight the wind with a blade, Henry."

"Well, I will fight what can be fought with a blade, and when I'm waiting, I won't sit up in a tower with a box of rags. I'll make new friends and hear stories and drink ale and play games."

Grey nodded, for she couldn't argue against such a plan except with bitter logic, which seemed an insult to a boy's ideals.

"Think on what you'll need to take with you. Colin could give you some lessons on that."

Henry nodded.

"Colin's taught you well enough to read and put down marks. You could be a Bailiff and carry a ledger!"

Henry pulled his head back and narrowed his eyes in disgust of such an idea.

"Why does Colin write down about who people's grandfathers were and how many sheep they have?" he asked, trying to sound more disdainful than curious.

"People like to have things written down about themselves."

He stood up, shaking his head, already thinking about a more interesting place to be than with his mother.

Grey's eyes filled with tears. "If you go on, then, son, I'll miss you," she said. "But I want you to go where you need to go and bring back good stories to tell me. But don't tell me everything. I am your mother, after all."

"You've had adventures," Henry said.

In the shadows of the old tower room, Grey leaned back and closed her eyes. Her son's face was a lingering image in her mind as she said, "I have not been far. You know I was born in Finnistuath, where you were a Lord's son for a short while. And you know the story of how I got you and put a hole in the Lord's boot."

"Pinned his foot to the earth!" Henry said, looking out the window at the farthest point he could see.

"And you know that I was at the Monastery before that, before the plague."

"And you saw carts full of dead people."

"You like that part too well," Grey said.

They were silent, and a thrush came and sat in the window for an instant before soaring off. "Do you think of going to see your father?"

Henry shrugged. "I might."

"He loves you well, but he is a man of fear. He has seen too many horrors and clings to what he thinks is comfort. It's a fierce struggle, for he has to be blind to much, including his own heart."

Henry shrugged again; he didn't like to talk to his mother about his father. "I'm glad I'll be shearing the sheep. I like working with the Chieftain's grandsons."

"Most especially Seamus. I hear that you are jesters, the both of you, with your silliness."

Henry laughed, remembering to himself when he and Seamus pretended to milk a ram by pulling its penis, and when they talked about carving dolls for Seamus's sisters out of dried sheep dung. "With little stick arms and legs." The two boys had laughed themselves sick and got the Chieftain's son to struggle to keep from laughing as he scolded them. And even after all these years, all it took for the two boys to spill into laughter anew was to say to one of Seamus's little sisters, "Would you like a new dolly?"

"But shearing is just for a little while, and then there's not enough to do."

"But chores for me that you leave undone."

"While you're busy being a warrior, dozing up here."

"Ahh, a warrior, is it? With all my fierce enemies. And meanwhile, I keep the hearth and make your bread, don't I?"

Henry nodded.

"You don't have to be one thing or another, Henry. I've learned well that you can call yourself a number of fine things. One instant you're a holy man and the next a murderer and there's no final truth to either as far as I can tell. You just do what needs to be done and what you have the skill to do. I help with the wool, don't I?"

"You help, but you're not very good at carding."

Grey threw the arrow by her back at his leg. She stretched and stood up. Leaning out the window, she saw the first star of the evening in the sky.

Soon Grey heard Henry bounding down the stone stairs. She saw him when he was below her, running down the hill toward Old Mary's. She imagined that when she got old and died, this is how she would see her son, looking down at him from Heaven. Or maybe she would be in the Otherworld waiting for him, sitting at the big banquet table that Colin always described in his stories. She would wait for Henry there so they could discuss with each other what they would like to be next. That's how Colin said it worked before the priests came to Ireland.

Life was moving so fast. Time, like a horse that had at first walked and now galloped, was riding off with her life, and she could see, even without the plague, that death, and old age before it, were not so far in the distance. How had the years taken off with her? How had Henry just been two and now almost fifteen? He was still a boy, still her boy, always her boy.

But a mother does not fully know the identity of her child, though she thinks she does. She mustn't know everything, such as the amount of ale a boy drinks and how he vomited in the road and how Old Mary scolded him and Colin spoke to him about being a man and not a fool who didn't know when to stop lifting the cup. And most knew, and even Grey guessed, that at fourteen a boy will have some ale and listen to men speak about the thighs they have parted, or wish they had parted.

Henry had traveled more than anyone in the village knew except Seamus, the Chieftain's grandson, who went with him to a meadow over an hour's walk to the north where a girl tended goats. She was a dangerous angel, this girl, whose name was Alysse. Green eyes and black hair and white skin, all the elements that a boy might never forget. And though Seamus had kissed her once, Henry, without even trying, got a good look at her breasts, which she bared for him one day while Seamus was pissing against a tree. They were fine, those breasts, Henry thought. And he touched them.

Seamus came upon them touching each other and laughing and called Henry a pig's arsehole and went home, whipping everything he could with a long stick.

Henry was worried about Seamus, but worry wasn't as compelling as the feelings that Alysse shared with him. She had desires Henry had never known existed, and she believed in him as a man when everyone else saw him as a boy.

Henry made friends with Seamus after a week or two, when the Wheat Grower's daughter, who was five years older than Seamus and married for two years, called him in to help her lift a churn and ended teaching him how to fuck her from behind as she bent over that very churn. Seamus had no one to tell but Henry, and so it was that the two became friends again and Seamus agreed to tell Henry's mother that he was with him when really he was with Alysse.

Henry and Alysse made love while the goats watched, and then they talked about the kind of life they wanted together. They were going to be married. They were going to have children, and Henry was going to become the best sheep shearer in all Ireland and make money with his talent so he could drink ale and go on adventures and come home to Alysse in their big, soft bed.

He stayed away from his mother more and more, and she believed she saw Seamus on the road one day when he was supposed to be with Henry. But there was nothing to be done. There was nothing but to set him free and love him and mutter about the misery he caused her to whomever would listen.

Henry told Alysse about his real father, about how he thought about him more than he told his mother because he didn't want to see the look that came into her eyes. He told Alysse that his mother didn't tell him much about who she had been before she was his mother, and that he wasn't going to be that way with his children. He would tell them everything, because his life was going to be as full of pleasure as possible.

Against her soft ear where the down looked like silver filigree, Henry told her about the things he remembered, being on the back of a horse eating honey, a big black dog in the Chieftain's house, his mother teaching him to make and throw a leather ball. The time he was sick and she told him stories about rabbits that she made up, using different voices for each one. He told her about the time he saw his mother kissing Colin and it made him sick and angry, but then he started to like the man, whose eyes were like half-moons when he laughed and who listened well to Henry's complaints and shared his own as though they were two men talking of the world's troubles.

Henry's complaints were increasingly about the need to be treated like a man, to be set free by his mother.

He told Alysse that now he was a man, no matter what his mother or anyone else said, but sometimes he felt too tired to think about what a man had to do to take care of himself. "I love my mother," he said. "But it's time to be on my own."

"When will you marry me?" Alysse asked, cuddling into him and kissing his salty neck.

"I'll have to go home for a few days, and then get the good shearing blade from the Chieftain, and then go to the MacCulhain place for a few days of work."

Alysse pulled away from him, pouting.

"Come on, then. Don't be acting this way. I'll be back in a few days."

"Well, hurry, then," she said, rolling back into him and moving her lips against his cheek, "or I might find someone else."

"I'll hurry," he said.

54

"IT IS VERY SAD."

That is what Old Mary said, standing in the doorway at such a late hour, after dark, when she should have been tending her hearth, stoking it for the long night. It was all she could say, and she said it over and over, kept from her own weeping by a fear of what more direct words would do to the young man's mother. Grey knew, though, even though the words hadn't been said. She knew in her body.

"Oh, it is very sad," Mary said with her trembling mouth.

"Is he dead?"

"Oh, God help us, yes. Yes. He's dead. Henry is dead."

Grey fell down on the floor and Old Mary could not pull her up. She fell down and wailed, a hoarse and inconsolable wail, so that soon the Chieftain himself was trotting down the hill. He saw Old Mary trying to pull Grey up. Grey looked at him and screamed, "My son. My son. My son."

Tears came down Old Mary's face as though every pore wept. But she made no sound. The Chieftain said, "It must be a mistake. Have you seen him? It is a mistake."

"He's dead, " Grey wailed, because she knew, she felt it to be true and wanted no false hope.

Old Mary explained to the Chieftain, "He'd been helping with the shearing and was on his way home. A trader on the road from the west saw him fall and went to him. He held him in the road, but he was full dead. He was running with the shearing blade and stumbled. It went right into his chest, it did. Oh, God help us all."

Grey sobbed, shaking her head so hard that her hair fell all around her face wildly. Then still and quiet she whispered, "Henry, you careless boy, always so careless. Oh, my son, my boy." And she started weeping again.

Old Mary said to the Chieftain, "He is just now being brought up the road. I said to take him to your place."

Grey looked from one to the other and said, "I cannot see him. I cannot see his body become a corpse. My son, my Henry . . . I cannot . . ."

They looked down at Grey.

The Chieftain said, "Are you sure it is Henry?"

"It is," Old Mary said.

"I cannot see him," Grey kept saying.

"You don't have to," Old Mary said, soothing, still weeping. She and the Chieftain pulled her to her feet, but her legs were made of pudding. They dragged her to a stool and set her down.

The Chieftain asked Old Mary, "How could this have happened? He stumbled? There was no one accosted him? The trader? Who did this?"

Old Mary hissed at him, "The boy's dead. There's no one did it. It just happened, man."

The Chieftain rubbed his head fiercely and then pounded his temples with his fists. They could hear people coming, walking hard under the burden of death and pushing rocks down the hillside.

"Dear God," Grey said. "Dear God, it's my boy. My boy is dead."

The Chieftain left, and the two women could hear him say, "Follow me. Bring him up here. She can't see him yet."

"The trader was fiercely kind," Old Mary said, "just holding him there as though he were his own."

"Where is my husband?" Grey asked, suddenly calm.

"He is helping to carry the boy now."

"My child's body, his corpse."

"There now, oh, my girl."

Grey stood up.

"I have to be with him. I am his mother."

Old Mary took her hand and patted it. "If you're not up to it . . ."

"I'm his mother. I have to be with him."

Grey walked outside and up the hill toward the Chieftain's home. There were torches flickering around it. A shape in the doorway turned to her, and it was Colin who came and held her and said, "Oh, woman, oh, my woman."

Grey held onto his arm, clutching it, as they walked into the room. And there was Henry, laid out on the table and covered with a dark wool blanket. The Chieftain's wife and daughter were holding each other, standing in a corner making soft weeping sounds. The stranger among them, the trader, stared at Grey. He was trembling.

Calm, the calm of a mother who must do what is necessary for her child, came into Grey's body like a possessing spirit. She touched the man's arm and said, "Thank you for holding my boy for me."

The whole room became silent. Even Colin stepped away from the mother, who walked carefully toward her child as though not to wake him. Gently she put her hand under the blanket and held his arm. It was like meat that had been stored in a cellar, firm and cool, dead. His lips did not look like his, always slightly opened in concentration or winded breathing. They were sealed together by dried blood.

"You are dead," Grey said to him, gently, for she felt his confusion. "I am here. My beautiful boy."

She kissed his eyelid, the eye also hard and dead underneath it. Then she walked around the table, touching his legs, his feet, feeling for the shape of him underneath the blanket.

"I am with you. I will be with you wherever you go."

She sat in a chair and stared at her boy, leaning over and placing her hand over his thin wrist, pushing the blanket aside. His long fingers had faint bruises on them. No one spoke.

"I am afraid," Grey said, looking up at the sickened faces surrounding her. "I am afraid of the grief of it."

Colin was behind her and put his hands on her shoulders. The Cheese-maker and the Watchman with his plump wife were now standing in the doorway. Then the Priest, with tufts of wool still stuck on his clothing, came in.

Grey grabbed him, holding him, clinging to him, and she wailed, "Where is my boy? Where has he gone?"

The Priest shook his head.

Grey left the women to wash and prepare her son's corpse and for the Priest to say prayers that, for all she knew, might help Henry, who had almost been a man. The Priest asked if the boy had been baptized. Grey looked up at him and said, "His father was an Abbot."

55

AT THE FUNERAL in the small church, Grey watched from the back, her usual position. A sheep wandered into the aisle, and no one bothered to get it out. It stood stupidly, content, sheared.

As the Priest spoke, Grey looked around, feeling that someone was trying to get her attention. Colin was at the front of the church, his face swollen with sorrow as he was ready to help carry the heavy oak coffin that had been made to hold the Chieftain. Grey looked past him to the crucifix. Jesus' face was still turned down, fallen forward in his suffering, and she heard the Abbot's voice saying, "My God, my God, why hast thou forsaken me?" And she thought of how careful she had been to bring Henry up as one of the faithful, though she had no certain faith herself. Was it because of her lack of faith that her son had been so senselessly taken? Would God do such a thing as to punish a mother by taking the son, having him fall in the road and bleed to death?

She stared at Jesus' face and saw the weariness and pain, the horror at what a human had to go through. She and Jesus, they both felt God's cruelty, His coldness. Now Grey understood. He had suffered so badly on the cross, had tried so hard to endure. She gasped, aware that she had not understood before, had not understood the suffering and Christ's taking it on, taking on all the suffering. Some turned to look at her. She sank down on her knees; a herder held her upper arm in case she were about to tumble into the well of grief and drown.

## 56

COLIN SAT in a chair by the hearth so that whenever Grey came in, from the tower or from getting cheese or picking cabbage, he was there, just sitting. As she passed by him he grabbed her wrist.

"I am getting some supper ready," she said, pulling her arm away.

Henry is walking down the road. He is alive walking down the road, and he is tossing the blade. He stumbles. No, Henry. You can step to the side; you can keep from stumbling; you can fall ever so slightly differently and not die. Please, Henry.

Colin watched her, stared at her as she tore the cabbage and put pieces of it in a pot, as she poured water from a jug over it, as she spooned some mutton fat into the water. Finally, he said, "We will have a child; we will have as many children as you want."

She did not even look up at his face when she asked, "Why?"

Henry is a corpse, his hands bruised. His lips are sealed with blood. Henry, please stop being dead, son.

Colin waited a moment, and then his words pushed forward. "We can have another child."

"There is only one child. There is only Henry." She kept working.

Henry as a three-year-old is playing in the dirt with a cup, holding out a cup of dirt as though it would quench my thirst. Henry is a ten-year-old and com- poses a song to a dog that is barking at him in the road, "Doggie, doggie, this I beg. Do not bite me in the leg." You cannot be dead, Henry. You cannot be dead.

"All right, then, I will stay here and let you brood and beat my back with your fists. I will hold you firm, or I will go and be a wanderer for a while again and leave you to be with Henry until you can let him go on. But I will come back to you. I will always come back to you."

The blade is falling; Henry is stumbling.

Colin stood up and went outside. Grey threw the pot against the wall. White chunks of cabbage and lumps of fat stuck on top of the dirt as the water soaked in.

Henry is stumbling.

Outside the wind was blowing so hard that the herds all faced in one direction and didn't even move their heads to graze. Colin shivered. Grey was soon beside him, her hair and skirts flailing about.

"I am not a wife," she said. "I cannot now try any longer to be a wife."

He put his arms around her, pressing her hard against his chest.

"You are Henry's mother still, and you are my other self, the part of me that is most free and most in pain, too."

Tears slid all over Grey's face, dripping from her chin.

Colin stared out, facing the wind so his hair, a tangle of gray and dark brown, was blown away from his face.

Grey walked like a ghost back through the doorway and found a cloth satchel that Henry had used before he had made a better one out of sheepskin. She put in it a cup, a small knife, the rest of the cabbage, some cheese, and a ball of yarn. When she passed by Colin, she stopped, pausing and looking back, for perhaps he would say something good, something like, "You were a good mother."

And he said, "You were a fine mother, Grey. He was a lucky lad to have had a woman like yourself as a mother."

He took the cloak from his own back, put it over her shoulders, and watched her walk on the road, going east out of town. She said over and over in her head, "Jesus help me. Jesus help me."

In their home, Colin sat by the hearth sobbing with his face in the palms of his hands.

Grey traveled east until she came to the riverside where the young man had shared a rabbit with her and Henry years before. She wanted to find him and tell him that the boy he had seen her with had died, had been killed in a careless manner when he had survived the plague and all other manner of danger. Perhaps in a discussion with someone she would come to understand what his death meant. Someone would say, "Oh, that occurred because of the vapors coming from Mars," or, "Oh, you will die soon, and his death spared him from the grief that you have taken on." But she would hurl a stone at anyone who said, "He is in a better place, in Heaven with God," for there could be no better place for Henry than with her, with his mother who loved him as not even God could love.

She had a dream that night by the river. It was a stunning dream in which Henry came to her and said that he needed something from her. He needed certain maps. Grey awoke after she had told him, "I love you. I miss you." When she woke up, she splashed water on her face saying to Henry, "I cannot read. I know nothing about maps. You must tell me more, tell me how to get them."

Grey walked on toward Tarmath, for she was making a pilgrimage to Henry's father, the Abbot. In Tarmath there was commerce again, and Grey traded some yarn for bread. Sitting against the Baker's shop, she watched people come and go. She watched their faces and could see their deaths there. She thought of all the mothers in Tarmath who had lost their children, including those whose children died during the great plague. Why had she not understood then what their suffering was? A great compassion came over her as she saw them, sincere in their efforts to survive and busy with their hopes and fears. How fragile and tender, these lives. What terror they held at bay.

But she had no terror about death, not anymore. Henry was dead; if he could do it, then surely his mother could. It was as though he had leapt from a high cliff into the water, a child showing up the adults who were still afraid. What was there for her to fear? It was worse to think of living to an old age—living twenty, ten, even five more years without being able to smell Henry's skin, to hear his voice. "Hey there, Mum," she heard him say in her memory—now only in her memory. No, she had no fear of death. In death was her only chance of being with him again.

57

the Monastery doors were open, and strangers, new monks, were tending to a garden of cabbage and herbs. One of these monks, curly headed and just a few years older than Henry had been, stepped in front of her.

"Women cannot enter here."

"I have come to speak with the Abbot," she said.

"What business do you have with the Abbot?"

"His son. His son is the business I have with the Abbot."

The monk looked her over and then said, "Wait here, then, and I'll see if he will come to you."

She waited, breathing deeply, feeling now that she was too weak to say the words to the Abbot. She sat down on the threshold, bending over to put her head on her knees. She could feel monks pass her to go inside, the wool-smelling breeze they made with their pious movements. Then she felt someone standing behind her. For a moment she was relieved to imagine that the Abbot would be a new man, not Henry's father. But she lifted her head up and twisted around to see the young monk standing beside the man she had known many years ago. His face was lined beyond his years with bruises under his eyes. She could not get up. She took his hand and sobbed.

"Go on. I will tend to her," the Abbot told the young monk. "She is stricken." He pointed to his head. The young monk bowed a little and went back into the darkness of spiritual seeking. They heard the chanting begin before they spoke to each other. The Abbot pulled her to her feet and said, "What have you come here for?"

She held onto his forearms and looked down at his robes.

"I am here to tell you that your son, that Henry . . . is dead."

The Abbot shook her slightly, or perhaps his arms trembled. Grey looked into his face and said, "It was a mishap. He was playing with a shearing blade and stumbled."

"What?"

"He stumbled and . . . a shearing blade . . ."

"When did this happen?"

"Only a few fortnights ago."

He embraced her, holding her as she wept hard, liquid coming from her nose and soaking into his robe.

"We survived the plague," she sobbed. " I thought it was a miracle, my child, my Henry, alive when so many died. I would make a deal with the Devil this moment to have my son back"

The Abbot let go of her and his eyes became opaque and flat.

"He is in Heaven. I baptized him. So he is in Heaven." The Abbot's face twisted against the tears he felt behind the skin.

"I don't want him to be in Heaven. That is too far away," Grey wept. "That is too far away from me."

She begged the Abbot, "I want to make a bargain. I want you to call Satan here now. I want my son back."

The Abbot was trembling.

"Why are you talking about a bargain with the Devil? You don't understand," he said. "The boy is in Heaven with Jesus." And he pushed her from him and walked away.

Grey followed the Abbot, running after him, only saying, "Please," and he went into his cell and closed the door hard. She leaned against it, repeating only the word "Please" over and over again. "At least talk to me about our son, remember with me when he was small, when he was alive. Please."

When someone came to remove her, she looked up and saw the Kitchener's kind eyes in a nest of lines and creases. He said, "Here, now. You must leave." But he took her to the frater and gave her some water and bread. They did not speak until the Kitchener, who now had a limp, asked her, "Where can you go to rest?"

And Grey answered, "Do you know if the blind Midwife in Tarmath is still alive?"

"I do not, but I could send for her," he answered. He called over a wiry, freckled boy who was standing in the doorway holding a pail of water.

Like a small child, like a little girl, which she had never been, Grey said, "Will you send for her, for the blind Midwife?" She could not stop the tears coming from her eyes. The servant boy stared at the distraught woman and she stared back, remembering herself in his place. She smiled and reached out to touch him, to touch her past before she knew the cruelest of sorrows. The boy stepped back.

"Go on to Tarmath," the Kitchener said to him. "Go on and fetch the old blind Midwife there. Go tell her she's needed here."

Just after dark, the Midwife came with her walking stick, amazed that before she died she would be led into the Monastery. Grey said to her as she gripped her slim hand, "My boy is dead." The Midwife put her hand on Grey's shoulder and said to her, "Come on with me."

They walked together in the dark, which was not an impediment to the blind Midwife. Before midnight they were in Tarmath, in her cottage, where she traded in dried herbs.

After Grey told the Midwife about the Abbot, the Midwife explained, "Some men betray their sons to satisfy their pricks. Their pricks lead them away from their family and into some woman's bed who has no love for his children by another woman. The Abbot betrayed his child for a virile image of himself in a different way, as a man of authority, as a man with God's authority." She stopped, considering whether or not to let the next words out into the air. Then she said, "I've been at the birth of other children with the Abbot's smell on them."

Sickening rage gurgled in Grey's throat. She emitted a growling sigh and sank down.

"I wanted to remember with him, to remember Henry with him. I wanted him to help me as Abbot. I was willing . . . I am willing to make a bargain."

"He cannot hold his image of himself in the same container with memories of his child whom he held and then abandoned. Such a memory is too heavy for a man. His heart does not grow larger with stimulation as his penis does."

"Where is my son? Where can I find him? For I know that I cannot live without him."

"But you are, you are living without him! So you can."

Grey got on her knees and put her folded hands in the Midwife's lap so the old woman could feel the posture of her pleading.

"I want to make a bargain. I want you to get the Bailiff so he can write down the bargain, and I will sign it. I will learn to sign my name, and I will sign it."

The Midwife just stroked her head.

"I want my son back. I will do anything."

"There is nothing you can do, sweet mother," the Midwife said.

"I can give my soul. I can promise my soul to the Devil in return for . . ."

The Midwife lifted Grey's chin and asked, "And why would the Devil want your soul?"

"Please. I want to try. Please get the Bailiff so he can put it down in his ledger."

"I will not get the Bailiff," the Midwife said. "You must make a different bargain, one that will work. You need to make a bargain with Henry."

Grey sat back on her heels and watched the blind woman's face.

"What can you do to be with Henry?" the Midwife asked. "What bargain could you make with Henry?"

"I can die. I can be with him in Heaven."

The Midwife nodded and said, "Good, good. And what will you do while you wait?"

Grey looked at her own hands in her own lap.

Henry's face is so clear to me, the brown eyes, merry and sad at the same time, the wide mouth and the wool cap on his head.

"Do you remember carrying his body in your body?"

"Yes."

My belly is taut with him, his restless desire to live free of the confines of a womb.

"Perhaps you can carry him in you now, in a different way. You are still his mother."

"But he would want to be free, not always to be with his mother."

Henry is telling me that he wants to stay the night with Seamus, to sleep with him outside on the hillside with the sheep. I ask him what about his dinner, and he promises that he will eat something.

"Sometimes you will carry him, and sometimes others will carry him. And when he lives in you, what kind of a life will you give him?"

Grey folded down and shook her head. "I have been many things in my life, and whenever I knew with certainty who I was, I changed into something else. Only as Henry's mother did the name I was called fit my body and my spirit."

The Midwife said, "There is nothing certain but change. That is what I know. Think of the transformation the world has gone through, think of the mothers who lost their children here in this town, lost their children to the black death, and think of the mothers whose sons fight for kings and die with spears in their throats."

Grey stood up.

"I do not like this world."

"Perhaps Henry is free, then, free of this sour world," the Midwife said. "And perhaps there is a chamber inside you that you can prepare for him, a place of joy and strength, free from your mournful ethers, where he will want to come from time to time. While you are waiting to die, perhaps you can prepare this place to carry him inside of you."

Grey thought for a moment and laughed.

"My Henry would not like silk pillows so much as a fierce horse to carry him."

"Then you must prepare your backside for a fierce ride."

58

COLIN WAS THERE when she came back. He was not sitting by the hearth but playing a drum to the music of two men who had come to Rosconen to trade. One, with unruly hair and a constant grin, played the harp, and the other whistled through his beard. They were having a fine time. Grey waited until they had stopped their tune and the whistler was laughing about his mouth being tired, and then she went in and greeted her husband. He stood up and smiled and said, "I am glad to see you."

"I have just tended the boy's grave. It needed tending." She wanted him to have no illusions about her priorities.

"I am glad to see you."

The two guests sat and looked at the floor. The whistler finally said, "What are you going to fix for supper?"

And Grey answered, "Your arse in a pot with some cabbage."

The man nodded as though it seemed reasonable to consider this, and then he stood up and stretched, saying to his comrade, "We'd best be going, then, and see to the Chieftain's request."

"All right," Colin said.

Grey looked around the room. It was kept well, new pegs put in the walls and new things hanging on them. There was a new table, small and occupied by ledgers and quills. As soon as the two men were gone, Grey went to Colin and let him hold her.

"Oh, hard this life," he said several times in her ear, and she held him tightly around the neck. "Hard it is, and so many think someone can fix it."

"People come to you, do they, to do magic with words and ledgers? There's no writing can fix me."

Colin said nothing, and Grey moved away.

The next day, Grey took the black horse and rode it far to the west, and then came back, passing that place in the road where Henry had died. The horse entered a conspiracy of freedom with his rider and pounded the earth, flying forward with all its strength. Every day Grey took the same ride, until the day when she finally forgot, just once in passing it, to notice the place where Henry died. After that, she rode the horse on explorations of the region.

When she was in Rosconen, Grey spent many hours up in the Chieftain's tower, sharpening the arrow blades again and practicing hurling stones at bushes from the tower window. Everything she saw from that window was Henry, every breeze was Henry, every change in the light, every bird's feather or fox. And so, if everything were Henry, then she must be Henry, too. She closed her eyes, and with the fixed stare she gave things whose spirit she wanted to see, she looked for her own spirit, looked for eyes to open inside her. And they were Henry's eyes.

When she came home in the evening, Colin was often there, listening to the whispers of some distraught or angry man who kept pointing to the parchment where he wanted his words put down. Sometimes Colin was making up songs with his two musician friends, who had decided to stay in Rosconen. If Colin had been drinking ale, he made them swear to sing the song he had composed about a boy named Henry who had arced across the sky like a fast-burning star wherever they went, and Grey would pull at his arm and say, "Leave the poor men alone, Colin. Leave them be."

Despite his outbursts of sorrow and his rants about the old wisdom of Ireland, Colin had become known in the village as a fair and steady man, whereas there were some, such as the Cheesemaker's Wife, who whispered that Grey was possessed and addled. Whenever Colin heard this, he would let his fist fall on a nearby barrel or table and say, "She's stronger in mind and body than any here, excepting myself, and you'll have to stand nose to nose with me if you have any disagreement with my opinion." This made everyone sure that indeed Colin was of that rough MacRaignaill clan, which several people were related to by way of a cousin.

When the Chieftain died, Colin was made the new Chieftain. Now he and Grey went to the Priest's Masses and sat in the first row, Grey always staring at the crucifix.

"There's great pain in dying on a cross, poor man," she muttered, thinking for the millionth time that she was glad Henry had come to a quick end.

Soon after Colin became the Chieftain, another Chieftain, to the West, tried to come in and procure for himself and his family additional herds and lands. He had heard that the old leader of Rosconen was dead and came along the road on horseback with three of his men, also riding horses. But Grey spotted them from the tower, met them on the black stallion before they had passed the first herd of sheep, and said, "You'll only come into Rosconen as guests of the New Chieftain, or you'll leave as corpses."

They laughed at her until she took a stone from a bag slung over the horse's back and hurled it at one of the men so that it hit his nose and caused blood to flow from it. While he was wailing, she lifted her lance and waited. The would-be usurper said, "Hold, now. We're just here to make toasts and share some ale."

"Whose ale?" Grey asked.

"We've got goods to trade." And so they did, having prepared for the possibility of having to shift at the last moment from foe to friend. But Grey figured that they would soon see that hers was actually the only horse in Rosconen, and since they had at least four, there was no telling what resources they had to bear against them. So she said, "You'd best go home to your own ale," and chased them, hurling stones at their horses' flanks so that soon they were well on their way back where they came from.

One evening, returning to the house, she heard the music and laughing going on in there and stopped in the dusk to listen. Grey listened from outside, hearing the way people can make bold plans as though boys didn't die; as though a mother's only child, a beloved fellow survivor of plagues and cruelty and other dangers, couldn't stumble into death in one irretrievable instant. Colin would get over Henry's death in a way that she never would, never would even want to. But he would want her to, of course. He might grow weary of the grief she held, as though it were Henry himself.

When his friends left the house, they didn't see Grey sitting against the wall, staring at the line of trees where frogs and insects shrieked at each other. They did not see her head fall against her knees as she wept. But Colin came out soon after to look for her and was soon squatting with his back to the frogs and the forest, his hands on both her shoulders. She lifted her head.

"It's no good for you here anymore, my girl, is it?"

She shook her head, and he sat down and held her, pressing her head against his chest.

"When I'm away," she said, "I think I might see him; I can feel him just around the bend, or feel that he was just a minute ago there by the stream. But here he's dead. He is always only dead here."

"Then you have to go on. I'd do it with you if I weren't . . ."

"You're the Chieftain and all. You're a fine man with your writing and advice and all your songs. You've a good home, here."

"I'm not fit as I used to be when I was young and able to wander about with all kinds of burdens on my back."

Grey moved more closely into him and said, "I can't pretend to be who I was."

Colin put his forehead on the top of her head. She began to cry and said, "I'd rather spend my life looking for Henry and not finding him than spend my life not looking."

Colin cleared his throat of tears and kept his voice steady. "You can go and still have my love. There's no other way to do it, though it be hard on us both. I'll not wheedle you into staying to turn bitter and rough."

"I'm still your wife," Grey said, no longer weeping. "And that will be one of the things I'll always be, and I'll tell you that I will understand if you need another man's wife to . . . no, listen to what I'm saying, man."

They stayed together there, outside with the frogs and trees and insects and sleeping birds—entwined, still, quiet—while Grey slept and Colin thought of how this moment was the hero's part of his story. And tomorrow he would be drinking ale and posing as a Chieftain with a legend for a wife.

In the morning, Colin was gone and the horse was standing nearby, ripping at the grass with some annoyance at the oddness of humans. Grey pulled him down to the ale house, where Old Mary, who always leaked tears when she saw Grey, helped her find some trousers and a warm wool tunic. She gave her some good saddlebags, which she stuffed with food and wool clothing.

Grey rode for a fortnight, speaking mostly to the horse. And she came to a place where there was a great emptiness after the hills and trees. It was the ocean, a thing she had heard of but not seen or even imagined as anything but a lot of water. But here were also gull calls and a fine salted mist in the air; scattered strips of seaweed, dark brown and glassy.

Vast it was, with a relentless and mesmerizing rhythm of thunder and silence. She slipped off the horse and led him down a path to the beach. Perhaps two hundred yards south, a fisherman was sitting on his small boat turned over on the sand; he was repairing a net. Otherwise, Grey and the horse were alone, overseen by the ghosts in a tower ruin on a jut of land to the north.

The ocean went on and on, until far in the distance, in a muted line, it met the sky.

"There it is," Grey said. She let the horse stand with its tail and mane blowing against its body. She walked into the froth and kept walking forward. How long would she have to walk? The water was deeper as she went; how deep would it get? Could she walk to the place where it met the sky? She listened for Henry's voice. She called out to him, above the sound of the waves and the wind. "Henry! Henry!" she called. There was no answer between the thundering of the waves, but he was there. For sure, he was there.

She pushed on, turning to the side and standing still to take the breaking waves and then wading hard beyond them. The freezing water made her tremble. But she kept pushing against the green glassy sea, remembering what Bartholomew said about the tribulations one had to endure to make the journey to the place where Heaven and Earth meet. The water swelled against her chest and she tasted it. It was not like the water she drank from pools and wells. It was not like that water at all, but like tears or sweat.

This was the collected tears and sweat of all the gods and beings and humans from all time. It was the sweat of their effort to make their way through suffering and the tears from when they had to stop and endure it. And sure there were many who drowned in that water.

She stopped and, with her teeth chattering, looked back at the horse, who looked at her. *What will happen to the horse?* Henry's voice asked inside her. The swelling waves, on their way to break on the shore and then returning, rocked her hard back and forth. She turned again to see that place—how far away?—where the two worlds met. The waves kept breaking and returning. The fisherman kept mending his net.

Perhaps he has some fish I could eat, Grey thought, and she pushed the great ocean out of her way and went back to the shore.

And from that time, Grey spoke directly to God about a number of things, and occasionally spoke to Henry or heard him speak in her head. Sometimes Grey was a man, hurling stones in a contest for coin; sometimes she was a woman who crept into bed beside Colin in the dark of night and left before dawn; sometimes she was a beggar standing in the rain in Naas asking for a cup of soup; sometimes she was a singer in a Lord's Manor, drinking good ale and eating roast pork until she could eat no more; sometimes she was a spirit gathering hazelnuts in the deep woods, watching the whorl of white-and-black wings when a magpie took flight. Sometimes she was a warrior, though she still didn't know what her true cause as a warrior was. Perhaps it was simply living each day without succumbing to bitter sorrow over the pain of being human; perhaps it was fighting to savor what one has and to honor what one has lost.